The Balance Wars

Book I
Deviance

Robert C Littlewood

For
Marilyn – my constant support

and Ian Andrew – valued friend and mentor

The Balance Wars

Deviance

Book 2 – Convergence – Coming soon

Book 3 – Equilibrium – Coming soon

GLOSSARY

PLANETS, MOONS and SUNS

Name	Meaning	Pronunciation
Tarvuli	The Mother, home planet of the Graaven peoples	TahFOOLee
Avlar	"Brightest" – one of the two suns of Tarvuli	AFlar
Colunda	"Fading Star" – second of the two suns of Tarvuli	KoLOONdar
Halidar	"Queen of Night" – moon of Tarvuli, the first to rise and set	HARleedar
Barask	"She Who Shines Coldly" – moon of Tarvuli, the second to rise	BAHrask
Orvasne	"He Who Waits" – moon of Tarvuli, the last to rise and set	OrVASHhneh

SEASONS

Name	Meaning	Pronunciation
Hordeth Gar	Season of Storms	HorDETH Gar
Veremis Gar	Season of Weeping	FerEEMish Gar
Talloch Gar	Season of Renewal	TAlock Gar
Carminac Gar	Season of Abundance	KarMEEnac Gar
Nahver Gar	Season of Waning	NahVEER Gar
Techmun Gar	Season of Desolation	TeshMUN Gar

THE SEVEN PROVINCES of the GRAAVEN EMPIRE

Name		Pronunciation
Percassia		PearCASHeeah
Dermoch		DAREmock
Voenia		FoEENeah
Kassarin		KashARin
Storluth		SsDORlute
Tashlak		TARSHlak
Crosh		CROWsh

THE TWELVE VASSAL STATES of the GRAAVEN EMPIRE

Name		Pronunciation
Perduvia		PearDOOfeeah
Phalandrel		FARlandrel
Lazmark		LATHmark
Murdeen		MOORdeen
Borv		Borf
Venlish		FenLEESH
Herdax		AIRdarz
Gromdesh		GROOMdesh
Derfon		DAIRfoon

PLACES and LOCATIONS

Name	Meaning	Pronunciation
Kareem Vastar	A City State	KAReem VASHtar
Palluvia	A City State	PaLOOveeah
Paxal	A City State	ParkSHARL
Tekla Xemik	The Great Water Lake	TEKlah SHEMik
Ter'Malloch	Silver Water Lake	TEar MAHlok
Firma	Large island set in the waters of Ter'Malloch	FEERma
Cheptosi Gem Hallach	The Thunder Water Falls	ChepTOsee Ghem HALack
Sharana	The Black Water River	ShaRARnah
Xerfun	The Underworld	SHERfoon
Tarmech	Capital city of the Graaven Empire	TAHmesh
Camchak	River of Life	KamCHACK
Steppes of Portis	Unconquered lands to the north	PORtish
Plains of Clarist	Desert region to the far east of the Empire	CLARisht

PRINCIPAL GRAAVEN GODS BEFORE the FALL

Name	Meaning	Pronunciation
Slax Ar Terrun	Goddess of Death	**SLArx ar TERoon**
Bekkor	The Seven-faced God	**BEKor**
Bringarell	God of the Underworld	**BrinGAHREL**

GRAAVEN MEASURES of TIME and DISTANCE

Spahn	Roughly equivalent to 12 inches	**SHParn**
Talit	Roughly equivalent to one inch	**TARlit**
Persangh	A Graaven mile	**PearZang**
Chaal	A Graaven hour	**CHarl**
Dak'chaal	A Graaven day	**DAHK CHarl**
Meh'chaal	A Graaven week	**MURK CHarl**
Bach'chaal	A Graaven month	**BAHR CHarl**
Sem'chaal	A Graaven year	**ZEM CHarl**

GRAAVEN MILITARY STRUCTURE

Name	Meaning	Pronunciation
Shu Tek	Greatest of 25	**SHOO Tek**
Shu Mut	Greatest of 50	**SHOO Moot**
Shu Lan	Greatest of 100	**SHOO Larn**

GRAAVEN MILITARY STRUCTURE (cont.)

Name	Meaning	Pronunciation
Kalvak	First of 500	**KULvark**
Met Stragosh	"Little" General	**Met STRARgoash**
Stragosh	General	**STRARgoash**
Impisch	Unit of 10 000	**IMpeesh**
Impisch tarn	Unit of 1000	**IMpeesh TAhn**
Praka	Unit of 25	**PRAka**
Praka xem	Unit of 50	**PRAka SHEM**
Praka vek	Unit of 100	**PRAka Fek**
Praka haram	Unit of 500	**PRAka ARam**
Hoplex	Graaven foot soldier	**HOplecks**
Sagit	Graaven archer	**ZAYgit**
Baran Mec	Imperial guard	**BAHrarn Mek**
Zaltec	Supreme military leader	**SAHLtek**

PROLOGUE

Gratish was a farmer whose life was hanging by a thread. Not that Gratish had any inkling this was the case. On the contrary, all he knew from his race memories was that his clan had always been farmers. He was in no doubt that this would continue for as long as the Empire stood.

Gratish grew terrax, an innocuous legume that was difficult to grow but had the advantages of being high in protein, easily transportable, and tasty on the palate. It could be prepared in a variety of ways so was a foodstuff in demand and Gratish was a genius at growing it, a skill he had inherited from his sire.

Here, in the vassal state of Gromdesh at the western extreme of the Graaven Empire, he had become moderately wealthy as the quality of his crop and the regularity of its supply to surrounding areas underpinned his success.

He sat quietly in his favourite chair after a long day in the fields and over a beaker of brandy mused about the ripening crop and its impending harvest. So successful had he been in his own modest way that he had been given permission to mate with Fronta, a member of the Xermish clan, somewhat higher in station than his own.

In the rigid caste system of the Empire this was a notable achievement, and he and Fronta had spawned four offspring – two males and two females – for whom he had high hopes. Now they were all asleep as the night stretched on.

Something had drawn Gratish from his rest and he had sat sipping brandy for some time when the sky above him suddenly lit with an eerie glow. He rushed outside and was able to observe a long, fiery tale arcing across the sky above him. The light rapidly diminished and was followed by a faint tremble in the earth beneath his feet. A sudden increase in light flared up momentarily afterwards and then died away. Whatever it was, it had apparently hit the ground somewhere to the west of his lands.

Hearing the door open behind him, he saw that Fronta, his mate, had awakened from slumber and was now peering at him through the gloom of the evening.

'What was that, Gratish? I dreamt of some creature flying above me and then a flash of light woke me up.'

'I am not sure, Fronta, but I don't think it came to rest too far away. Let the spawnlings sleep and I will go and investigate. Perhaps there may be some profit in it for us?'

Fronta smiled. 'You rascal. Ever thinking of profit. Yes, away with you, but be careful. You may be a commoner, but you are my commoner and I will not have harm befall you.'

Gratish smiled in return. He felt the familiar sense of affection and shared purpose which had grown between them and he knew he had been fortunate in being allowed to mate with Fronta, and more so that she had later agreed to cohabit with him.

Preparing him a pack with some food and water, Fronta waved farewell as he jogged off into the night.

Gratish was not old by Graaven measures, but he was not young either, and he was smugly proud when, after four chaal of steady progress with barely a raised heart rate, he reached the area where he perceived the light had first blazed up.

Around him the landscape was rugged. Here at the western fringes of the Empire it was semi-arid and rain came unpredictably, perfect for terrax growing but not so good for people wanting to make a living in other ways.

He noticed a glow that grew stronger as he pushed past some stunted pendal ferns that grew around the area. Finally, he came to a crater which radiated heat, and in the middle of which sat a spherical, metallic-looking object, easily the size of a house.

Cautiously he edged forward. The details of the object were hard to discern and Gratish stopped when he had closed to only some fifty spahn from the object. Finally, he could see that the skin of the object pulsed with a strange kind of luminescent light that flickered over its surface.

A warning voice screamed inside Gratish's head at the folly of approaching so closely to such an unknown object, particularly as the nearest Empire garrison was two days' journey away. But, as always with Gratish, the lure of profit conquered any rational thinking.

The sound of something sliding across the ground behind him brought all of Gratish's thoughts to one focused point. The tendrils on his neck flared red in alarm and his breathing became rapid and shallow as he turned.

What he saw was beyond his comprehension. Utterly alien. Black in aspect. Covered with a fetid slime. Gratish stood rooted to the spot in terror and his bowels voided as the thing approached him. He could find no voice to call out and, in the last few moments of his life, his mind filled with precious images of his mate and spawnlings. His last conscious thought was that they, and the whole of the Graaven Empire, were doomed.

CHAPTER ONE

Two suns hung in the sky above the world of Tarvuli. Avlar – the brighter of the two – had passed its zenith, whilst Colunda approached the horizon. The vault of the sky contained no cloud and a violet haze shimmered in the heat that radiated from the surface below.

A raptor glided silently on leathery wings in a warm thermal current and surveyed the terrain far below. Discerning movement, the raptor tilted one leathery wing and changed direction to glide above what appeared to be a long, silvery animal traversing the desert plain far below. A cloud of dust rose upward as the silvery thing progressed. The raptor, with keen eyesight, assessed its potential as prey, gliding for some time along the length of it. If any part of the "animal" noticed the shadow that flickered weakly across the ground, no account was taken of it.

To anyone looking up into the sky the predator would have been the merest black dot, despite its actual size and girth. No-one on the ground, however, took the trouble to survey the steely vault above. They were more preoccupied with simply placing one foot in front of the other in an endless succession of steps.

Having recently gorged on a careless herbivore the raptor was merely curious as to what this thing was; but nothing within its considerable experience as a hunter gave any clue. Finally, the creature decided that whatever it was, it was far too big to tackle, even despite its own size. The raptor banked further and continued its silent flight above the arid plains below, slowly disappearing into the glare of the brighter of the two suns that hung in the sky.

Far below, the thing continued its dogged progress. What seemed to be a continuous and unbroken line from high above was revealed to be a long line of individuals whose silvery aspect was due to the light chain mail coat that each wore. Both male and female, each humanoid individual stood over eight spahn tall. An outsider would have considered their aspect to be striking, both from the regularity of their features, which was pleasing, to their musculature and physical dimensions, which were impressive.

Closer inspection of their faces, however, would have exposed the exhaustion that all endeavoured to hide. The visage of each wore expressions that were haggard through lack of rest and appeared haunted by a fear that seemed to hang over them like a cloud. Here, then, were the last remnants of the Baran Mec, the elite Hoplex and Sagit imperial guard of the Graaven empire, harried and hunted by an alien enemy. Perhaps to their utter destruction and the extermination of their race.

Surveying them as they passed the rocky outcrop that he had climbed upon, was their commanding Zaltec. Grimly he watched them walk on and noted their weariness and despair. It was with a sense of forlorn pride that he noted that as each Hoplex passed him by, they stood a little straighter and strode onward with greater determination.

Menkh ab Dur rubbed a surreptitious hand over his belly as they passed in a vain effort to dispel the constant pain that, increasingly now, could reduce him to writhing agony. The lump he felt under the bones of his fingers had grown alarmingly and he knew that his days were numbered, and short.

A slithering of small stones behind him indicated that another had climbed to his vantage point. Without turning he knew that it was his second in command, Tishan Dar.

'Zaltec, our water situation is dire,' she informed him as she, too, gazed out as the Hoplex tramped past.

He chuckled grimly, 'Our entire situation is dire!' and he received a curt nod in response.

'Our scouting party should be returning soon, perhaps they will have some good news for us?'

'That would be fortuitous, given matters at hand.'

'Zaltec, what of the rearguard?'

Menkh returned a blank stare and Tishan sighed and nodded.

A disturbance in the column ahead drew their mutual attention as a dust-covered Hoplex appeared, running down the column, with figures pointing out the Zaltec to him. Menkh and Tishan watched calmly as the Hoplex ran to the rocky outcrop they stood upon, sweat pouring down his face and breathing laboured. The Hoplex stood straight and peered up at them but it was clear that no breath was currently available to deliver the message.

'Stand easy, catch your breath. We will join you momentarily.'

Menkh turned to Tishan but grimaced as a lightning bolt of pain hit his body and he could not suppress the groan that escaped from his lips. Tishan put out a hand and fought to keep her expression neutral as the Hoplex passed by. She could not betray the quiet desperation in her voice. 'Do you require assistance, Zaltec?'

'Give me a moment,' he wheezed in pain. 'Smile and pretend to be speaking with me, don't let our people see.'

The wave of pain passed and Menkh was able to climb down unassisted. Again, as on numerous past occasions, Tishan Dar was moved by the steely determination of the Zaltec to appear at ease when she knew he was in deep pain.

'Report,' hissed Menkh to the Hoplex.

'Zaltec, a swift-flowing river a half meh'chaal's march further on. It is wide and deep but may be fordable. The country on the further bank appears to be more hospitable than here.'

The Zaltec reached out and gripped the Hoplex's shoulder. He stared for a long moment as the features of the Hoplex before him evoked a memory.

'You are Baen Sang, are you not, spawn of Prin Sang?'

The Hoplex stood even straighter and struck his left shoulder with right fist in the Baran Mec salute while replying, 'I have that honour.'

Menkh nodded, 'I thought so. Your mother was a great Hoplex. You have given me the best news in many meh'chaal, Baen Sang, and I thank you. Now, go and join the column.'

The Hoplex turned away and Menkh directed his remarks to Tishan. 'Stragosh, gather your messengers and inform the column that water has been found and increase the pace. We have enough light to reach this river before the suns set today.'

'Zaltec.' Tishan saluted and jogged off to gather her messengers.

The news, as it spread, had a palpable effect on morale and the pace grew perceptibly faster in anticipation.

'Now, you gods,' muttered Menkh, 'show us some benevolence and let this be the opportunity we have sought.'

It was not until the evening that the last of the column, including those civilians who had managed to survive the calamity and flight, came into the camp that had been hurriedly set up.

The river was indeed deep and wide, and it flowed at such a pace and with such force that even the strongest Hoplex could go no further than ankle depth. Beyond that, they would lose their purchase and fall, with the inevitable result of death by drowning as they were swept away.

The initial euphoria of having a plentiful source of water after many meh'chaal of privation could not allay the feeling of doom that permeated the camp. Knowledge of the Zaltec's condition was widespread despite the best efforts to keep it under wraps. The likelihood that they would lose him soon and were powerless to prevent it affected everyone badly.

Menkh ab Dur, the greatest living Zaltec of the Graaven Empire, the victor of countless engagements, was as wily as he was courageous. The man who should have been Emperor was both talisman and shield, and those who had followed him after the collapse of the Empire were only still living due to his genius for warfare. Now, it seemed, a battle was being waged that could only have one outcome; one which presaged disaster for all. The enemy that relentlessly pursued them was alien to everyone, without pity and without honour. Only the evening gave respite from the pursuit as the enemy became motionless till the suns rose once again.

The Graavens had used this time and continued to travel as rapidly as possible. Menkh ab Dur had employed his knowledge of Graaven lands to their advantage, destroying bridges where possible and seeking tracks that were difficult to follow. As time passed this had cost the Graavens, both physically and mentally.

In an attempt to seek some advantage, Menkh had planned a night attack, led by one of his most trusted officers, against those they named Dorath Mar – "black devils" in the Graaven tongue. The name sprang from an old Graaven tale regarding mythical creatures who haunted dark places and would steal unwary Graavens away, never to be seen again. These creatures looked remarkably like the fanciful descriptions that could be found in this tale, with their alien eyes and long, claw-like arms. They stood motionless but alert, as the Hoplex discovered to their cost. 150 of their people had perished in the darkness and no further attempt was made to attack them at night.

Menkh lay in the confines of the rough shelter they had made for him and listened to the camp noises as his people settled to find what rest they could. If no way could be found across the river, they were all doomed as the enemy would close on their position within a single dak'chaal. Menkh did not expect that the rearguard would have lasted more than a few chaal at best, despite placing them in the best position possible for an ambush.

The pain in his belly was such that he could barely control crying out and begging for release. He was filled with despair for what was left of his once proud people and their descent into the abyss. Restlessly, he fell into an exhausted sleep where the pain receded but stayed on the fringes of his mind, clouding all with its insistent presence. The dream that came was more a remembrance of events that had passed before than an actual dream brought on by sleep.

------O------

They had come for him in the earliest part of the dawn where Avlar's light had barely driven off the shades of night. Menkh liked to walk along the shingled beach where the waters of Ter'Malloch, the Silver Water Lake, lapped. The dull ache in his stomach was persistent and he found that walking soothed it somewhat.

Here on the island of Firma, in the centre of the lake, he lived in exile by order of his sister Pershiva. Stripped of all offices and rank, and housed in a small dwelling that had been built for him on the edges of the fishing village that he called home, he lived a solitary existence.

All was not as it seemed. His exile was part of a careful plan that he and Pershiva had formulated. Together they had exposed the nobles who had plotted the death of their father, drawing them out and setting up Pershiva as a puppet Empress – or so those fools had thought.

After the agreed time, Menkh would return from exile, taking up the role of Zaltec, overlord of all Graaven forces, and, together, he and Pershiva would reset the Graaven empire. They would reshape the rigid society of their people where the less talented were given precedence merely because of their family and status.

It would take time but, between them, he knew they could accomplish it.

Now, as he observed the boat that ground to a halt on the shingles and saw four Hoplex of the Baran Mec jump out and approach him, he knew that something was badly wrong.

The four Hoplex saluted him.

'Zaltec. By order of the Pohlan Kar you are to return with us at once.'

'And you are?'

'Forgive me, Zaltec. I am Shu Lan Naz. Zaltec, the Pohlan Kar was most insistent.'

'I am sure she was. Well, I have nothing here but some notes and a few belongings. Send one of your men to fetch them. You can see my dwelling from here on the bluff and I will board your vessel.'

There were ten rowers on the boat. They bowed their heads in fear as Menkh stepped aboard. He could tell by the markings on their skin that they were all of a lowly caste. To Menkh they epitomised all that was wrong in the Empire.

'You need have no fear of me. I will see that you are rewarded well when we have returned to the capital.'

Their mumbled thanks and his reassurances did not lessen the palpable fear that each individual gave off. This was more than fear of him; something as yet indefinable. Menkh knew that the guards sent to collect him would have been under orders to say nothing, so he stood by the prow of the vessel and gazed off into the distance.

------0------

Intense pain roused him from his fitful dreams. So focused on the pain was he that he did not, at first, notice the blue glow that began to manifest at the bottom of his sleeping mat. When he did become aware, he could only stare at it in numb disbelief.

Slowly a figure coalesced into clear view, although still

somewhat transparent and amorphous. At only six spahn tall it was small compared to the average Graaven, though stooped over and clutching an elaborately carved and ornate staff that seemed to be made of a kind of crystalline material. A heavy robe and hood masked its features.

Through gritted teeth Menkh gasped, 'Are you one of the gods who abandoned us come to finally claim me?'

The figure stayed motionless, though some hissing noises came from with the hood.

'Speak, creature. If you have come to take me then part of me will welcome the relief from my pain, though I despair for my people.'

Finally, a voice emerged from the hooded figure, sibilant at first but growing in strength as it spoke. 'Greetings, Menkh ab Dur. Forgive me, but I needed time to assimilate your speech patterns in order to speak to you.'

It gave off a wheezing sound that Menkh thought resembled laughter.

'As to your gods, if you can find any hint of their presence then I wish you good fortune. I fear that such omnipotent beings are sadly lacking in your current reality.'

'What do you want with me?' asked Menkh.

'Aaah, now that is indeed the question, but sadly the answer to it will take more time than you have. I need you, Menkh ab Dur, more than you could possibly conceive of at this time, but in your current state you are of no use to me or to your people. So, whilst my power in this form is limited, I am going to help you. Hopefully, I will give you the time you need to get your people across the river and away from what pursues you. In return for my help I will exact a promise from you. You are a man of great honour so I will know if you speak truly.'

'That will depend on the promise. I will do nothing that will bring harm to my people.'

'Understood,' the figure replied, 'but the promise is simple, and one easily fulfilled by you alone. You will promise me that once you have crossed the river you will come and listen to me and carefully consider the proposition I will make to you. No harm will befall your people should you refuse to accept my proposal, that I promise you. I will need your answer now, Zaltec.'

Menkh's thoughts were rushing wildly. He was not entirely sure that he was not sinking into some kind of delirium and that this was a strange dream that formed part of it. 'Whilst it may be that you seek to trick me, I cannot discern any evil from what you have asked me. If, by so doing, I can save my people, then you have my promise. I will come and listen to your proposal and I will think carefully on what you say.'

The figure stood silently for several moments and when it spoke it was with a sense of profound relief. 'Thank you, Zaltec, this will mean much to both of us. I think that soon you will recognise my good intent for you and for your people. Firstly, however, there is the question of your physical condition. The malignant growth in you has nearly conquered all, despite your valiant fight against it. As in life, you fight as obstinate a battle internally as you do your external foes. You must come and stand before me now and hold your arms towards me.'

Menkh did not question the instruction but it took him some time to comply as he could barely stand.

'Good, very good,' said the figure. 'Now, hold out your arms to me. I must caution you that you are going to feel some very strange sensations. I will shield you as much as I can from any discomfort. No sounds will be heard outside the confines of this shelter, all will believe you are sleeping.'

'The guards?' Menkh asked.

'Preoccupied with pleasant thoughts,' the figure responded.

'So much for iron discipline,' said Menkh, and the figure wheezed its quiet laughter as it reached out its staff to lay across

Menkh's hands.

The world exploded and Menkh screamed in agony. A thousand, thousand knife points sliced into his body and he whimpered at the scale of it as if he would burst asunder. But as quickly as the pain appeared it became muffled and a soothing voice spoke in his head.

'All will be well, Zaltec. What I am doing will stop this malignancy for some time, but it will not eradicate it completely. I cannot do this here and now. When you awake, remember this: when the river water level recedes, you must get your people across quickly. The waters of the Caxaphalc will only tolerate interference for a short time. You will have four of your chaal at most. When you have crossed you must not be any closer to the river than two spear casts. Remember this on your life and those of your people. We will meet again soon.'

Menkh awoke, and the light that came through the walls of his shelter was indicative of the early dawn. He sat up and gingerly felt his belly. There was no lump and he could not discern even a glimmer of pain. He felt stronger than he had for a very long time. He remembered all that had happened but, whilst it felt like a vivid dream, the physical result was clear, and welcome.

Climbing to his feet he called to the guard, 'Gresh, call for my aide and tell him I'm hungry!'

'At once, Zaltec,' came the reply.

Menkh could not wait for assistance but dressed hurriedly and, pulling out the fine chain mail he had been unable to bear over past weeks, threw it on. The hide flap that passed as a door was lifted aside and his aide, Majek, entered and abruptly stopped, staring at Menkh as he did so.

Menkh in turn stared back and spoke crisply, 'What in the name of the seven-faced god are you staring at, Majek? Must I dress entirely by myself?'

'My lord f … forgive me, but you look … well, you look—'

'Well, how do I look, Majek? Do I now resemble some poxed-up camp follower after a night in the rain?'

Majek rushed to assist Menkh and in an excited voice said, 'No, my lord, you look well, very well indeed, my lord.'

Menkh snorted but was secretly delighted, as this reinforced how he was feeling himself.

Without turning, as Majek tightened the cinches on his chain mail coat, Menkh called out once more to the guard, 'Gresh!'

'My lord?'

'Summon the Stragosh and all Shu Lan and Kalvak, a meeting in twenty semmit.'

'Yes, Zaltec.'

Menkh wolfed down a bite of stale terrax biscuit and some indescribable dried meat that it was best not to inspect too closely. He hoped there would be time to hunt game and rest once they were over the river. He was filled with an optimism that had been lacking from the moment the flight from the capital had started many cycles before.

Menkh arrived at the command post which had been set up a short distance from his small shelter. As he approached, he heard from inside a babble of voices which stilled abruptly as he entered. The silence continued as his staff officers gazed at him, some with a look of incredulity on their faces and others, no less surprised, with smiles spreading across theirs.

Tishan Dar spoke directly as a broad grin broke out like sun from behind a cloud. 'Zaltec, I speak for all of us when I express delight at your apparent recovery. You look very well, my lord.'

Menkh's gaze swept the room. 'Thank you, everyone, you are no less delighted than I and perhaps we may have time to discuss this in more detail later, but time is pressing if we are to successfully ford this river.'

Glances were exchanged between the assembled officers but Menkh pushed on, fixing his gaze on Varga, the most junior Shu Lan present. 'Varga, take two of your best Hoplex and move to the river. I want to know at once if you see any changes to it.'

'Changes, my lord?'

'Indeed, a drop in the speed of the water flow, a drop in the level of the water flowing past. Is that clear, Varga?'

Varga snapped a salute. Whilst he may have felt some confusion over the orders, he quickly repeated the instruction back.

'Very good, carry on. And, Varga?'

Varga stopped and turned.

'Any changes at all, I am to be informed at once.'

Varga nodded, turned, and left.

'Now, attention all, I want an immediate muster of our people. Bring all civilians to the front. Once the level drops, we will have four chaal, and four chaal only, to get everyone across. Stragosh Tishan will coordinate this part of the operation and you will report directly to her.'

Menkh ignored the questioning looks on the faces of his commanders. 'Ankh, you are senior engineer. You will accompany me to the river and reconnoitre the best crossing point.'

Menkh paused and took a deep breath. It was critical that he had the complete commitment of all around him. He smiled at the group and addressed them in a quiet voice. 'I know you have questions. I know that what I am ordering would seem to border on madness, but I want you to trust me without question and I will explain all later. We have come a very long way; we have each of us lost nearly everything. Today there will be a reckoning, today we will stand and meet the filth that has been tracking us to our doom and throw defiance in their face!'

Menkh paused for several moments and looked at each of the faces in the room. Many were missing, but those remaining had proven their worth on countless grim occasions. 'Will you stand with me one last time, comrades?'

As one, each individual snapped to attention and stared back steadfastly. Words in that moment were unnecessary.

Menkh nodded. 'Well then, you have your orders. Quick as you can, if you please.'

In the general hubbub as officers left the tent to fulfil their orders, Menkh spoke to Tishan. 'Send a praka to that rocky outcrop we passed on the way here, I want to know as soon as there is any sighting of the enemy. With luck we have several chaal yet, but they will not be far away. They never are.'

Tishan saluted and paused as if to say something but, hesitating, reached out and gripped Menkh's arm. 'The gods may have abandoned us, but our faith in you is strong, Zaltec. May good fortune smile on us this day.'

Menkh smiled and nodded towards the doorway. 'Get out of here, Tishan, and be careful today. I cannot operate without my right arm.'

Ankh coughed and moved forward from the corner he had been standing in. A diminutive figure for a Hoplex, Ankh was a superlative engineer and, in combat, was as good as any warrior, male or female, who stood in the ranks of the Baran Mec. 'Let us take a look at your river, Zaltec, and see what can be done.'

Menkh nodded and they exited together, two guards silently joining them as they walked down a steady incline to where the river flowed past.

They halted several paces from the edge of the riverbank and gazed at the other side, some three bow shots across.

'Look there, Zaltec,' said Ankh, pointing to a location on the further bank. 'The way the slope rises seems to me to be far too regular for a natural occurrence. I thought the same as we walked down to the riverbank on this side. I could also be quietly encouraged to believe that the difference in the way the vegetation is growing on the far bank could indicate an ancient roadway or some other formation below ground level. In fact, the more I look at those two humps of rock the more I think that they might also be the worn-down foundations of some bridgework that may have spanned this point at some time.'

Menkh stared where the engineer was pointing. 'Well, Ankh, I don't have your professional eyes, but I can see what you are suggesting. But if you are correct it must be ancient indeed to have been worn down so much.'

'That, or perhaps deliberately destroyed by some unknown force or power. In any event, Zaltec, it is pure conjecture, and unless, as you suggest, we can expect a falling in the level and speed of the water, there is no way that I could see how we may cross successfully.'

'In which case,' said Menkh, 'I will return to the command post and await reports on the mustering of our force, and I will leave you, Ankh, to make whatever preparations you deem appropriate for once we are across.'

Ankh saluted as Menkh turned away and watched as he made his way back up the slope.

'Yes,' mused Ankh to himself, 'you have something up your sleeve or some knowledge about this that is yours alone.'

Ankh sighed and abruptly turned to one of the remaining guards. 'Send word to Kalvak Tarax, he is to meet me in my tent with the map he has been keeping of our journey.'

The guard saluted and left Ankh staring at the far bank and the features that he had made note of.

In the meantime, Menkh was pleased at the ordered activity. He could see that as the civilian component made their way forward, other elements of the guard packed up their frugal belongings and mustered in the positions indicated by their Shu Lan. After many grinding bach'chaal in the company of the Baran Mec, the non-combatants were nearly as efficient in getting moving as the imperial guard itself, having been required to move quickly and at a moment's notice. Those who were unable to do so were now long dead.

CHAPTER TWO

Time passed rapidly after the early morning meeting and Menkh was concerned about the enemy coming up from behind.

Deciding nothing further could be gained by waiting, he determined to make an inspection of preparations. It rapidly became apparent that all was ready for as speedy a crossing as possible and he forced down the worry that any change to the river would be too late. At that moment he saw a female guard running at full pelt from the river towards him. Quickly coming to a halt, she waited for permission to speak.

'Well?'

'Zaltec, Shu Lan Varga's compliments, he wishes to inform you that the river level is dropping.'

Menkh felt an almost electric surge of energy whip through his body and he fought hard to remain calm. 'My compliments to the Shu Lan. Tell him that I will be with him directly.'

Menkh felt, rather than saw, Majek standing near him. 'Majek, find the Stragosh and tell her to sound the call to make ready, if you please.'

In answer, he heard the sound of running feet as Majek hastened away and Menkh made his own way down to the river.

He walked calmly and without haste, all the while fighting the urge to sprint, nodding to individual guards and civilians as he walked down. Occasionally he would speak: 'Not long now,' or, 'Ready to get your feet wet?' and at some he would simply smile.

Wherever he passed by, both Baran Mec and civilians would stand straighter or nudge each other when he spoke, or simply smile and nod back. Everywhere, there was a palpable lift in the spirits of all he met.

As Menkh came up to Varga and accepted his salute he could see for himself that the water level was dropping by the wet sand and gravel that was being exposed. Ankh came rushing up as word spread.

'Well timed, Ankh. Observe the river level and the moment you think we can start to cross, give the order. I will send an advance guard across first, then non-combatants and baggage, then the remainder of the guard. I will wait on this bank until the bulk of our forces are across. As quickly as you can, we had four chaal from the moment the river level started dropping.'

Ankh looked bemused. With upwards of 1000 Hoplex and Sagit, as well as 500 civilians and non-combatants plus assorted baggage to get over, there was great pressure to get the job done as quickly as possible.

After a short pause, he replied, 'It will be done, Zaltec,' quietly praying to any gods who had not totally abandoned them to look down with favour on this crossing.

Menkh returned to the camp site. 'Send a runner to the lookouts at the bluff, see if there is any sighting of the enemy and return to me at speed,' he said to one of the guards that accompanied him. Saluting, they ran quickly off.

Menkh saw Tishan coming towards him. 'You have heard the news, Stragosh?'

'Indeed so, my Zaltec, and all are in wonder at your clairvoyance.'

'We will discuss that later. I want you to cross over with the leading elements and set up a defensive line. Take our remaining Sagit to cover the ford. The line should be no closer to the river's edge than 300 paces. Is that clear?'

Tishan's eyebrows lifted in silent query above her angular green eyes. 'Will you not need them? They would be useful to slow down the enemy's approach.'

Menkh looked into Tishan's eyes. 'We don't have enough shafts. Across the ford and on the higher ground they will be of better use. I have my personal guard, they will suffice.'

When no further explanation was forthcoming and realising that any suggestion that Menkh cross first would be rebuffed, she saluted smartly and strode off to find her command.

Back at the ford, Ankh stood with Varga as they observed the lowering level. Every now and then Ankh would take a few tentative steps into the water to test it. He noted that the water flow, whilst still strong, was also decreasing.

Finally, after what seemed an eternity of waiting, he waded out and determined that he would keep going. He called to the four Hoplex who gripped the rope he had tied around his waist, 'You motherless spawn hang on tight. If I drown, I will haunt you for the rest of your miserable lives.'

They smiled in response but appeared to take a firmer grip. Ankh stepped out into the water. The footing underneath was regular, and he surmised that the usual speed and strength of the water flow was such that any potentially dangerous rocks or tree remnants would be washed downstream where the flow was slower and more benign.

The water slowly rose up his body till it was almost to his chest. Crossing was the most difficult here, but he began to feel that he had reached the deepest point. Now approaching midway between the two banks, he felt through his feet that the river bottom was beginning to rise towards the further bank.

Ten more steps confirmed this, and he reasoned that the water level was still dropping. Turning, he called back to those gathered on the bank, 'Commence your crossing!'

Tishan stepped forward with a picked band of troops and struck out for the far bank. Menkh heard the noise as the assembled civilians stood in groups talking amongst themselves. Some were lucky enough to have family members still living and they all stood together glancing anxiously at the ford. With the order given, after picking up and hefting personal belongings, they began to move forward.

They stepped into the water, gingerly following after Tishan's small force. By now the water level and speed had reduced even further and crossing was not overly difficult, although care was needed when placing one's feet. In places the tips of hitherto unforeseen boulders, worn smooth with the passage of years, were exposed. They made good time as they crossed and as the last of them stepped into water, so the first praka of Hoplex stepped out behind them.

Tishan, having completed the crossing ahead of the civilians stood on the far bank and watched their progress. Three praka xem had crossed with her and set up a defensive ring, with their backs to what appeared to be the remnants of a path that led up and out of the deep gully where the ford was located.

No-one had any knowledge of what might lie just out of sight, and she preferred to take no chances with any nasty surprises that may lurk unseen, so she had sent the bulk of a praka, some twenty Hoplex, to scout along the path behind them. Interestingly, the terrain on their side of the river seemed to suggest a considerable change from the arid and desolate country they were now leaving. She could smell the scent of grass and ferns being blown towards her on the wind that was coming steadily from out of the east.

Meanwhile, Menkh had walked out towards the desert and peered into the haze that was rising as the heat of the day increased. He was anxious for news from the squad left as lookout but was relieved that, thus far, no runner had been sent with the news of a sighting. Every semmit was precious in getting across the ford in the time specified by the strange creature that had visited him. He had too many other concerns to have dwelt overly long on the circumstances around both the visitation and his miraculous recovery.

Behind Menkh, the last surviving Hoplex of his personal guard stood motionless. These men and women were the cream of his force, proven in battle and fiercely loyal. Each individual standing at the minimum nine spahn in height sported the swirling tattoos over their blueish skin that denoted them as elite Hoplex. Pitifully few of the two praka haram that had fled the fall of the capital with him.

Each individual carried a heavy mace in addition to the short stabbing sword they were equipped with. Each was protected by an oval shield of stoutly seasoned wood from the giant volgon fern, renowned for its hardness and durability. This wood was overlain with leather from a treloth, a giant herbivore that inhabited lands in the north of the Empire. Their accoutrement was finished with a knee-length, light chain mail shirt and knee-high, metal-reinforced boots.

Menkh was interrupted from his musing by the sight of the runner he had dispatched approaching from out of the desert and he stiffened momentarily – the news from the runner might presage disaster. As the runner approached, he directed course towards Menkh, pulling up in front of him and saluting.

'Report,' said Menkh.

'The enemy has been sighted, Zaltec. The Shu Mut wishes to inform you that he believes they will reach her position within one chaal.'

'Very well,' replied Menkh. 'Who commands?'

'Shu Mut Drax, sir'

'Inform the Shu Mut that she is to fall back to the ford here ahead of the enemy, keeping them in sight. She is not to engage them unless she receives specific orders from me, is that clear?'

The messenger replied in the affirmative.

'Good,' replied Menkh, 'now, how long did it take you to reach me here?'

'From the time I left the Shu Mut, forty semmit at a steady run, Zaltec.'

'Very well, return to the Shu Mut and deliver my message. Stay with her and assist as you can.' Menkh returned the messenger's salute.

'Shu Lan Carsa,' called Menkh to the Hoplex behind him, and a tall female Hoplex strode up to him.

'Zaltec?'

'The enemy will be up to our position very soon and it is likely that we will be making a fighting withdrawal to the ford. Send a runner back to the crossing. Check with Varga how much longer is needed to effect the crossing and then report back to me.'

Carsa snapped a precise salute and strode off to carry out the orders she had been given.

Meanwhile, Shu Mut Drax looked out from the bluff on which she was standing and observed the dust cloud that was moving steadily towards her position. As yet, individual figures of the enemy could not be discerned, only a darker shadow at the centre of the dust they were raising as they approached. She could see the messenger returning and estimated the turnaround time that it had taken for the message to be delivered and the return journey to their position.

As usual, the enemy approached steadily, marching uniformly at a rapid walking pace – a pace which never varied, even when marching into battle. For the thousandth time she wondered who and what they were and where they had come from. What terrible crime had the Empire committed that it should be laid low by these pitiless creatures?

Jet black in aspect, each one was a standard height of just over six spahn. Six arms extended from their upper torso, four ending in a razor-sharp curved surface whilst the other two arms, lower down, had extrusions that resembled three fingers and an opposing "thumb".

Their lower bodies had four powerful "legs" – two of which were versatile in close combat as they had a vicious claw which extended forward. Whilst they appeared as if they could move at speed, Drax had never seen this. Even in battle they were methodical, and their apparent lack of speed was a deadly miscalculation that had cost innumerable lives.

The head was angular with four large, bulbous eyes, two set atop and to each side of their heads and two set lower and more forward. The acuity of the topmost eyes prevented any attempt to sneak up on them from behind in battle. It took up to six Hoplex working together to bring one of these creatures down. Not one had ever been captured or a dead one retrieved from the field. They were a deadly mystery and they had reduced the might of the Graaven empire to nothing in just a few seasons, slaughtering the proud Graaven people and their vassals in their millions.

No demands from these creatures had ever been received, no reason was given as to why they pursued their deadly course. Only Menkh ab Dur had achieved any success in thwarting them by wily use of terrain – but at the costs of thousands of the lives of those that had fled the fall of the capital with him.

The Graavens cursed the Dorath Mar to their gods, without their gods ever appearing to have heard their prayers – or cared.

After receiving her orders from the Zaltec, Drax issued quiet instructions to her praka. 'We will begin our withdrawal ahead of the enemy. Keep it steady and quiet, we want no accidents this day.'

Almost silently, the Hoplex climbed down from the bluff and began to fall back towards the river.

In the meantime, Menkh had returned to the ford and stood observing the river crossing. There had been a few minor incidents in the crossing but nothing major had occurred to hold up progress. After almost three chaal since the water level had begun to diminish, the bulk of his people and associated baggage were across and the last elements were now entering the water. Menkh beckoned Ankh over to him.

'Well done, Ankh, how much longer do you think we need?'

'All being well, Zaltec, another half chaal and then only you and your guard will remain on this side of the river.'

'Very well, finish any last duties and cross over yourself.'

Ankh saluted and strode off to ensure that nothing was overlooked.

Shu Lan Carsa approached Menkh. 'Zaltec, we can see Shu Mut Drax's praka approaching and a large dust cloud rising up behind them.'

'Very well, hold your position and once the Shu Mut comes up to you, direct her and her praka over the crossing, then prepare to withdraw.'

Carsa saluted and, turning smartly, returned to her command.

'Now,' thought Menkh, '*assuming the creature was accurate in what he said, timing is everything.*'

After Drax's Hoplex had passed him by, Menkh made his way up to the 100 guards that made up the single praka vek of his guard, all standing immobile. The enemy, now clearly discernible as individuals, approached. Menkh could never get used to their silence. They never called or made noise of any kind even when brought down although, admittedly, that was a rare occurrence. It was eerie, it was disconcerting, and it was demoralising to engage an enemy that appeared so indifferent to the outcome of the fight.

Menkh spoke aloud to Shu Lan Carsa in a calm and matter of fact tone, 'Prepare.'

Carsa's voice bellowed out in response, 'Prepare!'

Shields were hefted from their resting position and cracked into place against the body of each Hoplex.

'The guard will defensively withdraw 100 paces on my order,' called Menkh and, after a few moments, 'Execute.'

'Defensive withdrawal,' boomed the Shu Lan.

With practised ease, fifty Hoplex turned and withdrew 100 paces before once again turning to the front.

No sooner had this been achieved than the fifty Hoplex who had remained motionless turned and withdrew the allotted 100 paces, slotting back into the now perfectly-renewed ranks and standing immobile as before, at the ready, with Menkh accompanying them.

Menkh judged his position but needed more time to allow for his plan to work.

'Carsa, take two praka xem and engage the enemy, I want you in and out enough to slow them up. I will sound the horn for you to withdraw back to me.'

Carsa stiffened to full height and saluted. 'By your command, Zaltec,' then, turning her attention to her command, called, 'First and second praka xem, prepare to engage with maces. Form on me.'

Fifty Hoplex stepped forward, hefting their heavy maces and lifting their shields higher against their bodies.

'Rank will advance!' came the call, and they strode off towards the enemy.

Menkh lifted his arm in salute as each Hoplex passed him. He had no doubt that some would not come back to him, but he hoped that the attack would slow the advancing enemy down and gain the additional time he judged necessary.

He watched as they moved off briefly, halted, gave a lusty cheer, and then ran full pelt into the foremost ranks of the enemy.

Menkh had chosen a point where the terrain compressed between two rocky outcrops as it descended towards the river. This meant that the front was limited and only a few of the Dorath Mar faced his Hoplex. There was a huge crash as the guards swept in with their heavy maces. The Hoplex had learned that the only vulnerable places were the creatures' eyes, and any damage to them could cause serious disruption to the creatures' movements.

The enemy line halted while they fought off their attackers and Menkh could see more than one guard go down under the scything arms of the enemy.

'Sound withdraw!' Menkh snapped at the trumpeter, and the brassy notes rang out from the curved instrument that sat upon his shoulders.

His Hoplex broke off the engagement and, where they could, snatched up the wounded, dragging them clear before the enemy could complete their deadly work. They withdrew back to the waiting guard, whilst the enemy, who had briefly halted, renewed their order and after a few moments resumed their advance – now somewhat slower than before.

Carsa, a large and bloody rent in her chain mail, came up to Menkh and saluted.

'Well done, Shu Lan, that was a well-executed manoeuvre. Losses?'

'Five dead, Zaltec, we could not save their bodies. Around thirty badly wounded.'

'And you, Shu Lan?'

'A scratch, Zaltec.'

'Hmmm,' replied Menkh.

Four more times Menkh gave the order to engage and withdraw, slowly bleeding his guards in a desperate bid to delay the advance down whilst the enemy was confined. Of the 100

Hoplex that made up the combined might of the praka vek, he had now lost thirty dead, and every one of the remaining troops carried a wound of some kind. After her third wound, Menkh had sent Carsa across the river, under protest, and taken personal command. By his estimation three of the enemy had been taken down, a notable feat, and the attacks had slowed down their advance considerably.

It had now been almost four chaal since the water level had begun falling. Menkh turned to his waiting warriors.

'No Zaltec at any time in the history of our people had better Hoplex under his command. You have my thanks and that of our people, whom you have given your blood and lives to protect. Now, it is time to withdraw across the river.'

On Menkh's command the remaining Hoplex threw their shields over their backs and, turning as one, moved away from the enemy as quickly as they could, some limping badly and supported by their fellows.

The Dorath Mar continued their slow advance but showed no signs of increasing their pace, even though the Graavens in front of them were retreating rapidly and in obvious difficulty. Splashing through the water and reaching the far bank, Menkh ordered his Hoplex to march up to join the Graavens who had assumed a defensive position above the ford on higher ground.

The enemy continued their advance in their silent way towards the water, spreading out a little as they passed through the bottleneck where they had been slowed down.

Menkh reached the higher ground, climbing up the now-beaten path where everyone had crossed before. Tishan Dar had moved the civilians and baggage much further away from the river, guarded by the twenty Hoplex she had sent to scout the path. She had placed all remaining Hoplex and Sagit across the narrowest point as the path led up and away from the river, some 320 paces below their position.

Moving towards Menkh as he came up the pathway towards her, she could see that almost all the Dorath Mar had now entered the water and were nearly halfway across the ford. There were hundreds of them and, as they progressed, they spread out further.

By her calculations, four chaal and twenty semmit had now passed since the river had begun to fall.

Tishan Dar saluted Menkh. 'Your orders, Zaltec?'

Menkh studied the position they occupied. 'You have done well, Stragosh. Here we stand, we retreat no further.'

Raising his voice, he called to the Hoplex standing nearby, 'Pass the word; we stand, and we fight, and we send this filth back up Bringarell's shithole where they came from!'

There was a muttering through the ranks as the name of the Graaven God of the Underworld was heard and some nervous laughter, then the strident calls of the Shu Lans and Shu Muts as the ranks were ordered to stand steady and all became quiet.

Menkh turned to observe the enemy, now fully committed to the crossing with their lead ranks, 150 individuals wide, some two thirds of the way across. Menkh gritted his teeth. Everything now was dependent on the warning the creature had given to him. Once those things were across, his people would make a good fight of it, but they were doomed no matter how well they fought, and Menkh battled a wave of despair that threatened to engulf him.

Fighting these negative thoughts down, Menkh turned towards Tishan. 'I see you have positioned our remaining Sagit to the front. You had the same thought as me, I think. You may order them to engage.'

Tishan turned and, nodding towards the waiting Sagit, beckoned to their Kalvak, a grizzled veteran of many years. 'Kalvak Vorsted, let fly on the enemy!'

Turning to the line of Sagit behind him, he called out the command, 'Nock, draw, and prepare to loose!'

150 bows rose in unison and sighted upon the enemy crossing the ford.

'Loose!'

150 shafts sprang away from the Graaven longbows with a whistling noise that had presaged the doom of many a foe. The Graaven war bow was nine spahn in length with a heavy gut string that only those with a lifetime of training could bend and release. The arrow, longer than an adult Graaven's arm and with a hardened tip made of hemmel alloy, struck with tremendous force into the lead ranks of the enemy. A noise as of a thousand hammers clattering against metal arose, followed by another tremendous crash of sound as a second and then a third wave of shafts impacted the enemy.

Here and there the arrows smashed into the eyes of the Dorath Mar, causing them to weave drunkenly and collide with others alongside them so that the advance slowed and became ragged. Creatures in the third and fourth rank were forced to turn aside to go around those who had been thrown down by multiple impacts or were staggering about with temporary loss of control.

Still the enemy came on, until the lead ranks were but ten paces from the bank. Menkh had to stiffen his resolve, as it seemed inevitable that the Dorath Mar would complete the crossing and begin their climb towards them.

'Prepare to receive the enemy,' said Menkh to Tishan. 'Sagit to the rear.'

Menkh did not turn as he heard the orders given. His Hoplex hefted shields and their long spears came down to the horizontal. He would hold the remnants of his personal guard with their heavy maces as a reserve once engaged.

It was then that Menkh felt a trembling under his feet which, at first, he thought was imagined. Glancing at Tishan Dar, he could see that she, too, had felt it. The tremor grew in power and strength and a moaning sound, like a thousand tormented souls, came from the direction of the river, accompanied by a cold wind. The Hoplex around him were moving uneasily and their Shu Lans angrily called on them to stand at the ready and hold.

The Dorath Mar continued without pause. The lead ranks were now stepping from the water, but the tremor was such that footing was becoming difficult where they stood. The cold wind increased. The roaring scream had built to a continuous roar when, with a mighty crash, the waters of the river swept back down into the ford in a wave of enormous power.

Tons of water, racing at terrifying speed, smashed into the Dorath Mar, instantly sweeping them away before grinding them into pieces against rocks and carrying them downriver. The water rose up toward the position the Graavens held until it seemed that they, too, would be swept away. The noise and fury were such that to witness it reduced all to a state of frozen incredulity and fear. Powerless to move, the water rushed toward them like some ravening animal intent on their destruction. It reached a peak some several paces from where the Graavens stood and churned and frothed as if in impotent rage that it could not wreak destruction upon them.

The noise and wind slowly died down whilst the river flowed by. It may have been just a few semmit, or many chaal, that everyone simply stood and watched the waters, each caught in their own silent thoughts. The wider implications of what had happened were slow to emerge. Individual Hoplex looked at their comrades and grasped each other's arms, clasping hands in sheer relief at having survived such an onslaught.

Menkh turned towards Tishan Dar. 'Well, that was something,' he said to her in glorious understatement.

Tishan Dar stared back at him, speechless, an unfathomable look in her eyes. Slowly she nodded her head and then turned towards the Hoplex behind her. Flinging her arms into the air she called out in a strident voice, 'Menkh ab Dur! Menkh ab Dur!'

Soon, the chant was taken up and Hoplex and Sagit alike hefted arms, spears, maces, bows or anything else that could be lifted, and joined the chant until there was a sound that nearly equalled the screaming of the river in its fury.

Menkh allowed their calls to wash over him. He realised that this was a form of release from terror. Terror of the river, terror of the enemy, and of grief and despair for all those that had been lost and for all that was and would never be again.

Slowly he made his way through the ranks, smiling and nodding until he had passed through the assembled throng.

Turning, he raised his arms towards his gathered people until the sound ebbed and died and all stood silently around him. 'The time of flight is over,' he called out. 'Now we shall rebuild our lives in a new land. All of us here have fought and bled and lived in fear and despair. No more! Let us go forward now and leave behind the blackness. Will you follow me towards a new beginning?'

If it were possible, the roar around him exceeded that of the river and was joined by the civilians further down. Menkh ab Dur strode down the path into the new land. He had no idea where he was going but he felt a sense of sureness and certainty that had been absent for a very long time.

CHAPTER THREE

The country they now entered was very different from the arid and virtually waterless plain they had so recently spent weeks in crossing.

Verdant grassy plains stretched out before them, and in the distance a mountainous range loomed with some peaks evidencing a hint of snow which reflected the light of the suns.

Everywhere, great herds of grazing animals could be seen moving off unhurriedly as the Graavens approached. It was apparent from the behaviour of these creatures that contact with people was so rare as to be a cause of curiosity and caution, rather than the expected rapid flight that such animals would have exhibited within the borders of the Empire.

The colouration of the grazing herds was strange to Graaven eyes, passing from a dusky shade of blue to a pale yellow which blended into the surrounding grasses. These were intermixed with more familiar herbivores, long-necked bernash and three-horned pertan, their huge size a case for much discussion and pointing. Comments about fresh meat and the roasting of joints were common as this was a greatly anticipated occurrence that had been, until now, merely a dim memory.

Tishan Dar walked alongside Menkh and surveyed the country around them. Scouting parties had been sent ahead to spy out terrain suitable for a camp as the intention was to rest for several days and take stock, now that the immediate danger from the Dorath Mar was over.

'The size of these animals amazes me, Tishan,' Menkh mused. 'Perhaps there were creatures of this size and number in the very beginnings of the Empire?'

'It's the size of the predators that concerns me, Zaltec,' Tishan responded. 'Anything tackling these creatures would either have to be of daunting size itself or of a number sufficient to ensure success.'

'Quite so, which is why we are travelling in close order with our Hoplex in a protective cordon around our civilians. We have several chaal of daylight left so, with luck, we can find a defensible place for a camp.'

'If I may suggest, Zaltec. If we have no news within the next three chaal, then we make a travelling camp and fortify with ditches. We can collect fuel for fires and – hopefully – see out the night in safety.'

'Agreed.'

Well within the three-chaal time limit a scouting party could be seen jogging back to the main body. They reported that a rocky outcrop with a small stream nearby was close, with ample room to set up a camp and defensive perimeter. An old stand of cycads and other strange trees could provide dry fuel. Menkh immediately diverted course, led by the scouting group.

Sometime later, after a flurry of concentrated and coordinated activity, a marching camp had been established. A series of fires had been lit around the perimeter and Ankh and his team had been busy in setting up rudimentary defences utilising, as far as possible, the outcrops of rock that surrounded the summit of the small hill where they had established the camp. Whilst somewhat cramped, it was sufficient for a night before pressing on towards the mountains in the distance.

Hunting parties had been successful in bringing in game and the smell of roasting meat filled the still air as dusk descended, setting mouths to watering in anticipation of what seemed a feast after many bach'chaal of privation and short rations.

Menkh walked around the perimeter of the camp, talking to the Hoplex who had been placed on guard and were staring out into the rapidly increasing darkness. The calls and cries of night life echoed around them and the Hoplex echoed his thoughts that it would not be a good thing to be alone out in the darkness. Once or twice dark shapes were dimly perceived passing by below the hill and the vibration of the ground under heavy feet could be felt, but nothing came within the circle of light cast by the fires, which were to be kept burning throughout the night.

After ensuring that all was under control and after partaking of a share of the meat, which was succulent and flavoursome, Menkh retired to rest in the shelter set up for him. It was not his intention to sleep for long and he was aware that, after the tumultuous events of the past days and the removal of the threat that had dogged them throughout their flight from Tarmech, it would be easy to become somewhat complacent. However, they were in a strange and new land so far beyond the borders of the old Empire that nothing could be taken for granted.

As Menkh lay down a thousand thoughts and unformed plans and ideas played through his mind, and he drifted off into sleep unexpectedly. His sleeping mind wandered into the past until he once again stood in the Great Hall before the throne and looked up into the eyes of Pershiva.

------0------

Bowing low, he looked about the vast hall but saw only a few nobles garbed for war. Pershiva herself, dressed in shimmering mail, wore a helmet that also held the royal diadem, a blazing white crystal, long an heirloom of the House of Dur and symbol of kingship. Menkh's alarm grew.

'Pohlan Kar, the streets are thronged with our people who spill out from the city into the east. The waters of the Camchak are filled with vessels heading downriver and I see an impisch, gathering for war. What calamity befalls us here in the heart of the Empire?'

Pershiva al Dur stood up from the throne. With dignified steps she descended from the dais and stood silently before him. Her eyes, filled with tears, looked upon Menkh as if trying to fix in her mind all his features and hold them close. Then, beyond all protocol and thought, she swept into his arms. Menkh embraced her in surprise and alarm.

Menkh held her without words and he felt her gather her strength. Pershiva was short for a Graaven, but she had the features of their mother and the strength of their father. Her eyes, when they looked up into his, were haunted and she spoke quietly. 'Menkh. Dearest brother. The Empire …' here she battled another emotion and choked out the last words, 'the Empire is undone.'

Menkh drew back in alarm and confusion. 'Undone? How can this be, Pershiva? I have been gone for less than two sem'chaal. What has done this? How has this happened? Why did you not call me sooner?'

'All good questions, Menkh. An alien force utterly unknown to us. They have rolled over our forces, Menkh. All of them. News has been slow in coming to us. Our impisch mustered to defend, all annihilated. The people have a name for these things – they call them the Dorath Mar – and now the last of our forces muster at my command.'

'So, you have called me to lead our forces out to defend the city? I will do my duty as you command. If you send the Kalvaks to me, I will prepare.'

Pershiva placed a finger on Menkh's lips.

'Hush. It is I, the Pohlan Kar, who will lead our last impisch against the enemy.'

As Menkh made to protest, steel came into her voice. 'Menkh ab Dur, will you heed the command of your Pohlan Kar?'

Now it was Menkh from whose eyes bitter tears fell. 'I am ever the servant of the Pohlan Kar. What is your command?'

'The Baran Mec is mustered by the Eastern Gate. Take them and flee the city. Take with you any of our people that you can, Menkh. Your skill in war is their only hope for survival and the final hope of the Empire. I will give you as much time as I can. Tishan Dar, your Stragosh, awaits you. I have given you the best commanders we have left. Go, Menkh, my beloved brother. Go and may the grace of the gods go with you.'

'Surely there must be another way?' Menkh said desperately. 'Is all so hopeless?'

'We are never without hope. You are our hope. Do this for me, Menkh. Do this for all our people. Live for me. That will be enough.'

They embraced and at the last touched foreheads in the way of Graaven affection. Pershiva finally drew back.

'Go, Zaltec. You have your orders.' Turning without a backward glance, she swept out of the hall, followed by the few nobles who remained with her.

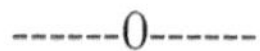

Menkh turned in his sleep and snorted awake, disoriented so that, at first, the coalescing blue light at the foot of his travel cot did not register. When it did, he sat up slowly as the strange figure that had visited him before took on a more solid reality.

'Greetings, Zaltec. I see that you orchestrated a safe passage over the Caxaphalc and your enemies are destroyed – at least, for the time being.'

'Yes, and for that and so much more I and my people shall be ever in your debt. It would seem apparent that you have not just come to congratulate me on a safe crossing?'

'Indeed, no. Given the circumstances involved, there was little time for me to speak with you and the drain on my power was overly great. Here I am more able to speak with you and, perhaps, to answer any questions you may have?'

'I have ten thousand questions, though I think if we spent all night and all day you would still have not answered them all. Firstly though, who are you to whom I owe so much, and what land is this that we have crossed into?'

'As to who I am, I think that would take one of your dak'chaal to discuss, and perhaps then we would only have scratched the surface. I have had many names over time – some I remember with fondness and some, with sadness.'

'Are you a god, then?'

The response was some quiet laughter which seemed to Menkh tinged with a degree of irony.

'No, Zaltec, I am not. If there is one thing I have come to know across the cosmos, belief in the gods, any god and their divinity, is the root cause of some of the greatest calamities and evil deeds ever to be perpetrated upon intelligent life. For with belief comes "religion", and within that concept lies a terrible path to corruption and domination.'

The intensity and passion with which the words were uttered carried a weight of anger and sadness and Menkh could sense an ocean of bitterness that lurked behind them.

A silence ensued that Menkh did not wish to break. At last, the creature issued a long sigh. 'My apologies, Zaltec, perhaps there are things that at this time we should not discuss. Let us move on. You may call me Crixac which, translated into your tongue, means friend. I hope that we will be good friends no matter the circumstances. As to the land you are sitting upon, it is ancient and once, eons ago, was the home of three great civilisations that flourished here until their fall. It is fitting that you chose this rocky outcrop to camp upon. Once it was used as a place to observe the stars and, to some extent, it stood guard over the road that led to the ford over the Caxaphalc. Its energy still echoes here despite the long years since its ruin and most creatures will avoid its slopes. As to any gratitude you may have, this is accepted with thanks, but remember that I have set a price upon the "gift" – if that is what you want to call it. Soon, now, we will meet in person and I will not have to rely on this projection. Then we will discuss my proposition.'

Here Crixac mused for a few moments before resuming. 'Continue your journey towards the mountains. There is still the trace of a roadway that takes you towards them. Follow this. It will be hard to discern in some places but the vegetation that grows upon it will be stunted and sparse compared to that which grows around it. Your scouts should be able to pick the route for you as they go ahead.

Other than some large predators, which you should endeavour to avoid and take precautions against, there is nothing in this land that should cause you any problems. Whilst large, the creatures that graze the plains and woodlands hereabouts have little knowledge of people, so hunting food should not be a problem. Many of the plants and fruits you will also recognise as you travel. These, you can gather.'

'How long will this journey take us? You can appreciate that my people have been hunted and harried for a long time. The thought of stopping and perhaps now having some kind of a future other than death is beginning to take shape. I cannot continue to drive them on without some semblance of a plan.'

'Yes, I do understand. I would estimate that in a week, or what you would call a dak'chaal or so of your time, you will arrive at a place where all that your people need and desire will be able to be satisfied. Trust me on this, Zaltec. You have come here for a purpose. Whilst matters have proven your gods' non-existence to you, there is, nevertheless, a power that manifests itself for good or for evil dependent on the nature of the individuals that focus their will upon it, even unknowingly. In the circumstances you find yourself, Zaltec, you yourself are a prime mover; yet you would not think of calling yourself a god, I think?' The last was said with some degree of dry humour.

Thoughts whirled in Menkh's head and some of the concepts that Crixac had spoken of challenged a number of the beliefs that Menkh had based his life upon, whilst others seemed to confirm some of the ideas that had formed as he had lived his life in the Empire.

'So, I will leave you once again, Zaltec. Sleep now, all will be well, but you will face a challenge in the morning light. Follow your heart in dealing with it.'

'Thank you, Crixac. A cryptic comment but I will endeavour to do so. You have given me much to dwell upon, but I would ask one thing of you before you leave.'

'And what is that, Zaltec?'

'That you call me Menkh. If we are to be friends, then I would have you use my name.'

A deep silence ensued after Menkh had spoken and the voice, when it returned, had some unfathomable emotion tied to it. 'Thank you, Menkh. A name is a powerful thing and your words are as a cherished gift to me. It has been time out of mind since I have called or been called, by anyone, friend.'

As the figure vanished from sight the last words echoed in Menkh's head, 'Remember, at the sun's rising ... follow your heart.'

Menkh slept deeply and if he had dreams, he could not recall them later. His slumber was disturbed when Majek shook him awake.

'Zaltec, there is a disturbance on the perimeter. Stragosh Tishan calls for your presence.'

'Yes, yes, very well, Majek,' mumbled Menkh, coming blearily awake. 'There is no need to shake me like a fern tree in a high wind, I am, as you can see, awake.'

'My apologies, Zaltec, but the message is urgent.'

'Very well, I will go there. Help me with these boots.'

Menkh followed two agitated guards to the "disturbance", where Tishan Dar was pacing up and down. Thirty Sagit stood with nocked bows and 100 Hoplex armed with spears had formed a phalanx with shields up and facing outward.

Tishan spun around at Menkh's approach.

'What in the name of the gods is happening, Stragosh? Has the enemy miraculously swum back up the river and joined us?'

Tishan pointed back over her shoulder beyond the perimeter. 'No, Zaltec, they are the problem.'

Menkh peered out into the dawn light to what, at first glance, appeared to be several very large, tawny-coloured boulders. It was only when one of them moved that he realised they were living creatures.

"Imposing" and "majestic" did not appear to be adequate terms to describe these creatures. Tawny fur with reddish stripes covered their bodies. Powerful front limbs with huge, padded feet and claws extended into long and graceful legs, which ended in massively muscled shoulders. Equally powerful hindquarters had bony spurs which would be useful for taking a tight grip on the megafauna that it obviously was adapted to hunt, all ending in a stub-like tail. But, however impressive in sheer size, they were also magnificent to look upon with four large and intensely blue eyes that reflected intelligence. Their jaws were of equal proportion to their body mass and, even at rest, the size and quantity of their teeth gave confirmation, if any was needed, that these were efficient and deadly predators and pack hunters.

'Well, well,' said Menkh, 'somewhat like a Percassian vitran, only bigger again, wouldn't you say? Have these creatures made any overtly hostile moves towards us?'

'No, Zaltec. The guards report that they came somewhat closer and appeared to be sniffing the air. Apparently satisfied, they then lay down as you see them now, but to what purpose one can only surmise.'

'Waiting for something, perhaps?' mused Menkh.

'Aye, but what?' responded Tishan Dar. 'We cannot break camp with these creatures in such close proximity. If they decide to attack, we will be extremely hard-pressed to contain them.'

'Well, we may not have to wait too much longer. Look there.'

Tishan Dar followed Menkh's pointing finger. As one, each of the creatures rose up and emitted a deafening roar that hurt the ears. So primal and savage was the sound that there was not one person who did not feel their heartbeat increase and their stomach shrink. Yet, at the same time, a strange sense of freedom and utter joy came with it, so that the two feelings seemed to clash with each other until one could not tell if it was fear or something else entirely.

From up out of the slight mist that lay at the bottom of the hill another creature approached. Unlike those on the hill, this one was completely white and, if anything, half as big again as the others. Whereas those on the hill had blue eyes, as the creature came forward Menkh could see that its eyes were a deep and compelling green. A long, sinuous tail flicked over its hindquarters and as it passed each of the others they rolled on their backs and exposed their bellies to it in submission.

'Well,' remarked Tishan in a quiet voice, 'here is a king of beasts indeed.'

'Agreed, Stragosh, but I think you will find the word "queen" more appropriate in the circumstances.'

The creature continued its advance towards them, moving unhurriedly, with its eyes fixed on the point where Menkh and Tishan stood.

'Sagit, stand to!' snapped Tishan Dar, but Menkh turned towards them and raised his arm, bringing his hand down in a calming gesture.

'Stand easy and wait for my command.'

The beast continued its approach until it was within a spear cast and then sat its hind limbs on the ground and tipped its head to one side. A low rumble of sound came from its mouth. All the Graavens who had gathered looked at each other in astonishment.

'Is it talking to us, Menkh?' Tishan Dar's surprise was so complete that she had forgotten to use the formal address that she invariably used when in public.

'It would certainly appear that its immediate intent is to communicate rather than taking us on for a meal. Of course, it could just be enquiring as to whether we are tasty,' replied Menkh drily.

Tishan turned to Menkh in surprise but a smirk appeared on her face. 'She may find us a little hard to swallow.'

Menkh stared at the creature, his thoughts in a whirl. All instincts said that this was a wild and dangerous creature, and yet its actions belied this. It sat and looked at them, its head to one side and apparently at ease.

The words from the previous evening came to mind – follow your heart – and Menkh resolved to take a risk.

'Stragosh, I will endeavour to communicate with this creature. You will not shoot or take any offensive action unless that creature attacks.'

'But, Zaltec, surely you cannot be serious?' an incredulous Tishan Dar responded.

'You have your orders, Tishan. I understand your concerns, but I sense no aggression in this creature.'

Before any further protest was forthcoming, Menkh stepped forward beyond the perimeter. A wave of murmuring from the assembled Hoplex was immediately stilled as officers issued terse commands for silence.

Menkh pondered as he approached, *'How do you open a dialogue with a wild animal with huge teeth, extraordinary size and an unknown disposition? It feels strangely like walking into the presence of the Emperor. Hmmm ... now there's a thought.'*

Menkh considered the protocol of the Graaven Court, the precise distance that must be observed before the Emperor and the degree to which the formal bow was set.

Menkh continued in an unhurried pace, outwardly calm, inwardly seething with disquiet. He halted fifteen paces from the creature. He then bowed low and held that position for a slow count of ten before standing back up with his hands open and arms crossed before his chest.

'Greetings. I am Menkh ab Dur, the leader of these people. We mean you no harm and seek to cross your hunting grounds peacefully, with your permission.'

It was difficult not to feel like a fool addressing a wild animal in formal Graaven speech but Menkh simply felt that this was correct.

The creature had become totally motionless as Menkh spoke. After some seconds it stood very slowly. At fifteen spahn at the shoulder, it towered over Menkh's paltry eight spahn. Menkh prayed that Tishan did not do anything precipitate, whilst at the same time a small voice conceded that, if this creature pounced, he would be dead before any arrows could strike home.

After reaching its full height it stretched its massive neck and lowered itself down till its head was level with Menkh's, bowing its head before standing once again.

Menkh had never in his life been so relieved, astonished, and gratified all at once.

Turning away from Menkh, the creature issued a huge roar followed by a series of grunts — as one, the other creatures rose, turned towards where Menkh was standing, and repeated the bow that their queen had displayed. In turn, Menkh bowed low once more. The magnificent creature then turned with sleek grace and moved back down the hill. Her companions stood silently as they, too, calmly moved off behind their undoubted leader.

It was only then that Menkh's legs began to shake uncontrollably and he abruptly sat down on the grass. A huge sound of chatter and cheering rose up behind him, and the sound of running feet came as Tishan and Ankh approached, pulling him upright.

'By the seven faces of Bekkor, Zaltec, I think you have just created a story that will go down in legend,' said Ankh. 'How in the name of the gods did you know what to do?'

Menkh laughed shakily, 'I thought it was like approaching the Emperor and took my lead from that. Did you ever see such a creature? See such dignity and grace in a wild animal? Surely this is a most wondrous land that we have entered.'

Some chaal later, as the Graavens continued their journey towards the mountains, the creatures could be seen following behind in the distance.

Majek was pacing along behind Menkh and spoke aloud, 'Do you think they are keeping an eye on us, Zaltec?'

'Undoubtedly, Majek, as would I in their situation. Be so kind as to advise the hunting parties to ensure that they do not approach the creatures and to kill only what is needed for our survival.'

Majek saluted in response and jogged off to find the Kalvak coordinating the hunting parties.

Only once in the ensuing weeks did the creatures show any sign of aggression and ferocity, and that was in defence of the Graavens, when a huge and solitary predator came roaring out of a heavily wooded hillside that they were traversing.

For some inexplicable reason, the creatures had moved much closer and even somewhat ahead of the Graaven march. Now it seemed clear that they had sensed the attack as the creature appeared. It had four powerful legs with two arms ending in long claws, and a hide that appeared thick and tough and covered with scales. A huge jaw and needle-like teeth were supplemented by a long tail with a barb-like protrusion.

The pack led a coordinated and skilled attack, feinting and advancing with amazing speed which confused the creature. One of them was fractionally too slow and the claws of the predator left a bloody gash in its flank but, after what seemed like an age, the frustrated predator turned and ran back into the woods to escape the harrying of its attackers.

The pack gathered around their injured companion who issued a muted groan that was piteous, given its size and strength.

Menkh called for Grakh – the only Graaven who had any formal medical training – to accompany him and approached the gathered creatures. They protectively shielded their companion and issued a low but unmistakable warning to the two Graavens. The one the Graavens referred to as the queen emerged from the group and advanced towards Menkh and Grakh, who was valiantly trying to control his fear.

Menkh bowed low and dragged Grakh down with him.

'We thank you for your protection but see that one of you has been injured. Might we offer you assistance? My friend Grakh here is a healer,' said Menkh, indicating to Grakh and then pointing toward where the wounded beast lay.

The queen once again paused with its head to one side. It then repeated the bow that Menkh had given and, turning to one side, issued a series of low growls which Menkh deemed were instructions as, following these, the creatures opened up a path to the wounded animal lying on the ground in their midst.

'Pull yourself together, Grakh. Take a look at the wound and see what you can do. You've been on a battlefield. This is no worse.'

Hesitantly, the surgeon approached and inspected the wound which was reachable because the creature was lying on its side. The wound was clean as the other animals had applied their tongues to it, but a large flap of skin had been torn and was hanging down.

'I can stitch the skin with gut and apply a salve, Zaltec, but the creature will have to lie still, and it may be uncomfortable for him as I stitch.'

Menkh grinned humourlessly. 'Very well.' Turning to the leader and bowing again, Menkh said, 'My friend can stitch the wound closed but you must tell your companion that he must be still. The stitching may hurt somewhat.'

The lion turned its head to one side and issued a series of deep breathy sounds that Menkh was sure was laughter. Once again, he was mystified at the intelligence of these creatures and wished he understood them more.

The white queen touched noses with her wounded companion and issued a series of low growls, then dipped its head to Menkh.

'Proceed,' said Menkh.

Half a chaal later the job was done, and with the salve applied they were ready to return to the Graavens who had paused in their march. As one, all of the creatures bowed to Menkh and Grakh. Grakh was surprised when the very large, wet, and raspy tongue of the wounded animal he had assisted was applied to the back of his head. Menkh and Grakh bowed again in return and made their way back to the Graavens who were anxiously waiting for them.

'Well, well, Grakh, it seems you have a new and grateful patient.'

'Yes, Zaltec,' said Grakh as he wiped away the sticky saliva that covered the back of his head and neck. 'I am certainly grateful that he decided not to take my head with it!'

Menkh laughed and patted Grakh on the back. 'You did well.'

CHAPTER FOUR

The weather began to change for the worse as the seasons turned and the time of Hordeth Gar, the storm season, approached. Having endured one such season already, the Graavens were less than keen to go through this time again as they had suffered greatly being exposed to the elements. Whilst snow was a rarity, the temperatures, combined with storms of great intensity, posed a danger to any traveller without shelter.

The mountains, majestic and awe-inspiring, loomed above the Graavens as they made camp in the foothills. They had followed the roadway successfully, though at times the scouts had to cast back and forth to find its last vestiges as the undergrowth slowly covered it.

Eventually, the road ended at a deep ravine over which a huge and ancient stone bridge spanned the chasm in a single arch. A river could be seen far below, rushing through the ravine, fed by a magnificent waterfall which could be clearly discerned in the distance, threading its way down a cliff face.

Ankh had surveyed the bridge and crossed over it several times, testing its capacity to bear the weight of the Graavens as they crossed over. He remarked on the strange symbols that were carved into the stones, which in many places were obscured by mosses and similar plant-like growths that had become established over time. The single span of the bridge was wide enough for four Graavens to walk abreast with some room to spare, but it was not for the fainthearted as there were no outer walls on the bridge. A misstep near the edge would result in a long and terrifying fall to the river and rocks far below.

'Whoever these ancient beings were, they knew how to build,' remarked Ankh to Tishan Dar after completing his inspection. 'It's incredible that such a structure should have survived in such condition over the years.'

'Let us hope so, Ankh, because I don't fancy a long dive into the river below us,' replied Tishan Dar in a wry tone.

In due course a scouting group of ten Hoplex was sent over the bridge to assess the terrain on the other side. The path that led up on the other side disappeared between cliff walls not far from where it exited the bridge proper.

After only a single chaal or so, a lone scout returned and reported that at no great distance the path opened out into a flat area, continuing to run along a valley that was situated between a range of hills on either side. A stream of fresh, clear water ran alongside the path and no immediate or obvious danger was discernible.

After a brief conference with his commanders, Menkh gave the order to advance over the bridge and the Graavens moved forward. The Hoplex, moving purposefully, kept well away from the sides of the bridge, whilst the civilians huddled together as close as they could to the centre of the span as they crossed.

Behind them the giant creatures that had escorted them so faithfully moved closer before sitting on the ground. The white queen approached and, bowing gracefully, gave a series of breathy grunts before turning her head away from the bridge.

'I do not think our friends intend to accompany us further,' remarked Menkh to Tishan after responding to the creature's bow.

'Perhaps we are leaving their hunting grounds?' quizzed Tishan.

'In any event, we move forward.'

Menkh bowed low once more to the now departing queen and, turning, moved towards the bridge. The creatures watched as the Graavens marched away before themselves turning back without a further glance.

The bridge was crossed without incident and, in due course, a marching camp was established along the trail. It was a further happy event that led the Graavens to discover that the stream contained a plentiful supply of fish of appreciable size, and great activity resulted in a number of Graavens coming up with various ingenious ways to catch them.

As it was, the fish seemed to be unwary that they were being hunted and, as a result, a fine haul was duly caught. The smell of their cooking was soon smelt throughout the camp.

Bara Desh – one-time tavern owner from the Province of Dermoch – huddled by the fire with his surviving daughter, Mertain. They both looked hungrily at the two fish that were being roasted over hot coals and both were remembering happier times when they still were a family, with other siblings and Mertain's mother, Teremal, before the fall. Many a tear had been shed. Only the constant need to be on the move and fighting a battle merely to survive had kept them from a paralysis of despair. At last a sense of hope, still small but growing, had begun to form.

'By all the gods, Mertain, I wish your mother and brothers were with us to share this meal,' Bara Desh's voice was muted and soft, with an expression of infinite regret and loss.

'She is with us in spirit, Father, as are Grana and Rutha,' replied Mertain, squeezing her father's hand. A long and silent look passed between them. An acknowledgement of loss and a growing expectation that a new day was coming. A sad smile was exchanged and, with a sigh, Bara Desh reached out to skewer some of the cooked fish, depositing it on a wooden platter. 'Come, daughter, let us eat and offer our thanks for this food.'

All across the camp similar tableaus were happening as individuals exchanged smiles and occasional laughter, subdued but no less heartfelt.

'The people are beginning to believe that they have a future,' Tishan Dar mused to her companion, Baransi. 'I sense a change in everyone.'

'Yes,' replied Baransi, 'the Zaltec's recovery and his leadership throughout has been an inspiration and a beacon of hope amongst all the despair. I truly thought that we were doomed, though I would not say it aloud.'

'Yes, I felt the same,' replied Tishan as, smiling, she and Baransi shared a meal together.

Over the course of the next few days the Graavens, at Menkh's command, constructed more substantial shelters using the abundant wood and natural materials that were present in the area. Latrines were dug and, in all respects, a solid and defensible marching camp was established that provided a degree of comfort and shelter that had not been experienced since the flight from the capital.

Menkh had determined that the land should be scouted well in advance. He devised the makings of a plan for advancing into this new land for, as Tishan Dar observed, the land may appear empty, but of natural obstacles and native peoples they had no knowledge.

Shortly before the scouting parties were due to head out Menkh had retired to rest, but sleep eluded him. He felt restless but could not place any particular reason for it. As he lay on his cot going over things in his mind, he noticed the blue glow that presaged the arrival of Crixac and sat up in anticipation. As a figure coalesced into form, Crixac spoke. 'Greetings, Menkh, it appears that your people have settled in well to this place.'

'Indeed, Crixac, hope springs anew and we regain our strength before we move on. Perhaps you may be able to assist with our plans?'

'You come to the heart of it, Menkh. I now will ask you to fulfil your part of our agreement. Two dak'chaal from here lies an ancient city, long abandoned but perhaps ready for reoccupation by your people. It lies under my protection, but I would ask that you come here alone first. There are reasons for this which will become clearer to you when you arrive.'

Menkh paused while he absorbed this information. 'I am happy to accede to your request, Crixac. You have been true to your word and I can do no less. However, coming alone will be a problem as my people will demand that I take an escort. I cannot simply disappear into the night.'

'Very well. Select your escort, but no more than five of your Hoplex. I would ask you not to convey the information I have given to you at this time, but you have my word that all will be well. This land where your people camp is unoccupied, save for the animals that call this their home. There are predators that you need to be careful of, but nothing that you cannot prepare for or which would lie outside of your Hoplex's capacity to deal with.'

'We have already encountered some magnificent beasts, intelligent, powerful, and magnificent. Do you know of them?'

A dry chuckle issued from Crixac, 'Ahh, the encounter I warned you of. You did well indeed. You have encountered the last of the gonverdeem, as the inhabitants of the city called them – though that was an age ago, now. Bred for their intelligence and strength they were used as mounts for a time, if such a word can even begin to convey their true role. Able to communicate and understand complex concepts, they are unrivalled in battle, and feared; but they are also intensely loyal and affectionate to those with whom they bond. It was no mean feat to approach their leader as you did. Her pack will not forget you, and I sense may have a part in what is to come.'

'And what is to come, Crixac?'

The voice began to grow fainter as if diminishing into the distance. 'As to that, Menkh, we will discuss at length when you are here. Do not tarry, however, my time grows short and I have much need of you.'

With that, the light faded and the glow of the lamp once again dimly illuminated the cabin.

The next morning Menkh gathered all his senior commanders for a conference to relay his intentions. After listening, Tishan responded to Menkh, 'Zaltec, are you sure about this? We cannot afford to take unnecessary risks or face losing you.'

A nodding of heads accompanied this statement from the gathered assembly.

'I understand your concerns, all of you, and appreciate them,' Menkh's gaze swept across the faces in front of him, 'however, I need to see the land myself rather than at third-hand. I have told you that I will take an escort of five hand-picked Hoplex – you can choose them yourselves. I promise you that I will take no unnecessary risks but expect me to be gone for at least three to four meh'chaal. Then, when I return or if I send you word, be ready to move. This should give you the time needed to prepare our people.'

Ankh sighed, 'Zaltec, it appears that your mind is made up, and we know from experience that it is easier to move a Vorenian sloth than you once fixed.'

A dry chuckle went around the meeting room.

'Thank you, Ankh, and the fact that a Vorenian sloth is as hairy, large, and ugly as your backside has not escaped my notice!' responded Menkh.

The chuckles turned to outright laughter and eased the tension in the crudely made hut that was being used as the command post.

'Tishan, you will be in charge until my return. Coordinate the scouting parties and manage the needs of our people as you see fit, but make no mistake, everyone,' Menkh's gaze lingered on each face, 'we will be moving upon my return. You have all done well. Now, return to your duties, you are dismissed.'

The gathered commanders filed out, talking amongst themselves and nodding at Menkh as they passed, but Tishan Dar lingered.

'Zaltec, there is so much happening that you are not telling us, going back to your recovery and the crossing of the ford. None would question or doubt but there is much conjecture.'

'Do you perceive this as having a bad effect on morale, Tishan?'

'Assuredly not. I cannot conceive of any act or omission on your part that our people would not accept coming from you. Their faith in you is unparalleled. To have come this far, to have survived at all …'

Tishan's voice faded into silence and Menkh could see that she was overcome with an emotion that could not be formed into words.

'Thank you, Tishan. I am humbled by what you have said. But the cost of my personal adulation has been at the expense of many Graaven lives, all given in sacrifice to the hope that we might survive. It is not "I" but "we", all of us, who have gotten this far. No leader, no Zaltec in our race's history, could have expected and received more from his people.'

Tishan looked into Menkh's eyes and nodded. Without looking away, Menkh's voice quietened so that only Tishan could hear. 'No leader or Zaltec could have wished for a finer Stragosh, not in loyalty, not in courage, not in devotion, not in brilliance. No, Tishan, Menkh ab Dur may enjoy the adulation of the people but you enjoy mine.'

As if it were a natural progression, Tishan entered his embrace and for a long moment they clung to each other, each responding to a depth of feeling unrecognised till this moment, tempered in the furnace of adversity and moulded with mutual respect and admiration.

As was the way of the Graaven people, they touched foreheads and looked deep into each other's eyes.

'Menkh,' said Tishan in a whisper, 'if we arrive at a place of safety, if it should be that I am still capable, would you do me the honour, could it be that …?'

Menkh placed a finger on Tishan's lips. 'Tishan Dar, it is you who honour me. If …' Menkh's voice lingered on that word, '…if all should come to pass as we dare hope, then when you choose the time of your quickening, should you still wish, we will conjoin and together we will bring forth a new life and a new hope.'

Tishan bowed her head and Menkh himself was overcome with emotion. He thought of his sister and her needless death and all that they had planned to achieve, and for a time was lost in his own thoughts.

Finally, after squeezing Menkh's hands, Tishan stood back. She nodded to Menkh with an unfathomable look and, clearing her throat, spoke loudly, 'Thank you, Zaltec. I will ensure that preparations for your departure are in hand.'

Without a further look Tishan departed, leaving Menkh in a strongly reflective mood.

Next morning, after completing the formalities of placing command in the hands of Tishan Dar in front of the assembled Graavens, Menkh left with his five guards, sending two forward to scout, one as a rearguard, and the two others to stay near him as they progressed.

Menkh had conferred with Tishan throughout the evening and left detailed instructions as to the preparations that needed to be made. This included foraging for edible plants and fruits which could also be dried and stored now that the people had time to do this. The healer, Grakh, had set off in search of medicinal herbs which he was hopeful of finding in the fertile place they had encamped, and a number of Graavens who had knowledge of home remedies and cures, along with an escort, accompanied him. The weather had consistently remained unseasonably mild and warm even though the storm season was upon them and this, too, boosted everyone's spirits.

Menkh's five guards were well known to him, all proven and capable Hoplex. Votlas Fen, as the senior Shu Lan, organised their small troop in accordance with Menkh's wishes and all seemed to anticipate the journey ahead which surprised Menkh, considering the harrowing travels they had so recently completed.

Desh, the only male Hoplex in the group and big, even for a Graaven, brought up the rear, whilst Horven Var and her sibling Mareen stayed in close proximity to Menkh himself. After a brief conference Votlas, accompanied by Ardesh Pen, jogged ahead along the pathway that continued to rise into the hills leading up from the camp.

They travelled mostly in silence as was the Graaven way, occasionally remarking on a waterfall or other landmark either for its beauty or its grandeur. The country they passed through was verdant, with tall forests of giant ferns and other succulents slowly giving way once again to plains of tall grasses. Large herds of grazing herbivores ignored their passing after assessing them as no threat.

They recognised many plants, along with strange blooms of deep purple and shades of red. Such was their abundance that despite the many flying beasts of varying size that sought to gorge on them, they had little problem in picking fruits and nuts as they journeyed by.

Once, as they passed under an overhang of rock, a herd of giant herbivores grazing off to their left, the males with impressive horn-like protrusions on their backs, became greatly agitated. They bellowed deep-throated cries and milled around on the edge of panic so that a number of individuals became somewhat separated from the main herd. With an enormous crash and searing scream, a giant raptor suddenly plummeted out of the sky and fell upon one of these individuals, tearing at it with its long beak whilst using its wings to maintain a position above the struggling creature. The rest of the herd scattered in alarm, the hooves of their pounding feet sending a tremor through the ground that the Graavens could feel even from where they were.

The Graavens halted under the protection of the overhanging cliff where they stood and stared in amazement at the sight. The raptor, folding its massive, leathery wings, sank long claws into its prey and tore out its throat in one deadly bite. Even viewed from a distance, the Graavens could see that its beak was full of huge, serrated teeth.

'Never in my life have I seen such a beast. It dwarfs any creature seen or heard of in the Empire. Even a giant mountain shamdar would be dwarfed,' remarked Horven Var in a quiet voice.

'What land is this where such creatures exist and fall from the skies?' asked Mareen in wonder.

'Well,' replied Menkh no less astonished, 'wherever we are and whatever these creatures are, we had best start looking upwards in open country. I am sure none of us would want to end up like that.'

'Not that we would be much more than an appetiser, Zaltec,' remarked Horven Var.

'True,' said Menkh with a wry smile.

With that, the huge, winged raptor hefted its prey and, wings straining, lifted the carcass of the slain beast and slowly flew off. It gradually gained height as it went, while the frightened herd turned as one and rushed deeper into the tall grass, the thrumming of their feet on the ground slowly diminishing.

Some days later, as their path lead them towards the mountains, Votlas Fen came jogging back to Menkh from her scouting position some distance ahead.

Saluting Menkh with a clenched fist to her chest, Votlas described an encounter. 'Zaltec, a strange humanoid creature lying somewhat off the trail. It appears to be intelligent but wounded. We have not approached but deemed it best to report.'

Menkh nodded his head, 'Lead on, Votlas, and let us see this creature.'

After a period of time under the two suns – Avlar, the younger and brighter went past its zenith, and Colunda sank towards the horizon – Menkh and his party arrived at the spot. Ardesh, squatting at the side of the path, rose when she saw Menkh approaching and indicated the direction of the creature a short way off the path but obscured by some tumbled rocks.

As Menkh subsequently observed, it was these very rocks that had brought the creature to grief as its leg had been caught and twisted with a broken limb the result. Menkh observed the creature, which he estimated was barely five spahn tall, curiously. Sparely built, it was nevertheless well-proportioned with long, grass-coloured hair tied into many plaits that were gathered in a leather thong. Swirling blue tattoos covered its torso and large, intelligent eyes – calm, despite its obvious pain and distress – stared back. Well-made clothing of furs and other accoutrements made of animal hide and bone could be observed. A sheath of arrows that it carried had spilled and its bow had fallen just beyond the range of its hands, which Menkh noticed had four fingers and an opposing thumb, unlike the three fingers and thumb of all Graavens.

As Menkh approached, the creature let out a hiss. A string of strange sounds, obviously meant to be threatening, issued from its mouth. However, these were stilled as Menkh came closer and a look both of incredulity and wonder came across its face, presaged by an open mouth and staring eyes.

Menkh approached slowly and quietly and crouched down just beyond the creature, who was now silently and intently observing him.

Smiling, in what he hoped was a non-threatening manner, he indicated the creature's damaged limb. 'You are hurt,' he said.

A cock of the head and a narrowing of eyes followed this statement, along with another string of sounds which sounded less threatening to the Graaven's ears as they gathered around. The creature looked around fearfully as Menkh's guard approached. Without taking his gaze away from the creature, Menkh addressed the party quietly, 'All of you return to the track, except you, Ardesh Pen, we may need your healing skills.'

With nodding of heads, they followed Menkh's instructions, with the creature looking around as they all departed.

Menkh touched his chest and said clearly, 'Menkh,' and then pointed at the creature. A puzzled expression followed and Menkh repeated the action and his name. This he repeated twice more until the creature's expression cleared and he pointed at Menkh.

'Mursh,' it repeated in a surprisingly deep baritone for so small a creature.

'Close enough,' said Menkh with a smile.

The creature pointed at Ardesh Pen and said, 'Mursh,' with an upward lilt that seemed to form a question.

Menkh shook his head. 'Ardesh,' he said. The creature's head tilted and Menkh repeated, 'Ardesh.'

'Dreths,' repeated the creature. Menkh nodded and smiled and then pointed at the creature with a questioning look.

The creature also nodded, eliciting a stream of words that could scarcely be understood, so rapid was it. The creature smiled and then grimaced in pain as it moved inadvertently and, speaking much slower, made just one guttural sound touching its own chest; 'Draachnull.'

Menkh and then Ardesh tried to emulate the sound and, after several attempts, Draachnull smiled and touched his chest, repeating the sound.

Menkh pointed to Draachnull's leg and, indicating himself and Ardesh, made motions with his hands to indicate extricating the twisted limb where it was trapped between two rocks. Draachnull, obviously in great pain, closed his eyes and made a noise that seemed to indicate acquiescence. Menkh nodded and looking towards Ardesh said, 'We will extricate his leg, set the break and bind it. Any questions?'

'No, Zaltec. Though small he is not so unlike us, but it will be painful for him.'

'Hmm,' responded Menkh. Whereupon he broke off a stick and, putting it between his teeth and making a moaning sound, tried to communicate that the process was going to hurt.

A series of hiccups issued from Draachnull which, after some puzzlement, Menkh took to be laughter. The creature, however, held out its hand and took the stick, placing it firmly between its own teeth.

'Ready?' asked Menkh, and in response to a nod from Ardesh he positioned himself at Draachnull's shoulders, whilst Ardesh squatted near the leg.

Ardesh fixed Menkh with a firm look and, nodding, bent quickly to remove the rock. It was effortless for her but would have been impossible for Draachnull. Menkh grasped Draachnull's shoulders. Ardesh gripped the leg, straightened it, applied a bandage, and commenced binding it, all with military precision.

Draachnull writhed beneath Menkh's grip and emitted a long hiss before finally fainting from the shock.

Sometime later, the Graavens were seated around a camp fire as they prepared an evening meal. They had lain Draachnull on a blanket near the fire, a crudely fashioned crutch made from a tree branch and his weapons within reach. Alongside him, too, was a bowl of water and some of the stew made from dried meat and berries which constituted their evening meal.

Draachnull had been a matter of some discussion amongst the Graavens, being the first seemingly intelligent creature they had found since crossing the bridge over the chasm.

Discussion stilled when they observed him regain consciousness, sit up, and observe his surroundings. After drinking the water placed alongside him, he smelt the stew cautiously before dipping into the bowl a tentative finger. Bringing his finger to his lips, he made an appreciative grunt, and began to eat fastidiously after producing a wooden spoon from his pack.

The Graavens watched surreptitiously as Draachnull finished his meal, reached for the crutch that Horven Dar had made for him and, with a small grimace, rose to his feet with bowl in hand. He approached the Graavens, who were sitting across from him on the other side of the fire.

Seeing Menkh sitting to one side, he placed the bowl on the ground before him and, holding his arm out, made a curious waving gesture whilst vocalising some sounds, followed by a nod of the head. Menkh, assuming that this was his way of expressing thanks, slowly stood and also bowed his head.

Draachnull nodded and, for the first time, smiled openly, an expression that was made somewhat strange by his curiously pointed front teeth.

With no further communication, he returned to his place by the fire, rolled himself in a cloak he took from his pack and went to sleep.

'It seems he appreciates your cooking, Votlas,' remarked Menkh.

'Yes,' quipped Ardesh, 'Votlas's cooking is renowned amongst uneducated savages.'

Votlas grunted, 'And you would be an expert in that area, hailing from Tashlak Province as you do, Ardesh, which is also renowned for its mud-flavoured stews. A local delicacy, I believe.'

Ardesh smiled sadly, 'What I would give for a plate of that stew sitting in my family's tavern in Tashlak …' she trailed off into silence as all the Graavens grew quiet and reflective.

'Come, everyone, post a lookout and let us all rest, we still have some way to go into the mountains, may the good spirits watch over you.'

'And you, Zaltec,' they each replied.

Mareen banked the fire and, taking up a position somewhat away from its light, took up the first watch whilst the others settled to sleep.

Twice the guard changed during the night, each Graaven walking around the perimeter of the camp and listening for any sounds of danger. Whilst the calls and screams of night creatures echoed around the camp, their peace was not disturbed. The three moons of Tarvuli – Halidar, "Queen of Night", Barask, "She Who Shines Coldly", and Orvasne, "He Who Waits" – sank slowly, until the first tinges of light appeared on the horizon as Colunda raised his head and Orvasne reluctantly disappeared, always the last of the moons to set.

There was a great commotion when the Graavens discovered that Draachnull had left sometime during the night. The guards were shamefaced but all accepted blame and did not single out any individual for having failed in their duty.

Horven Dar sank to her knees before Menkh. 'Zaltec, we have failed you. Despite our skills the creature has gone and left no trace. We accept whatever punishment you deem necessary.'

Menkh looked down at Horven Dar, not speaking for some moments as the guards all shifted uncomfortably on their feet.

'Stand up, Horven Dar,' said Menkh quietly. 'None of you has failed,' he said, looking at each in turn and fixing each with a steady gaze. 'We shall not talk of failure after having come so far together. But let us all learn from this lest, in the arrogant belief in our abilities as Hoplex, we underestimate those we see as smaller and weaker than ourselves. Draachnull was not our prisoner but our guest, and as such has the right to come or go at will. We will speak no more of this. Let us prepare and continue on our journey and let us hope that our actions with Draachnull will reflect favourably upon us.'

The country the Graavens travelled through, whilst still verdant, became more mountainous. Frequent streams and cascades of water could be heard and seen, and they knew that the path they followed held true as stone bridges, ancient but still sound, crossed several of the streams that they encountered. Huge tree ferns now crowded close to the path and the calls of flying creatures, lizard-like and strange to Graaven eyes, flitted through them. The light of the suns was muted and the weather began to change, with a drop in temperature that was noticeable as the length of each day began to lessen. They were now fifteen dak'chaal out from the travelling camp and Menkh, though not certain, felt that they must be drawing near to the place where Crixac awaited his arrival.

As they journeyed on, a ridge of rock slowly rose alongside the path, growing gradually in size and height until it towered over the Graavens. Smooth and dark with flecks of crystal which reflected the light, there were no discernible cracks or other features that might be expected in a natural cliff face. The Graavens began to wonder if, in fact, the same hands that fashioned the stone bridges they had crossed had also fashioned the wall – for such they became convinced it was, even as immense and unbroken as it was for persangh after persangh.

At last they came to a place where a river flowed to one side of the path, with the cliff wall to their left, still unbroken and immense. Ahead of them the path forked, one branch turning right over another stone span which forded the river in one long sweep. Whatever road or path it might lead to was difficult to discern as it passed into the gloom of a dense forest beyond, composed mostly of tall fern trees.

The other path continued alongside the cliff face and it was here near the fork that the party halted. Horven Dar walked cautiously over the bridge, disappearing from view into the forest before returning some minutes later.

'Zaltec, the path that extends beyond the bridge is broken and rugged and then disappears completely into the forest.'

'It was in my mind that we should continue to follow the wall anyway,' replied Menkh. 'Let us camp here at the fork, there is ample water and perhaps some fish we can trap.'

Horven Dar clashed her forearm across her chest in the Baran Mec salute and began to issue orders to set up camp.

In the meantime, and after assuring the guards that he would not venture far, he walked further along the path, following the cliff until he could no longer hear their talking. He had not gone much further when he experienced a strange sensation of light-headedness and the air seemed to ripple around him. It was a disorienting experience that was not improved when a massive gateway, which he knew had not been visible just moments before, appeared in the cliff wall alongside him.

There were two huge doors made of some shimmering material which glinted in the light of Avlar, now high in the sky above. Surrounding the gates were stone pillars which were highly decorated with intricate carvings comprised of swirling linear designs and shapes that Menkh thought might well be words of some long-forgotten language.

Menkh was drawn to the gates which opened noiselessly before him. He passed through, drawn as if by invisible hands. He heard Mareen's voice call his name before the gates closed behind him – shutting him off from the path and the rest of the Graavens.

CHAPTER FIVE

As the gates shut fast, and Menkh could see no discernible mechanism that might open them from the inside, he chided himself for his stupidity. He could imagine the anguish that his guards would experience if he were unable to rejoin them.

Deciding that there was no other option, he turned his back on the gates and determined that he would go forward and take stock of his surroundings. The wall on the gate side still ran in both directions but now was so hidden behind vegetation that it could only be seen above the height of the trees and ferns that grew everywhere.

Trees bearing fruits of many kinds, some familiar and some strange to Menkh's eyes, could be seen, while herds of small, horned creatures grazed contentedly on the grasses and ferns that extended down from the gates.

The paved path he was on was well defined and sloped downwards, gradually descending through the grasses, trees, and ferns that grew along the path. The air around him felt moist but was warmer than the temperature outside the gates. His view ahead was obscured by the surrounding vegetation; but he suddenly arrived at a point where the path flattened out and a large, paved area of multicoloured stone gave a clear view overlooking the vista that lay below.

It was here that Menkh was truly amazed at the sight revealed to him. Seven streams now appeared in his view, flowing with considerable force out of tunnels built into the descending slopes, and into channels which were not naturally occurring. Most breathtaking of all, the streams converged upon a city which could be seen about a single persangh ahead.

The stream appeared to flow through the city, and from his vantage point it seemed that each of the seven channels then converged to a single point before disappearing under a building – perhaps a temple or palace – which, by its size, dominated the skyline.

Instinctively, Menkh knew that this was where Crixac was waiting for him. Presumably, this would also be his means of exiting the place he found himself in, and so he continued on.

As he descended one of a series of paved pathways that led to the city, he noted that there were no people of any kind that could be seen. Other than the rushing sound of the water and the call of birds and other flying beasts, the land all about was bereft of sound or any indication of intelligent life.

Eventually, Menkh reach the outer limits of the city proper. There were no defensive walls or towers of any kind. Strange-looking buildings of alien architecture seemed to simply rise up out of the ground. The buildings, like the water channels that flowed into the city, followed a logical layout with clear roadways leading deeper into the city. Everywhere there was a profound silence, broken only by the wind that moaned eerily between the buildings and the sound of the water which, in that place, was ever present.

The buildings themselves were a wonder – most looked like some mysterious force had melted and fused the materials they were made from. But given that each building, no matter its size or location, boasted carvings and decorations that were themselves undistorted, Menkh assumed that all the buildings were deliberately formed this way by some means unknown to him.

No weeds or plants could be seen investing the pavement he walked upon. Everything around him evoked a feeling of great antiquity, long deserted by those who had built it. Despite this, his surrounds appeared to be free of encroaching vegetation or dirt, and all was neat and clean, which would not normally be expected in a long-abandoned city.

Everywhere, there were bridges which crisscrossed the water channels at various points, allowing unobstructed passage into different quadrants of the city. Each bridge was built along similar lines with a single graceful archway that stretched over the water below, easily wide enough to cater for all manner of traffic whether people, vehicles or animals, in both directions

Menkh passed by large plazas and gardens, still green and lush with colourful plants and fruit trees, somewhat overgrown and tangled together, fed by waters cunningly diverted from the main channels. Whoever the people were that had built this place they had an evident love of open and green places, presumably where inhabitants could meet and perhaps hold contests or markets.

After two chaal of steady walking, slaking his thirst occasionally at the many fountains he passed by, Menkh eventually arrived at a causeway where it seemed that all paths converged, and which led to the large building he had seen from the distance. He assumed that it was of great importance as two enormous statues were placed on either side of the causeway entrance. To his eyes, they could have been representations of gods, perhaps revered by the vanished populace, so that this might once have been a temple; but he could only guess at that and the sighing wind gave him no clues.

The statues were of huge proportion and towered above Menkh as he stood gazing at them. Both figures, which appeared to be fashioned from the same material as the gates Menkh had passed through, looked out over the city. Their features, exquisitely carved, were utterly alien to his eyes. Strange helmets covered the heads of both figures while long, rope-like strands of hair flowed down over broad shoulders, leading down to a very narrow waist atop strongly muscled legs clad in what appeared to be a kind of stylised mail covering.

The figure to the left raised a gloved fist into the air whilst the other rested upon its hip, the second figure had both arms crossed over its chest, and both figures had strange accoutrements with a long, tubelike device which hung from belts crossing over their shoulders from left to right.

Like the Graaven people, they had three-fingered hands and an opposing thumb but the mouths of both statues, which were open – either in greeting or threat he could not tell – appeared full of sharp, needle-like teeth. They were unsettling to look upon and Menkh could imagine the effect they would have had on people approaching the huge building at the end of the causeway.

Stepping past the statues, Menkh felt a tingle that passed over all his body, almost like tiny insects had run over his bare flesh. The fine filaments on the back on his neck flared to a red colour, a sure sign amongst Graaven people of alarm.

However, no further sensations were apparent, and he continued his passage over the causeway. The causeway itself was paved in a white crystalline stone that glinted in the light of the suns. Wide enough to accommodate twenty people walking abreast, it rose, like all the other bridges in the city, in a single graceful span before descending towards the building beyond.

It crossed a vast channel that allowed the waters of the seven streams to conjoin as they rushed to this central point. Menkh, arriving at the centre of the bridge, gazed below at the turbulent waters. Looking at both ends of the causeway bridge, he thought that three bow shots from a Graaven bow would be barely enough to cover the width of the channel.

The noise of the rushing waters had steadily increased in volume as the seven streams converged, rushing together in a maelstrom of currents. They then flowed out and down into a culvert of enormous proportions that went directly under the building he was approaching. Menkh, descended as he was from a race of beings who prized grand architecture, could think of nothing that could possibly compare to the design and execution of the structures he had seen, and wondered again how such people might have vanished without apparent trace.

The air around him was filled with a fog-like mist from the waters below him as they crashed and foamed together, somewhat obscuring his view of the building and surrounds beyond, and which also lowered the ambient temperature of the air around him.

Finally, after descending from the centre of the bridge, he reached the end of the causeway and paused on the edge of an enormous, paved plaza. The plaza itself, paved in the same material as the causeway, was covered in mosaics of a complex design that appeared to mirror those that Menkh had observed on the gates he had entered and, in smaller proportions, on the buildings he had passed by.

Before him, a complex layout of many towers, rising to needle-like points, could be seen. One central tower, higher than all the others, rose into the sky, its pinnacle flashing in the light. Whilst the building was enormous it possessed a gracefulness and elegance of design that seemed to make it float above the ground from which it rose. Some 300 paces ahead, the building looming above him was approached by a massive staircase leading up to a portico and the main entrance. The steps were incredibly large and, even at Menkh's eight spahn in height, they presented some difficulty in ascending. Unlike the melted form of the other buildings Menkh had passed, this building was starkly different. It was uniform in shape and made from huge blocks of white crystal which glittered in the glow of Avlar and Colunda, reflecting their light and adding a luminous and magical quality to its appearance. The effect was altogether quite beautiful and was enhanced by many large windows which were glazed with a material that seemed to absorb the light, as a counterpoint to that which reflected off the walls themselves.

Reaching the topmost step of the entrance way he paused to gather his breath and looked directly down on the plaza. From his vantage point, now unobscured by the permanent mist present on the causeway, the swirling patterns could be seen for what they actually were, a complete representation of the stars of the night sky. Menkh recognised the constellations he had grown up with. Various pinpoints within the mosaic shone with a golden light, and lines of a silver colour appeared to connect them one to the other, for what purpose Menkh could not fathom. Again and again, Menkh had been overcome with a sense of awe at everything he had seen, but his sense of astonishment at the depiction which lay below him exceeded anything he had thus far experienced.

He was distracted from gazing at the mosaic by a slight rumbling sound behind him and, upon turning, saw that two ornately decorated doors were swinging outwards. Menkh noted that these doors, too, appeared to be made of the same material that the entrance gates in the cliff wall were fashioned from. Having opened relatively noiselessly they were now motionless. Beyond them, Menkh could glimpse a vast entry hall, the details of which could not be discerned as he stared from the light of the outside into the gloom beyond.

Having come this far and seeing no alternative, Menkh advanced and passed through the doorways into what he assumed was some enormous lobby. Upon entering, the gloom was lessened by luminous globes which appeared to hover in the air. The globes brightened and gave off a bluish light that gradually grew stronger. Large staircases led off in multiple directions deeper into the building proper and, as he looked up, he noticed that there was no ceiling; instead, the walls around him reached upwards till presumably they reached an apex at the top of one of the spires he had observed. Numberless floors could be seen at regular intervals but there was no indication of any staircases to allow any access to them, other than those which exited the lobby and rose to the first level above him.

Menkh was still observing his surroundings when the voice of Crixac echoed around the chamber. 'Greetings, Menkh, and welcome to the once mighty City State of Kareem Vastar, the "Place of Enlightenment" in your tongue. Impressive, isn't it? I am sure you must be brimful of questions. First, let me assure you that your fellow Graavens are aware that you are safe, although I am not sure that the method of my communication and my aspect gave them much reassurance. However, they have set up camp and now wait near the outer gates for further word.'

'Thank you, Crixac,' Menkh spoke aloud into the space around him, 'that is most pleasing as I was concerned that they might try to do something foolish. Yes, I do indeed have many questions, but I am here in fulfilment of the promise made when we struck our bargain. Shall we at last meet face to face?'

'To the point and direct as I would expect, Menkh. Yes, let us at last meet and discuss the proposal that I will put to you. Do you see, directly ahead of you, a staircase that leads straight up and does not curve or turn in any direction?'

Menkh looked ahead and saw the staircase referred to. He noted that all the others curved gracefully and turned left or right before disappearing into different sections of the walls through various doorways. Menkh also saw that each staircase was slightly different, subtly coloured in various hues from a rose colour through to a translucent blue, although appearing to be made from the same crystalline material as the mosaic and causeway bridge.

'Approach that staircase and climb to the first level.'

Menkh crossed the floor of the chamber and ascended the staircase. Whilst not of the proportions of the entrance to the building he had climbed earlier, they were still of a size that required him to take a significant step up each time. After climbing the stairway, he paused to collect his breath and stared at the wall in front of him. A magnificent frieze was painted on the wall, depicting a forest scene, mountains, and waterfall in wonderful detail, but the staircase itself did not appear to lead anywhere.

'Look to the right of the frieze at your head height. You should see a shallow depression in the wall near where the sun hangs in the sky in the picture.' Having had his attention drawn to it, Menkh could see the depression where Crixac had indicated.

'Place your hand palm-down in the depression,' instructed Crixac.

Reaching up and placing his hand as told, Menkh tried not to flinch as a tracery of luminous lines appeared around it. He could feel a slight vibration through his booted feet when, with a quiet hissing sound, a doorway appeared in the frieze. This opened into a very small room which again appeared to lead nowhere.

'Enter, Menkh, and do not be alarmed at what happens. You are perfectly safe.'

As he entered, the doorway closed with the same quiet hissing sound and then Menkh could sense movement, presaged by a slight lurch in his stomach, although whether that movement was upwards or sideways was difficult to tell. A series of rapidly changing symbols flashed with a pale blue glow on the inner side of the doorway. Menkh wondered if these could indicate where in the vast building he was, or at what level. Everything about the city, and this building in particular, was a perplexing puzzle that Menkh's mind grappled to deal with.

After what appeared to be quite some time, the lights slowed in their flashing and, with a quiet hiss, the door opened and Menkh stepped out into a much larger space.

Dimly lit, Menkh's first impression was that 10 000 trees had sunk their roots into the room. Apart from one clear channel leading from the travelling room he tentatively stepped out from, everywhere around him, from the ceiling – many times his own height above – and out of the walls, appeared long, snaking lines. Some of the lines were thicker than his wrist and some no wider than a blade of grass, but all of them seemed to either flow towards, or emanate from, a central point in the room towards which the path led.

The room was immense. Whilst not as big as the entrance hall to the building proper, there was an impression of cavernous space all around him. Any walls, however, were obscured by the myriad snaking lines that occupied almost the entirety of the space around him.

As he walked along the one clear path to the centre of the room, he saw that there was a space, some twenty spahn in diameter, where a raised platform sat above the twisting lines. In the very centre of the platform was what appeared to be a stylised tree trunk, upon which rested a large and magnificent crystal, some three spahn in length, which constantly pulsed in colour from blue to red. A large crack could be discerned in the body of crystal, below which the surface of the crystal was black and lifeless.

As he looked closer at the "tree roots" which surrounded him, he could see that they, too, pulsed with dim light; some with blue light pulsing towards the dais and others with red lights pulsing away. It was, to Menkh's mind, just another unfathomable curiosity in the strange place he found himself.

He could not avoid jumping and turning in surprise when a dry and sibilant voice said, 'Greetings, Menkh ab Dur, we meet a last.'

CHAPTER SIX

Crixac, for that was who it must be, sat across from him in an ornate chair that had not been there just moments before. Even as Menkh responded with his greeting, he looked closely at the hooded and robed figure seated before him. His first impression was of great age though he could not clearly distinguish any of Crixac's features. Even sitting, however, Crixac was hunched over and his breathing was laboured and wheezy.

'Please forgive me for not standing, I find that simply maintaining my will to exist all but consumes my power. My end, it would appear, draws near, but I thank you for honouring our bargain. My faith in you has been repaid. Please, do sit down. You must be weary after your journey here.'

Crixac indicated a space behind Menkh where a chair had appeared as if out of the air itself. Menkh cautiously sat down on it and it proved to be both solid and comfortable.

'May I offer you refreshment? A tisane or perhaps some water?'

'Thank you,' replied Menkh, 'that would be most welcome.' He was also intrigued as to how Crixac would conjure refreshment out of thin air. However, within a few heartbeats, Menkh heard the sound of footsteps and he looked in surprise as a strange creature approached from the direction of the travelling room.

It bore a tray upon which was placed a jug and some sort of fruit on a crystal plate. This was placed on the armrest of the chair Menkh was sitting on, a cunning latch holding the tray in place.

The creature was metallic, no more than five spahn tall and, in proportion, had a vivid similarity to Draachnull, the creature they had rescued on the journey here. The facial features were expressionless and after placing the tray on the chair, it turned and walked away – presumably back to the travelling room in which Menkh himself had journeyed.

'Curiosity after curiosity, Menkh?' enquired Crixac.

'A day of mysteries indeed, Crixac. I think if I had a sem'chaal to ask questions, we still could not answer them all.'

'Indeed, and I am afraid I do not have one of your sem'chaal or even, perhaps, what is left of the day. Please,' here Crixac indicated the tray alongside Menkh, 'refresh yourself, the tea is made from a herb that grows on the banks of Phalandrel, one of the seven streams you will have seen. It is refreshing and restorative and the fruit is a kind of melon that grows here and will complement the tea. While you eat, I will talk.'

Menkh politely poured some of the tea and ate some of the melon, which were both delicious and indeed restorative, as Crixac began to talk.

'There is so much that I can share with you about this city and its vanished people, and so many things you have seen as you fled your empire to journey here. But the proposition I spoke of when you were near death cannot be put aside. Know this, that you are free to choose your course and, if you refuse my offer, then your people are still welcome here. Here, at least for a time, they will be safe from that which hunted you. Also, I will eradicate the growth inside you permanently as I promised I would.'

Menkh slowly dipped his head towards Crixac. 'In all respects, Crixac, you have shown yourself to be both honourable and truthful and I deem a friend to all the Graavens who are left. Please make your proposition and know that I will give it my fullest consideration.'

'Thank you, Menkh. In light of what I have to say, that is most reassuring. You really are unique in your species, you know. Quite unlike any of your forebears in your thinking, as proven by the way you have journeyed here. There are few amongst your people who would have had the poise, the confidence and the sense of wonder that you have displayed thus far.' Crixac mused silently for some moments. 'So, to the business at hand. Let me say firstly that the creature you see before you, in the strictest sense, is both me and not me.'

Menkh crinkled his forehead in confusion but remained silent.

'Yes, intriguing isn't it? You see, Menkh, I — that is I who I really am — is what is called a "symbiote". In this sense, I cannot exist outside of a host's body.'

'So,' interrupted Menkh, 'you are some intelligent form of parasite?'

Crixac laughed humourlessly, 'Not the words I would have used to describe myself but, if you will, in some primitive sense then yes, but a benign parasite. Moreover, unlike a parasite which invades and feeds off its host to their detriment, I enhance my host. The host must be willing to enter into the arrangement, which is more a mutually beneficial partnership.'

'And you seek me as a host?' concluded Menkh.

'Yes, Menkh, yes, I do.'

Menkh leaned forward. 'Why?'

Crixac sighed. 'I am pleased that you have not crossed the floor and tried to kill me, at least,' he remarked wryly.

'I still have time for that,' replied Menkh, and in saying the words he wasn't at all sure that some part of that was not true. A part of him felt a revulsion but another part a strange fascination with the concept.

'Indeed,' answered Crixac, 'but before long that will have occurred anyway. The time that I can support my host is at last drawing to an end. But, to your question. I have asked you for the reasons I alluded to earlier; you are unique amongst your people. Intelligence, balanced with a keen curiosity about the world you live in. You alone of your people challenged the mores of your society and questioned their worth. Quite amazing when you think that you were the next in line for the throne, and a more blood-soaked throne has never existed on this world. Yet, you challenged it and set in motion a series of events that would, in time, have led to fundamental changes within your empire for the better.'

'My sister played a key role in the circumstances you allude to.'

'Yes,' pondered Crixac, 'her loss was another great tragedy, not just for you but for all of your people. It is interesting, Menkh, that there is no Graaven word for love. The whole concept is alien to your people. But you and your sister may have been the first Graavens to truly experience a profound love for each other. I don't mean in some carnal sense, but a true bond of deep affection and respect. It's no wonder the Council of Nobles didn't see the events that came to pass coming.'

'Your breadth of knowledge astounds me, Crixac, but, with recent calamities, all to no avail,' Menkh could not help a bitter tone entering his voice. 'Please, let us leave talk of this. The wounds are still there, only the flight from danger into danger has pushed the feelings away.'

'I am sorry, Menkh, it was ever a fault of mine to let my thoughts wander down other paths and distract me, even when the direst consequences are in balance. So, your flexibility of mind and your ability to challenge old concepts and consider new options are qualities that a host must have.'

Crixac's voice took on a more passionate tone. 'Menkh, together we can truly save your people. Together we can build a new home based on peace and strength in gentleness, not on constant war, bloodshed, and enslavement. I can show you things that will make your experience today seem trivial. Places and peoples that even in your wildest dreams you could not imagine. We can travel this world and your knowledge and understanding of life will expand to a degree you could not have thought possible. All this and more, Menkh. A true partnership. Not some parasitic invasion of your body where you lose your individuality and self-determination but one that enhances and nourishes us both. Through you I experience all the wonder and delight as if I, too, had not seen these things before. Through you, Menkh, I truly live.'

Menkh pondered these words and then responded, 'And what then, Crixac, if I agree but then change my mind later, what power will you have over me to dominate and control me?'

'Yes,' replied Crixac quietly, 'the greatest fear and one that I have only words to reassure you with.' Crixac looked directly into Menkh's eyes and spoke, 'It is true that I could seek to forcibly overpower your will and strive to dominate you. But I can tell you, from the experience of others of my kind that have attempted this, that only death for host and symbiote is the final result. Ultimately, the body and mind of the host will drive us out, madness and death the result for the host and obliteration for the symbiote. You are free to change your mind, Menkh, but we would work together to find an alternative host for me, at which point I would transfer to the new host and leave you.'

'And would madness and death be my ultimate fate as a result?' asked Menkh.

'Death, certainly,' responded Crixac, 'but in its own time, not through any directly negative result of my transference.'

'What of the host that you currently occupy, what conscious will does it have?'

'Virtually none at all.' Crixac grew silent and Menkh did not prompt him.

'In the long ago of this world, when this City was at the height of its power, there was a war. For a thousand years the three City States of Palluvia, Paxal and Kareem Vastar lived in peace and harmony. They developed technologies that to your people, as you have experienced first-hand, would seem like magic and which unlocked great knowledge and power. Wisdom, however, was another matter. Slowly, as the cycles of time went by, the people changed. Like some terrible and malignant cancer, greed and jealousy and the will to dominate others displaced compassion and kindness and gentleness. A war that should never have been erupted between them.

Finally, Kareem Vastar developed a weapon so powerful that in response, and in fear and loathing, the other two States allied and released a devastating attack, which, whilst nearly successful, destroyed only half the city.' Crixac paused and looked directly at Menkh who had sat listening in fascination. 'Yes, Menkh. Once, long ago, the city extended past the place where we now stand, another causeway leading into it like the one you crossed over to reach here. But, in the blink of an eye, all vanished, totally obliterated.'

Crixac again paused in thoughtful reflection and Menkh could only contemplate such a war and its terrible consequences.

'But,' began Crixac again, 'they had fatally underestimated the power of this City, for the Kareems had unlocked a force that was unprecedented in 1000 years of technological advancement. Their retaliation was not long in coming. A wave of energy was released, so powerful that the City States of Paxal and Palluvia were extinguished and utterly obliterated. Not a building, an animal, a plant or a person was left; it was as if they had never existed at all. Victory at last for the Kareems, so they thought: but it was short-lived. The backlash of energies was so huge and unanticipated that the crystal you see before you, the source of all power within the City, was fractured, and every living Kareem instantly annihilated in their turn. However, the Kareems had set up fail-safes as a precaution and, as inadequate as they proved to be for the Kareems themselves, what remained of the City after the attack was preserved, as was the plant and animal life that lived within its boundaries. Only the Kareems themselves were destroyed.'

Menkh sat in rapt attention and Crixac continued, 'My host and I at that time were travellers. We had entered this world by means of, to put it simply, a kind of gateway, and we were observing the Kareems as a first step to see if we could influence the circumstances that had led to the war in the first place. Together, we had theorised that there would be some kind of aftermath to the use of the Kareems' weapon, but neither of us anticipated what actually happened. We were attempting to leave the city when the aftershock struck. My host, like the Kareems, winked out of existence and I was thrown out.'

'How is it that you survived, Crixac, when all life was snuffed out?'

'Not all life, Menkh. I was disoriented and I had mere moments before I, too, dissipated.' Crixac responded to a look of puzzlement on Menkh's face, 'I cannot exist for long outside of a host, Menkh. But not all life was extinguished. Only the Kareems, not their animals. The poor creature you see before you was a kind of pet, for want of a better word. A creature of limited intelligence and barely sentient. I can tell you, Menkh, that it was only fate that caused the creature to be nearby when my host was extinguished. In desperation I forcibly transferred into the creature and thus preserved my existence.'

'I can appreciate your desperation,' mused Menkh, 'but surely transference into such a creature must have been limiting?'

The wheezing sound that Menkh took to be Crixac's laughter came to his ears.

'After my initial gratitude at having survived I came to realise that I was trapped in a kind of perpetual solitary confinement. It was impossible for me to leave the city or, even if that were possible, to journey beyond the boundary walls. This poor creature has poorly developed limbs for manipulating the technology of the Kareems – even opening a door is a challenge. But we managed, and the crystal, whilst damaged beyond repair, continued to function adequately having only half a city to manage.'

'So, the entire city is run by this crystal?' asked Menkh in astonishment.

'Indeed, Menkh. The crystal channels the energy required to power the systems which preserve the buildings and cloak the city itself. Everything within the outer walls, which run for many leagues is, in a sense, shielded. Without my opening the outer gates you would never have found this place at all. You are looking, Menkh, at the rarest form of crystal in the cosmos. Its properties have been the subject of research for millennia. It can change its state and manipulate forces around it. In a word, Menkh, it has its own intelligence, though on such a profound level that living and breathing beings can scarce comprehend it. The value of this crystal, as damaged as it is, is incalculable and there are forces within the cosmos that would seek to acquire it without thought as to the cost and effort required to do so. Even to the entire destruction of this world and everything that lives on it.'

'For every explanation, a thousand more questions arise, Crixac. But for our purposes now, answer me this: what are you and what purpose do you pursue?'

'Good questions, Menkh,' here Crixac paused, considering his response. 'In one sense, I am a form of energy. I have no form or shape of my own and yet I am an individual. I am not alone in the cosmos, but none exist like me on your world. There were never many of us and our origins are so far back in time that how we came to be, or even where, is a mystery now even to us. My purpose is to pursue knowledge and understanding, to seek order where there is chaos, and enlightenment where there is confusion. I have had many hosts across the ages, all with qualities like yours, but very different in form and aspect. I have been trapped here for so long that I despaired of ever having an opportunity to continue that purpose, but I have had ample time to contemplate the bitter failure of my host and I in preserving life. I have been observing you for a long time, Menkh, as the power of the crystal gradually wanes. But the explanation of how I did this must be one we pursue later – if there is a "later" for me. I would have liked to give you more time to consider your response but time for me grows desperately short and I must ask you now. If, as I fear you might, you refuse, then I will need time to prepare myself for the inevitable.'

Menkh stood and turned away from Crixac and, for a time, observed the pulsing red and blue lights that perpetually traversed the lines that fed into the crystal room. Crixac's tale was at once astonishing and intriguing and hinted at things that were so far outside of Menkh's experience that he felt like a small child. But he could not discern any harm or ill will in Crixac, nor could he doubt the sincerity of the words Crixac had spoken.

Menkh turned back to Crixac. 'I have listened to all that you have said. It is a tale of wonder and fascination to me. I have seen much on this journey that has challenged my beliefs and yet, at the same time, reinforced many of them. I was heir to the Graaven throne and heir to the greatest empire on this world, or so we thought. What arrogance and pride we Graavens had! Laid low by creatures we still do not understand. What irony that the destruction of our Empire delivered to us what many of the conquered within the borders of the Empire would see as some kind of divine justice, even at the cost of their own lives.

I saw the corruption within the Imperial Court and the plots that saw my father slowly poisoned. He was a traditionalist in many ways, yet he initiated some much-needed changes that were resented by our so-called "nobility".

My sister and I had plans of our own and knew that a coup would be attempted with herself as the puppet Empress. This would be after my own execution on charges of having betrayed the Empire when I refused to slaughter a valiant enemy after they had surrendered. But they underestimated us both, and the ruthlessness of my sister.

How I exulted when the nobles who had contrived the death of our father were themselves put down. Willingly, I went into the temporary exile that my sister and I had planned to appease the traditionalists, and to gain time whilst we enacted our long-term plans to change the very fabric of Graaven society. I, who had never wished for the throne, ceded it to my sister, a better administrator and ruler than I could ever be. Bitter as ashes was my return to an empire on the verge of collapse from a foe that we could not understand and were powerless to defeat. An empire 300 sem'chaal in the building, overthrown in a matter of months.'

Menkh turned to Crixac, 'And so, you see, my greater purpose was undone, replaced by a new and more urgent enterprise, the very survival of our species. Without your direct intervention I have no doubt that I would have died, and the last hope of our people been extinguished. Now you have presented to me a far grander vision and hint at things that are beyond my current understanding, which have caused me to reflect on what and who I am and what my purpose might now be. So, Crixac, I am willing to be your host, on one condition.'

Crixac said nothing but raised an arm to indicate that Menkh should continue.

'We must ensure the safety of my people. I would see them with a future and with peace and prosperity returned to them, so that the nightmare of the past months will dispel. If that means dealing with the creatures that have pursued us so remorselessly, then so be it. When we have achieved this, Crixac, then shall we have free rein to journey wherever you will.'

For long moments there was silence between them until Crixac rose slowly. 'Menkh ab Dur, I agree to your terms. Upon my honour we shall strive together to ensure the peace of your people, however long that may take. Know that my gratitude to you for agreeing to my plea knows no bounds. Together, we shall achieve great things and, in time to come, I will show you places beyond your imagination.' Crixac paused. 'Come then, we have much to achieve.'

'What do you need me to do?' asked Menkh.

'There is no great fanfare, ceremony or procedure, Menkh. In reality, the process is quite banal. Simply approach me and together with me take hold of the staff I carry. I will guide you from there. I can promise you that there will be no pain of any kind though the experience of transference will seem strange to you.'

'It will be yet another in the long list of strange experiences of these later days, Crixac,' replied Menkh wryly.

'Very well, come and take hold,' said Crixac, who lifted the staff before him with outstretched arms.

CHAPTER SEVEN

As Menkh reached down and took hold of the staff he observed that it, too, was made of what appeared to be the same or similar substance as the crystal that resided in the room. It felt cool to the touch, though a slight tingling sensation, which was not unpleasant, went through Menkh's body as he took hold. He now saw that the staff pulsed with the same light as the lines that entered the room of crystal.

'Now,' said Crixac, 'try to relax your muscles and empty your thoughts, and look into my eyes.'

Menkh observed that the creature Crixac was bonded to could now be clearly seen as the hood had fallen from its head. It was incredibly old, merely old paper stretched across bones. In appearance it bore a striking resemblance to Draachnull but its eyes were hypnotic. Not the black eyes of a Graaven, but a deep blue colour with flecks of red that seemed to swirl about in a constantly changing pattern which drew Menkh's own eyes deeper in until he felt that he was falling, trancelike, into a living dream.

A strange coolness followed by a sensation of warmth flowed up into Menkh's arms and flooded his body. It felt like he was a kind of vessel being filled with light and energy. Finally, he gasped as his vision blanked out into nothingness for the merest instant before returning. As his eyes refocused, he found that he could see everything with a greater clarity and precision than before, and he noticed that the pulsing red and blue lights that entered and exited the crystal were, in fact, layered by other colours that before he did not see.

A voice suddenly echoed inside his head, '*It is nearly done. I sense that you are not distressed by all this. Not long to go now.*' It was indeed a strange experience, like talking to someone who you knew was in the same place as you but in another room and just out of sight and reach.

The voice of Crixac inside his mind was more alive and fuller of energy than the voice which had emanated from the mouth of the creature before him. Youthful, yet with an edge of age and wisdom, and with a timbre that was both comforting and reassuring somehow. One that Menkh felt he could listen to for hours without growing tired of it.

'I am fine. These sensations are strange but interesting to experience,' replied Menkh aloud in a tight voice. 'Strangely, the process brings with it a range of emotions and unlocks memories that I have not thought of in a long time.'

'*Very interesting. Different hosts experience this in different ways. Perhaps this is your mind's reaction to my insertion. Very well. Keep a firm grip on the staff now and do not be startled by what you see, the transference is almost total and, once complete, my former host will transmute.*' After saying this, the flow of energy seemed to cease and the creature that gripped the staff with Menkh began to disintegrate before Menkh's eyes.

'*Keep hold now, Menkh, this will not take long.*'

In mere moments, the form that had been Crixac's host had been reduced to a mound of whitish powder that was almost concealed by the robes that had clothed it before they had fallen to the floor.

Crixac's voice took on a wistful tone. '*Well, it is done, and the years of my confinement have at last reached their end. I cannot express my gratitude to you, Menkh, but now we can begin to plan for the restoration of your people.*'

It was a strange sensation to have a voice speaking to him inside his head but only a few moments passed before Crixac spoke again. '*Come, before we make preparations to receive your people there is one thing I would like to show you. Leave my poor host's remains, they will be taken care of. Let us proceed to another level via the perach you arrived in.*'

As Menkh heard the word "perach", it was as if understanding of what it was unlocked inside his head, like it had always been present before but dormant. He understood that a complex series of perach accessed the various floors and levels of this huge building. Temptingly, Menkh could sense knowledge of the building proper but, like a name you can't quite recall, the knowledge remained just out of reach of his conscious mind.

As they entered the perach, Menkh spoke clearly, 'Level 1, Northern Quadrant exit.'

Once again, the knowledge of where they were going had come to him and Crixac's voice echoed in his mind, '*Interesting experience, isn't it? Slowly your erudition and understanding will increase as my knowledge filters to you and you are exposed to things that were outside of your cognisance before. But I will manage this slowly, otherwise I may cause you distress. Also, you should know that I am manipulating the organs of your body to increase your vitality and remove any pathogens or other harmful organisms. Almost immediately you should begin to feel the effects of thi*s.'

Menkh turned his thoughts inwards to himself and it was certainly true that he felt remarkably refreshed and full of energy. Considering he had not slept for an entire day, that was indeed an indication of changes within his body.

The perach moved smoothly and again movement was hard to detect, but Menkh knew instinctively that it was crossing and descending through the building. Before long, the doors opened with their customary hissing sound.

'Behold, Menkh, the great Northern Gates which once led from here to the northern half of Kareem Vastar over a causeway identical to that which you crossed from the southern half of the city. Let us proceed to the causeway and there you will see what I came to show you.'

The perach debouched onto a set of stairs identical to those he had climbed when he first entered the building and, similarly, descended into another cavernous room with many staircases leading up from the entry level.

As they approached the exit, twin doors made from a silvery metal swung outwards almost noiselessly. Menkh walked outside to stand on the portico above a set of huge steps that led down to a plaza that was strikingly similar to that before the southern entrance. Here another representation of the sky was set out, although to Menkh's eye these star patterns and constellations were unknown to him.

'This is still the night sky of your home world, Menkh, but it is that which can be seen on the other side of your world, should you journey there.'

Menkh could only stare in astonishment. It was yet another piece of knowledge that left him wondering.

His eyes left their exploration of the mosaic and lifted towards the causeway bridge. Unlike that of the southern side, this span seemed to end abruptly at its midpoint as if it were never completed or as if the builder had intended that it go no further but simply hang in midair.

With difficulty, Menkh descended the steps that led to the plaza and hesitantly began to ascend the bridge.

'Fear not, Menkh. The structure is still perfectly sound and as we ascend you will see what I wish to show you.'

As with his previous ascent, the noise of the waters thundered below, and a mist rose into the air around him. As he came nearer to the point where the bridge ended, he stopped in amazement. Now he could see that there was a dizzying drop into a chasm so deep that its bottom could not be seen.

Turning around he saw that the combined waters of the seven streams flowing out from under the building behind him abruptly poured over the edge of the chasm, the torrent of waters disappearing into the yawning fissure below. Looking up he could see, several bowshots away by his reckoning, the other side of the chasm where an impossibly smooth and sheer rock face extended roughly three persangh to the east and west. Looking down to his immediate left and right, the wall he stood above also extended in a similar direction, its face so sharp and smooth that it looked to have been cut with a knife rather than some natural occurrence of nature.

'Behold, Menkh, where once stood the northern districts of Kareem Vastar. The weapon of the enemy destroyed it utterly. In the blink of an eye half of the city and all those who dwelt there winked out of existence. The very ground beneath their feet vanished with them, leaving this vast chasm biting deep into the earth.'

Menkh's thoughts were tinged with a profound sense of horror. *'I cannot begin to conceive of a weapon that could unleash this kind of power and destruction. I have laid siege to great cities and I thought the destruction then was incomprehensible and pointless, but this?'*

'Yes, Menkh. And remember that the Kareems unleashed even greater force on Palluvia and Paxal and nothing remains of them at all. A vast lake now fills the crater where the city of Palluvia once stood. Including those that perished here in Kareem Vastar, we are talking of the extermination of an entire civilisation, Menkh. Countless numbers of people.'

Menkh was rendered speechless. It was one thing to talk about it, and quite another to see the effects and to weigh it against all the marvels he had seen so far of what remained of Kareem Vastar.

'Why show me this, Crixac? What purpose does it serve?'

'Two reasons, Menkh. Firstly, if you are going to live in their city you should know something of the beings that once inhabited it. Secondly, as your own knowledge increases, it is a salutary lesson about ultimate power and the arrogance of using it. Everything in the cosmos is about balance, Menkh. The

Palluvians, Paxals and Kareems had become unbalanced, so blinded by their fear and hatred that they undid centuries of peaceful cooperation. Their ultimate destruction, in a sense, restored balance, though in a fundamentally disturbing way.'

'But what about all the innocent people, those who didn't agree and thought that peaceful cooperation was possible? What about all the animals and plants who did nothing to warrant destruction? Is there not some power that works to preserve and protect the weak and innocent? A force for good?'

'Think, Menkh. Think about what you have said. When your armies conquered the peoples around you, where was the force for good that stopped the killing then? Your people prayed to your gods for victory and when you were victorious, you praised them and gave the credit to them.

What about the innocents that were slaughtered by your armies so that your empire could expand? Where were the gods they prayed to when you marched in? Where were your mighty Graaven gods when your empire was overthrown, and all its peoples laid low?

No, Menkh, there was no divine intervention from the gods or any other power. What the Kareems, Paxals and Palluvians did, they did themselves and they, and all with them, paid the ultimate price. You cannot ascribe concepts of "good" or "bad" or "right" and "wrong" to the Balance. It is not some sentient being that can be influenced by prayers, although the actions of all sentient life and random acts of nature that occur will impact upon it.

Trying to understand a cosmic force like the Balance is like some tiny insect trying to understand a mountain. Why did the Dorath Mar appear? What are they and where are they from? Why have they done what they did? How does their arrival affect the Balance? Questions that currently have no answers, Menkh, with no logic that can be applied to shed any light on them.

Knowledge and enlightenment may come with time, Menkh, but, ultimately, we must take responsibility for all our actions and do what we can. It would be good to try to avoid ending up the same way as the Kareems, don't you think?' These last words carried a tinge of humour that was underscored by a deep sense of sadness.

'*Crixac, there is so much here that I do not understand. Concepts now that my mind has difficulty dealing with. I will think on it. Through you I begin to perceive that this City may present some profound dangers for my people, but with your knowledge we can at least do our best to ensure that the ultimate fate of the Kareems can be avoided. The first step must be the preservation and protection of my people, which I swore to do. Perhaps these will be steps which influence the Balance in our favour. All I know is that we must act as best we can.*'

'*I agree, Menkh. As long as you are my host, my knowledge is available to you. In the same way, I have access to all your memories. You are a quick learner; in one sense I am "in your head", so all you need do is think the question or response and I will hear it. Knowledge of things will seem to spring into your mind as you encounter them in the city, and this will seem very strange to you at first. With practise this will become seamless.*'

'*Thank you, Crixac. I must hope that my questions will not drive you to seek another host as quickly as possible.*'

Quiet laughter was the response. '*Whatever your questions, Menkh, I will delight in answering them. For me, your arrival is like a traveller lost in a waterless desert stumbling upon an oasis. So, my friend, let us leave our musings regarding the Balance and see to our people and to their future!*'

So saying, they re-entered the complex and returned to the crystal repository room.

'*This room, Menkh, is located at the heart of this building. You may have thought of this as a palace or temple but in fact it is, or was, the very nerve centre of the city proper. Here the Great Council of Governors met, and it was also here that the Kareems stored their knowledge in vast libraries, as well as housing their research laboratories. Each floor of the building was set aside for a particular purpose, and this extends to areas below the surface. These areas were restricted to most Kareems, and it was here also that the most secretive of research was undertaken. It will take a long time for you to completely understand how this building works, and we are limited at this time due to the partial destruction of the crystal. Slowly, Menkh, the crystal itself will diminish in power until it fails. Whilst this is still some time off, we will have to find a replacement crystal and I am not sure if this is even going to be possible.'*

'How long do you think we have until that point is reached?' asked Menkh.

'Impossible to say to any accurate degree, but as it decays the rate of failure will increase, perhaps ten more cycles — that is to say, three more sem'chaal before failure is reached. Perhaps less than that.'

'And what happens then?'

'Then, Menkh, all of the systems that maintain this building and the City will fail and fall into ruin. The fail-safes that are built into this building will activate and everything inside will be destroyed. Or at least, that is what is supposed to happen. It may be that the process of destruction itself will fail, as the systems designed to activate are so old that they might not be able to activate successfully; but let us hope we have averted that possibility in the time to come. For want of a better word we shall call this building the Complex. It is as good as any and is as close as we can get in your tongue to the words the Kareems used. Now, I will take you to another room and you can initiate the arrival of your people.'

They exited the crystal room via the perach and after a short journey Menkh entered a long hallway that contained several doors. Following Crixac's guidance, Menkh stood before one, once again placing his hand on a depression in the wall. The door moved quietly to one side, opening onto a small set of steps that led downwards into the centre of a large circular room. The walls of the room were blank, devoid of all decoration but glowing with a muted bluish light that pulsed slightly. As Menkh reached the room's centre, a section of the floor lifted in front of him, stopping at waist height.

The top of the raised section, which was slightly angled towards him, contained a series of slight depressions which covered it in a semi-circular pattern. Above each depression were strange symbols that were some form of writing. A slight feeling of dizziness overcame Menkh as his eyes passed over the symbols which, incomprehensible before, suddenly had meaning for him.

'*Apologies, Menkh, I should have warned you that this would happen. I will endeavour to reduce the feeling of disorientation as the knowledge comes to you.*'

'*Remarkable, Crixac. With knowledge of the language, other concepts come into my mind. This is truly a unique experience.*'

As Menkh looked at the display before him a strange device appeared, seemingly out of nowhere, and rested on the panel in front of him. It appeared to be made from a series of small yellow crystals interconnected by fine, silvery wires. It was certainly beautiful to look at and Menkh thought he perceived its purpose.

'*Yes, Menkh, this is an interface between you and the display which you will see shortly. Pick up the object and fit it over your head. You will find that it will adapt itself to you and fit to the contours of your skull.*'

Picking up the object, which began to give off a yellowish glow as soon as he touched it, Menkh did as Crixac requested. As the device settled over his head the walls and ceiling around him also began to glow with the same diffused yellow light.

'*Now, Menkh, all you have to do is think of who you wish to make contact with or of an area that you wish to look at.*'

'*Well, if we are going to get my people here then I need to speak to Tishan.*'

No sooner had Menkh thought the words then the glowing light on the walls and ceiling began to swirl into a myriad of different patterns, making him feel as if he was being transported through the air. The colours coalesced into the light of a lamp inside a room and in front of him sat Tishan Dar, drinking from a beaker as she was writing notes. Tishan's eyes opened wide in amazement to such a degree that Menkh felt sure they would pop out from her head. The beaker fell from her fingers, its contents spilling over her notes, and strangling noises issued from her throat.

'Tishan, it is alright. This is just a projection of me. I am safe and well and have used a device to enable me to speak with you, there is nothing to fear.'

Tishan stood up slowly. 'Menkh, is it really you? Is this some kind of sorcery? By all the gods you have near frightened me to death.' Tishan collected her thoughts and took a deep breath.

'No ... all is well, I swallowed too much water and choked,' this last was called out to the guard at the door who had heard the noise inside Tishan's room.

'Tishan, listen to me. There is so much to tell you and the others. I have found us a new home! Gather together the people and make ready to journey here, it is not overly far but will take you some meh'chaal of travel. I will send Votlas back to you as a guide, but you will only need this once you are very close. Just continue to follow the path as we have done till now, you should not have difficulty following it.'

Tishan's eyes narrowed as she absorbed this news. 'But, Menkh, there will be questions. How will I tell the others that I have seen you? They will think I have gone mad,' replied Tishan anxiously. 'I am not sure that I haven't gone mad!'

Menkh considered her response. 'Yes, you may have a point. How much time will you need to gather the Shu Lans together and bring them to you?'

'Give me one chaal. It is late but not so late that they will need to be roused from their sleep.'

'Very well. I will return to you in one chaal,' Menkh responded, and as he said the words the vision of Tishan faded abruptly and the walls went back to their bluish glow.

Menkh now turned his thoughts to Votlas Fen and once again the walls and ceiling around him swirled with colours. They coalesced around a small fire where he could see Votlas and the other guards, seated, cooking something over the flames.

They all jumped to their feet as he appeared before them, hands going to weapons and bodies dropping into the ready stance.

'Do not be alarmed any of you. I am safe and well, this is a projection of me which enables me to communicate with you. Votlas, is all well?'

Votlas overcame her amazement in a commendably short period of time. 'All is well, Zaltec. I speak for all when I say it is good to hear and see you, however strange the meeting. We scouted along the wall and tried to find a way through, but the gates disappeared the moment you went through them. We made camp here, following the strange visitation of a creature who told us you were safe, in the hope that you would return the same way.'

'Good. You have done well, all of you. I have communicated with Stragosh Tishan in the same way I am speaking to you. It is remarkable but completely safe. Votlas, at first light I want you to take Ardesh and Desh and make your way back to the encampment. You will meet our people on the way back, journeying towards this place. Guide them here and lead them to the gates.'

Votlas clashed her right arm across her chest in the Baran Mec salute. 'As you command, Zaltec.'

'Very well. Listen to me, all of you. I know you must be brimming with questions. On the other side of this wall is a city, or at least what remains of one. It is habitable and full of quite remarkable things. Here we can rebuild and start anew without fear of enemies. Horven and Mareen, I will open the gates once Votlas has departed, so be ready. I will meet you on the other side and take you along the path that leads to the city. Any questions?'

This was greeted with a further salute and murmur of assent and as Menkh severed communications he could imagine the buzz of discussion and comment that would follow.

As the walls turned opaque once more, Menkh looked down at the panel in front of him.

'*Crixac, can I open the outer gates through the cliff wall from here?*'

'Yes,' came the response in his mind. '*Turn your mind to the gates, that will bring them into focus on the walls. Then place your hand in the depression below the gate symbol. All you have to do then is give the command.*'

'*I have a sense that the markings on this panel above the depressions is somehow in a script not easily understood by all. Am I correct in this?*'

'*Your senses do you credit, Menkh. Where we stand now was restricted to all but a chosen few because from here you can command the entirety of the City and all its resources. As your thoughts interact with the array on your head, so this is communicated to the panel. This will no doubt seem like magic to you, but everything in the city and everything around you is powered by the crystal. In its own profound way, the crystal is sentient. It can read and adapt your thoughts and translate them into action. The ancients who built this city created many wonders by channelling the power of the crystal. Today, it is damaged and failing — try to imagine what this place was like when it was whole.*'

'*If it is sentient then why did it not prevent the destruction of the other Cities? Why would it adhere to actions that would result in such a cataclysm and loss of life?*'

'*The crystal is not sentient in any sense that you or even I can understand. It has no concept of good or evil, it is what it is. Its power is limited only by the intelligence of those who interact with it and the moral code that binds them. It will interpret and translate any directed thought into an action. In this sense, the power of the crystal can be used to undertake profoundly good and profoundly bad things; but it is, at all times, supremely dangerous.*

But then, what is good or bad all depends on your perspective, Menkh. Your memories tell me that you commanded at the battle of Morkesh. How many enemy slain were there, half a million? And that's not counting the captives who were put to death later. How did you feel about that then?'

The words called up memories in Menkh's mind. He had led the Graaven army, some 100 000 Hoplex, and ambushed a huge force of rebel Perduvians who had defied the Empire. Trapped in a ravine, the enemy Zaltec was a fool who thought that the size of her force would prevail. Twenty thousand Sagit had slaughtered them as they milled around at the bottom, hopelessly trying to defend themselves. The slaughter had continued over two days. Despite cries for mercy, the Sagit continued to loose arrows until their supply was exhausted, even throwing down torches in the night to pick out targets. On the afternoon of the second day, Menkh had unleashed his heavy infantry. 50 000 highly-trained Hoplex advanced into the ravine and systematically dispatched anything left alive with strict orders that, if she still lived, the Perduvian Zaltec was to be captured and brought to him.

Menkh was young and the image of a true Graaven prince – the perfect Stragosh, both cruel and unforgiving. He had the enemy Zaltec dragged before him in chains. She had tried to take her life but botched the process. It took many chaal for her to die, but only after watching the slaughter of those of her personal guard who still lived.

Menkh was sickened by those memories. He had changed profoundly and was no longer the person he was then. *'Back then, Crixac, you know what I would have done if I had access to such power. We were mighty, we believed utterly in our right to rule and our pre-eminence as a race. So, I take your point. If this is what the Kareems became, it is ironic that Pershiva and I were attempting to redirect the Graaven people towards a more enlightened path. There is a part of me that believes that what happened to the Empire was some kind of divine retribution, inflicting on us what we had, in our arrogance, inflicted on so many others.'*

'Perhaps. The question of balance lies at the central core of this, Menkh, but come, let us leave the past and look to the future that we can build together.'

'Yes,' agreed Menkh, *'there will be time for reflection as we move forward. Let us see if Tishan has mustered the officers for us. I am anticipating their reaction when they see me.'*

Menkh turned his thoughts to Tishan and, once again, the wall coalesced into a range of colours which then drew into sharp focus. Tishan was now sitting amidst an array of commanders who abruptly ceased their talk as Menkh himself came into view before them. Open mouths and wide-open eyes expressed their incredulity at the sight of him and there was complete silence in the room.

'As you commanded, Zaltec, you see around me all of the senior officers. Judging by their reactions, they are as amazed as I was at your presence.'

'Thank you, Tishan,' responded Menkh. 'As ever, you have displayed your capacity to follow orders with the minimum of fuss and perfect professionalism, although I am interested to know what you said to get all of them together?'

'As to that, I said I had received an urgent message from you and that they should attend, posthaste. Of course, I did not intimate that the message would come from you directly,' said Tishan in a slightly amused tone. Menkh smiled in response and turned his focus to the assembly who huddled together in the command tent.

'What you see of me here is a projection coming to you from the room I am standing in. This room, my friends, is located in a city, long deserted but entirely habitable and filled with amazing things. There is plentiful water and food available, and it is situated behind a wall that even the Grand Army would have found impossible to assault. In short, I am ordering the Stragosh to break camp and have you all march here to take up occupation. Then, my friends, you will see for yourself this place and, like me, you will be reassured that we have found a new home. From here we can forge a new future and make plans, and I will be at leisure to answer the many questions you will have.

I am sending Votlas, Ardesh, and Desh back to guide you. You should meet up with them as they return. Follow the pathway as we have been doing. We encountered few obstacles, although we did come across and aid another being.'

An exchange of looks amongst the officers followed this remark.

'Yes, a rather diminutive but capable person who overcame his initial fear and communicated with us. A hunter by his dress and weapons. He disappeared into the night after we had tended to his injuries and fed him. You will appreciate that slipping past Votlas Fen and the rest of the party was no mean feat! Watch out for further contact with him or others of his kind as you make your way here.

From what we could make out, the creature's name is Draachnull. He posed no threat to us, but a larger group of our people perhaps might be seen as trespassers on his lands.'

Menkh turned his gaze back to Tishan. 'As usual, scout the way ahead and try to select those who are cool headed. None of us wish to start a conflict. I think we have all had enough of that for the foreseeable future.' This last comment was met with a nodding of heads and a buzz of talk. 'Now, I will leave preparations to you all – the long journey is nearly over, my friends. I look forward to seeing you all very soon.'

As Menkh severed the connection he saw his officers deliver the Graaven salute and heard the beginnings of a general discussion commencing.

CHAPTER EIGHT

As Menkh's form disappeared from view, the buzz of conversation grew loud again with amazement and speculation. Tishan rapped the table with a knife blade and the conversation abruptly stilled, with all eyes turned on her. 'Questions, anyone?'

It was Ankh who expressed the general feelings of the group. 'Well, Stragosh, we are all amazed beyond belief. But if this is not sorcery or witchcraft, I have no explanation for the Zaltec's appearance. Speaking for myself, if Menkh ab Dur commanded us to march off a cliff I would do it without question,' he said.

A general nodding of heads greeted this statement.

'It seems that wonder upon wonder presages our journey into this new land. What orders, then?'

Tishan stood and looked around the assembled officers. 'All of us have followed our Zaltec into the darkest pits of Xerfun and he has led us back into the clear light of day. Are there any here who will question his commands or believes that sorcery and witchcraft are at play?'

Tishan waited quietly and her gaze was met calmly by all in the room. Finally, Tarax spoke. 'I think I speak for all here assembled that, even had the Zaltec made a pact with Slax Ar Terrun herself, still we would follow his commands.'

Looks were exchanged as Tarax named the dread Goddess of Death.

'Very well,' Tishan spoke into the silence that followed and smiled at the group, 'we make preparations to break camp at first light and we march to join the Zaltec as soon as possible.'

So saying, Tishan made a movement of her head in dismissal towards the doorway. 'You all know what to do.'

A clashing of salutes followed, and a buzz of conversation rose once again as the group exited the command hut until only Tishan and Ankh remained.

'So, Ankh, it seems that you may yet have direct experience of your bridge builders and their craft.'

Ankh smiled at Tishan. 'Wonder upon wonder, Stragosh. I wouldn't be dead for a handful of golden merix.'

Tishan smiled in response. 'Much good that they would do you now, Ankh.' Her voice took on a more serious tone. 'That we are not all dead is down to one person. Now get out, Ankh, and get yourself organised, the Zaltec has just robbed me of a night's sleep.'

Ankh patted Tishan's shoulder and turned to leave. 'You know where I am if you need me.' But he only received a grunt in reply as Tishan strode out ahead of him into the camp.

------0------

'So, *what now, Crixac?*' asked Menkh as the image of the assembled officers faded and the walls before him tuned opaque once more.

'*Now, Menkh, it is time that you rested. Take refreshment and get some sleep. Whilst I can manipulate your body to diminish hunger and boost your vitality, to do so on a prolonged basis would be damaging and unnecessary.*'

They exited the strange communications room and, re-entering the perach, travelled to another section of the building. The doors opened onto a well-furnished room with enormous windows that looked back over the city, and thence to the place where Menkh had entered it several chaal earlier. A muted light illuminated parts of the city and from his vantage he could see the seven streams, reflected in the light of the moons, as they flowed towards where he stood.

Now that he had time to reflect, he realised that he was both tired and hungry. He walked into a smaller room set with a table and chairs and noticed that one of the walls was inset with panels that glowed with a green light.

'*Place your hand on the panel here and allow yourself to think that you are hungry and thirsty.*' Menkh followed this instruction and he concentrated on the feeling of hunger. The light of the panel grew brighter and a slight hissing sound could be heard. Finally, Menkh jumped back in surprise when the panel slid open and there before him was a cup and a bowl with steam coming from them, and eating utensils set to one side.

'*Here is your meal, Menkh,*' said Crixac in a mischievous tone and, as Menkh hesitated, '*Go on, take it out. It won't bite you.*'

'*How is this even possible?*' asked Menkh in a subdued tone.

'*After all you have seen and experienced today it is food and drink that captures your amazement!* Crixac exclaimed. '*Everything in the city, Menkh, is energised by and, in a sense, filled with the essence of the crystal. I have told you that the crystal is sentient, it can interpret your needs and manipulate the City's resources to supply those needs. The Kareems constructed the city and, as they developed their knowledge and understanding of the power of the crystal, established systems that could respond. In turn, the crystal itself modified what the Kareems did. A thousand years – imagine that, if you can. A thousand years to build a city filled with the living power of the crystal. Ultimately, there was no poverty. The Kareems practiced agriculture but developed machines to supply the basic food stuffs that the City then converted into meals. They pursued knowledge and formed guilds that specialised in specific areas of learning, and a golden age of technological advance blossomed. But knowledge does not necessarily beget wisdom, and in the end the pursuit of* knowledge in the name of power ruled. The gift of the crystal and the resources of the City led to indolence and decay and, eventually, into the catastrophe that obliterated them all.'

Menkh sat down with his meal at the table and after tentatively sipping the drink, which was a kind of tea, and sampling the stewed vegetables, he deemed them both delicious. 'Yes, a salutary lesson, Crixac. So, I am going to be curious to see how my people react when they get here.'

'Yes, it will require adjustment. But there will be work for them to do. The land around the city is fertile but neglected. There is much that needs to be done for the City and in return the City will nurture and protect your people. For now, though, you should rest. You will find a bed and there is a room where you may cleanse yourself. It even has a bath.'

'A bath!' exclaimed Menkh. 'By all the gods, that will be an even greater luxury then a bed to sleep in.'

The room containing the bath and other necessary equipment for bodily functions was well appointed. The Graaven people prided themselves on cleanliness and public baths and lavatories were a standard feature in cities across the Empire. Even the poorest had access to such amenities. So it was that, after some initial instruction from Crixac and after a lengthier process of removing his mail coat and undergarments, Menkh reclined in hot water and allowed its heat to soothe away tension and relax him.

Menkh slept dreamlessly and well, and awoke refreshed as the first rays of Avlar lit up the window in his room. He was somewhat disconcerted to find that his garments had somehow disappeared in the night. In their place, items of new and unfamiliar clothing were neatly laid out on a small bench at the foot of the bed.

'Do not worry, Menkh, the same servant that delivered your refreshment when we met has taken your clothing for cleaning. In the meantime, you should find the clothing here of a size to fit you.'

The clothing was indeed the correct size. There was a tunic made from a material that Menkh did not recognise but which

Crixac informed him was plant based, and which was worn over a kind of loose-fitting trousers. An ornate belt of a bluish-coloured metal, embossed with a swirling geometric pattern, was cinched at the waist. Finally, foot coverings made of a tough but durable leather with a silvery sheen completed his wardrobe.

'*Hmmm, you look quite the Kareem, albeit a smaller version,*' joked Crixac.

'*Yes, the size of the bed indicates that they were of a greater stature than your average Graaven,*' quipped Menkh. '*Again, I wonder at the capacity of the City to supply such things.*'

'*You will get used to it, Menkh. The City was assessing you from the moment you entered its boundary. There is nothing that escapes its attention; or, rather, the attention of the crystal.*'

Menkh nodded his head. There was so much here that he could not explain. It was truly magical, though Crixac took pains to explain these wonders away as "superior technology".

After breakfasting on a meal not dissimilar to the one he had consumed the previous day, and which Crixac later explained was reconstituted vegetables, Menkh picked up the staff that he now carried with him at all times and they made their way once more to the communications room. Again, they stood before the panel and the glowing walls that surrounded it.

'*You told your guards that you would open the gates. Whilst you can do that from here, there is another way I will show you which is more effective.*'

'*Yes, it is going to be tiresome if we have to come here every time I want to communicate with others or execute a request like opening the gate*s,' thought Menkh in passing.

'*Indeed,*' replied Crixac, '*and that is why you have that belt around your waist. If you now activate the central depression on the control panel then we may access something to assist us.*'

Completing this action caused a panel in the wall behind them to slide open and reveal an array of strange devices, all about the size of a Graaven thumb.

'*Of course, to the Kareems these were quite small. But they have different functions and you will find that they will sit quite nicely on your belt.*'

Menkh gazed in bewilderment at the metallic-looking devices that sat in rows on shelves lined with what appeared to be a kind of woollen material. Each winked with a different light, covering all colours of the spectrum. They were all beautifully made and, in all cases, looked like some ornate type of jewellery more for adornment than functionality.

'*So, Menkh, we are going to need a red, a green, and a blue to start with while you are learning. Pick up one at a time and hold it near your belt.*'

Tentatively Menkh selected a red device, which was remarkably light and thin. Its surface, too, was highly decorated in way that rather reminded him of the geometric design he had observed on his belt. As he lowered his hand to the proximity of the belt there was a brief but intense glow from both the belt and the object, and it suddenly disappeared out of his hand. Menkh couldn't help but jump in surprise.

'*So sorry, Menkh,*' said Crixac in a mischievous tone. '*I should have warned you about that.*'

'*Hmmm, you did that deliberately, Crixac, just to get me to jump. It would seem you are something of a practical joker.*'

Laughter echoed in his head. '*Well, now you know what to expect.*'

Taking a green and then a blue device, each one mirrored the same action. Menkh noticed that whereas before his belt was uniformly a metallic blue, now three different sections shone with the same winking light as each of the devices he had selected.

'*So, let us practise,*' instructed Crixac. '*The blue light initiates transportation. You must think deliberate thoughts here, Menkh. We wish to travel to the outer gates so you must fix this very clearly in your mind. I can help you with this. Once you have that thought fixed, place your hand on the blue section of your belt.*'

'*What's going to happen?*' asked Menkh.

'*It's a surprise*,' responded Crixac in the same mischievous tone as before.

'*Is it too late to change my mind about him?*' mused Menkh to himself.

'*I heard that, Menkh!*'

'*I know.*'

Fixing the thought of the gates and picturing them in his head, Menkh touched the blue-coloured section.

Menkh could not recall such a strange sensation. It felt somewhat like running at the fastest pace imaginable. Everything around him seemed to somehow go out of focus and rush past, yet his body remained motionless. There was a feeling of light-headedness, which was somewhat unpleasant, and then everything suddenly coalesced back into focus and he found himself standing immediately outside the gates. Menkh was rendered speechless.

'*I told you it was a surprise*,' said Crixac.

Menkh caught his breath. '*You did not exaggerate. Well, it beats walking*,' he reflected.

'*So now, a command. We want the gates to open, so fix that in your head. Imagine the gates opening and concentrate on that. Then place your hand on the red section.*'

Following Crixac's instruction, Menkh concentrated on this and, placing his hand on the appropriate section of his belt, saw the gates swing open seamlessly. Mareen and Horven Var came into sight, both in the crouched position they had assumed as they saw the gates appear, ready to react to any danger. On seeing Menkh, they sprang to attention and saluted. Relieved expressions were followed by broad smiles from both guards.

'Zaltec, we are happy and relieved to see you well,' said Horven.

'It was of considerable concern when you disappeared behind the gates,' added Mareen in a tone that had a hint of admonishment.

'You are right to scold me and I should not have left you all behind. However, it has worked out well. I cannot promise that I will not be so precipitate again in time to come, but you wouldn't want me to suddenly become boringly predictable, would you?'

Horven and Mareen exchanged glances. 'Actually, Zaltec, boringly predictable would be most welcome,' announced Mareen, accompanied by a solemn nod from Horven.

'Noted,' replied Menkh. 'Now, let me show you something that will make your jaws drop. Follow me.'

Menkh turned on his heel and walked down the path to the city that he had followed before. His guards spoke in subdued tones but pointed things out to each other as they noted items of interest. As expected, when they reached the place where the terrain opened out and they saw the city for the first time, they were rendered speechless and looked at each other and then at Menkh in surprise.

'Yes, my friends, I also stood in mute surprise. Behold our new home. You have seen the fertile lands that surround it and have glimpsed the animals that feed on the abundant grasses and plants around us. They are not unlike the civix, do you think? Perhaps they will yield a rich and creamy milk for us later.'

'But, Zaltec, what is this place and what of its inhabitants? Surely our arrival may not be welcomed?' asked Horven.

'The inhabitants are long gone; on that score you need have no concern. The city was once named Kareem Vastar but has long lain abandoned. Come, we will walk down to the outskirts of the city together and we will talk as we descend.'

So it was that they followed the path downwards and an earnest discussion about the city began.

-------0-------

Tishan was pleased with the progress they were making. Well-fed and rested, combined with the lifting of the fear of imminent death, had a wondrous effect on the speed of advance. The

Graavens observed huge herds of grazing herbivores, the like of which had not been seen within the confines of the Empire in living memory.

Occasionally a vast trumpeting sound would issue from individual animals, but whether male or female could not be discerned. Whilst some sported horns or tusk-like protrusions, different species appeared to graze together in close proximity. Some had long necks which enabled them to reach to the tops of the tallest ferns, whilst others grazed contentedly on the abundant grasses. They observed the passage of the Graavens with a degree of curiosity but seemed unperturbed by their passing and, after a long and considered look, returned to their grazing.

'Have you noticed something about these creatures, Stragosh?' asked Ankh as they walked past one herd.

'And what would that be, Ankh?'

'Look carefully as the creatures approach the edge of the forest. There, where the light changes and the grass changes colour,' said Ankh as he pointed to a family group of herbivores that had separated themselves somewhat from the main herd.

Tishan followed Ankh's pointing finger and observed them as they approached the point that he indicated. At first, she wondered what Ankh was getting at but then she noticed that the skin of the animals was changing colour. In just a small fraction of time their skin tone had subtly altered to reflect the changing light pattern and colour of the ferns. If Tishan had not been looking at them directly she would have had difficulty in seeing them when they stood motionless.

'Yes, quite fascinating isn't it?' said Ankh, who had been looking at Tishan's facial expression. 'I have noted that, to a greater and lesser extent, just about every species we have passed by has the same ability.'

'A naturally occurring ability to camouflage oneself, I could have used that many times!' exclaimed Tishan.

She had no sooner made this remark than there was a palpable shift in the demeanour of the grazing animals. As one, they had stopped grazing and heads were raised, smelling the air, whilst herds of like animals moved together protectively. A silence seemed to descend over everything – continuing for what seemed like a long time but was only moments – when suddenly the general peace was shattered.

A series of high-pitched screams, piercing to the ears, were heard, seeming to emanate from different points at the edge of the fern forest. At that exact moment, several creatures stepped out on the grass. Even at a distance you could see that these were a predatory species. Their hides were coloured in green and black stripes that imitated the dappled colour of the fern forest they emerged from. At twice the height of a Graaven, they had long snouts filled with rows of sharp teeth. Two powerful legs and a long tail for balance, combined with a sinuous body, gave the impression of both great strength and speed. Two long upper arms ended in three hook-like claws with bony protrusions.

As one, the grazing animals turned and fled with great cries of alarm, the ground trembling under their feet. The Graavens, standing as they were on an area of path that was shielded on one side by a long, wavelike rock formation that stretched before and behind, had no concern with being trampled in the rush as the creatures all headed across the grasslands to the safety of the forest edge, away from the creatures.

'Mellax!' exclaimed Tishan.

Here was a creature the Graavens knew and feared. Beautiful and deadly, although they had been eradicated from the Empire, they still remained a feature in Graaven horror stories.

'Shields!' yelled Tishan. 'Defensive formation!'

Like the disciplined Hoplex they were, the Graavens formed an interlocking wall of shields in rapid time. Spear tips, like the prickly spine of a giant Percassian sloth, poked out. Behind the shields, Sagit were positioned, though with virtually no arrows to speak of they were largely a token force. Behind them stood the non-combatants and baggage, hard up against the cliff face.

Varga ran up to where Tishan and Ankh were standing behind the shield wall.

'I am heartily glad we have the wall behind us, Stragosh. Orders?'

Tishan nodded her head without looking at Varga. 'Nothing to do but stand and wait, Kalvak. Return to your people and hold steady.'

Varga rattled off a quick salute.

'The Baran Mec will stand firm,' Tishan called out. 'They are after bigger prey than us this day.'

'I hope,' remarked Ankh quietly.

'We are unknown to them, Ankh. If we stand still, I am hoping that they will ignore us.'

The mellax went from standing still to tremendous speed in three steps. They had selected one large creature who had been slow to follow its fellows as they stampeded away. With wondrous coordination they isolated it and formed a loose circle around the creature. The Graavens waited for the inevitable rush that would bring the huge herbivore down and the ripping and tearing of razor-sharp teeth as the mellax devoured their prey. Instead, they just stood there.

It was Ankh's sharp eyes that spotted the diminutive humanoid figures that stepped out from the forest edge. Dressed in hides and with long, plaited hair, they carried short bows slung over their backs. The leading figure seemed to limp somewhat on one leg.

Several individuals, appearing to have their skin painted the same colour as the mellax, approached them as they stood gathered around their prey. Small tubes protruded from their mouths and a series of warbling calls and strange piping sounds issued from them. The mellax, far from turning and devouring these presumptuous encroachers, issued similar sounds and swayed their heads to the left and right at the same time.

The Graavens exchanged shocked looks and muttered amongst themselves.

'If I had not seen this with my own eyes, I would have said it was impossible,' said Tishan in a breathless tone.

'Indeed,' responded Ankh, not taking his eyes off the scene in front of him.

Now the rest of the humanoid creatures had come up to the group and whilst the trill and calls of the whistles continued, they fired arrows into the surrounded herbivore.

'Pah!' exclaimed one Sagit from behind. 'How do they expect to drop an animal that size with such puny arrows? They'll need a thousand of them and a sem'chaal to do it.'

There was a general muttering of agreement and some quiet laughter from fellow Sagit, accompanied by a nodding of heads.

However, after a remarkably short period of time, and what appeared to be very few arrows loosed, the huge herbivore lurched, issued a despairing groan, and dropped with a resounding crash to the ground.

There was a collective gasp of surprise from the Graavens and particularly the Sagit.

'By the fetid bowels of Bringarell,' said one, 'I have never seen or heard of such a thing.'

A Shu Lan's voice called out, 'One more word from you, Deng, and you'll be seeing stars you've never seen before neither. Quiet in the ranks and concentrate. If they start shooting arrows at us, we'll fall faster than that creature, I warrant.'

'That's my fear also,' muttered Ankh in agreement.

The humanoid creatures moved in, now many more in number. They swarmed over the fallen beast and, all the while, as the whistles continued to sound, the mellax warbled and swayed in response. In a coordinated and well-practised series of moves, the humanoids had opened the belly of the beast. Three of their party, actually inside the now-opened cavity, removed choice parts of its internal organs. These were loaded on wooden sleds and dragged away. Still others cut superior portions of flesh in other areas and soon they appeared to have taken all that was needed, moving off back into the fern forest.

Once this operation was nearing its apparent completion, the humanoid with the limp approached the Graavens. If it showed fear it was not apparent. As Varga drily remarked later, 'If I had seven mellax backing me up, I wouldn't be afraid either.'

The creature looked curiously at the Graavens behind their shields as he called out to them. The Graavens looked at each other.

'Is he saying "Menkh", Stragosh?' asked Ankh. 'It's hard to make out.'

'I believe he is, Ankh, and I also think that this might be the creature that Menkh referred to. What was it … "Draachnull"?'

Tishan didn't wait for an answer but, moving from behind the shields, she pointed and called out to the creature in a questioning voice, 'Draachnull?'

The creature tilted its head to one side and, touching its chest, nodded its head and said, 'Draachnull,' although the way it said it didn't sound much like Tishan's version.

Tishan nodded, smiled, and, touching her chest, loudly said, 'Tishan.'

'Shisshern,' responded the creature.

'Close enough,' responded Tishan with a smile.

'Menkh?' asked Draachnull.

Tishan could not think of how to tell him that he wasn't there so she pointed ahead in the direction they were travelling.

'Menkh,' she said and tried to indicate by gestures that they were going to meet him.

Draachnull seemed to understand. Also indicating the road ahead, he nodded and made a shooing gesture with his arms.

'Well, it seems we need to move on,' muttered Tishan. Waving to Draachnull she called out to the Graavens, 'Standard marching formation. Move out, at the double!'

With some tentative misgivings, the Graavens reassembled and moved briskly along the path away from Draachnull and the gathered mellax.

Draachnull watched them departing and after some time moved off himself, rejoining with his people at the forest edge. Behind him the painted whistle callers followed along and, upon entering the confines of the forest, quickly disappeared.

Freed from the spell of the whistles, the mellax once again screamed loudly and fell in a pack on the freshly killed herbivore. From a distance the Graavens heard the screams and, knowing what was occurring, increased their pace along the path by unspoken agreement.

------0------

In the meantime, Menkh had re-entered the city, responding to a myriad of questions from Horven and Mareen as they walked. After passing by the two figures that guarded the approach to the causeway, and having a similar unpleasant experience, they had accompanied him to the building which Menkh now referred to as the Complex, where he had installed them in a room not far from his own.

Menkh was surprised at the rapidity with which they had both adapted to their unique and wondrous surroundings. Reflecting that perhaps this was because Menkh himself showed a degree of familiarity with his surroundings and was relaxed in manipulating the workings of the building, they appeared to accept his explanation without question.

Over the coming days, he sent them to reconnoitre the surrounds of the city and report back to him on what they discovered. In part this was a ruse to keep them both occupied, as Menkh had full access to both the city and its surrounding lands via the interface he could manipulate in the viewing room, as well as the power of the belt he wore and the staff he now carried. It was also a way to reassure them of the safety of the city and the fertile lands that surrounded it. During these forays, Menkh — under Crixac's guidance — familiarised himself with the layout of the city and how to adapt this for the Graavens once they arrived.

Even though two thirds of the city had been destroyed, what was left would accommodate many times the current number of surviving Graavens. The city had been divided into precincts, each with a governing subcommittee responsible for all matters relating to the day-to-day running of the city. Whilst the Kareems had their own family dwellings, in each sector all meals were eaten in huge refectory buildings. These buildings usually had two stories above ground containing a meeting room and dining hall, but they also had several floors below ground level. No Kareem cooked or prepared food. This was done in a large, automated kitchen run via the power of the crystal. Farming produce was delivered each day to a huge loading bay where foodstuffs and livestock were placed in containers and taken into the heart of the building on a conveyor system.

Menkh learned more of the Kareem people as Crixac passed on knowledge and Menkh himself began to access some of the Kareem records. Initially, the Kareems had laboured in the fields and grown and harvested the food required to feed the populace. The arts had flourished alongside the sciences in a golden age. As their technology advanced through the power of the crystal, machines were designed to take over and the Kareems became increasingly indolent. Over time, the population of the city decreased as those in power made laws which prohibited the breeding of any Kareem below a certain intelligence level.

People of limited intelligence were gradually bred out. No-one was required to undertake simple manual work. As the City took care of all their needs, the requirement for a "working class" was totally eliminated. The arts were frowned upon as technological advance became an obsession, and millennia of cooperation with Palluvia and Paxal was replaced by jealousy and fear. Finally, this culminated in the catastrophe of the war which had exterminated the populations of all three Cities.

Menkh reflected on all that he was learning about the Kareem people as he stood in the meeting room of the refectory building within the precinct he had selected for occupation once the Graavens arrived. This was relatively close to the outskirts of the city, where fields and orchards were in close proximity. The fields, whilst neglected, could easily be restored and replanted. The orchards, overgrown as they were, still bore many different kinds of edible fruits. Menkh determined that there was enough expertise amongst the Graavens to manage the growing and harvesting required, and there were enough Graavens to supply the labour needed to weed out the fields and manage the orchards. In addition, large flocks of the small, goat-like creature the Graavens referred to as civix grazed in the lush grasses that grew near the banks of the seven streams. There was ample space to set up pens for these creatures as needed, and they were quite tame so herding them would not prove an insurmountable problem.

Menkh kept track of the progress of the Graavens from the viewing room. He had missed the incident with the mellax and the encounter with Draachnull's people, and it was not until sometime later that he learned of this curious event.

Gradually, over the intervening days, he had formulated plans for the housing of the people and had determined that an initial meeting would be held, especially as there was such an ample and well-designed space intended for this purpose, to help settle the people and allay any fears they may have.

Only one thing disturbed him, and this began to increasingly distract his thoughts, particularly at night when he lay down to rest. At Crixac's insistence, he regularly retired for a few chaal of sleep but, with Crixac able to monitor and manipulate his body's organs, the need for sleep was minimal. A voice, or at least the echo of a voice, began to pierce his thoughts. He knew it was not Crixac and as Crixac made no comment regarding this strange phenomenon, he surmised that he was oblivious to it. For reasons he could not adequately explain, even to himself, he did not mention the occurrence to Crixac. There was something about the voice that set up a longing in him he had never experienced before, but what the longing was for was a mystery to him. Nevertheless, it grew in intensity until one evening, some days after the Graavens had had their encounter on the road, he found himself standing at the door of the perach.

All was quiet, and he had a strange feeling he could only describe as an "emptiness" inside his mind. The presence of Crixac seemed entirely absent and yet Menkh did not feel perturbed about this. The other voice in his head seemed to comfort him and his feet were drawn inexorably into the perach. Moments later, the door hissed open and he stepped out into the room that housed the crystal itself.

Still, the blue and red lights pulsed along the cables that lay everywhere around, feeding into the crystal and flowing out again, renewed by the power that issued from it. The crystal, its lower third blackened and opaque, reclined in its throne-like structure. Tiny winking facets of light that Menkh had not noticed before flickered constantly over its surface. These lights were hypnotic in effect and, as he drew nearer, the flickering seemed to relax his mind, evoking a desire to touch the crystal's surface.

Menkh stood for long moments staring at the crystal, listening to the strange voice in his head that seemed to synchronise rhythmically with the lights pulsing gently over its surface. Very slowly, he lifted up his right arm and moved his hand to touch it. As his fingers touched the surface, Crixac's voice exploded in his head as if bursting out of a restraint.

'*No, Menkh! Do not touch the—*'

At the same time, the warmth he had felt was replaced by a cold numbness, his vision went dark, and he felt as if he had fallen forward into a pool of icy water. Down and down he felt himself falling, the echo of Crixac's voice receding with great speed. Still he fell, until time itself seemed to mean nothing and he had a sense of travelling a vast distance. As suddenly as it had started, the sensation of falling was replaced by the cessation of all movement. Utter stillness surrounded him and he felt cocooned, unable to move but strangely calm. He could not remember breathing for a long time, but as he did he perceived light.

Slowly, the light grew. He had a sense of himself but, on looking down, could see nothing. He felt encased, as if he were an insect trapped in some kind of sap which enclosed him and prevented all movement. This feeling receded and he felt space around him. There was a floor that seemed to run interminably in all directions from where he stood and a ceiling which mirrored the floor. Both floor and ceiling had the same crystalline appearance as the surface of the crystal in the city. No other living thing could be discerned. It felt as if everything that ever was or ever would be had no meaning, as if such things were but the dream of a dream.

Then he felt a rush of air and saw that there were walls, which at first were impossibly far off, but were moving towards him at tremendous speed. Curiously, he felt no alarm as they approached. He felt no threat as they rose up before him. As quickly as they had moved, they now stopped. He felt as if he was in a large room, perhaps a space as large as the room he occupied in the Complex. A window appeared in one wall and beyond the window he could discern a landscape, composed entirely of crystalline material, which mimicked the shape of trees and hills but was colourless and translucent to look at.

The floor in front of him bulged upwards, a viscous crystalline liquid devolving into a table and two chairs and, finally, the semblance of a humanoid form — but whether male or female could not be determined.

Words issued from the mouth of the form.

'Greetings, Menkh,' a myriad of voices echoed quietly around Menkh, mirroring these words.

'Please sit down, there is much to tell you,' and saying thus, the form indicated the vacant chair with a liquid arm that flowed out from its body. 'It has been long and long since any being visited our world.'

'Long and long,' a sibilant chorus of voices echoed all around him in agreement.

A face appeared in the shape in front of Menkh and smiled.

Menkh felt as if he should be considerably more unsettled than he was. Where he was and what was happening was so far outside the norm of things experienced in life that he felt he should be panicking. Yet he felt strangely relaxed and at ease, confused certainly, but he had no sense of physical threat or danger of any kind. His mind grappled with making sense of his situation.

He framed a question, but it took him some time to find a voice with which to communicate it. Whilst he felt as if he was sitting in the chair his body lacked real substance. Any movement he initiated seemed to cause a disturbance in the air around him. He felt movement but could not discern it. Eventually he managed to speak but the words sounded strange, as if he were trying to speak under water.

'Yes, yes, you have questions,' said the shape encouragingly. 'You have but to frame the thought and we will hear it.'

Menkh considered this. This was exactly how he communicated with Crixac and the City's interface, so he pulled his thoughts together and focused them towards the shape opposite him.

'Where am I?'

'A good question,' susurrated the voices in agreement.

'Yes,' replied the shape, 'a good question but one that is not easy to explain in terms you will understand. You are now "between" all things, Menkh. This place exists everywhere and nowhere. By physically touching the crystal you have allowed us to translate your conscious existence into our dimension. You are separate from what you perceive to be your reality and now inhabit ours. Yet our reality and yours interact with each other. There are other dimensions in the cosmos that interact also, but everything is in balance. Balance is all.'

'Yes, yes,' echoed the voices, 'balance.'

Menkh tried to turn his mind to the explanation, which was not a little confusing.

'How is it possible that our realities interact with each other?'

'Thoughts, Menkh. Your thoughts and desires interact with our reality. The thoughts and prayers of sentient creatures everywhere influence us. We can manipulate the Balance. Who lives and who dies, who wins and who loses, what is formed in perfection and what is crippled and dysfunctional. Be careful what you wish for, Menkh.'

'Careful, careful,' echoed the voices.

Still Menkh grappled with the enormity of what he was being told.

'But what of evil or good? If you can manipulate the Balance can you not oversee the end of disease, of famine, of war?'

'What is evil, Menkh, and what is good? From what you perceive as great evil can come great good. From great good can come calamity and death. We work to preserve balance in all things.

In the City, though, your direct thoughts physically manipulate us. The technology of the Kareems and the others allowed a direct interface between us. This disturbed the Balance until it was eventually restored.'

'*I am sorry, this is very confusing. How was the Balance restored?*'

'When the peoples of the three Cities were annihilated. Balance is all.'

Menkh was overwhelmed with the coldly dispassionate attitude expressed by the shape.

'*So, the obliteration of an entire race was necessary to restore balance?*' asked Menkh.

'Yes,' replied the shape.

'Yes, yes, yes,' echoed the voices.

'Think on this, Menkh. The Kareems exercised their free will to enact a series of actions that precipitated their demise. It was not us. We responded to their desires and allowed them power – that included the power to change what they were becoming. There was another path open to them, but they chose not to take it. If the balance had not been restored, the Kareems would have eventually visited death on systems far from their home. Without their destruction, your people would have no place from which to build anew. The City can help you bring enlightenment to your people. A new age of peace may yet come to pass.'

Menkh sat for a long time pondering what had been revealed. The crystalline shape pulsed gently but allowed him the time.

'*What are you?*'

'What are we?' echoed the voices.

'We are a manifestation of the "Intelligence", Menkh. The Intelligence permeates all life everywhere. The crystal that powers the City is dying and its contact with the Intelligence dwindles. Soon, it will be no more.'

'*Is the Intelligence a god?*' asked Menkh.

The shape melted and reformed.

'You cannot apply such concepts to the Intelligence, Menkh. Applying your knowledge and understanding to the Intelligence is like trying to visualise a mountain by holding a pebble in your hand. The Intelligence "is", and everything everywhere is a manifestation of the Intelligence, including us, including you.'

The shape flowed back and waited for Menkh to respond.

Menkh grappled with the concept and, like an unsolvable puzzle, pushed it to one side in his mind to contemplate later.

'So, why am I here?'

'Another good question,' echoed the voices.

The shape reformed into sharper features; a clear face and upper torso which leaned across the intervening table.

'Random events have disturbed the balance. Whilst random events are a normal phenomenon, in this case the consequences may be dire. The appearance of those you call the Dorath Mar on your world may be the harbinger of doom.'

Menkh sat back. *'Surely if it is a question of balance, then events will unfold so that balance is maintained or restored. I surmise the destruction of our Empire was a question of balance being restored?'*

The shape sat back. 'You may think so, and it is a logical deduction based on what we have told you. But their arrival was a random event that may lead to chaos. The odds against it occurring were astronomical. Your birth and that of your sister were events that would have restored balance over time. You would have set your empire on a course of enlightenment. You would have, albeit unknowingly, received our aid in ways that you would not understand. All of this has been overturned.'

'How?'

'The creatures that hunted you and which destroyed your empire are not the real menace. Rather, it is the being that caused their creation that threatens the Balance. Those you call the Dorath Mar are programmed to perform certain functions and cannot be manipulated or influenced outside of this. Their objective is to annihilate any opposition they encounter. The creature that created them feeds on life and drains the land and everything in it to satiate its constant hunger. You have been overwhelmed by its creations, Menkh, and they cannot think, plan or anticipate in the way that you do. You have outsmarted them using your natural ability, the knowledge you possess of your surroundings and the terrain to thwart them. The crossing of the river destroyed those who pursued you, but they are many and the being that created them fashions more of them as we speak. Soon, Menkh, it will expand its activities. If it gains access to the City, then the knowledge housed in the city archives will mean that it will have power over all life on this world.'

Menkh sat back, considering this ill news. *'But what is this creature. Does it have a name?'*

'A name, a name,' echoed the voices.

'We will not reveal their true name. Suffice to say it is one of a race of creatures – in your tongue you might call them the Talixit Ven, the "eaters of light". In a way they reflect what the Kareems might themselves have become had they not been obliterated. They are a race with a unique ability to corrupt the life essence of others and reshape it to their will in order to absorb and consume life itself. They are devoid of compassion and care only for their own species.'

'How is it, then, that the restoration of balance has not obliterated them like the peoples that lived here?'

'The Balance has kept them in check, Menkh. Some of the worlds they dominate ally or fight back and expel them. Light counters dark. Here, the random event we have explained sets up new parameters that are unique and deadly. It is worse still, Menkh.'

'How is that even possible?'

'Your world of Tarvuli is one of the Balancepoints.'

'Balancepoint,' whispered the voices.

'*Balancepoint?*' questioned Menkh, now completely confused.

'Yes, yes, yes, a Balancepoint. Balance is all,' echoed the voices.

'A Balancepoint is one where our dimension extrudes into yours. There are a number of them scattered throughout the cosmos. Our liquid crystalline form takes physical shape in your dimension.'

'*So, the City is one of these points then?*'

'No, Menkh. The crystal that inhabits your City was stolen by the Kareems and their allies from the Balancepoint thousands of cycles ago. Three Cities were established as a result and each held a crystal. The Balancepoint lies in a place far to the west of the City. If the Talixit Ven find the Balancepoint, then they have access to a force beyond your comprehension and all is truly lost. Every sentient creature in the cosmos will be subject to the wishes and desires of their masters, all balance will be destroyed.'

Menkh sat in deep thought before responding in his mind. '*So, in this possible chain of events that could overturn cosmic balance for all eternity, what role do you want me to play? Obviously, you have me here for a purpose, but I have not the means to understand what I or the remnants of my people can do.*'

'Yes, yes we must tell him,' echoed the voices.

'The random event has provided us with you, Menkh ab Dur. The unique circumstances and the threat the Talixit Ven presents to all sentient life means that, for the first time in countless millennia, we actively seek to influence events ourselves. To this end, we wish to recruit you as an Agent of Balance. Your presence here may yet act to avoid the terrible consequences we anticipate will occur. You have proven that the Dorath Mar and their master have difficulty anticipating your actions and, as yet, it has no inkling of the technology you now have access to. The City, Menkh, has weaponry that can neutralise the Dorath Mar and contain the creature that sits behind them. You and your people hold the key.'

Not for the first time, Menkh sat back pondering the momentous information he had been given. After long moments, he responded, '*My people have barely escaped with their lives. Even now they journey to the city on my orders, but I cannot anticipate how they will react to the wonders that they will encounter. It will take time for them to come to terms with this and not react in fright. I can and will do my best to explain the technology of the City but if they reject my explanations then I have no notion of how this could be managed.*'

'There is one alternative that you might consider, Menkh. To explain all that they will see as "technological advance" requires a certain level of intelligence, and either an understanding of how this can occur over centuries or the capacity to rapidly adapt and assimilate the knowledge provided. You are a rare person with that ability and there may be other individuals amongst your people with similar ability. But a simpler explanation is to base your explanation on "magic" and the magical powers of the City. Magic is a concept that sits in the folklore of countless races of sentient beings. You may find a readier acceptance of the wonders of the City based on magic than that of an alien technology. This may also assist in your explaining the Dorath Mar. Even now there must be those amongst your people who see these creatures as a reflection of dark magic or sorcery.'

'Yes, yes, magic,' echoed the voices in agreement.

Menkh sat deep in thought. He had been grappling with how to explain all that had occurred. By using magic as a reference point even Crixac's involvement could be included. Dreams and portents were a manifestation of magical elements and powers and his people had a rich folklore based on the concept of magic. '*You have given me much on which to think. But my people will still need time to adapt to the City, to re-establish some sense of normality. Even an acceptance of magic is going to take getting used to. I can think of a thousand things which will need to be done. How much time do we have?*'

'There are things which must be done between now and any confrontation with the Dorath Mar. The crystal in the City must be restored and you must journey to the Balancepoint to achieve this. One cycle of seasons, Menkh. One sem'chaal and you must be in position to confront the Dorath Mar. We anticipate that it will take them this amount of time to eradicate all final pockets of resistance. The Talixit Ven will gorge itself on life and the land will begin to die. You will need allies in this quest and your own unique abilities will assist you.'

Menkh tried not to be overwhelmed with the enormity of the task they had given him. There was no question in his mind of a refusal. Negating the Dorath Mar was the least he wished in memory of the millions of Graavens who had perished.

'You say the crystal needs to be restored. How am I to accomplish this? I don't have the first idea of what is required.'

The liquid crystalline form seemed to melt somewhat and then reform.

'Our time grows short, Menkh. The crystal loses its connection to the Intelligence. The Intelligence can be located within the Balancepoint. Only when you are there will you gain the understanding to achieve this. You must travel to the west, Menkh, and look to the mountains.'

The crystalline form began to ebb away, dissolving slowly into the floor.

'But what of Crixac? I cannot feel his presence in my mind, and you must have known he was inhabiting my body. If I am to achieve all this then I will need his aid.'

'Yes, the symbiote. We blocked his presence so he could not influence you. Your decision to assist must be of your own free will, Menkh. This is critical. Crixac and those like him have ever been strange beings, but in the main they have always worked to retain the Balance.'

'The Balance is all,' came the sibilant echo.

'Yes, balance must be maintained in all things,' the voice seemed to muse to itself, and Menkh was not sure if its words were actually directed towards him or were some internal reflection. 'Random events have provided two opposing forces with the power to affect all life. One in the form of the Talixit Ven and the other in you, driven into our arms by circumstances that could not have been foretold.' The creature suddenly reformed and its head shape drew close to Menkh so that he would have drawn away if he could. 'It is mysterious even to us who are the servants of Balance.'

The shape melted and only partially reformed as the table and chairs also melted away. 'When you return, the knowledge you have will be available to your symbiote. It will come as a shock.'

'*Why is that?*'

'Because to touch the crystal usually means death, Menkh. You will be the first to survive and return with your knowledge and it will open up new understanding for Crixac. Now, you must return, or you will be trapped here in our dimension. We can only preserve you in our form for a finite time. Bend your thoughts to us in time of need, we will aid you where we can.'

'Yes, where we can,' echoed the voices.

The crystalline form dissolved, and its voice came from far away. 'Farewell, Menkh ab Dur. The Balance is all.'

'Farewell,' echoed the voices.

As the walls receded, Menkh's vision darkened and he felt himself flying upwards at an ever-increasing velocity whilst all around him it was silent and utterly black.

Suddenly he lurched back into his body, his hand receding from the crystal before him, with Crixac's voice sounding sharply in his head as the shouted utterance that was framed just before he touched the crystal was completed, '—*crystal!*'

CHAPTER NINE

Draachnull sat with the other tribe elders in the midst of their village. They had feasted on fresh roasted meat and tubers and now the people were singing to the music of pipe and drum. The youngest of the people danced around the large central fire in the intricate steps of the Thanksgiving Dance. The strange people they had encountered had engendered much discussion and speculation – not out of fear but curiosity. No-one living could remember any interaction with strangers other than those they traded with who lived across the Mother Water. The Benshin had inhabited these lands time out of mind. A peaceful people, they farmed and hunted and lived as one with the land and the beasts, birds, and plants that coexisted with them.

Kohlikar, a fellow elder, turned to Draachnull after quaffing a gourd full of tek beer.

'What make you of these people, Revered One? Do they pose a threat to us?'

Draachnull considered his response carefully as befitted the seriousness of the question. Bellanscir, another elder, leaned in close to Draachnull, her voice raised above the laughter and singing of the people. 'Yes, I would know your thoughts on this matter also.'

Draachnull cleared his throat and nodded his head. 'I have given this matter much thought. I do not believe they are a direct threat to us; remember they could easily have killed me. But their leader, Mesh, instead assisted me, cared for my wounds, fed me, and gave me water. No, I believe their intentions are honourable. It is true they are clumsy and easily fooled and I walked past the guards that were set to watch me without their notice. But I think they were to watch over me for my safety, and not with any sense of threat.'

'Still,' replied Kohlikar, 'they cross our lands and we cannot truly know of their designs. They follow the ancient path but ultimately that path leads into the wilder lands beyond the lands of the Benshin. It may be prudent to watch them to ensure their peaceful intent.'

'What Kohlikar says has merit, Revered One,' exclaimed Bellanscir. 'Such an action would incite no hostility if they are peaceful.'

Again, Draachnull nodded his agreement. 'What you say is true. Kohlikar, direct your finest hunters to observe them. They are not to approach but make sure they are observed by these people. Let them know that the Shadow Hunter clan of the Benshin tribe watch them.'

Kohlikar bowed his head and made the clicking noise that indicated assent. Bellanscir smiled and nodded at this wisdom.

Draachnull looked at them both. 'I feel a change is coming to the land. Whether for good or ill I cannot tell, but we will meet it with our eyes open. Bellanscir, send word of these people to the Lightning, Smoke, and Thunder Water clans. Tell them that the Shadow Hunters watch only, and that these people may walk our lands in peace, at least for the time being.'

------0------

Since the encounter with the mellax the rain had, at last, set in over the past two days. They had been lucky and the weather till recently had been unusually dry, but now a constant and soaking rain made going miserable if not overly difficult.

Three days after the encounter with Draachnull's people, a Graaven scout ran down the column as they advanced up the road. Tishan Dar observed the runner's progress but it did not seem overly urgent, so she decided against her immediate response to call a halt.

'Report,' she called as the runner came up to her.

'We are being watched, Stragosh. Forward scouts have sighted observers on the heights above us.'

'Are they taking any action other than watching us?'

'No, Stragosh. They make no overt moves, merely stand and watch.'

'Very well. Return to your position. You are to instruct the others that no attempt at approach is to be made and no hostile act displayed. We march on peacefully, is that clear?'

'No action to be taken against them, continue the march peacefully.'

Tishan nodded and the guard saluted, turned, and jogged away.

Ankh, walking close by Tishan, spoke. 'A threat, do you think?'

'No, I don't think so. If these people were hostile, they could cut our throats in the night or shoot us with poisoned arrows, and I doubt we would see them. No, Ankh, they do as we would do with strangers. They observe and they let us know they are watching.'

'Hmmm, let us hope you are correct, Stragosh. I admit that the thought of a poisoned arrow in my nether regions is not one I relish. But then, seeing the control they had over those mellax, they would only need a couple of them to do the job for them.'

'Agreed. I am hoping that we will soon meet up with Votlas Fen and Ardesh. We must be close now to a rendezvous. Then we will have an idea of how much further we have to travel.'

------0------

Menkh's head whirled with dizziness and Crixac's voice became strangely silent. As Menkh wished for a chair, one materialised near him and he sank gratefully upon it. Behind him, the crystal continued its pulsating rhythm of colours and it appeared as if nothing had happened.

'*Crixac, are you there?*' Menkh whispered into the corridors of his mind.

'*Yes, yes, I am here, Menkh. Still absorbing the knowledge you have brought back with you. I have existed for time out of mind, Menkh, and thought that my experience of life had prepared me for everything, but here I am, incredulous. How is it possible that I did not perceive even a hint of this? That the crystals had enormous power, yes. That they were sentient, yes, but not in the way that you have experienced. Imagine, Menkh, a consciousness connected across the cosmos working to preserve the Balance.*'

'*I am becoming used to being overwhelmed, Crixac. Wonder upon wonder such that the fabric of all my beliefs has been shredded and reconstituted. Every new day has surprises in store and every day offers new challenges to my way of thinking. You have shielded me, I think, from becoming mad with the weight of such revelations.*'

'*To a degree, Menkh, but you have a surprisingly strong and agile mind. I was not there when you descended into the crystal dimension. Such an experience would have rendered most intelligent beings insane I believe. Yet, here you are, absorbing and redefining your perceptions. Truly, you are quite remarkable in your own way, Menkh ab Dur.*'

'*Be that as it may, we have a unique set of challenges in front of us. The first must be to settle my people into the city and to calm their fears. This may be no simple task, but it is our first priority. I still cannot grasp how we go about settling the people in. How are they to be fed, clothed, sheltered? The list is endless.*'

'*What you must understand, Menkh is that the City itself is sentient in the way that the crystal is. The City is, in many ways, a physical manifestation of the crystal. It interacts with you. How many times have you activated something whilst you have been here? Each and every interaction provides the*

City with information about you. Even when you sleep, your memories, your knowledge, your experiences, culture, personal likes and dislikes, everything that makes you "you", in fact, is fed into its matrix. What was the last meal you had? Was it not a dish that you were familiar with and liked to eat? The City produced that meal and caused it to be delivered to you.'

'But how does this work, Crixac? How does the City take my wishes for a meal and then create it and transport it and deliver it? How will it deal with all of the people when they arrive? It seems so impossible that I confess it really is magical to me. There is nothing within my experience that can even begin to explain it.'

'I understand, Menkh, and whilst I can explain that the City has a form of sentience, I cannot tell you the actual mechanics of what it does and the "how" of it. But I can tell you this. The City knows that your people are coming. It has learned of it through you and through its interactions with Mareen and Horven. In the same way, it is building its knowledge of you as an individual. Already it knows much of your culture and it is busy filtering this knowledge and adapting it to the workings of the City. This city once contained a million inhabitants and they all interacted with the City. So, if you cannot grasp how it will deal with a mere 1500 or so individuals, then apply that to a million individuals and see how you go.'

Menkh shook his head. *'I cannot.'*

'You and I, Menkh, have determined on a quadrant of the city for initial inhabitation. We will meet in the refectory building situated there. The reality is that the Kareems ate communally anyway and the City provided meals in refectory buildings scattered across the city. Likewise, communal bathing areas and sanitation areas were also contained in these buildings with facilities for visitors from other cities to sleep. In the short term, whilst your people are acclimating, they can stay there. Later they can choose individual habitations for themselves or have ones chosen for them.'

'This makes sense, as we discussed, but there are other changes which must also come. Graaven society was highly structured. I bear the colour markings of the royal family of the Garnesh clan. The markings on a Graaven's skin determined their status in our society and it was forbidden for any female of

higher status to have a lower status male fertilise her brood of eggs without permission. This must change if we are to rebuild. We do not have the population to effectively grow as a people if we stick to these old notions of society.'

'But is it not also the case,' responded Crixac, *'that your people have had to forcibly make changes in their thinking? Males and females from all levels of your society have been thrown together in adversity. Many owe their lives to individuals of so-called "lower status". You have fought, starved and died together, and I think that these bonds will prove stronger than you might think.'*

'I trust that this may be so, Crixac, but only time will tell — and that sooner, rather than later.'

'For now, let us observe the progress of the people. Surely they cannot be too far from us now?'

Somewhat later, Menkh was able to focus on the Graavens as they journeyed on the pathway that led to the city's outer gates. Menkh saw that Votlas Fen, Ardesh, and Desh had now joined the column and that, barring accidents, a further four dak'chaal would see them arrive. Interestingly, he could also see what he assumed were Draachnull's people observing the column's progress, and he focused on one of the figures that stood impassively on a hillock that overlooked the path to confirm this view.

Menkh recognised at once that he or she was dressed in the fashion he recalled Draachnull was wearing, and deduced that some form of contact had been made between the two peoples. He could see no overtly hostile moves being made and, from the lack of any defensive action on the part of the Graavens who passed by, that all was well.

Later contact with Tishan when they had stopped for the night confirmed this thinking and Menkh was apprised of all that had happened.

'You have done well, Tishan. You are no more than three to four dak'chaal now from the outer gates. I will be there to meet you all and show you the way. It will be a consideration for us to try to make further contact with Draachnull's people, but this will wait for a future time.'

Tishan nodded her agreement and, after some further discussion concerning the final stages of the march, Menkh severed contact.

Over the next few days Menkh continued to familiarise himself, with Crixac's assistance, in the workings of the City and the structure of the Complex. His facility with manipulating the crystal grew quickly and he regularly transported himself to various places, only occasionally with Crixac's guidance.

On the evening of the day before the expected arrival of the Graaven people, whilst Menkh was sitting in the building they had selected for the first gathering, Crixac made an observation. *'Since your return from the crystal realm there has been much to absorb us. I would know how you feel you are adjusting to having my presence within you.'*

Menkh laughed quietly. *'Surely you must know my thoughts, Crixac, and know the answer already?'*

'No, Menkh, I will not intrude into your personal thoughts unless some dire emergency leaves me with no option. We share body and mind, but it is important – nay, critical – that you maintain independence of thought.'

'This reassures me, my friend. At first it was strange. Now I feel there is a bond of friendship with you, Crixac. We have a monumental task in front of us and to achieve it we must trust each other and build on that bond. You have proven yourself true to all that you have said and promised. There is honour and dignity there, and there is also a trust and respect which I hope is mutual between us.'

'Yes, you speak truly. For years beyond count I endured in the city and I questioned my place in the cosmos. I was a prisoner trapped in perpetual solitary confinement. Now I perceive that the Balance placed me here in order to meet you, Menkh. I perceive now that a great task lies before us. The Balance is all. But I am humbled to be called friend – such words to me are

more precious than can be expressed. Together then, my friend, we shall endeavour to achieve that which has been placed before us.'

------0------

In the meantime, Horven and Mareen, other than reconnoitring the land immediately surrounding the city, had been harvesting fruit and vegetables from overgrown plots that surrounded it. An intricate system of metal tracks had been discovered that wound its way through the food growing areas. It had been a simple job to follow these tracks back to two huge bays that formed part of the refectory building that Menkh had selected, and others like it across the city.

From the moment that it had been decided that they would spend time in the fields, metal carriages had appeared on the tracks – moving silently, of their own accord, as if by magic. At first this was unsettling and a cause for great trepidation, but they posed no threat and the two Graavens rapidly adjusted to their presence. These metallic vehicles were open on the top and contained ten lightweight, open-mesh baskets made of a material which appeared to be some kind of smooth wood. Horven and Mareen presumed these were for the storage of the fruits and vegetables they were harvesting as they were easy to lift out and replace. Even full of produce, when they were lifted back into the carriage they weighed not much more than when they were empty.

The vehicles themselves were not overly large, being big enough to accommodate the ten baskets that each contained. They did not appear to have wheels but rather seemed to float somewhat above the tracks they moved across, and they moved off silently the moment the last filled basket was replaced in its compartment. Not for the first time, the guards exchanged looks with raised eyebrows to express their amazement.

On the first day of field work where they had both been rendered speechless by the silent arrival of the carriages, Horven had remarked, 'You know, Mareen, there is a part of me that thinks

I should run screaming from this place, yet I feel remarkably calm inside. As if I know that all is well and that no harm will come to me.'

'Yes, I know exactly what you mean. I have the same calming feelings. Do you think that it is the magic the Zaltec has told us of that is working on us?'

'I don't know exactly. But I will tell you one thing. Whatever the strangeness, it is infinitely preferable to a night in the open, running from the Dorath Mar.'

'You speak truly. So, let us see how we get on with picking some more of these fruits and vegetables.'

Mareen paused and chuckled to herself, 'As imperial guards, who would have thought that we would end up as field workers?'

Horven smiled, 'Yes, my guilty confession is that I am rather enjoying the experience.'

'Hmmm … a pity we didn't think about food and drink for ourselves when we came out here.'

'As to that, we can sit in the shade of these kumac trees. After all, there's plenty of fruit to eat and water not too far away.'

So, for the next few days this was the routine that they followed as carriages arrived from the city, empty, and went back full.

------0------

The outer gates swung noiselessly inwards. Beyond the doorway, a long column of bedraggled people stood as a steady rain fell on them. Inside the doorway, the sky was clear and no rain fell. Those who could see gasped in wonder and some drew back in fear, but the figure of Menkh ab Dur, dressed in a flowing robe and leaning on an ornate staff, flanked by Mareen and Horven Var with grinning faces, reassured them.

'Have no fear, any of you, step forward and be welcome,' called Menkh and such was the power of his voice that all heard his call.

Tishan Dar stepped through the gateway and smiled broadly. 'You are ever a source of wonder, Zaltec,' she said as she grasped his left forearm, followed by a crisp salute.

'Welcome indeed, Tishan Dar, make your way down the path,' said Menkh, indicating the pathway behind him, 'and follow Mareen and Horven, they will show you to a place where we may all gather.'

As the Graavens filed in, Menkh greeted them all. He noted the looks of wonder and fear and spoke reassuringly as the people passed by. As the last Graaven entered, the gates swung shut behind them and Menkh followed them down to the level place where the city could be seen. Making his way through the gathered people he looked at them and, holding his arms in the air, spoke in a loud voice, 'The time of running and hiding, of blood and despair, is done! Here in this place the Graaven people will build again. Put away your fears, put away your feelings of hopelessness. I know that this is all new and strange but follow me to the city. There we will eat and drink together and I will tell you of this place. You may ask me questions and then you will sleep, safe within walls, safe under a strong roof, and safe in your own bed!'

There was no cheer – the people were too wet and weary for that – but there was laughter that spoke of relief and reassurance and a swell of conversation as people looked at the verdant fields, woods, and flowing water all around them.

Later, in the main hall of the refectory building, the Graavens had finished the food that had been prepared. Horven and Mareen's efforts had ensured that, at least for a short period of time, the kitchens, located deep within the building complex, had enough raw materials to produce a meal. As the Graavens had entered the hall, dishes of stewed vegetables and prepared meats were already in place, running down the centre of long tables with bench seating on either side.

Any misgivings about the food, where it had come from, and who had prepared it were offset by the appetising aroma and the hunger of the people. With a minimum of fuss, the Graavens had seated themselves in places where eating utensils had been laid and set to. A quiet buzz of discussion continued as people remarked on their situation and many looks were directed at Menkh as he sat amongst them.

Menkh noted that the Graavens sat in groups that were very different from those that might have been expected in the Empire. There, Graaven society was strictly hierarchical. The swirling patterns that were a natural skin colouration repeated amongst family groups delineated the social standing of all Graavens. No imperial guard would have sat with a member of the merchant class for any reason. Once spawned, a Graaven individual was strictly limited as to the work that they could undertake and the position they could aspire to in Graaven society. All this Menkh and his sibling Pershiva had sought to change. Now it seemed the terrible circumstances of the destruction of the Empire had thrown the Graavens together in a way that no other circumstance could have done.

Slowly, Menkh stood and moved to a position where all could see and hear him. Raising his hands, quiet descended on all who were gathered.

'Now is the time for explanation, for questions and for answers. Here within the City we are safe; at least, for the foreseeable future. All of us here have endured, all of us here have triumphed over adversity. Together we have escaped calamity and together we will move forward.'

Around the room heads nodded but no-one interrupted Menkh's address. All sat quietly, listening intently to his words.

'Many chaal ago we travelled in despair across the Plains of Clarist. In despair we traversed that uncharted wasteland, still pursued by the enemy. Many of you knew that I had sickened even unto death.'

A low muttering could be heard as the Graavens responded to this.

'How, then, is it that I am here before you now, looking as if this had never happened? How is it that we sit now in this ancient city?'

Menkh paused and nodded his head as he gazed around the seated Graavens before him. 'Listen now. On the night that we encountered the river, a strange vision came to me in my tent. At first, I thought that perhaps one of the gods had finally come to us in our need or that perhaps one had come to claim me and take me into the immortal realms.'

Menkh paused but the silence in the hall was total. 'My friends, the truth of that vision was even stranger, if that is possible. It was not god or demon or sorcerer but the spirit of this City, who named itself Crixac, that had come to me. By the magic of this place was I cured. By the knowledge given to me and the power of the City, we crossed the river and dealt destruction upon our enemies. The spirit Crixac has guided us to this place. It is a place of magic. The pure magic of life and hope and new beginnings. A place of rebuilding and regrowth for all here.'

A hubbub of conversation began as the Graavens exchanged looks and views. Menkh looked around the hall and, raising his hands, waited for quiet to descend. 'Now is the time for your questions. Speak and let me answer them with you all here as witness to what I say.'

A hundred voices seemed to lift all at once and Tishan Dar stood up. Raising her hands, she called out, 'Silence!' and such was the discipline that had been established amongst them that the noise abruptly ceased. 'How can the Zaltec answer when you all call out at once? Raise your arm and we will deal with each question in turn.'

As arms were raised, Tishan indicated the individual who then stood to ask their question. First, one of the civilian survivors stood and looked nervously around her. 'With respect, Zaltec, how do we know that this "magic" you speak of is good? Weren't we all raised in fear of magic and witchcraft?'

Mutterings accompanied this question.

'You are quite right to raise that point and you are, of course, correct. There was much in the Empire that we were raised to fear. I would say this to all of you, do you fear me? Do I look evil? Does anyone here now feel threatened? Strange and inexplicable, yes, that I will grant you. How was the food you just ate? How safe do you feel in the city? I have been here for many days but perhaps Horven or Mareen Var might offer an answer, too?' and Menkh indicated with a nod to each of the guards as they sat there amongst their comrades.

Both of them stood and Horven spoke first. 'It is a good question, Marin. We, too, felt uncomfortable when we first entered the city but in all the days we have been here, we have seen nothing to fear – although there is much to be wondered at. Things that make your jaw drop but never anything that felt like a threat. In a funny way, you feel like the City wants you here and is almost listening to you. Why, on the second day, we had a plate of stewed tash root for dinner that was just how I remember my mother making it.'

'That's right,' responded Mareen. 'Why, the first time I saw one of the supply wagons moving by itself I damn near soiled myself! Begging your pardon, Zaltec. But we have slept and eaten better even than when we were at home in the Empire. No, what the Zaltec says is true. This place is beyond explanation, but you will see what we mean yourselves.'

A second Graaven stood and saluted. 'Zaltec, you spoke of this as an abandoned city but what of the inhabitants? Will they not come back and want their city back? What about them?'

Menkh nodded. 'Once, in times long since passed, there were three Cities, of which this was one. After hundreds of years of peace, war broke out between them. In that war, terrible weapons were used and the other two Cities were obliterated. This City, too, was damaged. When you explore the city, as all of you are welcome to do, you will come to a vast causeway. Once, this led to the rest of the city. Now, there is only a vast chasm where the waters of the seven rivers pour down into its depths in a never-ending cascade. The people who once lived here are gone, never to return, but the magic that preserved the part of the city that we now inhabit endures.'

A third individual stood. 'Zaltec, if we are to live here, what are we to do? In the Empire I was a cloth dyer; here, I don't know what I am.'

'Around the city there are fertile fields, orchards of fruit trees and livestock,' Menkh responded. 'If the City is to nourish us then we must supply the raw materials. The building we are in has counterparts across the city where we will eat our meals together. So, in the beginning we must tend the fields and orchards, which are overgrown, and herd the livestock. There are some among us who were raised to do these things and we must all help if we are to survive.'

A guard abruptly stood. 'Forgive me, Zaltec. Are you saying that we Baran Mec must also undertake this labour?'

'I am, Dresh. Just as Horven and Mareen have done whilst you were all travelling here. We must all realise that the way that the Empire was run cannot be supported here. No male or female will be segregated according to their family markings. We do not have the population at present. No Graaven in this city will be restricted from performing roles which heretofore they would be banned from. Do any here question this necessity?'

Votlas Fen stood and pushed Dresh back into his seat. 'Zaltec, I have been in the Baran Mec for forty meh'chaal and have had the honour to serve you for five of those. I cannot speak for the others but I would have you know that if you told me I had to work naked in the fields for the next five, I would simply ask when you wished me to start. I have followed you into the maw of death and you have led us out.' Votlas raised an arm and pointed, 'Over there sits Marga. In the Empire, she cleaned the filth out of the sewers. No guard would be seen dead sitting in her company, let alone share her food. When we destroyed the bridge over the Tasihk, I was the last to leave. As the foundations came down, I slipped and would have fallen to my death. Marga rushed to my aid. She held me while I got my feet under me and, together, we ran to rejoin the others as we fled. She is not the only Graaven "low life" to have put themselves in harm's way to help those in need.'

Votlas surveyed the room and eyed Dresh. 'Any Graaven here who offers her insult will suffer under my hand. I am proud to call her my friend and the Empire be damned!'

Around the gathered Graavens there was a general nodding of heads.

Menkh allowed the talking to subside. 'Thank you, Votlas. It is my view that the ways of the Empire held good people back, stifling those with gifts and talents that might have been better used – and the Empire suffered as a result. Yours is a fine example. But I will say this, none of you who do not wish to stay in the city will be forced to remain. You will be free to leave and strike out as best you can, and we will supply you with as much as we can. But if you stay then you must be prepared to work for the good of all and to adapt to new ways of doing things.'

There was a renewed burst of conversation but as there were no immediate questions, Menkh spoke again. 'This building will be our home for a short time whilst you get used to your surroundings. On the floor above us are baths and facilities to clean yourselves. On the floor above that are sleeping quarters.

Votlas and Mareen will conduct you and show you how these things work. In the morning we will eat together here and for all that day you will be free to wander the city and its surrounds. All meals will be here. After tomorrow you will be placed into groups and work in the fields will commence the day after tomorrow. Beyond that, I will speak with you all over coming days and we will plan our approach. If you have questions, then seek me out and I will answer as best I can.'

As people began to move towards where Votlas and Mareen stood, Menkh called out, 'Stragosh, you and our Kalvak and Shu Lan commanders, gather to me.'

After a short time, as the Graavens took the stairway to the next level, the commanders formed a group in front of him. Menkh looked over them and made eye contact with each one. 'What you have seen and heard is cause for amazement but the proof of what I say surrounds you. You will see much over coming days that will baffle and surprise you and will be inexplicable. But I assure you all that we are as safe here as we can be, barring unfortunate accidents. We have much to do – a whole society to restructure and make work. The roles that we all had, including mine, will change and there will be difficulties and challenges ahead. My confidence in you all is unbounded and I believe that, together, we can face any obstacle. More than ever, I need your trust and support. Each and every one of you plays a vital role in this "new world" we find ourselves in. I do not have all the answers, but I need to know, here and now, if you see yourselves as a part of this. For now, the time of war is over, and we must adapt to our changed circumstances if we are to prosper. What say you?'

Artax was the most junior Shu Lan present. Nervously he cleared his throat and all eyes went to him. 'Zaltec. For many chaal we fled the enemy and every day I expected to breathe my last. I would have been proud to lay down my life for the Empire but,' here he drew a long breath, 'the Empire is no more. All my loyalty now is to you, Zaltec. You have been the constant for all of us. Before we had no time to think of tomorrow. But for what it is worth, sir, you have my trust and commitment that I will do my best. Although, outside of being a guard I don't know what I can do.'

Menkh stepped forward and gripped both of Artax's forearms in his own. 'You are worth more than you can ever appreciate, Artax, and I thank you for your commitment. When you find out what else you are good at, let me know too. I have long pondered on what a redundant "almost Emperor" might be able to contribute as well.'

There was a small amount of laughter that followed this remark and Tishan Dar added her voice. 'Zaltec, I speak for all of us to echo Artax's words. You need never doubt our loyalty and we will all do our best. Your words regarding the old Empire and the rigidity of our society caught some by surprise, but the reality of our situation is that every Graaven is alive in some way due to the efforts of all. We cannot now return to the old ways, and few would wish it. With all the surprises we have in store in days to come, I doubt that many will focus on it anyway as we adjust to our new home.'

Menkh nodded. 'Very well. Then follow me upstairs and I will show you how this building works. Even running a bath will present you with some interesting questions.'

CHAPTER TEN

Several dak'chaal passed by, during which time the Graavens began to adjust to their new life. Perhaps most perplexing of all was the way in which the City itself began to interact with the Graavens as individual people. Slowly, the meals that were presented for consumption began to reflect Graaven tastes and cuisine, with some Graavens remarking that the flavours were even better than they remembered them.

Grakh, the physician, awoke one morning by himself in a strange location, and not the shared accommodations he had fallen asleep in. Upon calming his fears and leaving the small but comfortably appointed room he had awoken in, he ventured down a flight of stairs that was the only exit. He was amazed to find himself in rooms, the layout of which were remarkably like his surgery back in the capital. Shelves of labelled jars contained herbs and unguents neatly labelled in writing that uncannily mirrored his own script. A sniffing and surreptitious tasting of some of the contents reflected his own blends of medicinal compounds, developed over the years of his training. Gleaming surgical instruments were arrayed in drawers.

As Grakh explored his surroundings he could not hold back tears as he beheld cherished objects that he had left behind in the flight from the capital, but which remained vivid in his deepest memories. He caressed them lovingly with fingers that were shaking too much to allow him to pick them up. On venturing outside, he found that he was in a building no great distance from the refectory building which the Graavens inhabited. As he stepped away from the doorway, it closed with only a slight hissing sound behind him. He noted that there was carving around the doorway which depicted various medical procedures, a sure sign to anyone that was looking as to what the purpose of the building was for. Later, as he excitedly showed Menkh and other curious Graavens the building and its contents, he discovered that the door would only open when he laid his own hand in the recess to the right of the entry way. No other Graaven could access the building before him.

This event was a cause for huge discussion, wonder and speculation, but it was not an isolated one. Other Graavens had similar experiences and one in particular was the cause of great celebration.

Bara Desh and his daughter, Mertain, awoke one morning in strange surroundings which, upon exploration, were revealed to be an almost perfect copy of the tavern which the family had run in the capital. Not only that but, as they excitedly discovered, the barrels and ceramic containers behind the serving bar contained a range of beverages that, upon tasting, were exactly as he remembered them. Desh's Tavern became a popular place away from the refectory for the Graavens to reacquaint themselves with some of their favourite beverages.

Shortly after the miraculous appearance of the tavern, he made a wistful comment to Tishan Dar, 'The main difference here is that unlike the old place in the capital, here there is no charge for any of it. I dole it out and watch how much is being drunk but the next day all the barrels are full again. Nobody appears to be drinking to excess, they drink, they talk, they laugh, and they play Kavala. It all seems rather strange. Mind you, Stragosh, I don't miss cleaning up the vomit or breaking up fights with my cudgel. That is definitely an improvement!'

'It is good, Bara Desh. The nearest thing to home that we have experienced and, therefore, to be valued most highly. I must say, the Kassarin brandy is some of the best I have tasted so I have no complaints to make.'

Methodically the Graavens tilled the fields and cleared them of weeds. Orchards were pruned and the wandering livestock, which proved to be remarkably tame, were corralled. Menkh and Tishan organised the people so that work was rotated, also ensuring that there was time for weapon drills and sparring so that fighting skills were maintained.

It was Varga who made the next discovery as he, too, awoke in strange surroundings. For several nights he had been pondering how to make training more effective. Sparring between individual guards was all very well, but repetition led to a somewhat disaffected attitude and, without arrows, practise for the Sagit was impossible.

So it was that one morning he awoke to find himself on the floor of a small vestibule which opened into a large circular room, some fifty paces in diameter. Its pale blue walls seemed to gently pulse. In the centre of the room was a metallic rack which held a range of weaponry. Swords, maces, axes, and pikes reflected the pulsing blue light and Varga tested the weight and feel of each weapon.

They were strangely light and wickedly sharp. As he hefted a Palluvian broadsword, he went through a series of steps he remembered from his training days. No sooner had he selected a weapon than the rack disappeared, and the walls shimmered. They seemed to melt and reform into a walled garden, bathed in sunlight, and across from him, in full battle dress, was a tall Hoplex standing silently, hands resting on the pommel of a sword of similar dimensions. The visor on its helmet was closed and whether the Hoplex was male or female could not be told.

Varga stepped forward and realised that he, too, was now garbed in full battle dress – a flowing coat of mail, marvellously flexible and lightweight. Metal plate carved with intricate design covered his forearms whilst metal-reinforced calf-length boots covered his feet. An open-faced helmet encased his head. So real was the image that he felt yielding grass under his feet, a cool breeze blew, and he could clearly hear songbirds calling outside the confines of the walls of the garden.

The figure before him slowly lifted the sword and bowed in the traditional way before a duel. Varga mirrored the gesture. No sooner had he stood back upright when the opposing Hoplex sprang into the fight, delivering a blow with frightening speed and launching a sweeping and powerful overhead cut. Desperately, Varga threw up his own sword and the blades met with a ringing clash.

Varga felt the power of the blow smash into his arms. He had only just blocked that strike when the Hoplex pivoted with the speed of a striking viper and launched a huge cut at Varga's left side. On the verge of panic, Varga jumped back but, as the blade swept past him, the Hoplex pivoted again and followed with an oblique cut to Varga's neck.

Time seemed to slow and Varga felt the blade shear through his neck and down into his body. To say it as an unpleasant sensation was an understatement. For an instant, Varga had felt the blade pierce his body. Dropping his sword, he staggered back. The opposing Hoplex immediately resumed its stationary position whilst Varga frantically felt his body where the sword had appeared to enter. It was some time before he could be certain that he had sustained not the slightest injury.

'*By the fetid breath of Bringarell,*' he thought, '*that made me sit up and take notice?*'

He crossed his chest with his left arm and bowed to his opponent. 'I yield, my silent friend. For now.'

The silent Hoplex inclined its head, the image shimmered, and the garden disappeared as the walls returned to pulsing blue.

The discovery of the training room was significant. The room could cater for multiple combat scenarios and could seemingly provide any number of opponents. Any guard who initially came into the room and boasted of their prowess was rapidly humbled. It took genuine skill to defeat the opponents that materialised and every "wound", or worse, that the Graavens experienced was painful and unpleasant, even if only for a brief period. This had the effect of ensuring that any training session was met with the utmost concentration and there were cheers whenever an opponent was bested by a Graaven.

The Sagit who entered the room inevitably found themselves in a scenario where they were faced with a large number of foes of various kinds bearing down on their position. It was real enough that the ground trembled under the charge of mounted enemies and stampeding herds of horned herbivores. But, whilst the training was excellent in keeping their skills honed, it did not address the lack of arrowheads which was of pressing concern. Hopes that the City might produce arrows were not fulfilled and the Graavens had no current solution to this problem.

So it was that one day whilst Menkh was continuing his exploration of the Complex, that a strange sound began to echo throughout the building. It was not unlike the moaning sound the wind might make as it whistles through a slightly opened doorway, but much louder, rising and falling in intensity.

'An alarm, Menkh, from the gate. Something has activated the warning. Let us transport to the viewing room.'

Menkh was now adept at teleporting himself around the Complex in areas he knew well and within an instant he was standing before the panel. The exterior of the gateway came into focus and it was immediately apparent that a large group of humanoids were sitting patiently outside. Menkh could see that prominent amongst them was Draachnull.

Menkh materialised by the gates which silently swung open before him. He saw Draachnull climb to his feet with some dignity whilst those around him exhibited some degree of alarm as the rock walls before them revealed gates.

Draachnull peered at Menkh and a slow smile spread across his features as he made out Menkh's form behind the robes he now wore, and looked closely at the staff which Menkh gripped in his right hand. Draachnull crossed both arms in front of his chest and gave a small bow, whilst uttering some words.

The translator on Menkh's belt converted the words quickly.

'Greetings, friend Menkh. It would appear that our trackers did not imagine seeing your people disappear behind the wall. These are indeed strange times.'

Menkh bowed in his turn and spoke back in the Graaven tongue, though to Draachnull's ears it was as if Menkh spoke in the language of the Benshin. 'Greetings indeed, friend Draachnull. But even in strange times it is good when friends meet and renew acquaintance. I would thank you for allowing my people to pass peacefully across your lands and I would tell you that the Graaven people have no ill will or malice towards you and your people.'

If Draachnull had any surprise at Menkh's ability to speak the Benshin tongue – albeit with a strange accent – it did not show in his face. 'Your intentions were clear from the moment you helped me with my leg. A slight limp is all that remains after your good offices and those of your people. As to your people's passage, had we discerned any overt threat your people would never have arrived.'

His tone was matter of fact and, knowing what the Graavens had observed with their control of the mellax, Menkh knew that Draachnull was simply stating the reality.

'I see that where you stand, friend Menkh, the air appears warmer and drier than where we stand. May we enter your gates? I have with me a hand of my people. Rshak, a skilled hunter. Npath, my eldest daughter and one of our healers. These two who stand with me are Mrellin and Dthar, who come from the Lightning and Thunder Water clans which inhabit to the south and east of here.'

Menkh bowed again. 'You are all welcome here,' and, gesturing with his left arm, beckoned them forward where they followed him down the path that led to the city. The Benshin talked quietly amongst themselves, remarking also on the benign weather conditions which prevailed, when outside the gates the Time of Storms held precedence over the land.

There was complete silence when they spied the city for the first time, in the same spot where first Menkh himself and then the rest of the Graavens had caught sight of it.

'So, our legends are true!' exclaimed Draachnull to Mrellin and Dthar. He turned to Menkh. 'Amongst our people, there is a story handed down from generation to generation of great cities that once stood near our lands. The legend speaks of many wonders and also of a terrible curse that befell the people who lived there. It would seem that there is at least a core of truth in this ancient tale.'

'Perhaps more than you might realise,' responded Menkh. 'And we have made the city, or at least that part that is left, our home. There are, indeed, many wonders; but you will see for yourself.'

'No, my friend. Your new home is basmerkh and is forbidden to us. That part of our legend is very clear and, in any event, the people of the Benshin live under the Great Sky. We would not venture into your city even if we could. To live trapped inside such buildings is anathema to us. No, you are welcome to it but, with no wish to cause offence, we would prefer to stay in the open lands around your city.'

'No offence is taken, friend. I will arrange for refreshments and we can sit comfortably while you tell me the reason for your journey, as I deem this is not simply a social visit?'

Draachnull nodded his head and smiled. 'You presume correctly but let us leave that discussion till we are seated.'

Sometime later a small pavilion had been set up and refreshments were arranged. Accompanying Menkh were Tishan and Ankh; as well as Bara Desh, who had supplied the refreshments, feeling a little awkward in the company he found himself.

'So, my friends,' said Menkh to the seated Benshin, 'what brings you here? We are all curious.'

Draachnull looked at his companions and each one slowly nodded to him. 'Trade, friend Menkh. Trade brings us here. The Benshin are a forest people. Our meetings with you have shown that you have knowledge of many things that we do not. In turn, we also have things that perhaps you may need, including these.' So saying, Rshak produced a beautifully embroidered, rolled bundle made of cured hide. As he opened it, the Graavens saw that three arrows were contained inside. Tishan exclaimed and Menkh looked quizzically at Draachnull.

'Please, pick them up and inspect them. The Benshin are master fletchers and making your arrows is not such a difficult task for us, even if they are many times bigger than our own. We found a discarded arrow with a split shaft that your people had left behind. We thought that perhaps you might trade with us for a supply of these.'

Ankh exclaimed over the arrow and exchanged looks with Tishan. 'These are as finely crafted as any that we could have made in the Empire. The arrowhead is sharp but of a metal that appears strange to my eyes.'

Draachnull anticipated Ankh's comment as he observed the Graaven reactions. 'The arrow heads are made of an alloy that the

Benshin discovered long ago from ore that we find nowhere else than in our lands. You will find them capable of penetrating most things but, naturally, you must try them first.'

'What is it that you think we have that we could trade?' asked Tishan.

'Our legend also says that there were cultivated fields and gardens that surrounded the cities. We can see for ourselves this is also true. As I have said, we are a forest people. Whilst the forest gives us all that we need, it would be good to have a supply of fruit and other things that the forest provides only on rare occasions. Would you trade with us?'

'I think if we did not, every Sagit here would be seriously questioning my judgement, friend Draachnull. We would be pleased to trade with you. I am sure there will be other things that will be worth considering. You say that your daughter Npath is a skilled healer. Perhaps much may be gained with an exchange of knowledge with our healer, Grakh?'

Draachnull nodded. 'You speak wisely. The forging of friendship between peoples is a weighty matter but one which may lead to the greater good of all. Let us discuss, then, how we may effect this trade so that we are all clear as to how it may work.'

The meeting and talks continued for the rest of the day. An evening meal was shared and the Benshins found they also had a taste for the potent Storluth brandy which Dresh had supplied, and which was also included in the list of trade goods after further consideration.

Menkh and the other Graavens learned that the Benshin had quite a capacity for strong drink and, as the evening wore on, the language barrier grew less. Other Graavens had come to observe the visitors and, at some point, music began to be played. The Graavens played on instruments that the City had provided them. The four-stringed sherm and the plaintive sound of the chalsid flute brought back memories of home and the people grew quiet as they listened.

The Benshin nodded in appreciation and then they also produced small flutes, such as the Graavens had seen when they encountered the mellax. A steady beat was kept on polished wooden clappers and the music was unlike any the Graavens had heard, evoking images of the wild forest, its rivers and mountains, at once ancient and stirring. The Graavens clapped their hands delightedly, to which the Benshin responded with broad grins, encouraging the Graavens to play more for them. It was clear to all that the basis for a strong friendship had been founded on that day.

At dawn the next morning Menkh and Tishan bade Draachnull and his people farewell in the knowledge that, in a short time, regular trading visits to which all looked forward would commence. Menkh presented Draachnull with twelve medallions made of a bluish-coloured metal. He explained that these medallions would allow a visitor to pass safely through the outer gates.

Crixac had already explained to Menkh how to activate a defensive shield that would allow entry only to those who carried a medallion, allowing the gates to be left open. Whilst the number of medallions limited the size of any trading party, it made it more convenient to any of the Benshin who came to trade. Without a medallion the defensive curtain would prevent entry.

This curtain of energy could be just seen, shimmering in the air in the broad light of day. Any living creature who ventured to enter would experience an unpleasant reaction which grew in intensity if they persisted in trying to enter. Unwelcome or unannounced visitors who continued to push into the barrier risked death.

With trade and friendly relations established, Menkh and Crixac turned their thoughts to the task laid before them by the crystal entity. It was clear that any journey must venture towards the location of the vanished cities and to the lands that lay beyond. Knowledge of these areas was limited, and so many sem'chaal had passed since the Cities were at the height of their power that any records available from the city archives were deemed to be of little value.

Menkh brought Tishan into the deliberations, providing a plausible story around the need for the journey and showing her the crystal room inside the Complex.

'This is just another wonder of the City, Menkh. But other than the need for the journey to restore the crystal, our information is so limited as to the lands you will need to cross as to pose serious concern. There is no telling how long a journey like this will take on foot. It could be many cycles before you return – if you do return at all.'

'These are things I have pondered myself, Tishan. Information I have found in the Complex vaults indicate that a vast forest once lay to the east of the city, and beyond that an area of rolling grasslands. The Cities established smaller satellite towns which grew produce they supplied to their respective communities. But that is so distant now in time that the layout of the land may have altered dramatically. Perhaps the Benshin may have knowledge that goes beyond their lands and it may be that they will provide me with a guide, at least to their borders.'

So it was that, over coming dak'chaal, as Menkh pondered the risks involved in making the journey, questions were asked of the Benshin. After conferring with tribal elders, the Benshin agreed that they would supply guides and provide Menkh with what knowledge they had of the lands to the east and beyond the mountain range that stood as their ancestral border.

So, preparations continued until one day, still some days before Menkh had planned to set out, another alarm sounded from the gates. In a matter of moments, Menkh had translocated himself to the gateway and then stood in stunned surprise at what awaited him. Two tawny mountains of fur sat either side of their white queen whose penetratingly green eyes were focused on the curtain of energy that shimmered in the light.

'*Well, friend Menkh,*' Crixac's voice echoed in his head, '*like you I am burning with curiosity as to the reason for this unexpected visitation.*'

'Indeed,' responded Menkh as he bowed low towards the gonverdeem queen. His bow was returned gracefully by the huge beast. Menkh manipulated a crystal on his belt and the defensive shield vanished. Slowly, the creature entered the doorway, pausing slightly on the threshold as if to reassure herself that the shimmering curtain was indeed gone. She then advanced toward Menkh, coming so close that she towered over him. Then, stretching her neck, she placed her nose in direct proximity to Menkh's and sniffed.

'*I swear, Crixac,*' thought Menkh, '*that if you hadn't had my legs under control, they would have folded under me.*'

'*It was as much as I could do to hold us steady, my friend. Only the knowledge that she could overtake us in a heartbeat had she intended us harm stopped me from turning us both around and running,*' Crixac responded wryly.

A series of grunts and other sounds issued from the creature's mouth and instantly the crystal on Menkh's belt flared into life. As the sounds continued, images and speech patterns began to form in Menkh's mind and slowly understanding grew.

'A dream came to me. The white faces were in the sky and my children were sleeping. Your face came into my thoughts. A long journey. Strange voices called to me and I felt a longing to travel far from our range. I called to my children and left. Two who also felt the call journeyed with me. I am here. We will journey together.'

Menkh was astounded and Crixac's voice spoke in his mind. '*Did I not say that I felt these creatures had a part to play in what was to come? It seems that I was correct.*'

'I am honoured,' said Menkh, bowing. The red crystal translated the words, so it appeared that the speech uttered came directly from Menkh himself and the creature's head twisted to one side as she listened. Other than this, Menkh could discern no visible reaction to his speech.

'If we are to journey together then you should know my name. I am Menkh ab Dur, the last of my clan. Might I be permitted to know your name?'

The creature emitted a low rumbling from its throat which was its way of laughing. 'What name would you have for me, Menkh ab Dur? I have many. I am She Who Hunts. I am the Roar that Shatters. I am She Who Walks Unseen. All packs bow down to me. What name would you give me?'

'There could only be one name in my tongue. I would call you Fendrax, a white flower of surpassing beauty. But the sap of the fendrax is a deadly poison so it is a plant that you must be respectful of. Admired from afar but fatal if mishandled.'

There was a momentary silence as the creature's eyelids closed until they were mere slits. The coughing, grunting sound came from the creature's two companions. Suddenly the creature's eyes opened fully.

'A fitting name. My children agree that I am indeed like your plant. Henceforth, you may call me Fendrax. I am pleased. My children and I will hunt and scout out the land that sits outside of this place. When you are ready to leave you will find us waiting. Then you will come to know what it is like to ride on the back of the wind.'

'How will you know that I am ready?'

'You have much to learn, Graaven, you and your silent friend. You may choose two companions; they will ride on my children. As you prefer names, this one,' and here Fendrax tossed her head to her left, indicating a tawny male with black spots in its fur, 'is the third son of my tenth litter. You will find that he says little,' turning her head to the other side, 'and that one is the sixth daughter of my ninth litter.' Fendrax indicated a female whose tawny fur was more golden in colour with subtle russet stripes. 'Her, she likes to growl a lot. Makes her feel important. So, Menkh, what name would you give them?'

Fendrax's eyes focused intently on Menkh and her head turned slightly so that Menkh understood that the answer was one that she was interested in.

'Well, in my tongue he who stands quietly would be "haran kesh va", so I would call your son Haran. Then, as to your daughter, our armies employ a large drum to signify our approach and to terrify our enemies. This drum is called the "kuhltar", the voice of thunder. So, her I would call Kuhltar.'

Fendrax leant her head close to Menkh and delicately sniffed his face. 'You are clever, Menkh ab Dur. I approve. Now, we will leave you to hunt. We will see you again soon.' So saying, she and her two children abruptly turned and walked back through the gateway, leaving Menkh standing quietly.

'I feel like we just passed a test and I don't think I would like to know the consequences of failure.'

'Yes, I know exactly what you mean, my friend. What you were not aware of is that there was an intelligence that was probing me even as it spoke with you. This is a dangerous creature with abilities that, until now, I was completely ignorant of. Happily, they appear to see themselves as allies in our quest.'

'Yes, and if our new-found companion Fendrax and her kin are offering to carry us, that will make the journey somewhat easier on us, I think. So, let us proceed with our preparations. We still have much to prepare.'

By agreement with Crixac, Menkh determined to bring Tishan into their deliberations. It was to Tishan that overall governance of the Graavens would fall during the time of Menkh's absence and there could be no guarantee that his return was preordained.

Tishan had a sharp mind and was not inhibited by any prejudices relating to the old ways of the Empire. Like the other surviving Graavens who had been through the crucible of fire as they had battled an unknown enemy, and seen all that they had known ripped from them, she had embraced change and viewed the workings of the City as a wonder that did not scare her or challenge her view of life.

After being taken to the crystal room for the first time, she was amazed at the beauty of the pulsating gem and recognised it as the source of the magic which permeated the City. Her fascination with the building complex and the race that had once inhabited the city grew into a thirst for knowledge of that earlier and distant time. Like Menkh, she began to spend many chaal accessing the various archives that occupied space in the Complex and to become familiar with the layout of the building proper.

The archives alone were a thing of wonder. There were no books or scrolls such as may have been found in a Graaven archive or library. Instead, row upon row of silvery metallic balls, no bigger than would sit inside the palm of her hand, occupied shelves. To activate a sphere, she sat in in one of the cubicles that dotted the archive and placed it in a slight depression on a flat panel, somewhat like a small desk inside. Once that was done, the sphere would magically rise and begin to spin, issuing colours that rapidly coalesced into pictures, diagrams, and other illustrations. These floated in the air around her and a "page" could be moved forwards or backwards with a deft flick of her hand. A metallic sounding voice could be heard reading the text that accompanied each page. The language was translated by means of the crystal that Menkh had given her and so it was that she became acquainted with the rise and fall of the great Cities.

She began to realise that it was technical advancement and the harnessing of the power of the crystal that underscored the miraculous workings of the City, but her increasing knowledge only highlighted the vast gulf in her understanding. Silently, she acknowledged that the reference to magic when it came to the workings of the City was not a lie for the gullible but, in essence, contained a core of truth. She also developed a deep appreciation that, whilst the power of the City could be used for the benefit of the people, it was capable of being manipulated to more nefarious purposes, as the peoples of the three Cities had discovered to their cost.

CHAPTER ELEVEN

Time moved on. Tishan and Menkh made a multitude of plans, ranging from the formation of a governing council to the harvesting and cultivation of food and trade with the Benshin. The Graaven people adapted to their new life and slowly the horror and pain of loss became less sharp.

The time of departure drew near. Menkh had agreed with Tishan that no great announcement would be made regarding his absence. As it was, the people were more used to seeing Tishan than Menkh of late. It was determined that Menkh would take two companions with him if they were willing, and it was his preference that Mareen and Horven accompany him. They were the first Graavens in the city other than himself and had shown a remarkable capacity to adapt to its workings. They were also accomplished Hoplex and were, in their own way, devoted to Menkh.

They were approached secretly and Menkh spent some time emphasising the risks and likely dangers that they could face.

'We are honoured that you would ask us, Zaltec,' said Mareen. 'We will happily accompany you on this journey, my lord.'

'I am pleased. But there is one matter that we must cover and to which you must agree. On this journey, we travel as companions and to that end, you will call me Menkh, not Zaltec.'

Horven smiled wryly. 'So, is that an order, Zaltec?'

Menkh smiled back, 'It is, Horven Var, and the last one I will give you. What say you both?'

Mareen and Horven looked at each other. 'We agree … Menkh,' here Mareen looked at Horven for assent, 'but you are still the leader and we will defer to your advice during our travels.'

'Yes,' said Horven, 'unless, of course, it is rash or foolish, in which case we will offer our direct opinion. Is that acceptable … Menkh?'

Menkh nodded thoughtfully. 'Why do I have the feeling that I have just created a monster?' he mused aloud. 'Yes, I find that acceptable. I wanted you along for your experience and common sense so I can hardly object if you wish to voice an opinion in the best interests of us all.'

'So, Zal— Menkh,' began Horven, correcting herself, 'when is the appointed time?'

'One meh'chaal from today. We will need to be equipped for this journey so tomorrow I will go to the Complex for this purpose, then I will make a time for you to accompany me once I have located what we need. Remember, say nothing of this to anyone. Our departure is to be secret, and we will leave without any fuss being made.'

The next day, Menkh quietly translocated to the huge anteroom that led into the Complex proper. Menkh and Crixac had spent some time in considering the potential dangers of the journey and what equipment they would need. It was Crixac, whose knowledge of the Complex and its workings vastly exceeded Menkh's, who determined that what they would need should be available in the first of the lower levels. For, as he had explained to Menkh, *'The lower levels — of which there are ten — contain armouries and weapon stores.*

Menkh had followed Crixac's instructions and had activated a metallic ramp which opened in a section of the floor. The surface of the ramp moved smoothly downwards as he stood upon it, the walls automatically giving off a steady yellow light which sprang into life as they travelled downwards. Some few minutes had passed when the section he had travelled on reached the lower floor level, decelerated, and stopped, allowing Menkh to step off the now-stationary ramp.

In front of him a white panel, several spahn across and double that width high, slid open to reveal a long hallway with a series of doorways placed at regular intervals down it. Each doorway had a series of symbols above it which Menkh, now thoroughly familiar with Kareem script, saw was a descriptor of the contents of the room.

'Some of these rooms contain weaponry that will not be required for our journey. In any event, some is so technically advanced that they would prove a danger to the user without detailed training and familiarisation, for which we lack the time, so we should access equipment which has some degree of familiarity, if possible,' remarked Crixac.

'That applies to Mareen and Horven, Crixac, but what of me? With your knowledge, mastery of these weapons would surely not be an issue?'

'You have the staff, Menkh. You will find you need nothing else. In fact, it is probably one of the most sophisticated devices in the whole city. You have much yet to learn, my friend.'

Menkh had become so accustomed to carrying the staff wherever he went in the city that it had become like an extension of his own body. He had not considered any offensive or defensive capabilities it might have and determined that he would explore this further.

They spent several chaal exploring the rooms to ascertain what might be usable. Suits of metallic clothing and helmets of intricate design occupied one room. These were displayed inside transparent cubicles made of some semitransparent material.

'How do we access these, Crixac? The cubicles appear to have no openings or access point.'

'It is not necessary to access the equipment inside, Menkh. Place your hands on the surface of the cubicle and you will see how it works.'

As Crixac had directed, Menkh placed both hands on the front panel of one cubicle. In response, a myriad of blue lines appeared on the surface. These glowed and pulsated and a tracery of light swept over and around his body. In moments, the opaque surface of the cubicle became transparent and was illuminated by a clear white light. Menkh was amazed to see a perfect image of himself clothed in the suit that was on display. The image rotated through a complete circle so he could clearly see how it fitted and various parts of the suit back and front. As the suit turned, a display lit up to one side of a panel that sat flush with the surface of the cubicle and a series of symbols appeared, presumably highlighting and explaining different parts of the suit.

'Can you understand this, Crixac? What does it say? I have not encountered this script before.'

'This is technical information relating to the suit and what it is used for. It is the first time that we have encountered this particular type of text. The Kareems developed it as a kind of shorthand of their tongue which was adapted for this purpose. Give me a moment and you will be able to read it.'

Menkh experienced a brief sense of dizziness which caused him to close his eyes. When he opened them, the swirling symbols and diagrams now made complete sense.

'I am still fascinated as to how you enable me to comprehend this script, Crixac. Suffice to say you are a very handy companion to have around.'

'My dear friend. I have hardly even started with you! But let me not spoil future surprises for you. What do you think of this suit?'

'No, I think not. Given the read out it has some qualities that are useful, but it is too specialised for what we need.'

After inspecting several suits that looked promising, Menkh finally found one which matched their purpose admirably. Lightweight and highly durable, it was capable of providing protection from projectiles of all kinds as well as enhancing the strength of the wearer. The readouts also provided information as to complementary items of protective headwear and footwear that supplemented the suit's protective powers. Having determined that these were the articles required, Crixac explained how they could now be selected.

'Place your hands for a second time on the panels. This will confirm your selections and the information will be transferred to a disc for you to use later.'

Having followed this advice, and after a further array of lights flickered brightly for some moments, an aperture appeared in the front panel and a small blue metallic disc appeared, which Menkh retrieved. The aperture disappeared as Menkh picked the disc up.

The same process was repeated with the choice of weapons, packs and other equipment that would be used on the journey. All in all, Menkh considered it to be one of the most fascinating "shopping trips" he had ever been on. 'So, what is next?'

'For now, let us return to the city proper. We can take the next step once your companions are with you.'

Menkh was beginning to understand that Crixac had a wry sense of humour and greatly enjoyed surprising his host. For, as Crixac explained, 'I do so enjoy experiencing the wonder and surprise with you. It is like a first time for me too, so you will excuse my delight in withholding information from you. After all, it would spoil the surprise for both of us.'

And so, despite repeated questions, Crixac would not be drawn.

Returning once more to the city, he arranged to meet with Horven and Mareen outside the refectory building the next day. It was still early when they set off to the Complex. A light shower of rain had fallen the previous evening, making the crystals in the pathways glimmer in the light. As they travelled, the noise of the waters rushing through their respective channels reverberated everywhere. The Graavens, having now grown so accustomed to the sound, no longer noticed it. They crossed several bridges and here and there Graavens emerged from dwellings that had "adopted" them, nodding and smiling. Menkh reflected how far the people had come in relinquishing the horror of their flight and how much they had adapted to their new life.

Finally, they stood before the two statues that guarded the entryway to the Complex.

'You know what to expect as we walk past these statues.'

Mareen and Horven exchanged looks.

'Just saying,' said Menkh.

As they stepped forward the air shimmered and, immediately, Mareen and Horven missed a step but then continued on.

'Blah! that was truly disgusting, Menkh. I felt like I was going to vomit,' stated Horven with Mareen nodding her head in agreement and taking a few deep breaths before saying, 'You would think that having passed this point any number of times the experience would become less unpleasant.'

'Indeed,' replied Menkh, 'I still haven't determined if passing through this is a kind of test or some manner in which a person is cleansed of any contaminants they might have. Look on the bright side, you two. If the City had discerned any evil intent, then vomiting would have been the least of your worries,' he said with a grin.

'Don't be smug, Menkh. If it weren't for me manipulating your physical reactions, you would have felt the same. Perhaps I should let you, anyway?'

'That would be far too cruel of you, Crixac. Besides an ex-Emperor is allowed to be smug on occasions.'

Entering the antechamber, it was not long before they stood together at the bottom of the ramp. Horven and Mareen conversed quietly as these new mysteries were unveiled.

'Well, Crixac, here we are again. What now?'

'Now we proceed to the arming room which is located at the end of this hallway.'

'And you couldn't tell me this before?' quizzed Menkh in a wry tone.

'Come, come, Menkh, don't be petulant. I know you will find this part of the process entertaining.'

'Are all symbiotes as annoying as you, I wonder?'

'Menkh, you cut me to the quick!'

As Menkh continued his silent, internal conversation with Crixac, Mareen and Horven accompanied him down the hallway, keeping up their own quiet dialogue between them.

It was not long before they stood outside of a doorway with a descriptor that matched Crixac's advice. Once the panel had slid open, they entered a very large room. Circular in shape, a table large enough to have seated several people occupied the centre of the room. Spaced all around the walls were doorways which were curved to fit the shape of the walls.

The top of the table contained a large recess of rectangular shape. Whilst the table was white, the material on the bottom of the recess was black. Two indentations on the tabletop, either side of the recess, could be clearly seen.

'You know what they are for, Menkh.'

Menkh placed a hand inside them and almost instantaneously a panel rose upward out of the recess in the table. As it reached eye level the panel became motionless. A light appeared and an image of the room came into focus showing all the cubicle doors, each with a symbol underneath it. Menkh recognised that these were numbers and that there were twenty numbered cubicles in all.

'You must select three cubicles — you need one each — by touching a finger to their number. This will activate the cubicle which is where you will arm yourselves. Once you have activated the cubicles required, you will insert the disc you have into the panel. Do this now.'

The three cubicles that sat directly across from the table were numbered ten through twelve. As he activated them, the door panel of each opened first outward and then upwards, revealing a room beyond. When all three doors had opened, a drawer slid out from the panel. The drawer contained several slots which were obviously made to accommodate discs like the one Menkh had. Upon placing the disc in one of the slots the drawer retracted. A series of lights began to flash on the screen and after several seconds these steadied to an unwinking silvery colour.

'You may proceed now into each arming cubicle. The door will close automatically once you are inside. There are two rooms. In the first room you must disrobe completely. Once you have done that you may proceed into the next room. There is a depression in the floor that you must stand in. Nothing will happen until you have done this. Once there, well … you will see for yourself.'

Menkh explained this to Mareen and Horven, who exchanged looks. Horven said, 'Well. As long as it doesn't make me feel like throwing up again, I am happy to go ahead.'

Menkh waited until they had entered their cubicles before entering his own.

Upon walking through the outer door, it closed behind him with a quiet hiss of air. A cool white light illuminated the interior of the outer room. A further space — the light from which was much dimmer — could be accessed via another open doorway.

Once the outer door had fully sealed, a panel in the wall alongside him slid open to reveal a set of shelves with hanging space.

'Here you disrobe. Store your clothing here, you will be able to access it again when you come out of the arming room.'

Menkh followed Crixac's instructions and, naked, walked through the interior doorway. As he entered, the light gained in intensity and he noticed a depression in the floor at the centre of the room which, like the main area outside, was circular.

'Now, stand in the depression and keep your attention on the wall. It will help if you can stand still.'

Menkh avoided the temptation of asking Crixac what was going to happen as he knew he would, at best, get a cryptic response.

As he took stance in the depression a series of coloured lights, similar to the ones that he had experienced when selecting the equipment, began to trace over his body. On the wall opposite, a perfect image of himself appeared and slowly rotated. The longer the lights moved, the more detailed the image became. In addition, items of the equipment also appeared with a series of symbols flashing alongside each item and piece.

'This is measuring me, isn't it?' Menkh asked.

'Indeed. Now that you have selected the equipment you require, all three of you are being measured so that the items issued are exactly matched to your body size and muscle mass.'

'Remarkable,' observed Menkh.

After several minutes, the lights faded and the room was once again illuminated in the cool white light from before. Just as Menkh was about to ask what to do, various panels, which before had not been discernible, began to be outlined in the surface of the walls surrounding him.

First, a panel on the left slid open and a large drawer appeared. On inspection it contained what Menkh assumed were some type of undergarments made of a material that was soft and pliable but lightweight. The first item was a shirt that he slid over his head, followed by leggings that reached from his waist to the tops of his feet. The garment fitted him so perfectly that it was like a second skin. No sooner had he donned these garments when a second panel opened, this time revealing the metallic-looking suit that he and Crixac had selected.

This, too, comprised a shirt and leggings. Remarkably, it felt as pliable as the undergarment and Menkh wondered if he had made an error in selecting it or if he had misinterpreted the readouts that gave the suit specifications. Next, boots were revealed. These had a thick and durable sole of a material that Menkh had never seen before and which proved to be extremely comfortable to wear. Finally, a helmet. This had a silvery hue and certainly appeared to be metallic, given the ringing sound it made when Menkh rapped his knuckles on it. The interior of the helmet was coated in a thin layer of a black-coloured substance that was soft like the undergarment he wore and which yielded to the push of his fingers, but then sprang back into shape when the pressure was released. Upon placing it on his head, the helmet appeared to adjust itself to the contours of his head. No sooner had this been done than a transparent visor appeared over his face. How this occurred was another marvel, as it was self-activating and Menkh, on later inspection of the helmet, could not see any aperture or other feature that showed where the visor appeared from. Adding to this mystery, as his eyes moved over the interior of the visor, he could see a tracery of symbols which Crixac explained provided all sorts of information relating to the terrain that was being traversed.

Final accoutrements included gloves and a backpack, made of a material that appeared not dissimilar to the helmet and which by some means devoid of straps "adhered" itself to the back of the suit once positioned there. Later use showed that the backpack each Graaven carried was capable of storing quite a quantity of supplies, more than might be indicated by its external size. And, additionally, no matter what was placed inside it, it hardly weighed anything at all.

Once he had retrieved all the items provided and clothed himself fully, a further door at the back of the room opened revealing yet another room.

'*Before we enter that room, Menkh, I suggest you retrieve your staff and gem belt. You may as well get used to having all your kit together.*'

'*Very well, Crixac. I suppose there is little point is asking you what is in the next room?*'

Only silence met this question.

'*No, I thought not.*'

Once Menkh had retrieved the staff and set the belt that held the coloured crystals in place, he entered the third room. This room was much larger in proportion than the arming room and the light here was much more yellow, which reflected the colour of the walls. As the door closed behind him, the light grew brighter and the walls flickered. Menkh felt slightly disoriented just for a second and he suddenly found himself standing on sand in the middle of a desert-like terrain. Alongside him stood Mareen and Horven, also fully kitted out in the gear he had selected for them. Both of them carried a mace-like weapon, which, when he picked it, had seemed to be not unlike the weapon which the Baran Mec favoured.

'What is happening, Menkh? Dressing in this equipment was strange enough, but where are we now?' asked Mareen.

'I think we are still in the room but, by some craft, we appear to be in a desert which seems eerily like the Steppes of Portis,' replied Menkh, 'and, if I am right, I think that very soon we are going to have our gear tested most thoroughly. I suggest we don our helmets and await developments.' Having done so, Menkh tentatively called loudly, 'Horven, Mareen, can you hear me?'

Sounds of pain echoed in his helmet.

'Do you have to shout, Zaltec? I mean Menkh. I can hear you very clearly. How about you, Horven?'

'I will tell you when my ears cease ringing!'

'Well, that satisfies the issue of communications,' remarked Menkh drily.

In the distance, a horn sounded, and grunts and cries could be heard, growing in volume as something approached.

'If these are the Steppes of Portis then we might expect drokhounds and their oh-so-pleasant handlers to welcome us,' remarked Horven quietly, 'and, as they like to surround their prey, I suggest we circle around to cover each other's backs.'

Without further discussion they assumed a circular formation with weapons poised. Menkh had not used the staff in combat before but his heightened senses, pending imminent conflict, caused the staff to glow with a greenish light and Menkh could feel it vibrating with energy through his gloved hands.

As the first of the drokhounds appeared it became apparent that the three Graavens had been standing on top of a dune. The drokhounds launched themselves without a moment's pause into a ferocious attack. Diminutive in size for most creatures that inhabited Tarvuli, they were not to be underestimated. Three spahn high at the shoulder they had massively muscled forequarters. Two pinkish-coloured eyes were deep-set in a long face, finished with a protruding jaw containing powerful bony plates that could crush the hardest bone into fragments. Their hide was rough to the touch and patterned in a reddish colour that allowed them to blend in with the desert terrain.

Emitting a fearsome howl, they leapt upon the Graavens.

Mareen and Horven whipped their maces around their heads and smashed them into the bodies of the leaping drokhounds. The effect was stunning. The sounds of breaking bone and the painful yelps of the smitten drokhounds were heard as their bodies were flung nearly twenty spahn into the air from the impact.

If the two Graavens were amazed at the force that the two weapons had emitted they had no time to express it, as they spun around to deal with other drokhounds who took the place of their defeated companions.

In the meantime, Menkh had swept his staff in a horizontal move which he thought would knock the attackers away. Instead, a flash of green light exploded outward from the staff. The energy bolt swept out in a flat and concentrated arc and cut through several drokhounds, severing their bodies in a gout of purple-coloured blood.

'*Surprise!*' said Crixac with dry humour, '*aren't you glad I didn't spoil the fun?*'

Menkh grunted, '*You and I need to have a serious discussion regarding the concept of fun.*'

Mareen and Horven had dispatched more of the creatures and the remainder had drawn off, circling slowly around the three Graavens. They sniffed the bodies of their fallen comrades and emitted long howls which sounded eery in the desert air.

'*So, Crixac, I understand that this appears to be a scenario designed to test our equipment and gain facility with the weapons we have, but how long will this continue?*'

'*It will continue, Menkh, until you have satisfied the objectives; that is, to defeat your opponents, whilst avoiding defeat yourselves.*'

The sound of horns, raucous and harsh, were heard and the drokhounds slunk away. The three Graavens stood together awaiting the next challenge.

'Menkh, this mace is a wonderful weapon. I thought that being so light it would hardly deliver a telling blow but the power it unleashes is unlike anything I have experienced previously with any weapon.'

'You speak truly, Mareen, it is a wondrous weapon – but have you noticed that our suits have changed colour during combat?' responded Horven.

Menkh and Mareen looked at the sleeves of their mail coats and their bodies. The colour had indeed changed from the lustre of silvery metal to the dull russet red of the surrounding sands.

'Well, that will be very worthwhile if the suit can match the surroundings we find ourselves in as we travel,' remarked Horven.

Barely had she made this observation when three figures rose into view.

'Mensch nomads,' hissed Mareen.

'Yes, that was predictable as soon as we saw drokhounds,' said Menkh. 'You never get one without the other.'

As his vision focused on the approaching foe, Menkh's helmet visor changed focus and gave him a close-up view of them as they approached. Exclamations of surprise showed that Mareen and Horven had the same experience.

Not tall like the Graavens, at an average height of six spahn the males were massively muscled. Whilst not a stupid people, their minds were closed to any concepts that were alien to their way of life and to anything that brought into question their steadfast belief in their gods. Three Mensch now stood and observed the three Graavens before them.

As Mareen had noted, the Mensch were a nomadic people who inhabited the Steppes of Portis, far to the north of what had been the Graaven empire. Pacified but never fully subdued, the Mensch were a fierce and independent people who tolerated no incursion into their tribal lands. Savage and cruel, they had long tamed the drokhound, fierce predator of the Steppes, and used them to hunt prey and kill their enemies.

Menkh had never seen such looks of unalloyed hatred in any opponent. He had heard of the Mensch and read of the expeditions the Graavens had undertaken to conquer them but had never seen them in the flesh – or in this case, a reconstruction of them in the flesh.

'*Crixac, how accurate is this scenario and where is the City accessing the information to create this?*'

'*The City draws on all of the stored data in the archives. Whilst much of the city was obliterated, the archives were mostly housed in the Complex. Also, it draws on your knowledge and memories. This is as real as if you were actually there, save that you cannot actually die as a result of combat. Though, as you already know, you will feel pain if a hit is made and the pain can be enough to render a combatant incapable of action for a short time.*'

The Mensch wore a tunic made from the tanned hides of some desert creature. Sturdy vests of leather provided protection for their upper torsos and a light helmet of the same material capped their heads. These were decorated with the teeth of some large predator and each Mensch wore a necklace made of the same. Stout sandals covered their large and horny feet and their bare arms, decorated with swirling tattoos of intricate design, had leather shields covering their forearms. They each had a long spear and carried a heavy blade and knives in a woven belt around their waists. A slit mouth was surmounted by the smallest slit of a nose and above that eyes, as red as the desert sands that surrounded them, gazed unblinkingly. Strangely for such heavily muscled and brutish-appearing beings, their speech was high-pitched and birdlike, and they spoke in muted whispers that could not be clearly heard from where Menkh stood.

'*Your name is curiously similar to the name they give themselves,*' remarked Crixac.

'*Deliberately so. The Mensch were never conquered, they are a wily and cunning people who simply melted away into their desert fastness. The Graaven name is, in one sense, a grudging tribute to them. It means "cunning and fierce", quite appropriate in the circumstances.*'

Menkh turned his attention to Horven and Mareen. 'Caution now, they are planning something and there is no possibility that they will simply back away.'

He had no sooner spoken when, with a ululating cry, the Mensch went from a passive stance to leaping into a throwing position and with a vicious heave launched their spears. At once it became clear that their target was Mareen. By crippling her, they reduced the odds and as they completed their powerful casts, they drew their heavy blades and swept into an attack focusing on Menkh and Horven.

There was no possibility that Mareen could dodge the flight of the spears, so accurately were they thrown, each covering the space that separated the parties in mere moments. As she braced for the collision her suit emitted a blue aura and as the spears verged on impact, they were deflected away, flying off some distance to skitter across the desert sand. Mareen still staggered back somewhat and, whilst off balance, three drokhounds darted in to attack her.

In the meantime, the three Mensch leapt into an assault. Menkh's staff blazed into light as he lifted it to two of the assailants who leapt on him, raising their blades to strike. This time there was an audible thump as energy was released and the Mensch were hurled away into the air, like limp dolls, to crash lifelessly onto the sand.

The third assailant swung with such ferocity that its blade slipped past Horven's lifted mace and swept straight down onto her helmet. As with Mareen's suit, a blue aura sprang into being and the blow was deflected at the last minute, though Horven was still forced onto one knee. As the Mensch nomad swept his blade around into a backhanded cut, Horven pushed up from the ground and her mace connected with the creature's midriff. With a grunt, the creature fell back two paces – enough for Horven to launch her own overhand swing. The creature desperately threw up its blade to ward off the blow but the mace smashed it down, driving into the Mensch's face both its own blade and the head of the mace, pulverising it into a bloody gruel as the body collapsed.

Meanwhile, Mareen was having a hard time fighting off the three drokhounds. One had latched onto her left arm and, whilst the suit prevented any penetration, the weight of the creature swung her off balance, allowing the other two drokhounds to enter the fray.

A pulse from Menkh's staff was enough to throw the two drokhounds away and finally Mareen could then bring her mace down on the hound which gripped her arm. The creature fell to the sand and the other two, howling piteously, dragged themselves away.

The Graavens experienced a sudden lurching sensation and found themselves once again standing in the yellow glow of the outer room. All vestiges of their recent combat were now gone.

Mareen sat on the floor nursing her arm. 'By all the gods, my arm hurts where that creature grabbed. If that was pretend, I'm glad these are not the real thing.'

'Well,' said Menkh, 'as you know from similar combats in the city, if there is no pain or consequence then the lesson does not really hone in.'

Over the next few days, they returned several times to the arming and combat rooms. The simulations left them bruised and battered but they rapidly learned the power and limitations of their weapons and equipment. The suits could deflect ranged attacks from spears, arrows, and all manner of launched or thrown projectiles, but the wearer could still be thrown back as a result of the averted impact. In close-in fighting, an arm could still be grabbed or a leg tripped. The suit absorbed penetration from all kinds of weapons or the jaws of predators but a painful bruise on the skin could still occur.

Thus, preparations continued until the appointed dak'chaal had passed and Menkh, in mental discussion with Crixac and consultation with Tishan, determined that all was as ready as possible.

Near to their time of departure Menkh addressed Horven, Mareen, and Tishan, who had gathered for a meeting in Tishan's private dwelling. This was yet another of the surprises that the City seemed to throw at them. Internally, the dwelling was an accurate reconstruction of the home she had dwelt in as a newly emerged Graaven in the Empire, and it held fond memories for her.

'As near as we can tell, given that the weather in the vicinity of the city generally remains mild, the Time of Storms has mostly passed by outside the walls and the Time of Renewal draws near,' said Menkh. 'We have arranged for a Benshin guide to take us through their lands and, if Fendrax is to be believed, they will await us once we leave the gates. Are there any final questions?'

'None, Menkh. All is in order and the people appear happy and contented with our plans going forward. Some of our females have mooted that they wish to invoke the quickening and, as is usual, the City seems to have provided a perfect facility to support hatchlings. So, naturally, there is much excitement, particularly as the Time of Renewal approaches.'

'Good, then if Mareen and Horven have nothing further?' Menkh turned a questioning look to them both and on receiving a negative response added, 'Well then, we shall meet at the gates before Avlar rises, two dak'chaal from now. I bid you goodnight and, other than the details of our journey remaining secret, you are free to spend your time as you will.'

Mareen and Horven smiled and nodded, a trip to Desh's Tavern for a convivial drink foremost in their minds. As they left, Tishan turned to Menkh.

'A moment of your time, Menkh, if I may?'

'Of course, Tishan, whatever you need.'

Tishan looked directly into Menkh's eyes and spoke quietly. 'I spoke of the quickening earlier. Menkh, I too have felt the stirrings in this settled time.' Looking down, she smiled shyly. 'It seems I am not too old after all.'

She returned her gaze to his eyes. 'There was a time that a joining between us would have been impossible. But would you honour me by——?'

Menkh interrupted her by gently lifting a finger to her chin. 'Tishan Dar, it is I who am honoured. I will gladly join with you and I have no doubt that the hatchlings that result will be all that any Graaven could desire. So, time is short, and Phags Par takes several chaal if it is to be honoured. What is in your mind?'

'Meet me at dawn tomorrow. The City has provided us with a facility perfectly adapted to our purpose not far from the refectory. There, we can observe all the requirements,' she paused and looked deeply into Menkh's eyes. 'Thank you, Menkh.'

Menkh gently touched his forehead to Tishan's. 'There shall be no talk of thanks between us, Tishan. Till the dawn then.'

CHAPTER TWELVE

The building comprised a single storey located not far from one of the many bridges that crisscrossed the seven streams as they flowed endlessly towards the Complex. Unlike many other buildings, there were no ornate symbols or patterns that decorated the frame of the entry. Instead, the single Graaven symbol for regeneration sat squarely above the centre of the frame atop the door. As was usual with all buildings of the city, entry was gained by placing your hand in a depression located to the right of the doorway. Upon doing so, the door opened with the expected slight hissing sound.

Whatever Menkh was expecting to see, the space he entered was totally surprising. Where he had presumed that he would enter some kind of room or rooms, instead, the entire inner space was verdant with ferns and other flowering foliage which emitted a heady scent. It seemed as if a cloudless violet sky soared above him, and the calls of animals and insects accompanied the sound of water running nearby with a melody that was pleasant to the ear. The air was warm and humid, and the surrounding forest was reminiscent of the natural environment of Venlish Province where Tishan was spawned and had lived her formative years.

Already the tunic and boots that he wore felt hot in the steamy atmosphere of the room. As he stepped forward and entered the space, a robe made of a light and gauzy material could be seen hanging from the branch of a fern which, upon closer inspection, turned out to be a kind of storage space cunningly designed to resemble the ferns and plants which made up the scene around him.

'It would appear that a change is in order, Menkh. Your raiment is completely out of place here,' remarked Crixac, *'and, before you ask me, I will absent myself from your thoughts and presence. I have no wish to intrude on your ritual.'*

'Thank you, Crixac. Although I cannot see how you can "absent" yourself in such a way when you are a part of me.'

'A part, yes, but also separate in ways that, in time to come, you will appreciate. It is complicated, but I can be apart from you as well — at least for periods of time — without affecting our bond. So, for a short time I bid you farewell.'

Upon hearing these words, Menkh did indeed feel a slight sense of "shifting" inside himself. A feeling of absence where something warm and comforting had suddenly been withdrawn. He had no doubt that Crixac had indeed absented himself and, whilst this was to a degree unsettling, Menkh nevertheless was glad. The ceremony of Phags Par was primordial and its effect on Graaven males and females could be unpredictable.

Not knowing what else to do, Menkh donned the light tunic after divesting himself of his other garments. His staff he lay against the storage fern, having no concern that it would be disturbed and, barefooted, stepped forward into the forest around him.

Almost at once a muted glow highlighted a narrow, grassed path that led deeper into the ferns and flowering plants before him. For some time, he quietly followed the path and the sounds of flowing water. Around him, the chirruping of insects and the muted calls of birds and other creatures was soothing. He felt that he had walked a distance that was many times the size of the building he had entered, and yet there seemed no end to the path he followed which at last began to descend towards the sound of falling water.

There, by a small pool just above the point where the water cascaded down some rocks, sat Tishan.

Her tunic lay to one side and, as Menkh approached, she stood, naked, and awaited his arrival, raising her arms up to him in the ritual greeting. Her eyes were wide and black and the swirls and colours that every Graaven exhibited under their skin, delineating their clan and kin, were engorged and raised like welts. Like Graaven females before her judging the time to be right, Tishan had invoked the Stelik Xin, the quickening, making her body ready to spawn. The pores of her skin emitted a thick and musty odour which Menkh's body immediately reacted to. In turn, the patterns under his skin also engorged and lifted in hard welts. He too raised his arms in the greeting, fighting to retain control of his body and mind. Rational thought began to be displaced as the ritual of the Phags Par took hold.

Advancing into the pool, Tishan beckoned to him to join her. There were no words. Looks and gestures were all that was needed. Menkh also stepped into the pond. The water was pleasantly warm and proved to be only as deep as to rise to the midpoint of his shins. Sinking down to his knees opposite Tishan's kneeling figure, he felt her arms rise to his shoulders, gripping them tightly. Menkh did the same to Tishan.

Now there was nothing but the rhythm of Phags Par. Tishan's breath came in panting gasps as her body expelled a bluish-coloured, translucent egg into the water. The size of a clenched fist, the egg was jelly-like in appearance and hung suspended in the warm water between Menkh and Tishan's bodies. Menkh's own body responded involuntarily to the appearance of the egg and emitted a clear, viscous fluid which enveloped the newly produced egg, whereupon it sank gently to the bottom of the pool. Both the production of the egg and its fertilisation were intensely pleasurable sensations. Both Graavens, maintaining an intense and fixed stare into each other's eyes, were oblivious of their surroundings, such was the intensity of the experience.

Over the course of several chaal Tishan produced two eggs to be fertilised. At last, she released Menkh's shoulders and turned her attention from her body and the eggs that she had produced to Menkh's eyes. They touched foreheads in the Graaven way of affection and, in a manner that required no words, expressed their deep respect and admiration for each other. Gently they stood, leaving the two eggs lying in the warm water of the pool.

As they donned the robes they had discarded, Menkh spoke, 'You will be alright? I may be gone for some time.'

'All will be well, Menkh. We will both know when our progeny emerges, and I will be here to greet them. They will be amongst many new hatchlings who will be native to the City. I have no doubt that we will find new ways in which our home will adapt itself to their arrival.'

'Yes, the City continues to surprise us all with its ability to cater to our needs and wants. I have great confidence in our future and hope that my journey will ensure it for all Graaven people.'

'You have told me its purpose, so all my thoughts will go with you, in hope that your journey is successful and that you return to us safely. In the meantime, I will progress the plans that we have made.'

'Then I will depart. Remember that you have access to the viewing room now, so we can communicate and keep apprised of eventualities, at least for the first part of the journey.'

Tishan nodded and, touching foreheads for a last moment, they parted, Menkh back along the path to where he had first entered, leaving Tishan as she turned her attention back to the pool and the precious cargo it now contained.

Just before dawn on the appointed day of departure, Menkh relocated himself to the paved area which overlooked the city. He did so surreptitiously, as only Tishan at this time knew of his ability. Rightly or wrongly, he deemed that disappearing and appearing at will might be a cause of alarm and possible suspicion. Nor did he want Mareen or Horven to see him materialise out of thin air, and he had determined that this was the best area to achieve his purpose. Having done so, he walked up along the pathway towards the gates where he soon saw his two companions waiting quietly.

Like him, they were fully kitted out in their equipment with packs full of supplies and other necessities for the journey ahead.

'Greetings, Zaltec,' said Horven.

'Greetings, Menkh,' said Mareen with a sidelong glance at her sibling, 'we are ready on your command.'

'I expected no less,' said Menkh with a smile, 'so let us proceed. Remember that the crystals I gave you will assist in translating any strange speech we may encounter. Like the magic which pervades all the city, I cannot explain how it works, only that you should wear your belts at all times. Finally, something I haven't told you before.'

Both Horven and Mareen exchanged looks

'Indeed?' said Horven with a quizzical look, before Mareen responded, 'We are all ears, Menkh.'

'We will have other companions on our journey. You will recall our tawny friends on the journey here?'

Both siblings nodded their heads cautiously.

'Well, their queen and two of her children accompany us. I should add that I did not seek their assistance and can give you no explanation as to how they found us, how they knew of our journey or why they wish to accompany us. The fact is they are here, and they are coming with us. I, for one, will be glad of their presence but we should obviously exercise caution. Giving them offence would not be the wisest move, I think.'

'Always I believe that I am beyond surprise after the last few months, and always I am mistaken,' stated Horven.

'Well, this journey grows ever more interesting,' added Mareen, looking at her sibling.

'So then. Let us venture forth and see what awaits us,' and, so saying, Menkh silently commanded the gates to open. The dawning light grew ever brighter as Colunda peeped over the horizon. Outside the gates three massive, tawny shapes rose up from where they had been lying and watched the Graavens approach.

Following Menkh's lead, all three Graavens bowed deeply, an action mirrored by the three gonverdeem.

'Greetings,' purred Fendrax. She turned her eyes on Horven and Mareen, who had exchanged sharp looks as the words of the gonverdeem were translated and seemingly appeared to come directly from the mouth of Fendrax.

'These are two of my litter, as I agreed with Menkh. This one you may call Haran,' indicating with the motion of her head a male with russet stripes. 'This one you may call Kuhltar,' indicating a slightly smaller female with greyish-black spots.

'I will take this puny female,' rumbled Haran, indicating Horven. 'That leaves the fat one for you,' and here he turned his eyes towards Kuhltar.

Mareen's eyes squinted dangerously. 'A wise decision, pup, you look far too weak to bear me, even if I agreed to ride on your back.'

A silence descended on the three gonverdeem. Haran turned his black eyes on Mareen and advanced towards her till their noses were almost touching. Mareen defiantly held her ground. Menkh and Horven said nothing, but their stances became tense as Fendrax also turned her gaze on Mareen.

Haran sniffed loudly, his penetrating gaze fixed unblinkingly on Mareen's eyes. Then, suddenly, he issued a series of breathy grunts. He broke his gaze to stare at Fendrax. 'I like her. She has spirit. She can ride on me,' he said to Fendrax and then, turning his gaze back to Mareen, 'I will do my best not to collapse under your weight.'

Mareen bowed her head graciously.

'Do not mind my brother, his high opinion of himself is only to compensate for the lack of size of his male parts,' added Kuhltar.

Haran issued a further series of grunts. 'My mates find them adequate, sister, so your barbs do not pierce my hide.'

'That is true, daughter,' agreed Fendrax. 'Enough with our play, lest we embarrass our new companions. Let us move, I sense a Benshin scout not too far from here awaiting us. Perhaps you will ride now, so as to get used to the motion?' This question was directed at Menkh.

'As you will, Fendrax.'

'Then let your friends imitate your movements in climbing up.'

So saying, Fendrax lay her head low to the ground. 'You will find a bony plate just behind my ear. Grasp this firmly and swing your leg over my neck. You cannot hurt me, so grip strongly. As you do this, I will lift my head and body up.'

Following Fendrax's instructions, Menkh found it a little awkward at first but, once he had perched himself behind Fendrax's head, he discovered her pelt was smooth and thick around the neck and the position quite comfortable, if odd. In fact, it was quite secure, there being a number of bony protrusions which allowed him to place his legs firmly without in any way impeding her head movements. In rapid succession, Horven and Mareen took up their positions and the three gonverdeem moved off at a steady walk. The three Graavens found the motion not unpleasant and it was a thrill to sit so high above the pathway.

'I could get used to this, Menkh. I feel invincible sitting here. Truly these are marvellous creatures, indeed.'

'I agree, Horven. But tell me how marvellous it is after you have ridden for a day using muscles you didn't know you had.'

'Yes, sister. Not to mention hanging on when our companions break into a run. Walking I can handle, but we have all seen how fast they can move. Talk to me then about how "invincible" you feel.'

'Yes, yes. I take your points, but that doesn't take away the thrill. This journey was worth it just to experience this.'

They now followed the path that continued alongside the cliff wall that surrounded the city. On the other side of the stream that meandered alongside the path, the dense fern forest seemed to smoke as the slowly-increasing warmth evaporated the dew of the night before. The songs of birds and calls of other animals could be heard but rarely was any creature seen. In the far distance a mountain range could be discerned, whose distant peaks were wreathed in snow and mist. All in all, it was a beautiful morning to be setting out and so they continued in companionable silence for a chaal or so, always with the cliff wall on their left and the stream murmuring over rocks and small cascades on their right.

The path began to descend somewhat until at last it reached a small ford. Here, shallow water from a smaller flow joined the main stream. The water chattered across the ford and the long fronds of a yellowish aquatic plant swayed rhythmically in the flowing water.

Two Benshin guides, who had been heating some water over a small fire, had risen to their feet at the sound of the Graaven approach. Their eyes widened in surprise at the sight of the riders and their mounts. Both dropped to their knees and made deep obeisance, their arms stretched above their heads with the palms of their hands upward, at the same time making grunting noises at the back of their throats. The three gonverdeem continued their steady approach until Fendrax, towering over the prostrate Benshin, gently touched their heads with her snout. To Menkh's eyes the gesture, from such a huge predator, seemed almost affectionate.

Fendrax drew back somewhat and the two Benshin stood upright. They both smiled in delight at the three gonverdeem. As they arose and looked up, Menkh now saw that the two Benshin, though similar in height, were male and female.

'Greetings, Menkh ab Dur. I am Kexin, and this is my sister Shartuk. Draachnull sends his greetings and told me to tell you that we are to be your guides over Benshin lands. When we tell him that you were borne on the backs of the Tamut La it will be a source of great wonder.'

Menkh and the two Graavens dismounted as the gonverdeem bent their heads low.

'Greetings, Kexin and Shartuk. These are my companions, Horven and Mareen. We are pleased that you will be guiding us, but you speak of the Tamut La, and obviously you know of our travelling companions. Perhaps you can tell us how this is possible?'

Shartuk turned her gaze from the three huge creatures. 'Those we call the Tamut La, "silent death", have long been the friends of the clans of the Benshin, though our contact now is rare indeed and almost they are become legend. Once, in the long ago, the Benshin often journeyed to the lands of the Tamut La and they to ours; then the forest grew, and the open plains receded. The Benshin do not forget and it is also in the nature of the Tamut La that, once a friend, always a friend. To us they are sacred creatures. In many ways they are like us, fierce and proud – their family groupings are liken to ours also. But the white Tamut La, they are rare indeed, the most sacred of all. We were happy to act as your guides; now, we are honoured that once more we travel in company with our ancient friends.'

Here, both Shartuk and Kexin bowed deeply once again and the three Tamut La also bowed.

'It is a good thing to meet old friends again,' purred Fendrax. 'Our Graaven companions have given us names in their tongue. I am Fendrax. These are two of my litter, Haran and Kuhltar. I find the names pleasing and you may call us by them whilst we journey together.'

Again, the two Benshin bowed.

'You understand their language as well?' Menkh asked in surprise.

'The Benshin know the ways of all creatures, they are one with us and we with them,' and, having responded to Menkh, the Benshin turned to Fendrax, issuing a series of grunts and coughing sounds which the Graavens understood by dint of the crystals they each carried.

'It shall be as you say, Fendrax,' replied Kexin. Then, to the Graavens, 'We have heated water; we will make tea to celebrate your arrival and then journey on to a village of the Thunder Water clan. For a Benshin, that is two days' walk from here as we measure it. We had supposed that this would take longer with you on foot, but the Tamut La can easily match our pace, and this will make our journey that much quicker.'

Whilst the tea was prepared, Fendrax, Haran and Kuhltar went a little way up the stream to drink and bathe. The Tamut La, as the Graavens in the fashion of the Benshin now began to think of them, were fastidious creatures and the opportunity to swim and bathe was never overlooked.

After drinking the tea that their guides had made and becoming somewhat more acquainted, the party drew together and the Graavens remounted.

'We shall journey now till we come to a place where the path divides. This will take us till Tarrat, the second sun, which you call

Avlar, I think?' here Shartuk looked at the Graavens, and Menkh nodded silently.

'Then, when Avlar reaches his highest point, we should arrive at that point and there we will stop for a meal before proceeding. Follow us now.'

So saying, the two Benshin turned and jogged off across the ford and up the path that now turned away from the cliff wall and plunged deeper into the forest. They did not pause for breath and their steady pace continued unabated. The path was wide enough for the Tamut La to follow in single file. Their steady walking pace increased only slightly in order to keep pace with their two Benshin guides. Menkh noticed that the ferns and cycads which surrounded them grew larger, and the forest denser, as they journeyed on.

Crowns of flowering blooms, yellow and red in colour, were in evidence and small creatures flitted amongst the trunks of the plants and disappeared into the dappled light of the forest. The air barely moved under the canopy of the plants and the atmosphere was both warm and humid. Time seemed to stand still. One chaal inside the forest felt much longer. Within this ancient growth, only the change in seasons gave any indication that the passage of time had relevance.

As they journeyed on, a feeling grew amongst the three Graaven that there was a watchful presence all around them. The more they concentrated on that feeling, the more aware they became of it, almost feeling that if they turned their heads fast enough they would see something or someone looking out from amongst the trunks of the trees. But no matter how quickly they looked, there was never anything to see; just that feeling of quiet observation that stayed with them. Not exactly hostile but neither entirely benign. At last, they came to a natural clearing where the giant ferns became sparser. A pool of clear water bubbled up from the ground and delicate mosses and small flowering plants grew in profusion around it. Warm sunlight dappled the area which was altogether peaceful. The only disturbances were huge black and purple insects which delicately floated around the plants, stopping to sip nectar from them and then flitting off back into the forest proper.

Kexin turned to the Graavens as they climbed down from the Tamut La. 'Here we will rest and refresh ourselves for a short time. You may drink from the pool; the water is said to have healing properties and this place is shared by the Lightning, Smoke, and Thunder Water clans. When we start our journey again, we pass into the lands of the Thunder Water.'

'Why Thunder Water?' asked Mareen curiously.

Kexin smiled. 'Soon you will know the answer, friend Mareen.'

The Graavens nodded their understanding and Menkh asked about their strange feeling of being watched. Shartuk nodded and smiled. 'You feel the presence of her who the Benshin call Varthansh Mek, the Keeper. We leave offerings to her so that our passage through the forest is safe. Those who offend her often find their path blocked or end up lost and wandering through twisting paths far from their intended route. Also, people who offend her have died when a heavy branch unexpectedly fell as they passed by.'

'So, it is a spirit then. But you have said "she" – how do you know it is female?'

'Did her presence not feel like that to you? Almost like a mother watching over her children, and her children are all around you. We gather no wood and make no large fires in the heart of the forest. To do so is to invoke her anger. Travel quietly, respect the forest, and all will be well. Or so we believe.'

Fendrax nodded her head. 'We feel that presence, too. But to us it is both wild and free, a presence that soothes us and sings of time gone by. Much like the music of your peoples' flutes, which are like the echo of her voice.'

Now Kexin smiled. 'You speak truly, it was Varthansh Mek who taught us the music of the flute. You will hear that tonight. But for now, let us journey on. Soon we will come to a mighty river that cuts through the forest. Our path leads over those waters and up into the hills beyond. We still have several chaal of travel ahead.'

'Yes,' said Horven, 'and my rear parts are beginning to let me know that riding on Haran isn't what they were designed for.'

'I will refrain from saying "told you so",' said Mareen smugly, but a grunt was all she received in reply.

Mounting up, they followed the Benshin back into the forest depths where they again felt the presence of Varthansh Mek. Knowing the beliefs of the Benshin, however, gave them a more benign feeling than before. More like a watchful presence against danger than one which plotted them harm.

Again, after what seemed many chaal, they reached the banks of a broad and fast-flowing river. Here an ancient span made of great blocks of black stone swept over the river in a graceful curve.

'Tell me this is not the work of the City dwellers. It is like to those we have seen before. There must have been a road here in times past — this is far too solid a structure to stand simply as a way across the river in the middle of the forest,' observed Menkh to Crixac.

'Most assuredly, Menkh. There were roads that once connected all three Cities. But my knowledge of the land is limited and gleaned only from access to the city archives. My former host's original mission was with the City itself and our travel outside was extremely limited. Also, the land is much changed in the many hundreds of sem'chaal, as you Graavens count the years, since their fall. There is no reference to any other humanoid races at all. Whether they existed or were so far beneath the notice of the city dwellers, I cannot say. Certainly, there is some vestige of knowledge tied up in legends that surround the Cities themselves.'

'Strange, then, that you knew of the gonverdeem. How is it that the archives contained information regarding these creatures?'

'That is because the Kareems delighted in dabbling with breeding creatures that were adapted for their use. Originally mindless predators, the Kareems utilised their superb killing skills and interbred them with another species of predator. The scientists of Kareem Vastar, through their arts, honed the gonverdeem's intelligence so that they could understand language and develop a sense of themselves. They did this so well that some of the gonverdeem slaughtered their masters and fled far from the City into lands that they claimed as their own. But, Menkh, their race memories are handed down from generation to generation and their knowledge of the City and their origins remains clear to them. That is how they knew where the City was. On top of that they have a mysterious connection to the crystal, perhaps as a result of what was done to them, but they have their own reasons for being here. It is clear that the Benshin know and recognise them, so at some time in the past their paths crossed, and they earned their name of the Tamut La. Let us not forget that Fendrax senses my existence and the duality that exists between us. That has left me much in thought.'

'Yes, let us hope, then, that their goals and ours are the same.'

'Do not fear treachery, Menkh. The fact that they have allowed you to ride them is a wonder and has not occurred in living memory. You can trust them: it is not in their nature to betray friendship once freely given. Clearly they sense that their aid is important in your quest to maintain the Balance.'

'Well, we shall see what unfolds as we go forward.'

As Menkh had carried on his internal conversation with Crixac, the party had halted while Kexin had crossed over and briefly scouted the path that now plunged downwards back into the forest. Returning, he waved his arms and the group moved over the bridge, the water rushing by.

'Does this river have a name, Shartuk?' asked Horven, as she and Haran plodded along the bridge behind her.

'We call this the Sharana, the Black Water, and it can be treacherous. He flows for many of your Graaven persangh and eventually leaves our lands, flowing at last into a vast lake of black waters, the Sharana Nek. There the lands of the Xotic begin.'

'He?' remarked Mareen.

'Yes. Strong, powerful, and not to be trusted,' quipped Shartuk, eliciting a chuckle from Horven and Mareen.

'Ha,' growled Haran, 'females need a strong male to keep them in line, but he who cannot be trusted is worthless.'

'The river does not care, Haran. Whether we live or die is of no consequence to him; but his waters are treacherous to the unwary and they can rise and fall rapidly. If the waters of the Black River were like you, friend Haran, I should spend all my days swimming and fishing in them without fear.'

'Many females have drowned in my waters,' boasted Haran with a grunt, although there was a humorous tone in his words.

Shartuk, Mareen and Horven all laughed at this response.

'I will remember that boast, Haran,' called Kuhltar. 'I am sure that your mate, Fire in Her Eyes, will also find it very funny.'

'Fire knows that I am a braggart, dear sister, so you go right ahead. I look forward to hearing her comments when we return to our range.'

Now the party stepped off the bridge and their pace once again lifted to the tireless jog that the Benshin guides could maintain for chaal after chaal. The path plunged downwards into a deep depression but, whilst the giant ferns and cycads were everywhere, now huge boulders also began to appear. These were overgrown with vivid carpets of a red fungus whilst climbing plants festooned their sides and grew in profusion in the spaces provided by the stony outcrops. The group began to rise out of the depression and the terrain became interspersed with dense patches of forest and rocky outcrops. When they emerged onto higher ground, the mountains ahead loomed larger, their peaks covered in snow which the Benshin tried to describe to the Graavens. The Graavens were fascinated, having seen snow only from a distance, their only knowledge of it being what they had learned from stories. The Benshin regaled them with descriptions of its coldness and traps for the unwary as they jogged along under a clear violet sky.

The day was drawing to a close when they at last stopped in a small clearing surrounded by the cycads and fern trees that had been their constant companions. Here, two Benshin elders stood silently. They bowed low to the Tamut La and their riders, and turned smiling faces on Kexin and Shartuk.

'You are welcome to our village. We apologise for the humbleness of our dwellings, but this is a travelling camp. We of the Thunder Water clan dwell here only during the seasons of regrowth and burgeoning in order that we may gather the medicinal plants and herbs that thrive at this time. Please, make yourselves at home. We have set aside a larger dwelling place for you as our normal shelters would not cater for you. My name is Dermok and this is my life partner, Threnarh,' the male said, indicating a tall female standing alongside him with red hair, strange to Graaven eyes, tied in intricate plaits. 'Welcome, welcome,' she responded with a smile.

Here Dermok and Threnarh opened their arms in the traditional Benshin greeting, and all at once a gaggle of people seemed to appear out of thin air from amongst the trees. Had it not been for this movement, the Graavens would have thought that Dermok was playing a joke as there was no evidence of anything even remotely approaching a village in their immediate vicinity. However, on much closer inspection, they saw that the Benshin dwellings were so cunningly intertwined amongst the trunks of the trees that they seemed to form some kind of natural plant growth. Indeed, as the Graavens soon discovered, the dwelling places of Benshin travelling camps were more "woven" from vines and creepers than they were built of wood or other materials. The cycad and fern trunks acted as the main supports and, like the webs of spiders, the tough vines of the xemak were plaited and secured to form the walls and roofs of the dwellings.

These were fashioned to accommodate the shape and girth of the trees that supported them and so they took a form that, whilst pleasing to the eye, conformed to the shape of their surroundings rather than being fashioned to dominate or stand out from the landscape in which they were built.

Later that evening after they had rested, they joined the Benshin elders and the tribe for a meal where the word "feast" would not have been out of place. Although the fires that were lit were small and contained in ceramic pots out of respect for the forest, there was much laugher and dancing to the playing of flutes and pipes. The food and company were convivial and the music haunting.

'You have still many of your meh'chaal to journey to reach the mountains, my friends,' said Dermok, during a lull in the playing.

'Yes,' agreed Threnarh, 'and you must travel cautiously. In another day or two of travel the forest will begin to thin out. Soon, you may encounter creatures not so friendly, and there has been a whisper of something else. Two of our gatherers have not returned to us and this is worrying. With your permission, our son Churmah,' and here a tall and well-proportioned Benshin stepped forward and nodded his head, 'will accompany you some of the way. He is a canny hunter and if there is trouble then he will bring news of it back to us.'

Menkh nodded his head in reply and noted the ritual scars that were etched into Churmah's features. 'Are you not concerned that Churmah will not return if there is trouble?' queried Menkh.

Churmah, Dermok and Threnarh shared a knowing look and chuckled quietly.

'Our son is a Spirit Tracker of the First Mark. If he does not return, then the danger is such that we are in great peril. No, friend Menkh, our son has all the skills he needs, and he may be of assistance to you also.'

'Then he is welcome indeed.'

'Thank you, Menkh,' said Churmah in a surprisingly deep voice for a Benshin. 'It will be my honour to journey with the Tamut La and my cousins Kexin and Shartuk. If acceptable, we will leave just after dawn. We have far to journey.'

'As you wish,' assented Menkh. So saying, the three Graavens excused themselves and made their way to the accommodations set up for them, the Tamut La having disappeared into the forest for the night. They drifted off to sleep to the sound of Benshin flutes and drums as the villagers continued to dance and sing. The sound was comforting, evoking images of the forest and its inhabitants in the haunting melodies that were played.

The next morning, they arose early and met Churmah by the rebuilt fire. The village was quiet but Dermok and Threnarh joined them over a simple breakfast.

'Safe journeys to you, friends. May the spirits of the forest watch over you and keep you safe,' said Threnarh, presenting each of the Graavens with a small parcel of foodstuffs and other things.

Dermok nodded and, in the Benshin way, reached up to grasp the forearms of each Graaven in farewell. Finally, Churmah, Dermok and Threnarh stood with their arms encircled and chanted a small prayer, calling on their clan Spirits to send Churmah safe home. Without further ado, the Graavens mounted the Tamut La, who had silently returned at the appointed time, even though, as Menkh commented to Crixac, they were nowhere near when the arrangements with Churmah had been made.

'*Yes, it is uncanny,*' mused Crixac. '*If this was the City, I could surmise they had a device of some kind; but here we see some kind of innate ability that defies such easy explanations.*'

'*After the wonders I have seen over recent times, it is just another to add to the pile for me to ponder. Let us see now what the day ahead brings us,*' responded Menkh as, once again, the three Benshin settled into the steady, ground eating jog that they could maintain all day.

CHAPTER THIRTEEN

Two days passed uneventfully. On the early morning of the third day they appeared to be climbing steadily towards the mountain range far ahead. At times, the forest around them appeared to thin out, and then would again become denser in pockets. Lithe and inquisitive creatures of diminutive size, alien to Graaven eyes, with long, black-skinned arms and legs and furry tails which clung like a long finger to the trunks of trees, peered at them, chattering noisily as the Graavens passed by.

'We call these creatures tatha. There are several kinds that roam the forest. They move quickly and have excellent hearing but sometimes their curiosity can lead to danger from predators. They eat mostly fruit and their flesh is quite succulent, but we rarely hunt them unless in great need,' explained Churmah. 'They are intelligent and gentle creatures and cause no harm, so it does not sit easy with us to kill them.'

'Do you care for all the forest creatures in this way?' asked Horven.

'Mostly we look to keep the balance,' replied Churmah, 'but there are some things that we would eradicate if we could. Fortunately, these are few and mostly found a long way from here.'

Now their path led downwards beside a chattering stream of clear water, and small plants grew in profusion. They slowed their pace as they reached a picturesque dell where the water formed a pool of clear water near a small waterfall.

'Let us stop here to rest for a time. We can heat some water and drink tea to refresh ourselves. Soon you will learn why Churmah's clan is called Thunder Water,' said Kexin with a smile.

As they dismounted, Fendrax sniffed the air warily, the fur on her body bristling in alarm, as did that of Haran and Kuhltar.

'Something disturbs this place. It is watching and waiting and means us ill, but I cannot place its scent although my kind have encountered it before. Be wary, it is near,' warned Fendrax.

'Should we not just leave then?' asked Mareen as she hefted her mace in preparation.

'I cannot, friend Mareen,' said Churmah quietly as he fitted an arrow to his bow. 'This may be what I was sent to find. Perhaps here is where my people lost their way. As gatherers they would have been drawn to this place.'

Churmah had no sooner said this when a plaintive call could be heard from amongst the trees that grew around the dell. Here the woods had become thick again and it was somewhat difficult to pinpoint exactly where the voice came from.

'Help us, please help us!' came a plaintive wail. It was clear that there was considerable distress and pain in the timbre of the voice.

Several things happened at once.

Churmah called out, 'I am coming, Nazash, hang on!' and leapt into the trees.

Shartuk and Kexin, similarly disturbed, called out, 'Draachnull, Draachnull, we are here! We will come to you!' and they, too, sped off into the trees, though in a somewhat different direction to Churmah.

Horven and Mareen looked at each other in shock and surprise. 'It is our brother, Zeftah. He is here! Zeftah, Zeftah, we are here, we are coming!' and then they also ran off.

For just a moment, Menkh could swear he heard Pershiva's voice, desperate and in pain. In that moment, all logical thought at the impossibility of this was banished from Menkh's mind and replaced with the single urgent need that he had to help her. Had to save her from her obvious pain and torment.

Around him, the Tamut La howled in anguish and ran around in panicked circles, seemingly without control over themselves.

Then, in an instant, the voice was gone and Crixac's voice echoed in Menkh's head. *'It is an illusion, Menkh. I have put a block into your mind. Whatever is making the call is powerful and means harm to everyone. We must act quickly before actual harm befalls them all. We can follow the sound of the voice. You will not find it so pretty now that I have established the block.'*

'Thank you, Crixac. I have never experienced such a complete loss of thought. I could only react to the sound of the voice, so like Pershiva's.'

Now in its place there was only a shrill and high-pitched cry, like some lost soul calling in torment from the bowels of Xerfun itself.

Gripping his staff and leaving the Tamut La's anguished howling, Menkh sprang into the trees and made in the direction that the sounds emanated from. To his left there was a scream of pain, instantly silenced, evidence that at least one of the company had encountered serious trouble. Menkh's desperation increased as he ploughed through the trees. As he ran, the staff began to glow with a greenish light and Menkh could feel energy surging in the touch of his hands.

Suddenly he burst into a clearing where he was stopped forcibly by an invisible shield which would have winded him had Crixac not interceded. Between two large trees there hung a black form. It rippled like the surface of a pond disturbed by a passing wind.

Strange moaning sounds emanated from it, along with a stench like decomposing flesh. Now he could see Shartuk lying lifeless on the ground immediately before it and slowly, like the viscous flow of liquid mud, her body was being drawn over the ground towards the curtain of blackness. So, too, Horven and Mareen, somewhat farther back, were also being drawn, whilst emerging from the tree line, walking in a trance like state, were Kexin and Churmah, still calling out to the people whose voices they could hear inside their heads.

'*What is this thing, Crixac?*'

'*A creature of legend, Menkh, and one I had supposed long since obliterated. Once, they were common, so it appears that, somewhere, a pod has emerged from out of the slime. Explanations later. Focus the staff, you need to send a bolt at it and sheer the curtain asunder.*'

'*What of the shield that protects it?*'

'*It should not expect any kind of attack from an energy device. Quickly now.*'

Menkh focused his will on the staff and directed a bolt of energy at the writhing curtain. Shartuk's left hand was almost in contact with the veil as the bolt surged out from the staff, ripping through the shield, and leaping across the space between to slice completely through the black mass writhing between the trees.

A screech ensued, so high-pitched that the ears rang painfully as it grew and grew in volume before diminishing to a moan. Crixac had blocked Menkh's ears to protect him from a noise that would otherwise have incapacitated him.

Churmah and Kexin collapsed to the ground, and all of the company lay unconscious. From between the trees emerged a nightmarish creature, black ichor leaking from a savage wound that scored its body.

Black as night, several tentacular arms extended from its torso. It moved, not so much on legs, but as some sort of jelly-like substance that flowed across the ground as it progressed. At nine spahn in height, it exceeded Menkh's stature, and its head contained a huge mouth full of sharp teeth, surmounted by four eyes; two large ones set above two smaller ones. The whole body oozed a black, slimy coating. From its mouth issued sounds that needed no interpretation and it approached Menkh with surprising speed.

Menkh readied the staff once again but before he had time to issue a further surge of power, three tawny shapes burst out of the trees and fell on the creature. In seconds they had torn the thing limb from limb, ripping it to pieces with primordial savagery, the tearing and crushing going on long after the creature was utterly obliterated. Then Fendrax, Haran and Kuhltar urinated on its remains, the strong smell of their bodily fluids almost like perfume after the corrupted stink of the creature.

Fendrax approached Menkh and bowed low. 'Please accept our deepest apologies, friend Menkh. We should all have recognised this filth for what it was, and we were caught unawares, exposing you to much danger. It will not happen again.'

Menkh bowed low to all three Tamut La who hung their heads in shame. 'Amongst friends such apologies are unnecessary. On such a journey danger is to be expected. We are honoured to have the friendship and trust of the Tamut La.'

'You are generous, friend Menkh,' responded Fendrax. 'Let us see to our companions.'

Crixac's voice echoed in Menkh's mind. *'They should be relatively unharmed but will sleep now for many chaal and awake feeling very cold and weak. I fear Shartuk's hand may have contacted the veil. If so, she will need healing.'*

'What was that thing, Crixac?'

'Once, as I said, they were common. The Cities combined their forces to eradicate them long ago but only after they had examined and experimented with them. Obviously, they were not as successful as the archives would have us believe. There is no word for such as they in your tongue. The Kareems called

them the crasmoch vesh, their words for "black veil". These creatures can read thoughts and somehow manipulate the space around them to entice and seduce their prey. Any creature under their influence will perceive the "veil" as something that has meaning to them. Perhaps a loved friend or parent. The power of the crasmoch vesh overrides reality. The fact that a person may have been dead for years, and any other rational thoughts, are overwhelmed. They see only what their heart desires, and once they have pierced the veil they are doomed.'

'What is the veil, what happens when you push through it?'

'You die. Presumably very unpleasantly. This is how the crasmoch vesh feed and, as nobody who has disappeared into the veil has ever returned, we cannot really say what happens. However, the scientists of the Cities were fascinated by the power and abilities these creatures had. Much of the advances they made in later developing the technology to interface with the crystals came from their research and experimentation on these creatures.'

'They are evil indeed,' remarked Menkh.

'Evil?' mused Crixac. 'I think they follow their instincts. They hunt and trap prey and, certainly, the end for any that they trap is unpleasant. But they do not kill indiscriminately, nor do they seek to conquer and subjugate. It is understandable that any sentient creature would perceive them as evil; after all, they are ugly to look at and have no redeeming qualities that alleviate our feelings towards them, so they are an object of fear. But "evil", I am not convinced.'

'Well, you think about that, and in the meantime, I will stick with my instincts in this matter till you convince me otherwise.'

'As you will, my friend. Now, let us look to Shartuk and see what we can do for her.'

While Crixac and Menkh had been holding their internal conversation, they had dragged the sleeping bodies of their companions into a circle with the help of the Tamut La. Shartuk's hand had blackened and the skin had begun to bubble and slough off.

'*We must act quickly, Menkh. Through me you have learned how to use the power of the staff to channel healing energy. We need to do this now to prevent further spread of this infection. If, indeed, that is what it is.*'

Menkh held the staff over the blackened arm and concentrated his thoughts on healing. There were no specific thoughts in his head other than the desire to eradicate the infection and heal Shartuk's arm. The staff, attuned to Menkh and Crixac's combined concentration, responded, emitting a purplish glow and growing warm to the touch. Shartuk tossed fitfully in her unconscious state and groaned aloud but did not waken. In the light that enveloped her arm the blackness appeared to retreat, slowly at first and then with gathering speed, until it had disappeared from view. Menkh grew tired as he strove to maintain his focus and he felt Crixac's power join with his to maintain their combined willpower.

The flesh on Shartuk's arm began to reconstitute itself until the blistering had also disappeared and healthy new skin had formed. Shartuk ceased to move and settled into a deep slumber, her breath now even and deep, and a slight smile formed on her lips.

Finally, Menkh broke off his concentration and staggered upright. Fighting dizziness, he felt weak for a moment, but then new energy swept through him and he recovered quickly. Crixac's voice echoed in his head, '*I have manipulated your metabolism to remove your fatigue. It was a mighty effort, Menkh, and we conjoined forces well in helping Shartuk.*'

Menkh sent out an acknowledgement of thanks and, as his attention once more focused on his surroundings, found he was the object of rapt attention from the three Tamut La.

'It would seem, my children, that we have an Adept in our midst and the old legends come to life before us,' said Fendrax. 'You have given us even more reason to journey with you, friend Menkh. It would seem that momentous events are afoot.'

'I have no understanding of what you speak, but I am glad I was able to help. Tell me, Fendrax, how is it that the Tamut La knew of this thing and that you were able to overcome its call?'

'That is a long story. Suffice to say that the origins of our species lie with those who built the Cities. Yes, Menkh,' said Fendrax in response to the look on Menkh's face, 'we were partly bred to hunt and capture or destroy the crasmoch vesh in the time before times, when our race was newly formed. It has been many generations since the last was hunted down and destroyed – or so we wrongly thought. Our minds are immune to their call, but they are capable of stunning us if we are not prepared for their scream. It is fortunate that you were able to unleash your power as this gave us the time to break its hold and come to your aid. We shall not be caught unawares again.'

Several chaal later, after healing sleep and a meal, there was a general discussion of what had occurred, and the travellers made ready to set off once more.

'Now that you have discovered the source of your missing people, I am sorry, Churmah. It would seem that your gatherers perished most unpleasantly. How will the Benshin hunt down any others, knowing the power they have?'

'As to that, friend Menkh, I and my children will aid the Benshin in this task. These creatures cannot be allowed to spread. With our help we can eradicate any threat.'

The three Benshin bowed their heads and gave the Tamut La their thanks, leaving the details to be discussed later. Having reached this conclusion, they packed up their temporary camp and set off once again, more wary then before. After several chaal of steady progress, Churmah turned to the Graavens. 'Soon we will reach the chief village of the Thunder Water clan,' he said. 'Even now you can begin to hear the call of the waters and you will see something that few outside the Benshin have ever seen.'

As they travelled further, they could feel a slowly intensifying vibration through the earth beneath their feet and a persistent sound, like a distant drone, amplified until they had to speak in a loud voice to make themselves heard. Eventually they largely abandoned speech, so great was the noise. Finally, they emerged from dense woods into a clearing. Abruptly before them the land fell away into a maelstrom of rushing water, churning in such fury that the volume of sound deadened the senses with its fierceness.

Above them and extending for as far as they could see to left and right, a huge cliff wall towered, its heights lost in a mighty spume of water vapour. Water fell in torrents down what appeared to be hundreds of cataracts. It was altogether an astonishing and breathtaking sight. Churmah turned to them and spread his arms wide whilst nodding his head. No words were necessary as Chaptosi Gem Hallach, the Thunder Water Falls, delivered millions of gallons of water every moment into the torrent beneath, that swept in a flood through a chasm that defied any living creature's ability to cross.

Churmah pointed downstream, indicating that they should move that way, and they set off, following the waters as they rushed downwards. All of them became drenched from the spray and spume that filled the air. After one chaal had passed, travelling downstream at the steady pace set by their Benshin guides, the noise of the falls had diminished to a level where a conversation could be heard, albeit in a louder voice than one might otherwise employ.

Churmah indicated a halt and, turning to the group, said, 'The main village of the Thunder Water clan lies a half-day further south. I propose we push on till we reach them, and we can then rest and recuperate fully.'

Menkh and the others indicated acceptance, and so they continued. The breadth of the waters had widened considerably, and this allowed for somewhat calmer conditions, although they still flowed at a pace that even the Tamut La would have trouble maintaining.

The banks of the river were relatively flat, and they walked over rock that had worn smooth with the passage of time. Once again, dense forest drew close by and Menkh noticed that the trees here were changing from the ferns and cycads to others that were strange to Graaven eyes. These had long limbs and leaves and in places reared up to impressive heights. The understorey was filled with smaller ferns that preferred the dappled light that came through the canopy.

Small creatures with smooth skin and long limbs, resembling the tatha they had seen earlier, could be seen sitting on branches or swinging from tree to tree with alacrity. A constant chatter of noise could be heard, and it was obvious that the party was a thing of interest to them from the inquisitive looks they received as they drew closer.

'These we call semak, cousins to the tatha,' remarked Kexin. 'They are harmless creatures and can make good pets. They are very curious and are particularly drawn to bright coloured things.'

'Have the Benshin ever hunted them?' asked Horven.

'Perhaps once, but no longer. They are not good eating because when frightened they emit a terrible odour that permeates everything. Besides, they are easily trapped and defenceless, other than their smell, and the Benshin have long considered them to be friends. They have intimate knowledge of the forest and can be followed, with care, to where fruits and berries can be found in abundance.'

The time passed in conversation with the Benshin acquainting the Graavens with stories of their peoples and the different clans and tribes that inhabited the area.

So it was that with the mighty roar of the waters behind them, they drew near the chief village of the Thunder Water clan. Here, the flat, rocky ground that ran alongside the banks of the river they had followed extended further still, and the forest drew well back. Unlike their forest-dwelling cousins, the Shadow Hunter and Smoke clans, the people of the Thunder Water dwelt inside buildings cunningly constructed from easily located river rock and driftwood. Menkh saw that the village sat on high ground, several persangh from the river. Here the river formed a sharp bend which allowed for the collection of rocks and small boulders, as well as timber that had been carried downstream in the torrent of water.

A welcoming party stood on the pathway that led to the village proper and, as they drew closer, they could see that it consisted of an imposing-looking man and woman clad in capes that shimmered silver in the rosy twilight and appeared to resemble the skin of a fish. Surrounding them were several males and females, dressed in cured hides intricately embroidered with coloured beads and leaning on long spears which had pronged tips.

They came to a stop some few spahn away as both the man and woman raised their arms and spoke in singsong voices together, 'Kethra and Penash of the Thunder Water clan bid you welcome to our village. You, our cousins, and also you, friends of the Benshin. Honours to you and to the Tamut La who accompany you. The Thunder Water clan bids you enter and be rested.'

The eyes of the party turned to Menkh, who dismounted from Fendrax. Bowing to the two clan elders he responded, 'On behalf of all our party, I thank you. My name is Menkh and these of my people are Mareen and Horven. The others you know. We are pleased to be in the lands of the Thunder Water clan. We thank you for your hospitality and generosity in welcoming strangers.'

Kethra and Penash smiled and spoke in unison again, 'Well-spoken, friend Menkh; however, word of your deeds in assisting our people precedes you. We welcome you as friends. As to our hospitality and generosity, this is a mark of all Benshin, so you would have experienced with our cousins here with you. Come, enter in peace and judge for yourselves the depth of our welcome.'

The village itself, as Menkh later discovered, was located at a midpoint between the waters of the river and the shores of the mighty lake, which the waters fed as they swept around the bend. It contained some fifty dwellings, with the most imposing being the meeting hall where the Benshin gathered for meals and storytelling. The whole was surrounded by a wall of rocks, some nine spahn high, that encircled it.

Over the course of the next few days the party was treated well and made to feel very welcome. The Thunder Water clan were expert fishers, and the three Graavens accompanied them on a fishing trip to the great lake, known by the Shadow Hunters as the Sharana Nek and by the Thunder Water as Tekla Xemik, or Mother Water, where the waters of the Sharana collected after their tumultuous journey from the falls. Here they hunted and caught giant pettak, a huge fish known for its tough and resilient skin and delicious, meaty flesh. Catching one was no mean feat and required highly refined cooperation between several groups.

The Thunder Water clan built huge canoes utilising the skins of the giant fish which were used to cover a skilfully-constructed wooden framework – light, but strong and flexible. Harpoons made of fire-hardened wood with metal tips, for which they traded with the Shadow Hunter clan, were attached to sturdy ropes made of keffler vines. By means perfected over generations, the pettak were lured into shallow water, harpooned, and dragged onto the shoreline. However practised the Benshin were, a thirty-spahn-long pettak could smash a canoe to fragments, and death and severe injury were not uncommon. Once out of the water, the pettak quickly suffocated, but the Graavens were impressed at the military efficiency of the clan people both on the shore and in several canoes on the water.

Later, over a feast celebrating the latest kill, Dthar, one of the clan's fishermen, relayed a story that had become the stuff of legend. After downing a third beaker of brandy, Dthar spoke to the three Graavens and their Benshin travelling companions. 'One day, several years ago, I was in a canoe with some twelve others. We had harpooned a real monster, some forty spahn in length.'

'That's five spahn more than the last time you told the tale!' interjected another.

Dthar sat taller and in a dignified tone said, 'Ignore my sister Eclona. She is obviously addled and jealous of my fame.'

There was general hilarity to this response.

With a sharp look at the laughing Benshin, he continued, 'As I was saying, this fish was at least fifty spahn long. Suddenly, despite the fact that he was pierced by several harpoons, it appeared that only the harpoon from our canoe had retained its rope. Before any of us could move, the fish had turned and swept back out into deeper waters.'

'You should have seen it, friend Menkh,' interjected Eclona. 'They moved off like a storm wind, towed by the pettak. We all thought we had seen the last of them. No-one has ever returned from the deep waters.'

'So, this happens a lot?' queried Horven.

'Often enough to know the danger. Usually we all jump out and swim back to shore; but not Dthar and his friends. We laugh now, but it was a great sadness in our hearts then.'

Dthar leant forward and put his arm on Horven's shoulders. 'It was a new canoe that we had built ourselves and we were loath to let Tekla Xemik have it for her own. So, for three days and nights the creature swam, with us towed behind. We cannot know why it did not swim down into the depths of the waters, as that would have been our undoing. Perhaps our harpoon had rendered it incapable. But, however it was, on the third day we noticed that the creature had swept in a great circle and was towing us back to the very spot where we had harpooned him before.'

'It was the hand of the spirits,' said Eclona gravely, to much head nodding in agreement. 'One of the children playing on the shore saw them and ran back to tell us. We all ran back to stand and watch.'

'We saw them from the canoe,' said Dthar. 'Without pause, the creature ran aground right in front of them, and there died, with us still in the canoe.'

'To this day,' said Eclona, 'we celebrate their return and give thanks to the spirits for watching over them. Now the skin of that creature forms the hull of our largest canoe, but we only use it on special occasions and during our thanksgiving ceremony. My stupid brother,' and here Eclona placed an affectionate hand on Dthar's knee, 'and his friends who were with him are great and legendary heroes and favoured by the spirits.'

'This is true,' responded Dthar, 'but, my friends, you should know that other than standing on the beach and helping drag the catch in I have not hunted from a canoe since. One does not tempt the favour of the spirits too often,' and, nodding his head gravely, took another gulp of brandy whilst simultaneously falling backwards into a deep slumber.

This was accompanied by a chorus of laughter and general raising of gourds and beakers to the now comatose form of Dthar.

So, for several days the travellers prevailed on the hospitality of the Thunder Water clan. On the fifth day a council was held to discuss the journey and how best the people of the Thunder Water might assist the Graavens in their quest.

They met in the large communal building set aside for weighty deliberations, and the senior members of the clan were present, along with all the travellers and their Benshin guides. Such was the size of the building that Fendrax also sat within to listen to what was said. The people had grown accustomed to the comings and goings of the Tamut La over previous days and their initial awe had subsided, though they were still greeted with a degree of reverence by all the clan's people.

Kethra spoke to those assembled in a quiet voice which,

nevertheless, carried to all who sat within. 'The Benshin will aid your quest as best we are able, but now your path lies further westward. The mountains loom larger now but are still many days' travel distant. Your best path lies across the waters of the lake. To journey around it will take many weeks but our people can safely carry you across,' here he paused and bowed his head deeply towards Fendrax. 'That is to say, we can convey Menkh, Mareen and Horven, our Graaven friends who, whilst taller than the tallest Benshin, may yet ride safely. The majesty of the Tamut La could never be conveyed within our canoes and here we have a dilemma. I trust that I have offered no offence to you, Fendrax.'

Fendrax lifted her head and fixed Kethra with her green eyes. 'No offence is taken, Kethra of the Thunder Water clan. You only speak what is true and, in any event, neither I nor any of my kin will travel over deep water.'

Here Fendrax turned her eyes on Menkh. 'For a time, friend Menkh, we must part company. It is in our mind that we will now return with Churmah to aid his clan in routing out the crasmoch vesh. As we discussed, they are a danger to all who journey within the forest and only we, the Tamut La, have the means to effect their eradication.'

Here Churmah stood respectfully to address the group. 'It has been a good trail with you all. I must return now and warn my clan of the danger. I hope that we may not encounter another of these crasmoch vesh but at the least we will know what we deal with. It warms my heart that the mighty Tamut La will aid us in this. I speak the truth when I say that I could not think of a way that we Benshin alone might hunt these creatures.'

Shartuk and Kexin also rose and bowed to the three Graavens and the assembled elders as Shartuk spoke, 'We, too, must return to our clan to spread the word. We are now come to the ends of the Benshin lands and our friends venture into lands beyond the knowing of the Smoke, Lightning, and Shadow Hunter clans. We send a voice in four directions and to Varthansh Mek, that they return safely to our lands where what is our is also theirs.' So saying, they bowed low and resumed their place.

'So, friend Menkh, we see there are many partings, what say you to the words you have heard?' asked Kethra.

Menkh stood slowly and looked around the room before speaking. 'The Benshin are a people with honour and courage. We Graavens have been truly blessed to have gained the friendship of the Smoke, Thunder Water, Shadow Hunter, and Lightning clans. We could not have come this far on our quest without their help and that of our mighty companions, the Tamut La. Our quest leads us to strange lands beyond our knowing. The counsel of Kethra seems wise, and we accept the offer to travel across the lake. My heart tells me that we draw near to reaching our goal and we, too, hope to return to you, our friends, in the time to come. We are sad that our travelling companions must return to their peoples, but we thank them for their guidance and wisdom.'

Here, Menkh bowed, as did Mareen and Horven, before sitting quietly.

Fendrax turned her head towards Menkh. 'Our journey together does not end here. We will await your returning and give you our aid in that future time. The blessings of the Tamut La also go with you, Menkh ab Dur. We sense a shifting in the Balance, and much is yet to come, though for good or ill we cannot yet tell.'

Churmah then stood and said his farewells, along with Shartuk and Kexin. Bowing to the Tamut La, they took the hands of each member of the party in the way of the Benshin and made promises to look out for the Graavens' return.

Penash clapped her hands together. 'So, a parting has been agreed. In two days, then, we will prepare two canoes to take our friends safely across the Mother Water.'

She spoke then directly to the Graavens. 'The journey will take five days, five of your meh'chaal, as you say it. There are some islands on the way which the Thunder Water know and use when the Mother becomes too rough for safe passage. Once there you enter the lands of the Xotic, the People of the Wind. We trade with them for ivory and seeds and they covet the fish hides which we use for our canoes, though they use them for a different purpose, as you will no doubt see.' Here Penash and Kethra exchanged a knowing look. 'Their lands are vast. Great, grassy plains upon which they travel. Though they are not unfriendly they are wary of strangers. It is our hope that they will see you across the plains where you may journey up into the mountains.'

Later that night after the council had finished deliberations and all were resting, Menkh turned his thoughts to Crixac. *'You have been very quiet of late, my friend,'* said Menkh in the quiet of his mind.

'I had not much to say or tell you after our encounter. This is all new to me as well. The city archives have little to say about the Benshin, or any humanoids for that matter, and much has changed since the time they were written. Like you, I feel drawn to the mountains that lay to the west. In my view, the Balance draws us on. We are now so distant from the City that the crystal shards we carry should have lost their power; yet, they have not. Why then? Does this mean that we move toward a greater source of power?'

'We can both only surmise, Crixac. It has been several dak'chaal since I tried to communicate with the City and Tishan Dar. I think I shall try this now before we cross the lake.'

So saying, Menkh sat up from the pallet on which he lay and, taking up his staff, focused his mind on Tishan Dar. He felt Crixac's mind bond with his own and his concentration multiplied. There was a sensation of lightness in his head and a swirl of colours across his vision, and suddenly Menkh felt himself standing in a room. He could see Tishan sitting, drinking something hot out of a cup she held, and her attention was drawn to a window that looked out over the city. As the vision grew into focus and gained deeper clarity, Tishan sat up straighter and turned around. First her eyes widened, and then a smile broke out. 'Menkh, you are alive! I felt that it was so, but it has been long since you communicated. Is all well?'

'I am so sorry, Tishan. Much has happened, as you can imagine, and there are many strange and wondrous things to tell you.'

Menkh and Tishan spoke for a long time, exchanging news and asking and answering many questions. Menkh learned that all was well in the city. Trade with their Benshin friends was now firmly established and the Graaven people had adapted wonderfully to the City. New fields had been planted and fruit trees and other edible plants propagated ready for planting.

'What of our offspring?' asked Menkh at the last, though they were not least in his thoughts.

'All is well, Menkh. The eggs have grown in size and I can sense a growing presence within each. There is much excitement amongst the people. The time for the first of our new hatchlings to break free is fast approaching. Truly, this will bring renewed hope to all of us here.'

'New life and a new beginning,' said Menkh. 'Let us hope my journey will also deliver a new beginning for the City.'

They spoke for a time more and then, saying farewell, Menkh broke the connection.

'I should have done that a long time ago, Crixac, I am remiss. It is a great comfort to know that all is well at home.'

'Home, friend Menkh? Truly, are you becoming a citizen of the City?'

'The Empire and all that we have lost sits heavy in my mind, Crixac. But it is the City and you that have given all of us a new beginning.'

'Yes, for me also,' replied Crixac, *'and I admit to a sensation of excitement and anticipation for the next phase of our quest. There is nothing like spending a thousand years in one place to give you an appetite for travel!'*

Menkh's laughter reverberated in his head. *'Well, then. Let us rest this body of ours and be refreshed for the coming journey.'*

CHAPTER FOURTEEN

The Graavens used the following day to prepare for the next phase of their travels. The suits that the City had fashioned for each of them were a thing of wonder. They showed no signs of wear or damage and were as clean now as the day they were put on. Unlike the traditional fighting garb of the Graavens, after days of continuous wear their skin under the armour was not covered in sweat and there was little odour. They were relatively easy to take off, with minimum assistance required from others in the party, and the more they used them the more comfortable they became to wear.

They had had little opportunity or need to place the helmets on their heads. The incident with the crasmoch vesh had happened so quickly that there had been no thought of wearing them and the Graavens speculated as to the outcome, had they been wearing them when the attack occurred. Whilst they, too, were far from uncomfortable when worn, their visage was so alien to the Benshin that they felt it would have been both rude and unsettling to wear them. Now, before the journey recommenced, they had removed themselves somewhat from the village and had each donned them in order to refine their use.

They had already noticed that, unlike conventional Graaven helmets, their City-made helmets did not restrict their view. An internal array displayed both forward and behind. The wearer had only to focus on a particular object or location to find that their view was rapidly magnified to an amazing degree. Their ability to communicate with each other was also enhanced. One had only to speak aloud to have their voices heard inside the helmets of the others. They had not been in a position as yet to see if there was a limit in how far they could be separated to hear each other. Twenty semmits of steady jogging in three separate directions had not affected the capacity of the helmets to convey and receive their vocal contact, and they also discovered that the helmets could magnify a sound, in much the same way as it could focus the user's vision. Focusing intently on a particular sound resulted in that sound becoming filtered and thus heard with greater clarity by the wearer.

'I can think of a number of situations in the past where this helmet would have saved me from some cuts and bruises or enemies creeping up behind me,' remarked Mareen into her helmet.

Menkh and Horven indicated their agreement. 'An army fitted with our suits, helmets and weaponry would be most difficult to vanquish, if not impossible,' agreed Horven.

So the day was spent in preparation for leaving. The Thunder Water clan prepared a farewell celebration and there was much merriment in their final evening with the clan's people. In the morning, many Benshin walked with the Graavens to the lake and gathered on its shore to see them off.

Kethra and Penash raised their arms in ritual farewell whilst the people chanted a blessing that their journey over the water be safe. Clasping hands with the tribal elders, the three Graavens climbed into the two canoes that had been prepared and were then pushed off by the willing hands of the people on the shore. Each canoe was manned by six paddlers who, with lusty strokes, pivoted the canoes and then headed off in a westerly direction. The morning was still and the waters of the Mother calm as the paddles bit and the shore slowly dwindled.

The Thunder Water clan paddlers laughed and chatted and told the Graavens many stories about the lake. Their first stop, as the Graavens found out, was a large island a day's journey away. Once a small breeze had risen, each canoe raised a short pole to which was attached a modest sail, cunningly fashioned from woven grasses. The sails caught the breeze which propelled the canoes comfortably, leaving the rowers free to rest, but for the one who used their paddle as a rudder to keep them on course.

So it was that this pattern continued throughout their days of travel on the lake. Each of the islands rose abruptly from the water, rocky outcrops covered in low vegetation with small shingle beaches where they camped during the nights. Only on the fifth day, as they neared the opposite shore, did the wind begin to mount and the waters of the lake began to swell. Fortunately, they were not far from their final landfall and the large bay they entered had a calming effect, so that the wind pushed them towards the shore until they were able to furl the sail and the paddlers resumed their steady stroking.

As the shore grew closer, they could see that it was composed mainly of shingle and the Graavens could see some small buildings set up a short walk from the waterline. From their limited view, the landscape had changed, and they had glimpses of the grassy plains which the Benshin had told them were a feature of the lands of the Xotic.

Finally reaching the shore safely, they climbed out of the canoes and made their way to the buildings they had seen as they approached. On closer inspection, the buildings appeared to be temporary and formed from panels of woven grass that could easily be disassembled. Manchek, the senior member of the

Thunder Water clan rowers, remarked, 'These are common. When the waters rise after storms the building can easily be relocated, but they are snug and dry and only the fiercest storms pose any threat.'

The Thunder Water clan had carried with them several tightly-bound roles of fish hides and arrow heads for trade. 'We shall light a signal fire and let the Xotic know that we are here to trade. There are always some Xotic camped nearby for such a purpose, even though they are a nomadic people for the most part,' commented Durtan, another of the Thunder Clan paddlers. So it was that they built a large signal fire on the beach using green plants to ensure much smoke, and they waited for the arrival of the Xotic.

During this time, the Graavens ventured some way inland from the shore. Here they could see vast, flat grasslands stretching out before them. In the distance they could see a herd of grazing animals and, using their helmets, were amazed at the visual clarity these provided. The creatures, which could barely be seen with the naked eye, were brought into sharp relief. They had long, shaggy coats of hair which mirrored the colour of the grasses around them. On their heads could be seen a huge spread of flaring horns and long, whip-like tails flicked occasionally over their rear ends, which were much more compact than their heavily muscled forelimbs.

'We must ask Manchek what these animals are called,' remarked Menkh into his helmet. 'They look placid enough, but I wouldn't want to be cornered by one.'

Something had disturbed their grazing, as they turned their attention towards where the Graavens stood. Standing motionless for some seconds, they suddenly turned as one and moved rapidly off, deeper into the grasslands, till they disappeared even from the enhanced view of the helmets.

A steady wind blew across the long grasses making them bend and weave, and it was Mareen that first noticed something that was rapidly approaching from out of the south of where they stood. When they turned their eyes towards this, they were all amazed at what they saw. Glinting with a silver sheen in the light of the suns, a strange-looking vehicle approached them, seemingly propelled over the grasslands by the aid of a large silvery sail. The sail billowed in the wind and pushed the vehicle, which had six large, spoked wheels, over the ground with considerable speed. The main body of the vessel was suspended on ropes tied to an outer wooden frame that housed the wheels. The frame also supported the mast with a tracery of ropes, later proving to be plaited from tough and fibrous reeds which grew on the shores of the lake. The sail, fashioned from pettak skin traded with the Benshin, was carried on a spar which was cunningly held aloft on the mast. The body of the craft, being thus suspended, was able to absorb much of the bouncing and jarring that the wheels encountered as they traversed the ground, so that those travelling within it were not unduly thrown about. The ride resembled a voyage over water more than across hard ground.

Several of the Xotic could be seen clambering over the outer frame adjusting ropes, quickly lowering the sail as the craft slowly trundled to a stop near where the amazed Graavens stood. The top of the wooden frame stood some twenty spahn above their heads, with the six elaborately carved wheels also reaching to that height. The inner part of the vehicle resembled nothing so much as a huge canoe, the frame of which, as the Graavens later learned, was fashioned from the bones of huge flying raptors, light but incredibly strong. The hides of animals, cunningly sewn together, were stretched over the entire frame. Altogether, the vehicle was a feat of great craftsmanship and cunning engineering. Even Crixac was impressed with the ingenuity of the vehicle.

A rope ladder was dropped down the side and the Xotic crew began to descend. They were a strikingly different race from the Benshin. Whilst their height was nearly a match for the Graavens, they appeared skeletally thin with long, tapering fingers and feet that were split into two long toes that proved to have remarkable dexterity.

Two large and intelligent eyes with enormous pupils of a mauve colour sat above a virtually noseless face, atop a mouth that lacked teeth, having instead bony plates. Large, fleshy ears drooped somewhat over a long neck and the Xotic looked up warily at the Graavens.

The Benshin held two hands up, palm out, in a gesture of greeting and spoke in a strange patois that contained hissing sounds and the odd grunt.

The crystal gems rapidly assimilated the speech patterns and what at first had been an unintelligible babble rapidly became clear.

'Greetings, Shashn of the Xotic. The Benshin once again come to trade and have brought our friends, Menkh, Mareen, and Horven with us, who seek to travel across Xotic lands. The Benshin speak for them and will stand surety that they, too, come in peace.'

Shashn turned his gaze upon the three Graavens. 'Never have we of the Xotic seen any being as tall as our people. These are strange times, but,' and here Shashn smiled, revealing reddish-coloured gums, 'a friend of the Benshin is welcome to travel our lands in peace.'

The three Graavens bowed to the Xotic leader. 'We thank Shashn of the Xotic and confirm that we come in friendship. But,' and here he quickly glanced at his two companions, 'my friends and I have never seen such a magnificent vehicle as the Xotic possess. We have no words to describe it and stand in awe of your peoples' ingenuity.'

No sooner had Menkh begun to speak than the Xotic also exchanged surprised looks and words. 'Your words are gracious, Menkh. But never have we met strangers like you who could speak our language so well. Even our Benshin friends can only manage an approximation. We look forward to exchanging stories with you, for your appearance is as strange and fascinating to us as ours is to you.'

The Benshin had understood the gist of what was said. 'Well, you are certainly full of wondrous surprise, friend Menkh,' said Manchek, somewhat wistfully. 'You speak their language yet have never seen them before. Truly, you have a powerful magic about you, and it is as well that we are all friends.'

'You need never have any fear on that score, friend Manchek, if it worries you,' replied Menkh. 'The Graaven people honour their friends and your people have shown us nothing but kindness and an open heart.'

Manchek nodded, whilst Shashn looked on curiously. 'Come,' he said, 'what have the Thunder Water clan brought for us to trade? On board we have ochre in five colours and bags of hemmish seeds, ready for planting.'

So it was that the parties later sat around a large fire, sharing tek beer and gourds of clshmik, a Xotic beverage made from the petals of a grassland flower, fermented in the sticky sap of that same reed which grew along the shores of the many lakes that dotted Xotic lands.

'Yes,' remarked Shashn to a question from Mareen, 'Xotic lands are flat, yet clean water flows to the surface from underground streams. Our grasslands support many herds of animals, from giant lizards and the raptors that prey on them to herds of smaller grazing beasts covered with hair and fur. The horned creatures you saw we call tran. They are generally quite docile but are unpredictable during their mating time. Then it is wise to give them a wide berth.'

The Benshin and Xotic had satisfactorily concluded their trading by the next morning and the Benshin bade farewell to their Graaven friends, bidding them a safe and speedy journey as they climbed aboard the canoes. The three Graavens stood on the shore with the Xotic as the Benshin slowly disappeared, with a last wave from the paddles which they held up in the air.

'Come, friends. Now you will see what it is like to ride across the plains and I think you will find that it compares to riding on the backs of the Tamut La that you told us about. I, for one, would like to experience that myself. Like you, they are creatures of wonder and legend, or so our friends the Benshin tell us,' and he laughed good naturedly.

Turning, they followed Shashn up the ladder and on to the outer frame of the Xotic craft. Now at closer inspection they could see that the canoe-like section of the "ship" was suspended on thick straps made of cured hide which allowed it to move freely, absorbing the impact from uneven ground. A cover, also made of the skin of the pettak, could be stretched over the centre section and tied down on the outer frame when it rained. Located forward on the outer frame was a lever which allowed the front two wheels to be steered and above each wheel there was another lever which could apply a brake when required. The sail could quickly be lowered and raised and most of the time, as Shashn explained, the Xotic were able to lower the sail and cruise to a slow stop. Large, lightweight frames extended out from the sides of the vessel. Here the Xotic could clamber out over the woven inner matting and lean their bodies to counterbalance the power of the sail whenever necessary.

There were eight male and female Xotic crew members who, with practised efficiency, loaded and stowed the trade goods, drew up the ladder and took their appointed stations, ready to assist with the passage of the ship.

'The Xotic word for this craft is poctech. It is the most common land sailer we Xotic use and has room for up to twelve of our people. The Xotic travel the Great Plain in family groups, although every year we gather together in a great festival where marriages take place and there is much storytelling and renewal of friendship. Here we hold our Courts, too, and punishment is dealt out by our elders.'

'So, you are hunters then?' asked Mareen.

'Yes, but we also plant crops. Our staple food is the vorux, a plant which we grind for flour and which we use for many other purposes. It is quite slow growing, so every year different families take it in turns to watch over their growth whilst others follow the sacred routes and hunt. We have settlements scattered across the plains, but no Xotic likes to stay in one place for too long. So, our lives are spent partly living in the settlements when it is our turn to watch, and then in our vessels traversing the plains. It is a good existence.'

'How vast are these plains that we are set upon?' enquired Horven.

Shashn laughed. 'If we set our course to the east and did not stop for a moment, and if the wind never failed, it would take many hundreds of days to reach the edge of the plains. To the west we are bounded by the Mother Water and the lands of the Benshin. To the north the mountains lift up from out of the plain and before you reach their mighty shoulders you will enter a land of foothills, where our craft cannot go. Far to the south lies a great water that stretches from horizon to horizon. I have never seen it, though I have travelled many days to the south. No Xotic sets foot on open water.'

'Why is that?' asked Menkh.

'It has always been so. We prize the great skins that we trade for with the Benshin, but we dare not travel as the Benshin do. To us it is kocharlin. I do not think your people would have a word that means what this does to the Xotic. I have no words to explain it to you, suffice to say that a Xotic would rather die first.'

Now the Xotic crew lifted the sail and the vessel began to move off, slowly at first and then with increasing speed in the fresh breeze.

'Do the winds always blow across the plains?' asked Horven, as she looked at the sail bellying and straining against the ropes that held it.

'Always,' replied Shashn. 'Sometimes the merest breath and sometimes with great force, but unceasing. Xotic in our tongue means "People of the Wind" and we have ever used its power. Now, my friends, we will journey north towards my home settlement and there we will talk about your journey to the mountains. We can carry you into the foothills but no further. From there you will be on your own devices. But, I warn you, we Xotic feel almost the same about the mountains to the north as we do about open water. There is something about them that makes my skin shudder, although perhaps it will be different for you.'

Leaving Shashn near the steering bar watching their passage forward they accompanied a Xotic, who Shashn identified as his daughter Tlkcha, to the canoe-like section. Slightly shorter than her father, she had softer, more rounded features. Two breasts, somewhat hidden behind an ornately woven chest piece of startling colours and design, were an object of fascination for Horven and Mareen. Graaven females did not suckle their young and so lacked the breasts that typified Benshin and Xotic females. As the Benshin females wore clothing all the time and were covered from observation, Tlkcha's garb provided Horven and Mareen the opportunity to look more closely – if surreptitiously, for fear of giving offence – and they exchanged looks with raised eyebrows.

Using a small bridge made of plaited vines with side supports that swayed with the motion of the vessel, they crossed over the suspended canoe. A deck was fashioned from woven mats, made from the tall stems of the vorux plant, set above a cunningly constructed framework of flying raptor bones.

Tlkcha bade them sit on cushions upon the deck and disappeared down a set of steps leading below, returning with a gourd and some carved wooden cups.

'May I offer you some hrotha?' she asked. 'It is something like the tek beer that the Benshin make but ours is made from fermented vorux sap. It is quite refreshing.'

'Thank you, Tlkcha, we would be pleased to drink with you,' replied Menkh.

She filled three cups and passed them out, finally pouring herself one. Dipping her head to the Graavens, she took a sip and smiled at them.

Menkh sniffed his cup curiously. The aroma that met his nostrils was something akin to the smell of damp earth following a rainstorm after the ground had been parched for a while. Tasting it, the flavour was unusual; not unpleasant, but unlike anything he had tasted before. Swallowing the liquid, it left a lingering aftertaste that reminded him sharply of the golden wine of Lazmark Province, a taste that brought back many memories.

He smiled, 'Thank you, Tlkcha, it does not remind me so much of tek beer as it does a particular wine of my homeland which, until now, I had not thought to taste again.'

Tlkcha sat up straighter and in a direct voice enquired, 'Then perhaps we might trade it with you in time to come?'

Horven and Mareen nodded in agreement. 'That is a good suggestion to consider,' said Horven and Tlkcha topped up their cups as they began to ask questions about the Xotic and were asked questions in return.

They traversed the plain with a steady pace that ate up the miles. For the next three meh'chaal they travelled with the Xotic and talked with the crew who, by marriage or blood, were all related. As Shashn had told them, the wind blew steadily, sometimes just a small breath that barely moved the poctech and at other times and most often, a steady breeze. They passed great herds of grazing animals who seemed unperturbed at the passing of the Xotic craft, other than to look curiously upwards or draw back with some degree of alarm if they came too close.

Shashn or Tlkcha and others of the Xotic would point to different animals and give them their names in the Xotic tongue. They varied from the horned, four-legged creatures they had seen from afar near the lake shore, which the Benshin had called mursk vek, to reptilian-like two-legged animals with smooth, yellowish-coloured hides who ran with great speed over the plains.

They stopped in the early evening of each day to light fires and cook a meal on the ground but slept aboard the craft. Watches alternated to replenish the fires they kept burning throughout the night against nocturnal predators. As Shashn remarked to them, 'We avoid travelling at night unless it is particularly bright and there is a strong need. We Xotic have spent generations following the same wind paths and we can navigate by the stars, but going too far off the paths can lead to serious accidents and in the dark it is easy to lose one's way.'

On the third day Tlkcha spoke to them. 'One more camp tonight and, with the wind staying steady, we will reach our village by mid-morning.'

The wind during the day freshened and in the late afternoon they sailed right through a herd of grazing deer-like animals. They raised long snouts, and large, delicate nostrils tested the air as they passed by. Their coats were a dappled red and white and they had long, powerful legs that enabled them to see above the grasses that grew so prolifically around them. The poctech sat well above the tallest of the herd who moved out the way with alacrity as they sailed by, but without any strong sense of alarm.

'These we call kakesh. They are beautifully made creatures who can run like the wind when startled but they are quite used to us passing by. Their flesh is delicate and tender and, if needed, we will pick off herd members who are somewhat removed from the main body. That way, they do not become overly frightened. Although if we were to stop and move amongst them they would rapidly disappear, it has always been the case that the appearance of our craft do not alarm them overmuch.'

'They must see this craft as some kind of lumbering creature that offers no particular threat,' remarked Horven to Mareen as they stood near the steering arm on the outer frame. It was fascinating to stand and watch as they sped over the ground but if there was a path, as the Xotic claimed, it was only visible to Xotic eyes as they journeyed on.

On the evening of the third night their slumber was disturbed by Tlkcha shaking them awake and placing a long finger across her lips to indicate silence. A strong breeze was blowing around them and the sighing of the wind in the grass masked any noise they made. The Xotic moved as quietly as possible, releasing brake levers, drawing up ladders, and loosening ropes ready to lift the sail. Out in the night, beyond the light of the fire, a coughing grunt could be heard, answered by another further away.

Barask and Orvasne hung in the sky, giving off a silvery light that provided some vision of the area immediately surrounding them, but no clear definition.

'Prepare yourselves,' said Tlkcha, 'we will attempt to move away at speed. You can hear the calls of gravosh as they hunt. It is likely they stalk the herd we passed through today sleeping nearby; but it is also likely that we could get caught up in the middle of it all.' Leaving them, she moved off to help her fellow Xotic finish preparation for leaving.

'What is our best position, Menkh?' asked Mareen.

'Here, out of the way. Once we are moving, we may be able to move to the outer frame but for now, we sit and wait.'

Again, a coughing grunt was heard, and sharp eyes could discern some stealthy movement at the extreme limit of vision in the moonlight. For now, the gravosh were staying clear of the watch fires.

Suddenly Shahsn's voice called out, 'Up sail!'

With practised and sure movements, the sail seemed to leap up the mast, and the poctech went from stationary to rapid forward motion in the blink of an eye. The sudden sound of Shahsn's voice had alarmed both the predators and their prey out on the plain. As they sped by the place where they had discerned movement, a huge, tawny form leapt out, trying to catch hold of the vessel. The spinning wheels threw it down and by the time the creature had recovered, they had swept on.

Grunting roars could be heard behind them as the gravosh regrouped and ran in the direction of the startled herd which was racing off in the same direction that the Xotic fled.

Now the danger from the predators was replaced by the stampeding herd as the poctech careered through the frightened animals. The vessel lurched as dozens of bodies banged into its sides or were crushed under its wheels. When this happened, there was a mighty crash as the wheels ran over the bodies and the craft lurched heavily. Still, the frame held. The wheels had suffered no particular damage yet, but the danger of a burst wheel was foremost in everyone's minds. The roars of the gravosh grew fainter but the speed of the poctech was still rapid as they kept pace with the frantically running herd. Desperately, the Xotic tried to stay on the path that only they could discern, but the herd that flowed around them were pushing them, in their panic, in an entirely different direction.

'Tlkcha, run to the mast and have them start to slowly lower our speed, we must turn with the herd or risk severe accident!' shouted Shashn. No sooner had he uttered the words than, with a huge crash and lurch that threw the three Graavens to the deck, one of the central wheels shattered and exploded outwards.

Fortunately, the craft did not lose its stability and, with the lowering sail and decreasing speed, the strain on the outer frame was reduced, preventing further damage. The stampeding herd continued to flow past the decelerating craft. Now that they were moving with the herd the beasts no longer slammed into the frame although there was still occasional buffeting by them as they ran past into the moonlit darkness. After several semmit the last of the creatures had gone, following its fellows and snorting heavily as it moved away. Dust kicked up by the massive herd blew past the Xotic as they stood at their posts. Finally, Shashn gave out orders in a crisp voice. 'Check for damage. Have we lost anyone over the side?'

The crew began to move purposefully. Other than the obvious damage to the wheel and its housing, the craft had withstood the slamming and buffeting it had received with remarkably little issue.

Meanwhile, the three Graavens had made their way to where Shashn stood next to the steering lever.

'What of the gravosh? Do you think we are safe from them, Shashn?' asked Menkh.

'I have no doubt they would have picked off some of the herd in the confusion, not to mention those that we ran over who would make easy pickings for them. No, I think we are safe for some time. Dawn comes soon and we can ship a new wheel and be on our way.'

Tlkcha approached them. 'Father, we have lost Gremma. There is no sign of her and Tovasch thinks she was near the wheel when it shattered.'

'Well,' responded Shashn in a quiet voice, placing his hand on Tlkcha's shoulder, 'we will see if we can find her once repairs are done.'

'Yes, Father. I hope she has survived the fall and ...' with a soft cry, Tlkcha turned quickly away as hot tears flowed for her friend and she went off to help with repairs.

'Shashn, we will go and look for Gremma. We are useless to you here and it may be that us going now may be the difference in her living or dying on the plain.'

Shashn looked into Menkh's eyes. 'That is gracious of you, all of you, but what of the gravosh? I cannot accept your generous offer and expose you, our guests, to such danger.'

'As to that, we are aware of the risk, but we are all skilled warriors and our weaponry is such that we can manage matters, should we encounter them.'

'It will take us some time to ship a new wheel. There are risks but I accept your offer gladly. Will you be able to find us again? We may have lost Gremma; I could not countenance losing our honoured guests.'

'Have no fear for us, friend Shashn,' said Mareen, 'my sister Horven is a great tracker. We will find Gremma and, if the gods allow, we will bring her back alive to you.'

'Go, then, with our good will, and may Den Har, the Sky Father, watch over you.'

A short time later after collecting their helmets and weapons, a bag of medicines, and some trail food and water provided by the Xotic, they set off. With their helmets on they began jogging back the way they had come, their vision enhanced by their helmets and their direction displayed on the faceplate.

'My muscles are stiff,' said Mareen, 'it has been too long since we travelled like proper Hoplex.'

Menkh's voice echoed in Mareen and Horven's helmets. 'Spread out. We can cover more ground and with these helmets we can comfortably communicate. Watch out for those gravosh, there is no telling where they might be.'

What had seemed mere moments in time from when they had lifted the sail to escape the gravosh, in speeding away with the stampeding kakesh, the distance they had travelled covered many a persangh. Mareen had moved some way off from the others and, moving off the trampled ground, she entered a small dell surrounded by the tall grasses and sheltered somewhat from the wind that ceaselessly blew. In Mareen's helmet display a warning sounded, a humming vibration that could not be ignored. At the same time, the silhouette of a gravosh was displayed.

Stopping abruptly, she spoke into her helmet, 'I may be in a spot of trouble here,' as three gravosh slowly stalked around her with menacing, low-pitched growls.

Horven and Menkh stopped at the same time and surveyed their surroundings. A growling, grunting sound could be heard from out of tall grasses some distance to the west of the churned and trampled earth left by the passage of the kakesh. 'That doesn't sound the same as the noises they made in the evening,' said Horven.

'I agree,' said Menkh. 'Let us move on warily. Keep talking Mareen, we are coming to you.'

'That is pleasing, Menkh. I think the only reason these brutes haven't attacked me as yet is because they are confused. They certainly will have seen nothing like me in their hunting. Nor will they have experienced the sting my mace will give them when they try,' she added.

Resembling the gonverdeem, these creatures were somewhat smaller, though still with huge and powerful forequarters and jaws. Unlike the gonverdeem, whose eyes reflected intelligence and a kind of deep wisdom, these eyes showed intelligence and unbridled savagery. In an instant, from a silent stalking action to blinding movement, one of the gravosh sprang at Mareen, claws extended and massive paws ready to rend and tear. As its enormous weight bore down, a blue pulse of energy flashed out from Mareen's suit. The gravosh, in mid-leap, smashed into a dense but transparent shield with no discernible effect on Mareen who, stepping to one side, brought a crashing blow to the gravosh's head with her mace. The gravosh emitted a yowl of surprise and pain and the others howled in response. Then the ground suddenly erupted around their feet and rippled with movement. As one, the gravosh leaped into the air and, howling in fright, turned and fled into the safety of the long grass.

Menkh stood up from where he had slammed his staff into the ground.

'*Yes,*' chuckled Crixac, '*I've always liked that particular move. It delivers maximum surprise and consternation with gratifyingly little blood and physical damage to your opponent.*'

'*Truly the capabilities of this staff are amazing,*' responded Menkh.

'*Oh, my friend, you have but scraped the surface. You will see.*'

Making sure that Mareen was without injury, they drew away silently from vicinity of the gravosh and concentrated on scanning their surrounds. Sometime later, Horven's voice called out, 'Over here, I am picking up something on my helmet.'

The Graavens converged and, following Horven, came upon the body of Gremma, lying motionless on the ground. At first glance they thought she was dead, so battered and bloody her appearance. A broken leg, innumerable cuts and abrasions, and a deep gash on her head left a trail of blood on the trampled ground which stretched away behind her.

'She has courage, this one, to have dragged herself so far,' observed Horven.

'Not to mention lucky that the gravosh had gorged themselves. What a pretty plaything she would have made for them,' responded Mareen.

A piteous moan escaped Gremma's lips.

'Come, she yet lives,' said Menkh to Horven and Mareen.

Bending down, he gently turned Gremma over, wiping the blood and slime away from her mouth and pouring a few drops of water into her mouth. '*Can we aid her, Crixac?*'

'She is very badly hurt but we can try. You know how to use the staff to aid recovery. Her wounds will need time to heal but we can attend to the worst of it and then get her back to her people.'

Gremma came up out of a nightmare of pain. As her last strength had failed her, she had cried that she would never see Tlkcha again in this life. Then, as if in a dream, she felt herself turned and, blessing upon blessing, the taste of water, cool upon her lips. Opening her eyes, three strange creatures knelt around her. Their heads were of a uniform silver colour with a metallic sheen which glinted strangely in the light of the moons above. They had no faces but a blank black visage that focused on her. She felt strangely calm and knew without being told that these creatures meant her no harm. '*I am dead,*' she thought, '*and these are the Sky Father's children come to take me home.*' And, with that, she lost all consciousness.

CHAPTER FIFTEEN

It was sometime later that the Xotic saw the group returning. The still form of Gremma hung loosely in Menkh's arms. Soon, all of the Xotic had gathered around and anxious looks were soon replaced by joy when they learned that she lived. After the still-unconscious Gremma had been placed on a sleeping mat aboard, Shashn, Tlkcha, and all the Xotic gathered around the Graavens.

Shashn raised his arms and silence descended on all. 'When these travellers came with our Benshin friends we agreed to take them across our lands out of friendship with the Benshin, and in honour of their request. Today, in a foreign land amongst strangers, with no thought of their own safety, these three travellers put themselves at risk to aid us and one of our own. They have no kinship with us, no blood ties to bind them. What they did, they did out of friendship. They did out of honour. They did because they would not see one of us suffer if they could prevent it. I, Shashn, Palx Mer of the Xotic people, say that these travellers are strangers no more! I say that they are our blood and our kin. I say that they may travel freely wherever they wish in our lands and that all Xotic will aid them as best they can, as they would their own kith and kin. Does anyone here dispute this?'

A chorus of voices rose in unison, 'No-one!'

'Then, when we reach our village there shall be a feast such as we have not seen for many a year and we will make our new brother and sisters truly welcome! Come, my friends,' he said, turning to the three Graavens, 'we may not be able to feast now but we can drink a flask or two in celebration. Up sail!' he called. 'Let us go home!'

Gremma awoke to the rocking motion that reminded her of the land sailers of her people. When she saw Tlkcha's smiling face looking down on her she burst into tears which alarmed Tlkcha.

'Whatever is wrong, Gremma?'

'It is not fair, Tlkcha, that you should have died too. It should have been enough for the Sky Father to have taken me!' she sobbed.

'Hush, hush now, Gremma. You are not dead but safely back with us and we are even now drawing close to home. Soon you will be well again.'

'But how can that be? I saw them, Tlkcha, with my own eyes.'

'Saw what? Perhaps with all your injuries ...'

'No, no. They were all silver with strange heads and no faces. It was the emissaries of the Sky Father come to take me, Tlkcha. They were so gentle I knew they would not hurt me because I had suffered enough.'

'Shh now, Gremma,' said Tlkcha, placing a finger on Gremma's lips. 'What you saw were our Graaven friends in their shiny suits. They rescued you and fought off the gravosh, too. You are alive and you are safe, and you will be well again.'

'Truly?'

'Most definitely truly,' said Tlkcha with a smile, holding Gremma's hand tightly as she once more drifted into a deep sleep.

The wind continued to blow steadily and soon they drew near to a vast lake that seemed to stretch on forever. In its mighty waters the mountains, which drew ever closer, were reflected, along with the cloudless violet sky. The waving grasses and the distant mountains created a picture of beauty.

One of the Xotic crew called out and they could see that another craft was heading in their direction. As they drew closer, they called out greetings.

'That is Chalayla, my mother's sister's daughter. She also returns from a hunting trip so there will be much story telling tonight and you will be the centre of attention, without doubt,' said Shashn.

Whilst not a race it was clear that both Xotic crews were more attentive to their sail to get the best of the wind, and from the laughter of both crews and the friendly insults they called to each other across the gap between them, this was something that was a regular occurrence.

Shashn had a fixed smile on his face and every now and again he turned his attention to Chalayla's craft, checking that she was not overreaching on them.

'Look there, friends,' said Shashn, pointing. 'We draw near to Tramxa, our home village. You can just see our walls above the grasses.'

The Graavens peered ahead and, sure enough, they began to see a regular outline lifting above the plain.

'You build in stone?' queried Menkh.

'Yes. Over generations we have gathered stone and rock from the plains to make clear passage for our wind sailers. We also gather it from the foothills. You will see as we draw closer.'

Now, as they approached, they could see that the village was positioned on an island that was surrounded by a wide moat filled with lake water. A long channel, perhaps natural at one time, had been widened and straightened and could be seen extending from the lake body in the distance. A wooden bridge extended over the moat, wide enough for a Xotic sailer to pass safely.

'The wind is right for us today so we can cross without aid,' announced Shashn as he lifted his left arm straight up as a signal. From behind one of the crew blew a long note on a trumpet fashioned from tran horn. It was surprisingly loud and resonant and, after the third note, an answering call was heard from the now rapidly-nearing bridge.

'Reduce sail,' called Shashn, and the poctech lost speed. Now Chalayla's craft drew ahead and with wonderful control and agility the sail on her craft was lowered. Its residual speed carried their craft over the bridge, followed by Shashn's sailer.

Other poctech sailers and craft of a smaller size were drawn up outside the walls of the village, which Menkh now saw was much bigger than the Benshin villages they had visited.

The walls that surrounded the dwellings were wide and cunningly fashioned from stones and rocks which were dry-set and sturdy. The Graavens could see that one large gate led into and out of the village. As they descended from their craft many a Xotic stopped to look at them curiously and exchange hushed comments, pointing and gesticulating. Small Xotic children ran up to them and peered, open mouthed, until Shashn and Tlkcha shooed them away.

'Come, friends. Welcome to our village, let us show you to where you may stay,' said Shashn.

As they followed Shashn and Tlkcha they smiled to left and right, while Shashn responded to the many questions that were called out to the group as it passed by.

The street they followed ran arrow-straight through the centre of the village, leading to another gate they could see in the distance on the opposite side. Conical buildings in long rows, also made from stacked, dry stone, were set above, with roofs of woven grass matting. Smaller streets led off in other directions. Some of the houses had stalls set up, trading in various foodstuffs and other items which Mareen and Horven looked at curiously as they walked by. Overall, there hung a spicy aroma in the air which the Graavens could not place, but that appeared to come from large woven baskets set on every street corner and containing a reddish-coloured material.

Upon being asked, Tlkcha replied, 'It is taroq root, a staple of our cooking. The root comes from giant reeds which grow on the edge of the lake, and we leave it to dry out prior to grinding. It gives off a spicy scent, which we Xotic love, and it serves also to cover other, less pleasant, odours. You will find it in every Xotic village.'

The "less pleasant odours" mostly came from covered drains which ran down the street on both sides, carrying wastes and dirty water out to the moat.

Now they reached the largest building they had yet seen, shaped like a giant poctech craft. It, too, was made of stone that towered above them, with a vast roof made from thatched reeds. A large doorway surrounded by intricately carved leg bones from some giant creature led into a lofty hall. Above them a framework of carved bones supported the roof, and the ceiling inside was decorated with the dusky skin of the slemmak, one of the lizard-like creatures that inhabited the plains. A wide stairway led up to balcony rooms on a second storey which stretched around the central hall, and small rooms could be seen occupying the space all around, reached by several stairways. In a way it reminded Menkh of the great atrium in the Complex. With its silvery ceiling and beautifully carved framework, the effect was quite stunning.

Four Xotic, two male and two female, their heads adorned with intricate head dresses made from painted and plaited grasses, stood to greet them.

'Welcome, strangers to our village. Pray, sit, and tell us of your journey. My name is Patchek, this is Rolona, Markesh, and Zhivona. We are the elders of Tramxa. Please, sit, sit,' said Patchek, indicating cushions and woven mats scattered on the floor in a space bathed in light from windows that pierced the outer wall at regular intervals.

After refreshments were brought, including a milky beverage which, though tart, was refreshing, Markesh said, 'Tell us about yourselves and why you have come to our lands.'

So it was that Menkh gave an account of all that had happened, with occasional comments from Horven and Mareen. The story was long in the telling for, unlike the Benshin, the Xotic had little knowledge of the Cities.

Finally, Menkh concluded the tale as the shadows lengthened outside. The four Xotic who had listened attentively, asking only the odd question, shared meaningful looks.

'A wondrous and remarkable story, Menkh. These events, though so far away from our lands and outside of our knowledge, have foreboding of what may come to pass.'

'We grieve for the loss of your homeland,' and here Zhivona looked at each of the Graavens. 'I cannot think of what would happen should a similar fate befall the Xotic.'

'And so, you seek this mountain as part of your quest to confront this menace?' said Rolona

'That is so,' nodded Menkh.

'We will aid you as we can. The mountains themselves are vast. No Xotic has ever climbed them and returned to tell the tale, though we journey to the foothills that lead to them to collect stone and to hunt. Will Shashn carry our new friends towards their destination, then?'

'I will,' said Shashn, who had sat silent throughout all of the discussions, 'and you should know that I have adopted them as honorary Xotic for their rescue of Gremma.'

Patchek clapped his hands and smiled. 'Aaah, another story for us, but one, I think, that should be accompanied by food and drink. Friends,' and here he turned to the Graavens, 'we thank you for your openness in telling us your story. Now you should rest while a meal is prepared and Shashn will tell all of us of the circumstances that led him to pronounce you as Xotic.'

So saying, the Graavens were led to individual sleeping places where, after refreshing themselves in the hot water provided, Horven and Mareen fell into a dreamless sleep.

Menkh sat in silent discussion with Crixac. *'I don't recall coming across any reference to the Xotic in the city archives. Was it something you encountered, Crixac?'*

'No. But that is not surprising because the archives hardly bear any relevance to current times. Whilst they are a font of information regarding the City and the circumstances that led to its destruction, the rise of the Graaven peoples, along with the Benshin and the Xotic and any other as yet undiscovered race, are things that will have no reference. Two thousand years is a long time. But, having said that, the Kareems in particular liked nothing more than to play with genetics. The archives contain records of their tampering in improving breeding stock and creating new genetic lines.'

'Ha, next you'll be telling me that we Graavens were genetically modified.'

A deep silence followed this thought. After some moments, Menkh sent out another thought. *'Crixac, what do you know that you haven't told me?'*

Eventually there was a response. *'I have been waiting for the right moment to tell you, Menkh. Yes, the Graaven people were genetically modified. In fact, they were bred by the Kareems to be fighters. Some notion at one time that an army of them could be unleashed against the other Cities. But, when saner minds took over, the Graavens became a kind of servitude race. Never very many, breeding was strictly controlled. But, well, that is how the Graaven peoples came into being.'*

Menkh's thoughts were confused and astounded. *'But what were we before this "modification"?'*

'That is unclear, though perhaps somewhat like the Xotic. In any event, before the calamity that befell the Cities, the archives note that a group of Graavens "escaped" – or at least failed to return from the task they had been

allocated to perform. Before the City could retrieve them, the war took its inevitable turn and there were no Kareems left to hunt them down.'

'But you were present then, with your host?'

'Yes, I was, but newly arrived and still endeavouring to infiltrate the Kareems and make connections. All too little, too late.'

'So these Graavens must have somehow crossed the Plains of Clarist, eventually finding themselves in the lands that became the Empire, and there established independent life.'

'Indeed, and whilst we are sharing this profound new insight, you should also know that the markings that lie on your skin, and which formed the strict hierarchy of Graaven society, were the means by which the Kareems delineated your usefulness. Your markings, for example, were those which indicated Graavens bred for warfare.'

'Stop, Crixac, stop! I need time to process this information. It is deeply ironic that the Graaven people were a manufactured product of a vanished race, subsequently vanquished by an alien intelligence from another planet. Tell me where the balance is in all that?'

'I cannot, Menkh. Only that we are caught up in circumstances that, when taken together, challenge all preconceived ideas we may hold about ourselves and our place in the scheme of things. I perceive that achieving the first part of our quest will enlighten us and open the pathway to achieving the ultimate goal, at least in the eradication of your Dorath Mar and the threat they pose to all the other life on this world. Rest now and let us see where the road takes us.'

Like the Benshin before them, the Xotic made their guests welcome. They applauded the rescue of Gremma and endorsed the adoption of the three Graavens into the Xotic people. They ate and drank and listened to the strange sounds of Xotic voices raised in song. The music of the Xotic was markedly different to the Benshin. Whilst the Xotic had instruments of a similar kind, they preferred the music of many voices in harmony and their voices produced sounds which, whilst alien to Graaven ears, were nevertheless haunting and mesmerising. Their voices rose and fell in complex harmonies that conjured up pictures of the grasslands and the very bones of the lands in which they lived. The Graavens lost themselves in the rhythms of the music and felt strangely refreshed when the singing reached a final chorus that seemed to echo on long after the voices had stopped.

For two days they remained as guests, becoming familiar with the surrounds of the village and frequently engaging with the Xotic in conversations regarding the daily business of living. Shashn and Tlkcha were never far away and it was a hesitant and grateful Gremma who approached them to thank them for her rescue. All in all, it was a pleasant hiatus from their journey and all three Graavens agreed that they could easily spend more time with their Xotic friends.

Then, after the first sun had risen on the third day, and Shashn's poctech sailer was fully ready, they made their farewells with promises to return. Each in turn was embraced by the four elders and it seemed that the whole village had turned out to watch their departure.

CHAPTER SIXTEEN

As the wind was against them, the sailer was drawn out on sturdy ropes over the bridge which had been let down with the coming of the dawn by willing Xotic helpers.

'There are many savage creatures in our homeland,' Rolona had told them on the first evening of their arrival, 'so the moat and bridge are a necessary defence, though it has been long since any creatures threatened our homes.'

Shashn's craft was positioned so as to catch the unceasing wind. With a last farewell, Shashn ordered the sail raised and they began to move away from the village. It was then that the assembled Xotic raised their voices in a song of farewell that caused the tendrils on Menkh's neck to lift in response to the harmonies and merging sounds. It was, he decided, the most beautiful and poignant melody he had ever heard, and the memory of those voices stayed with him ever after. Even Crixac was moved to comment that he had never heard such a primitive yet complex sound.

Now, as they gathered speed, they turned their course towards the towering peaks that sat on the horizon.

'We will make for the Gap of Crethic. This is known ground to us and where we gather stone for our village. There is a place some days' journey by foot from there which no Xotic will enter.'

'Why is that?' asked Horven.

Shashn looked thoughtful. 'Nothing bad has ever happened to those who come to that place, but it is a feeling that cannot be ignored. We think of it as a warning put there by the Sky Father. Those of us that have tried to go further fall sick and cannot breathe and must be dragged back.'

'So, there is a demarcation line? A point that you cannot go past?' asked Menkh.

'Yes, if you will. We Xotic now avoid that place but it seems to me that perhaps that is exactly the kind of thing that you might be looking for.'

'No doubt, friend Shashn,' replied Mareen pensively, 'almost exactly the kind of place shrieking of danger that we Graavens love to run headlong into!'

Shashn laughed quietly whilst Menkh, Horven and Mareen gazed out at the looming mountains and pondered the next stage of their journey.

'*This is exactly the sort of thing that would indicate we are on the right path. It is not the first time in my experience that those we meet on the way play a role in determining our success or failure,*' observed Crixac.

Menkh considered his response. '*Yes. It would seem to go beyond coincidence. We were promised help in this task and it would seem that this is a direct manifestation of that.*'

Several meh'chaal passed without incident. They left the shores of the vast lake behind and often encountered huge herds of grazing animals. As ever, different species – some horned and hairy and others smooth-skinned, lumbering giants – happily intermingled whilst consuming the abundant grasses.

The days passed without any significant danger arising and the grassy plain began to yield to rolling hills and rocky outcrops.

Eventually the ground became untenable for any further travel in the poctech.

Disembarking, Shashn and Tlkcha retrieved the packs and supplies that had been set aside for the Graavens and, after leaving the Xotic crew to gather stone and keep watch over the sailer, they journeyed on foot for two further days, passing into the Gap of Crethic. This proved to be a boulder-strewn valley that led towards the shoulders of two huge peaks, the tops of which were hidden in vapour and mist.

'Let us hope that our journey does not lead us high into the mountains. We are ill equipped to deal with such a height, not to mention the cold as we climb,' observed Menkh.

'Perhaps our suits will shield us from any weather extremes?' queried Mareen.

'Well, they have certainly been remarkably adaptive till now,' mused Horven, 'but I still don't fancy a long climb up an unexplored mountain.'

On the second day they saw the first of several flying raptors, whose vast, leathery wings carried them high into the air above them. The raptors' shrieking calls set the Graavens' teeth on edge, and they kept a wary eye above them as they moved.

'We call these flyers vorskh meh, "flying death". Their nesting grounds are high in the mountains and they hunt the plains. They tend to pick off the very young or very old and injured and, fortunately, they tend to be lone hunters.'

'Do they cause the Xotic any concern?' asked Mareen curiously.

'It is rare. They have been known to attack the odd sailer as it makes its way across the plains, but, generally, no. Sometimes you will hardly see any of them and at other times the sky seems full, but the plains are vast and the vorskh fly so high that even the keenest eye will have difficulty picking them out. The skin on the bottom of their wings is the colour of the sky and they can float for many of your chaal with hardly a beat of their wings. We Xotic harvest the dead. Their bones and skin are valuable to us in the building of our wind sailers but to hunt them whilst living calls for serious planning and coordination and no little risk.'

'But surely finding a dead one is rather hit and miss?' queried Horven.

'Interestingly, you would think that, being solitary, their remains would be scattered across the plains. In fact, there are three areas where the vorskh meh can be found in numbers. Two are breeding grounds far to the north and the other is their cemetery. Flyers from everywhere come to this one location when their time is near, and this is something that all the vorskh, who have not died from other means during a hunt or by misadventure, seem to share. Here you will find hundreds of bodies in various stages of decay. Each year, we Xotic organise an expedition to this place and harvest bones and other material from the bodies we find there.'

'Is that not a dangerous exercise too?' asked Menkh.

'No Xotic has ever been attacked on any of our expeditions and we have been doing this for generations. No healthy vorskh will go anywhere near the place and those who are there, well, they have little interest in us.'

When they made camp in the evening of the third day, the Xotic made plans to depart the next morning.

'We draw very near to the place we spoke of. We cannot proceed further with you but, once we have journeyed back, we will continue to camp in the place where we left the poctech. For fourteen of your dak'chaal, as you reckon the days, we will gather stone and herbs that grow in the area and we will wait for your return, but if you have not returned by then we will leave. In our place we will leave you a bavek so that you may return to us. The bavek is a small wind sailer. We carry its parts on board and we will assemble it for you, prior to our leaving, with a pole and flag to mark its location. It will carry four with ease and you have seen enough of how to handle the larger craft that this one should not be beyond you with a little trial and error. We will leave trail markers to guide your return, but head ever towards the suns as they set upon the horizon. If all else fails, light a signal fire and we or others of the Xotic will find you.'

'We thank you, Shashn and Tlkcha, for all your help. I cannot say how long until, or even if, we will return; but we will always cherish the friendship of the Xotic.' On saying this, Menkh withdrew a metallic disc from his pack. 'If you ever visit our city then this will open the gates. Present this to whomever you meet and be welcome.'

Shashn and Tlkcha looked curiously at the disc before they settled down to a last companionable meal in the gathering darkness. They spoke together well into the night.

With the coming of the dawn they made a cold breakfast and, after receiving directions, the Graavens stood and waved farewell as Shashn and Tlkcha made their way back to their starting point.

Dousing their small fire, Menkh turned to Horven and Mareen. 'Come, my friends, let us head off in the direction indicated and see what might await us.'

They walked at a steady pace all that morning. Small lizard-like creatures scampered over the rocks that surrounded them, and huge red and black insects fluttered on large wings, alighting on small, flowering bushes that grew everywhere in abundance, protected from any wandering herbivores by large thorns.

Other than the noise of these creatures, it was eerily silent after the constant sound of the wind. Here it was still and not even a slight breeze could be discerned. At midday they replenished their water flasks from a tiny brook that ran chattering across their path, and they made a small meal. As they journeyed on, the quiet became oppressive. Even the small animals that had been their companions had disappeared and the atmosphere became foreboding.

At last they reached a point where the simple act of moving forward became a burden. A thousand weights dragged their limbs down and even thinking coherently became difficult. Under all this, a strong desire to turn around and leave this place grew ever stronger.

'Menkh, hearken to my words. There is something here, presently unseen, and our passage has triggered its defence. Take the staff and anchor it into the ground in front of you and concentrate all your thoughts into it. Let us see what may be revealed to us.'

Menkh's thoughts were groggy but became clearer as Crixac threw up a protective mental shield. Mareen and Horven stood motionless alongside him.

Sweeping the staff before him, he planted the tip firmly on the ground. With both hands gripping it, Menkh concentrated all his thoughts into the staff. Red light pulsated and tendrils of visible force flowed out from the staff as it began to vibrate and emit a humming sound. In front of them, the energy encountered something, flowing upwards and around it in a slow and sinuous motion. Gradually the lintel, and then the capstone, of a huge doorway was revealed before them, slowly taking form and definition.

The frame of the doorway was as black as night, glinting with a thousand diamond points of light that shimmered in the air. As the doorway materialised, the feeling of lethargy left them and they stood blinking in amazement. No markings could be discerned on the surface of the stone that made the doorway, and through it they could see the boulder-strewn ground continuing towards the mountains beyond. Upon walking to the opposite side of the gateway, the path they had followed could also be clearly seen.

'So, my friends, it would appear that we have a gateway in front of us — but to where and to what, we cannot know.'

'Do we venture forward, Zaltec?' asked Mareen in a quiet voice, reverting to Menkh's honorific in the tension of the moment.

'Certainly, I feel that I must; but I will not command that either of you do,' he replied, looking at both Horven and Mareen.

'Prudence might dictate that at least one of us stay back to take word if the others do not return,' said Horven.

'*Any ideas, Crixac?*' thought Menkh.

'*A dimensional gateway, unactivated as yet. Not dissimilar to the one I and my host used when we first ventured here. This is of a material I have not seen before. You must order Horven and Mareen to stay behind, Menkh. You have me to deal with any unexpected occurrences and you can share my experience and knowledge, but the risk is unacceptably high for them. Once we have passed through, then we are in a position to know whether it is safe for them to travel also.*'

'*Very well.*'

Menkh turned to them. 'Now, you must trust me in what I am about to say. You both must stay here while I go forward,' Menkh abruptly raised his hand to silence their protests before they came. 'I have a power within me which will protect me but cannot offer the same to you. If I can return safely for you both, I will.'

'But, Menkh, how can we stand by and see you walk forward into the unknown?' asked Horven, with a nod from Mareen.

'I understand your feelings and your sentiment does you both credit. No-one can deny your courage and constancy, but this now is an order, and I will brook no argument. I can protect myself. I cannot protect you.'

'But, Zaltec, how can you protect yourself without us to watch your back? You do not know what you face either. What "power" do you refer to? Is it your staff?'

Crixac's voice echoed in his head. '*There is a simple way to end this discussion and reassure them both, if you are agreeable?*'

'*Whatever it takes, Crixac, I do not want a heated discussion or the probability that the moment I walk through, they will both follow.*'

Horven and Mareen took a step backward as a blue luminescence could be seen leaking out of Menkh's body in front of them. Their weapons came up in their hands as the luminescence coalesced into a vague, body-like shape, and a clear, musical voice could be heard.

'Greetings, Horven and Mareen. I am the power to which Menkh refers. He is as a brother to me, but we are connected in ways that you might have difficulty understanding. Suffice to say that Menkh is protected under my magic but I cannot extend it to you. I have travelled the gateways before, and they are not for the fainthearted.'

'Zaltec, are you … are you alright?' asked Mareen hesitantly.

Menkh smiled. 'I am perfectly fine, Mareen. Crixac is my friend and saviour; we are a part of each other. There is much I can share with you, but the time is not now. Will you now, please, do as I ask you to do?'

'Zaltec, you are truly full of surprises,' Hoven turned her attention to the blue form that shifted and swirled around Menkh, 'and you are Crixac?'

'I am.'

'What are you, a spirit, a ghost?'

'Ha, I am some of those things and none of them. I am a symbiote from the Cordelian System; but that will mean less than nothing to you. In fact, I'm not even sure if there still *is* a Cordelian System. But I digress. I will make sure that nothing happens to Menkh. What happens to him happens to me. One thing I can tell you is that, whatever might happen, you are not equipped to deal with it. Your presence will only make it more difficult if things go badly.'

Horven and Mareen exchanged looks. 'Very well, Crixac and Menkh. We do not like it, but we agree that we will wait.'

'Good, I am sure that Menkh will feel much better knowing you two are safe. Now, if you don't mind, I will return to Menkh. I always find these out of body experiences most unsettling,' said

Crixac, and the blue luminescence flowed back into Menkh who was left standing by himself, a tentative smile on his face.

'So, now you know. Do you feel better about things now?'

'Better is hardly the word we would use!' exclaimed Mareen. 'But we agree to stay and watch.'

'Good, then we will follow Shashn's plan. Wait here for several days. If I do not return, then make your way to the bavek and return to the Xotic village. It may be that I will join you there. I will try to get word to you. I have other ways of travelling and communicating which may work going forward. Now, there is no time like the present,' he said, turning back to the gateway.

'Any ideas on activating this gate, Crixac?' he thought.

'It may be as simple as touching the stone. Let's try that first. After all, anyone that can get around the defence has the ability to travel.'

Menkh removed the glove of his left hand and placed it on the left pillar. Almost immediately a coruscating light spread out from underneath his hand and ran up the pillar, across the lintel, and down the other side. Now, strange glyphs could be seen etched in the surface of the doorway and, from the central point of the capstone, a sudden draught of air blew outwards, accompanied by a low-pitched humming sound that vibrated through the ground under their feet.

Whereas before the space inside the doorway merely looked out on the terrain that continued towards the mountains, now a clear stone-laid pathway could be seen, which disappeared into a dense forest.

It was a strange effect as on either side of the doorway the landscape was unchanged and, as Mareen discovered, walking around the doorway the land continued on, although the space between the pillars was now opaque at the back and she could no longer see the others standing on the reverse side.

'Remember your promise,' admonished Menkh and, lifting up his pack and staff, he stepped through the doorway and vanished from sight.

Mareen and Horven jumped forward but the moment that Menkh stepped through, the gateway disappeared and reverted to its previous state. Repeated touching by Horven and Mareen elicited no response and, disconsolately, they made preparation to camp and wait out the agreed time.

Menkh stepped forward. Other than the slightest period of disorientation, there were no other discernible physical effects. On passing through, the doorway behind him became clear once more. The pathway he was on, and the surrounding forest, continued both before and behind him, flowing around the silent gateway.

'Where do you think we are?' mused Menkh.

'Hmmmm … well, of course, we could be anywhere, but given the hardly noticeable effect on us physically I think we are still somewhere on Tarvuli or in a location which is relatively close to your world. The air is the same at any rate, and the forest around us contains plants and trees that are familiar. Yet still, there is some essentially different quality to our surroundings that gives me pause. I think we can do nothing better than venture forward and see what awaits.'

Menkh nodded to himself and, agreeing with Crixac, stepped forward and moved along the path. It was quiet. There was no wind or animal sounds, no stirring of a leaf or anything else to break the eerie stillness. There was no impression at all of any danger, but it was nonetheless disquieting.

The path led around the corner and it felt to Menkh that it climbed steadily, though all around them the trees blocked any view further than a stone's throw from either side of where they traversed. Finally, however, after what felt like a chaal of steady walking, the path flattened out, the trees suddenly fell away, and they could see out across a deep valley to a single rocky peak that lifted itself above the forest canopy.

Menkh stood motionless. There was no doubt in his mind that this was what he had been sent to find. It was not the presence of the rocky outcrop but what sat upon it, occupying the entire top of the peak, that gave him this assurance. For there, merging with the contours of the rocky outcrop, stood a structure that appeared to be the mirror image of the great Complex in Menkh's City.

'What do think of that, Crixac?'

'Amazing. A duplicate or a reflection of its twin; or even, perhaps, the original building which the City unwittingly copied by some unfathomable means.'

'Well, whatever the means, it is some distance off and we will be hard-pressed to get there in daylight. Assuming, of course, that night exists where we are.'

Turning back to the path, Menkh stopped abruptly. A hooded and cowled figure stood upon the path, regarding him. Much taller than Menkh, it leant on a staff that looked remarkably similar to the one Menkh himself carried.

The figure gave no word and stood silently. It made no hostile move and an aura of calmness flowed from it.

'Greetings, stranger. I am Menkh and I have come to this place via the gateway back some ways along the path. I come in peace and am set on a quest which I believe may be fulfilled here. Are you able to aid me?'

The figure bowed to Menkh and, in a sibilant tongue, responded, 'Greetings, Menkh ab Dur, and to your companion, Crixac. We were aware of your approach as soon as you activated the gateway. You are welcome. Truly, we have been expecting you, though it has been an age and an age since the gateway was last opened. Come, I will take you to the City and much that was unclear shall be explained. My name in your tongue is Morgath. I am an Adept of the Red, though that will have no meaning to you as yet. Come, take my hand and we will journey together.'

Morgath lifted his left arm and extended a hand with six long and tapering fingers.

'All will be well I think, Menkh. I have no doubt Morgath means to transport us there, much as we did around the City.'

So, taking Morgath's hand, Menkh experienced the rushing sensation that transporting brought with it and, in less than the blink of an eye, they stood before a massive pair of gates that opened noiselessly inwards.

Now they were closer, Menkh could see that whilst there were many similarities between the two buildings, there were also substantial differences. They entered a massive atrium, just like in Menkh's City, but where stairwells led upwards to the first level there, here there were only open doorways. Inside each doorway luminescent pools of light shimmered and swirled but nothing could be seen beyond the swirling colours, so where they might lead was a mystery.

The atrium floor, liken to the mosaic that sat outside of Menkh's Complex, was covered in a massive depiction of what Menkh assumed was the night sky. It was disconcerting to look down because, when he did, it felt that he was looking out of a window into space into which he could fall forever. With some little imagination, he felt that the points of light slowly moved their position so that the overall picture constantly changed.

Morgath led Menkh to one of the doorways. As they were all identical in aspect and no signage could be discerned to indicate where each door might lead, Menkh mused as to how anyone could pick the doorway they wanted.

'Look carefully at the colours swirling inside each doorway, Menkh, and you will see a subtle difference in their configuration. That's the key, I think, but, of course, one must also know what each colour shift means. Perhaps as an Adept this is one of the things that one learns over time.'

Menkh looked carefully to compare the doorway immediately to the left of the one they approached and could see that Crixac was correct. There was a slightly different pattern to the swirl of colours that might indeed indicate purpose, but how this could be interpreted was beyond understanding at this time.

Now as they passed through there was a sensation of stepping through a slight resistance and the air, for just a second, was icily cold. They stepped into a large hallway. The immediate impression was of vast size. The walls seemed to be formed of crystal that glowed fitfully with a reddish light. Descending from the ceiling high above, a gigantic crystal, like some huge stalagmite, protruded into the space. It was so low that, with a stretch, it would be possible to touch it. Directly underneath this was a long table, capable of seating dozens of people. It was set with many chairs, all composed of a white, crystalline material. Four chairs were occupied by figures, cowled like Morgath but with their hoods thrown back. They stood quietly as Menkh approached behind Morgath.

Menkh paused a moment in deep surprise, for here were the living embodiment of the statues that stood either side of the causeway in his City.

'Are these people Kareems?'

'If not, they are closely related,' responded Crixac.

'Greetings to you, Menkh ab Dur and Crixac. In answer to your question, we are not Kareems in the sense that you mean it, though the descendants of the three Cities can claim lineage from us. Come, we have been made aware of your quest and would seek to aid you in this. My name is Frzath and I am the Kohnoor, the Abbott of this place. With me are T'klath the Kohnoor Maj, the Abbess, and these are Plakar and Denith, Adepts of the White and the Blue.'

Each figure bowed to Menkh, who returned the gesture before sitting in the chair that Frzath indicated.

'There is much here that is strange to you and much that you need to know, though that will be explained by other than us. The Intelligence has prepared a crystal for you but, in order to transport it from this place to your City, you must first seek to make the bond.'

'I am sorry, Frzath, but all this is bewildering. Where are we and what is this bond of which you speak?'

'We are sorry, Menkh, and we appreciate your confusion. These things we can answer. Then you must refresh yourself and we will prepare the bonding. In one sense, you have already experienced a kind of bonding when you laid your hand on the crystal in your City. Few survive touching a crystal. The fact that you did, and the Intelligence communicated with you, is significant. Where we are now is a Balancepoint. You have entered through one of the portals that lead here. Each of the Cities contained a single complex that, to a certain extent, mirrored this place. A longing for home, perhaps, or something like that. In any event, only within a Balancepoint does the Intelligence manifest itself in a physical form. Each Balancepoint is connected, though in ways that are difficult to understand. Everywhere else, the Intelligence is an invisible force permeating the very fabric of the universe. The Intelligence has a single purpose, to preserve the Balance in all things, without which there can only be chaos and destruction.'

'The Balance is all,' echoed the others.

'How, then, do you explain the presence of the three Cities and the crystals they used in them?'

'How indeed?' mused Frzath.

'There were once three siblings,' said T'klath as she took up the narrative, 'each a powerful Adept of the Red, the Blue and the White. As Adepts, we live for many lifetimes, imbued with the power of the Intelligence and ever acting as guardians of each Balancepoint. But, over centuries, the three siblings, Menath,

Kortsan, and Tambel, became corrupted with notions of power. Using means that even now we do not fully comprehend, they stole three small crystals and, with some followers enamoured of their power, exited the Balancepoint.'

'Could the Intelligence not have interceded to prevent this occurring?'

'Yes,' replied Denith, 'but who was to say that this was not a part of the Balance and that their actions were a necessary part of that?'

'In any event,' said Plakar, 'they left here and over many years they established their Cities and thrived. They made great advances and, for a time, lived in harmony. It was they that manipulated the genetics of some of the creatures they found on your world. You already know about your own peoples but there were others, too, who survive today. The Benshin and the Xotic and others.'

'But then the taint that had existed in the siblings and which infected their descendants gradually became more prevalent,' said Frzath. 'Eventually, the calamity which befell the Cities led to the destruction of two of the three crystals and the obliteration of the descendants of the three.'

'So, presumably restoring the Balance in some way?' mused Menkh.

'Perhaps,' agreed T'klath.

Frzath interrupted, 'And now, you must refresh yourself, your other questions will be answered in time to come,' and he and the others rose. 'Morgath will take you to some accommodations and you may eat and rest. The bonding will take place after that.'

Menkh burned with a thousand unanswered questions but it was clear that, at least for the present, no further answers would be forthcoming. So, following Morgath once more, he and Crixac departed and were led to a comfortable apartment in another part of the Complex.

After they were settled and whilst awaiting the bonding ceremony, Menkh mulled things over with Crixac.

'There is so much here that is beyond my comprehension, Crixac. What does your experience and knowledge tell you?'

'I, too, have learned much that I was ignorant of before, Menkh. My previous host and I came to the city, now home to your people, to try to head off a war. Neither of us realised how far along that path the Kareems and the others had progressed.'

'But how did you know of this, Crixac? What Frzaths and the other call the Intelligence told me that you were Agents of Balance. But what does that mean? Every time I get a piece of knowledge, my understanding seems to decrease. I admit to feeling quite overwhelmed.'

'That is entirely understandable. As to acting as an Agent of Balance, that is difficult to explain. It's not like we receive instructions or messages in the sky. Most of the time it is a feeling, a sense that something is not right, something is "out of balance". It is a poor explanation, I know. It is as much a surprise to me as it is to you that these Balancepoints exist or even that the Intelligence physically manifests itself in some places.'

'But if that is the case, how then did you follow these feelings? How was it that you were able to travel to this world from wherever you were when that feeling manifested itself?'

'The way always became available once you were attuned to the necessity of taking action. My host and I acted on what I can only describe as instinct. A sense that we were doing what was necessary and the strongest sense of "wrongness" when we took an incorrect path. Say, turning left when we should have turned right. Always, our steps were eventually guided to a place where travel was possible. The way was often difficult, but we always ended up encountering a portal, somewhat like the one we used to journey here.'

'That I can understand. When I touched the crystal for the first time, I felt the absolute certainty that it was something I needed to do.'

'Yes. For me that moment was one of the most frightening I have ever encountered. Everything in my experience screamed that certain death for both of us was upon us. Instead a new vista of knowledge was opened up. But mark

this, Menkh. If the Intelligence now seeks to directly influence our actions in a way that, as far as I am aware, has never been done before, then the reason must be dire.'

'Well, you know more than I do, even though you are feeding my knowledge and understanding.'

'Yes, but that process is a gradual one. To fill your mind at once with the weight of knowledge and experience I have could drive you to madness. You already have a feeling of being overwhelmed. Magnify that a hundredfold and you will glimpse an understanding of what would happen if I allowed this to occur.'

'Well, my friend. If the bonding we are to experience is anything like what I encountered in the City, then we should both prepare ourselves. Remember that the Intelligence was able to separate us effortlessly so that is a possibility here, too.'

'Yes. As you say, we must wait and see.'

Menkh dozed fitfully for a time until Morgath came to take him to the place where the ceremony was to occur. Returning once more to the atrium, they entered another portal.

'You may feel some slight disorientation once again as we enter the portal. Do not be alarmed, that is quite normal,' said Morgath.

So saying, they stepped through. Menkh encountered a feeling of dizziness and the same sensation of coldness that he had the first time. He closed his eyes briefly to counter its effects, and upon opening them registered that he had entered a gigantic cavern. The space had the same dimensions as the room where he had met Frzath but here the walls were covered in a myriad of fissures and protrusions of crystal. Several immense stalagmites of red, blue, and white crystal hung down, and here and there stalactites of crystal of varying size grew up from the floor of the cavern. All around him, at the very edge of his hearing, was the susurrating whisper of a million voices. A breath of air that flowed around the cavern, so subtle it could not be felt, resonated as it connected with the crystals. The only light came from the pale luminescence of the crystals themselves. To Menkh it felt as if a great and brooding presence, ancient and powerful, filled the entirety of the space. A presence that was neither benevolent nor threatening but was timeless and immutable.

'Here I will leave you,' whispered Morgath. As quiet as it was, his words echoed around the cavern and Menkh felt the presence shift and suddenly become more focused.

Menkh whispered in response, as if any speech above the lowest whisper was a desecration in this place, 'What do I do?'

'Whatever feels right,' came the response, as Morgath exited the cavern via the portal behind them.

Menkh stared around the cavern.

'*Close your eyes, Menkh, and listen,*' said Crixac.

As his eyes closed, Menkh noticed there was an immediate increase in the clarity of the sound that he had noticed in the cavern. This time he could discern voices that seemed to be all around him.

'*He is here,*' they said, '*he must choose, he must choose!*' And the word "choose" echoed around the cavern.

Opening his eyes, Menkh took a tentative step forward into the cavern. The pale luminescence in front of him flared a little at the step. Taking several further steps, he noticed the light increased and illuminated a path through the crystal stalactites.

'*It appears we are being led,*' Menkh remarked.

'*Indeed. Follow on, my friend, and let us see where it leads.*'

Deeper into the cavern they walked. The voices continued their whispering chant, '*He must choose, he must choose.*'

After what seemed an age in that place they arrived at a point where three stalactites of each colour rose from the ground in close proximity. Each was around six spahn in height and Menkh thought that he might just encompass each one with his arms wrapped around it.

As he looked at them, he saw that within the heart of each crystal swirling colours danced. Vague, indefinable shapes rose to the surface as if from great depths, and then sank back down once more as if pulled back by some unseen force. The colours changed repeatedly and all around there was an energy in the air that, whilst not lethal, nonetheless emitted a feeling that the slightest wrong move could have profoundly unpleasant consequences.

Still the voices whispered, but now they had changed somewhat, '*The choice is before him. Now must he choose.*'

Menkh became oblivious to the voices. If Crixac spoke, he could not hear him. Menkh's vision was focused wholly on the swirling, hypnotic patterns inside the crystals. He stood motionless, gazing long into each one so that whether he stood for a day or a year or a hundred years, the passage of time became nothing.

Slowly he was drawn more and more towards the red crystal. Like the others, it spoke to him in his mind – but whereas the blue spoke of power and the white of knowledge, the red spoke more of wisdom. Feelings of sadness and the regret of things lost were tempered by the potential of new realities and new life. After a long pause Menkh's thoughts and feelings led him to a clear decision and he reached out with both hands, placing them firmly upon the red crystal.

CHAPTER SEVENTEEN

He fell.

It seemed like forever but, in his mind, he could hear Crixac reassuring him that all was well. Eventually the feeling of falling dissipated and now he seemed to float along, suspended above a ribbon of red light which stretched endlessly before him.

Around him there was total silence and a darkness pierced by tiny points of light that, as he looked at them, were like stars in the night sky. As his senses sharpened, he saw that the ribbon of light on which he travelled passed by planets and moons which turned far beneath him. When this happened, it gave him a sense of how fast he was travelling. The worlds and their suns were left rapidly behind him to continue their lonely dance in space and he journeyed on.

As he passed living worlds, he felt the energy of life that emanated from them, sometimes tenuous and new, at other times vibrant and powerful, and on still others fading and decaying. He passed far above them as they turned slowly in the light of suns which brought them life and, once, he passed between several moons that hung over a world that he knew was dead.

He journeyed on and on until he felt that the knowledge of his past life was but a dream and that he would travel forever on the ribbon of light that drew him inexorably forward. Crixac was with him and his presence in his mind was comforting but remote.

Then, after an endless time, he passed out of the darkness as if through a veil and floated above a vast lake. The substance that formed the lake was not water. Nevertheless, it flowed and ebbed with a metallic sheen liken to liquid metal. In the middle of the lake rose an island composed entirely of red crystal.

Descending, he set foot upon the island and stood still at last. As he viewed his surroundings, he once again saw that Crixac had separated from him and was attached only by a tenuous thread of light that linked their bodies. Neither of them spoke. Around them was utter stillness. It was a place that gave the feeling that nothing happened there; it simply was, and always would be.

Before him part of the ground on which he stood became liquid and flowed upwards, forming a shape that roughly corresponded to that of a Graaven adult but was neither male nor female in aspect.

A voice reverberated inside his mind. '*You have chosen,*' it said.

The impact of the voice on Menkh sent his senses reeling. It echoed around and through him and beat down on his mind. An enormous weight impacted on his brain. When he tried to push back against it, he felt like he was trying to hold a landslide by pushing with his arms. He gasped involuntarily. Even with Crixac shielding his mind, it almost drove him to gibbering insanity.

The shape moved, flowing down and reforming.

The voice, when it returned, was at a normal level, warmer and more accessible, though with a weight of knowing that resonated still.

'*We are sorry, Menkh ab Dur, it was not our intent to hurt you. Is that better?*'

'*Much better, I thank you. Where are we?*'

'You are nowhere and everywhere, at the beginning and also at the end. We cannot explain this to you. You are here with us. It was necessary.'

'Who are you? Why am I here with you?'

'We are who we are. You may think of us as that which is the red crystal. This place where you are is a projection that you may comprehend. You chose us and now you must bond with us if we are to reset the Balance.'

'Have we not already bonded?'

'No. You have connected with us but in order to return to your dimension you must bond with us.'

'What must I do?'

'You must die.'

Menkh took an involuntary step back. 'I must die?'

'Yes. You must die in order to be reborn.'

'What of Crixac?'

'Your death will temporarily cut the bond. But you have no need to fear. It will not take long.'

'What will happen to me? Will I be different?'

'Different? You will be both the same and different. To reset the Balance, you must bond with us. You must decide.'

'What happens if I choose not to bond?'

'You will stay here. You cannot leave without the bond.'

'And the Balance. What will happen?'

'The Balance will not be reset. Without reset chaos will take hold. Eventually, a new Balance will be achieved. All living beings will be affected. Whole worlds will be destroyed.'

'So, my bonding will prevent this?'

'Nothing is certain. Either way, chaos may yet take hold. You have the capacity to reset the Balance and avoid this.'

'What say you, Crixac?'

'Take the bond, Menkh, I really don't wish to spend an eternity in this place. If there is a chance that, together, we can restore balance, then that must be a good thing.'

Menkh paused. *'Well, it would seem a waste to have journeyed so far here and in our own reality to step back now. What must I do?'*

'Step into us, Menkh. We will consume that which is you to create that which will become you.'

'Will it hurt?' he asked sheepishly.

'You will feel nothing at all.'

Menkh took a deep breath, nodded once at the form of Crixac alongside him, and stepped forward into the form before him.

Oblivion.

He floats in darkness and warmth. Utterly at peace and utterly calm.

There is no time, no place for thought. He is home.

A sensation of movement. A surge towards light. He struggles against the pull. A quiet, soothing sound comforts him and now he feels himself rising quickly, as if through water.

Opening his eyes, he stands once more on the red shore alongside Crixac, still attached to him by the cord of light.

'Welcome, Menkh. The bond is made. Now you may return.'

'I don't feel any different,' remarked Menkh.

'Other than your red, crystalline skin, you mean?' Crixac responded.

Menkh looked at his hands and those parts of his body he could see. The entirety of his body seemed to be now composed of a crystalline material that moved like skin and gave the same sensations but was patently very different.

'Well, that is going to take some time to get used to.'

The crystal ebbed and flowed in front of him. *'Your companion can change your appearance. Your covering will change to reflect the environment you find yourself in. Now you must leave. Things move towards a culmination on your world and you must be there to resolve them successfully. We will be with you. Now you will see what the City can do with its full power restored. Return to the cavern, retrieve the bonded crystal, and transport it to your City. In time all will be revealed to you.'*

'Thank you.'

'*Your thanks are superfluous. Follow your instincts, Menkh ab Dur. The path will be shown to you.*'

The shape sank back into the ground and once again all was utterly calm and still.

'*I should have asked how we were supposed to get back,*' remarked Menkh.

'*Well, as I feel that the blocks to my flowing back into you have been removed, I suggest we focus on the cavern and try willing ourselves back. Give me a moment.*'

With no discernible sensation, Crixac resumed his place.

'*You are not going to believe some of the internal changes they have wrought on you, Menkh.*'

'*Keep it to yourself, Crixac. I've had enough shocks for one lifetime already. Well, let's try this and see how we go.*'

Supplemented by Crixac's power, Menkh closed his eyes and, forming a vivid mental picture of the cavern and the place where they stood before the crystal, expressed his desire to return there.

He felt absolutely nothing. As he was opening his eyes and beginning to ask Crixac if he had any better ideas, he froze in shock. He stood in the cavern in exactly the place he had visualised. He had experienced no sensation of movement or of time as he had on the journey to the nothing place. Instead, he had seemingly winked out of one reality and appeared in another.

'*Still don't believe in magic?*' queried Menkh.

'*After recent events, I could be converted,*' responded Crixac.

'*Here is another change. All these doorways now have meaning. I know exactly where each one leads. Interesting.*'

'*You are developing a profound sense of understatement, Menkh. I agree, however. A pity we have such little time. This would be a most interesting place to spend a quiet lifetime or so. Let me just adjust our appearance. Returning to the City in our current form may lead to issues.*'

Menkh felt a warm sensation, not unlike standing under warm water. His hands resumed their normal colouration and the crystalline aspect and hue of his new skin returned to that of his Graaven inheritance.

With the transformation complete, they made their way to the entryway to the cavern. Morgath stepped through and, placing his two arms across this chest, bowed formally.

'We had warning of your imminent return, Menkh ab Dur. The Intelligence has communicated to us that your return to your own time and place is now urgently required. If you will come with me.'

Morgath re-entered the doorway with Menkh following behind. They emerged into the room where Menkh had first met the others. Only Frzath stood to greet them this time, like Morgath, bowing low to Menkh as they entered the room.

'That which you were is gone. That which you are now is revealed to us who can see clearly. Welcome back, if only briefly.'

Frzath indicated a large red crystal which stood suspended upon the table. The crystal appeared to float in the air just above the tabletop, seemingly without support of any kind. It was teardrop shaped, around six spahn in length and some three spahn across at its widest point.

'The Intelligence has made this shard available to you. It will replace that which is failing within your City. We would have made you welcome and shared stories with you. Alas, the Intelligence has indicated that you must leave us as matters approach a critical point. Our blessings go with you.'

'Thank you, Frzath and Morgath. I am concerned at this news and wonder how long we were away that matters have come to a head.'

'Time flows differently in different places. We cannot give you a precise answer. Here, seven cycles of time have elapsed. On your world this may be several years or merely several moments. In any event, it would appear that enough time has elapsed that you are needed.'

'Perhaps you might tell us how we transport the crystal with us. Carrying such an object would be difficult but I assume that such will be unnecessary?'

'Whilst knowledge will arise as you need it, Menkh, you are become Adept, reborn in the light of the crystal. Much that was inaccessible is now available to you, including travel on the threadway. Take the crystal in your hands and will yourself to your destination. The shard will journey with you.

Travel safely, Menkh and Crixac. Our goodwill goes with you. You can be sure that we will meet again in time to come,' said Frzath.

Menkh bowed to Morgath and Frzath after their fashion and, following Frzath's advice, placed his hands gently on the surface of the crystal. There was a warmth there and an energy which he felt through his fingertips. A voice shimmered and whispered in his head, forming intelligible thoughts, *'We travel?'*

'Indeed,' responded Menkh and, holding the image of the crystal room in the Complex, willed himself there.

An instant in time. A brief sensation of coldness and Menkh stood once more in the crystal room inside the Complex. As he materialised with the red crystal floating in front of him, Tishan Dar turned abruptly.

Menkh did not believe that any Graaven face could cover the range of emotions that flashed across Tishan's face. From despair to incredulity, astonishment to hope, Tishan's hand flew to her mouth, her eyes wide-open as the emotions flickered across her face. Then, in a totally un-Graaven-like fashion, she flew into his embrace.

'Menkh, oh Menkh,' she exclaimed, 'we had all despaired of your return when Mareen and Horven returned without you. Then the return of the Dorath Mar ...' Tishan fought to control her emotions. 'The people despair, Menkh. So much has happened while you have been gone. Where were you?'

Menkh held Tishan close and allowed the questions to flow out from her. That terrible things had happened were all too clear, but the details would come.

'I can hardly begin to tell you, Tishan. A journey to a place so distant that I have trouble comprehending it even though I was there. But all will be well. We will deal with the Dorath Mar once and for all now that I have returned.'

For some time, they simply stood together until Tishan had regained a semblance of control. Drawing back, she stood upright and looked him in the eye, a single tear still tracking down her face.

'Zaltec. It is good to see you back. You look different.'

Menkh smiled. 'There is much to tell on both sides, Stragosh. But first, let us see to the crystal and waste not a semmit more in finishing this.'

As they both turned their attention back to the crystal floating in the air before them, they could now see that tenuous lines of reddish-coloured light were extending out from its surface. Like questing fingers, they stretched out into the space around it, inexorably drawing closer to where the other crystal reposed.

'See, Menkh, the area of blackness has encroached much further into the old crystal. There is no doubt that its power is failing.'

Even as Crixac's words echoed in Menkh's mind, the lines of red light contacted the surface of the City's crystal. Fixing on it, the lines of light strengthened, becoming deeper and more vibrant. A low humming sound could now be heard and, slowly at first but with increasing speed, the surface of the older crystal began to glow. Brighter and brighter grew the red light and louder and louder the humming sound as it increased in intensity. Even though now both crystals pulsed with a light that hurt the eyes, neither Menkh nor Tishan could draw their gaze away.

The red crystal seemed to be shrinking, its essence flowing into the bands of light that extended from it, investing itself into the City's crystal. As the bands of energy from the red shard spread downwards from the top of the dying crystal, a black crystalline dust trickled out from beneath it, forming a mound on the floor.

Slowly the light faded, and the humming sound diminished until the red shard had totally disappeared, fully invested into the now rejuvenated crystal which pulsed with a red light. The mound of black crystalline dust which had formed on the floor now seemed to melt, forming a viscous liquid that flowed together, forming a black gem that glittered in the red light.

Menkh felt a brushing against his mind which, at first, he thought was Crixac. But Tishan looked quizzically at him and he realised that she, too, could sense it. Then a voice could be heard inside his head, the timbre and tone of which were neither distinctly male nor female but which echoed that of the Intelligence in the place he had first journeyed after touching the City's crystal. The words which formed seemed at times to him softer and more mellifluous and at other times more strident and harsher.

'Greetings, Menkh ab Dur, Crixac, and Tishan Dar. The first step has been completed and transformation has been achieved. Take up the black gem, Tishan Dar, it has power that we will use later. When you return to your dwelling place you will find there a worthy receptacle for it. The blocks that the renegade Adepts established to exert their control over my predecessor are removed. Now shall we unlock the power of this place. Now shall we begin the task of restoration of this City and together shall we work to regain the Balance.'

'It seems then that, unlike your predecessor, you are communicating directly with us? Is this because you have removed the blocks you have referred to?' asked Menkh.

'No, Menkh, it is because we are bonded, you and me. I am a Shard, separate from and yet still part of the Intelligence. I and others like me interact with our bonded agent — beings like you, Menkh — to actively intervene in events. We work for balance in all things. Balance is all. Now we must curtail our communication. I sense your Dorath Mar have crossed the Caxaphalc and

even now draw closer to the City. Whilst they suspect the existence of a threat to them, the City's defences have shielded it sufficiently enough to confuse them. They do not know what to expect but should not be underestimated.'

There was silence for a moment.

'Yet, I see that even your companion Crixac has not fully realised the nature of the Dorath Mar. So, I shall tell you that you may know what you face now. They are a creation invested with the life force of the beings that have been overcome. They, and those like them, are the tools of conquest for their master. These beings are your true enemy. They have a name for themselves but their language, which would be unintelligible to you, I would not utter anyway. We have told you that in your tongue you could call them the Talixit Ven, the Eaters of Light. You should know that as a race they are totally merciless. They lack compassion or pity and have no words or construct for such sentiments. They feed on the essence of life itself, absorbing the energy from all living things. Fortunately, there are not many of them. To say their coming here was an unfortunate occurrence is an understatement of epic proportions. If they were to get access to the City, the Balance would be altered irrevocably.'

'How did they arrive here? There must be many of them to have created such a disaster for my people.'

The voice laughed without humour. *'There is but one of them here, Menkh. One solitary individual. Somewhat like the Intelligence, its mind is connected to the others of its kind. Where one is so are all the others. They have absorbed the knowledge of the races they have destroyed, increasing their power and abilities such that they are now a threat that must be dealt with.'*

Tishan's voice echoed in Menkh's mind and there was an anguish in it that was unmistakable. *'But how is it that one single individual could conquer a race of millions in the space of a year?'*

There was a brief silence, then the voice of the crystal spoke again. *'Tell me, what was the one primal fear that all Graavens shared?'*

Menkh and Tishan looked at each other with a quizzical and confused expression.

'I cannot speak for all Graavens,' replied Tishan, *'but as a warrior it was ever the case that we feared to find an adversary that we could not defeat*

by force of arms. That we would find ourselves powerless and that, in despair, we would watch those we had sworn to protect, perish.'

'So, there you have it,' responded the Shard. 'From the first of your kind it/they absorbed, and all those later, was revealed that which you feared most, and it/they made it manifest. They spread like a disease, infecting their prey with their own essence, killing the body and robbing it of self will. Some they feed off, others they use to spread their contagion. Their taint spreads quickly, borne on the wind and carried in the bodies of those that have already succumbed. Some few prove resistant to the taint, but these are easily dealt with.'

'Then what are these things we have called the Dorath Mar?' asked Menkh.

The voice sighed but continued inexorably, echoing a profound sadness, 'They are the remnants of your own people, Menkh, trapped in a kind of living death. Animate but without will of their own. They are an abomination. Their life essence is forced to inhabit the shell of those you have named the Dorath Mar, trapped within them until their masters finally consume their energy. Caught between life and death, their silent screams bring pleasure to their captors. I am so sorry, Menkh and Tishan. The degradation of your people, and that of so many other races, is an affront to all sentient beings.'

A profound silence ensued, and it seemed an age before Menkh was able to speak. 'This news defies comprehension, like some malignant horror story. If Tishan and I and those who survived with us had not experienced it for ourselves, I could not credit what you say. What do I tell the people? How can the horror of this be grasped? It may be that those of their own kin now animate these things.'

'As to that, Menkh ab Dur,' came the voice of the Shard, 'do not tell them. It is enough that they are seen as the enemy. Defeat them and destroy the presence that sits behind them and your peoples' essence will be released. Leave such explanations for a later time if, indeed, there is ever a time that is appropriate for such an explanation.'

'*Very well,*' Menkh's voice was cold and fixed with a steely resolve, '*but know this. I cannot speak for my people, but I will wage such a war on these creatures that they will come to know one emotion. Fear. If it is the will of the Intelligence that the Balance be restored, then I act freely of my own will to do such things as I can to aid this. Tell me what must be done.*'

'*We three are bonded. In that bond you also draw on the power of the Intelligence as you act now directly as Agents of Balance. You, Tishan, are also chosen as a guardian of this City. Know that what you have seen and experienced is but a glimmer of the power that sits within the City and which I can release to aid our cause. I will need a little time to establish full control. I am sure that you will have much to prepare in the meantime while I do this?*'

'*Yes,*' responded Tishan, '*I was about to hold a briefing and there are things which I must communicate to Menkh.*'

'*Very well,*' mused the Shard, '*by the time tomorrow's dawn approaches, I will have established influence within the City at all levels. I will communicate with you again then.*'

The Shard abruptly severed communication, leaving Menkh alone with Tishan.

Grasping Menkh's hand tightly, Tishan spoke. 'Before we do anything more, Menkh, I have something to show you.' And with that she teleported herself and Menkh to another location within the city.

CHAPTER EIGHTEEN

'Y'ou have become adept at transference, Tishan,' remarked Menkh drily.

'That and many other things, Menkh. But we are here for a purpose which perhaps you will glean from our surroundings?'

Once Menkh focused on his immediate environment he realised that he was back in the place where he and Tishan had joined in Phags Par. Turning to Tishan, he raised a questioning eyebrow.

'Yes, they are both here. I can feel the bond with them, and they became aware of your return the moment you set foot back in the city. They wait for you just ahead. Go now and meet them, they are excited to meet you at last.'

'No less than I, Tishan,' Menkh briefly squeezed Tishan's hands and moved down the path that he remembered following before.

'I shall withdraw my presence, Menkh, and give you joy of your meeting.'

'No, my friend. Stay in the conscious, we have journeyed long together, and you will no doubt savour the experience.'

'Then I shall stay quiet and observe.'

As Menkh rounded a corner he came to the place where he and Tishan had performed the rite. Two individuals stood and turned towards him, standing quietly, watching and waiting. Menkh stopped abruptly as a hundred emotions flickered in his mind. When Graaven spawnlings hatch they emerge fully formed, though immature. Graaven offspring have immediate recognition of their parent and both parent and child establish an immediate mental bond on contact. This capacity was perhaps one of the reasons why the Graaven people had so ably adapted to the City and the influence of the crystal.

At five spahn tall, both male and female had much growing to do, but everything about them resonated sharply with Menkh and he drank in their features.

'Greetings, Father, I am called Drenyk,' said the figure on the left.

'I am called Pershivon, Father,' said the other. 'Do we please you?' she asked in a small voice.

Menkh knelt slowly, never leaving his gaze from their faces. On his knees he held out his arms and, formality forgotten, they both rushed into his arms.

'No Graaven has ever been more pleased,' he whispered, holding them close. 'Drenyk ab Menkh and Pershivon al Tishan.'

Tishan had quietly come up behind and smiled at the three of them. 'And now you have met your father, are you both pleased?' she asked playfully.

'Oh, yes,' replied Pershivon in a very serious tone. 'Are you back now to stay?'

'Certainly, for a time. There is much to do over coming meh'chaal but you will both be safe here.'

'Yes,' said Drenyk, 'the City is changing; we can both feel it, can't we Pershivon?'

Pershivon nodded.

'How do you know the City is changing?' asked Tishan.

'Because the voice that speaks to us, to all of us, has changed. When we hatched, the voice that greeted us was like an echo. Something from a great distance. This one is much closer, like someone is standing just next to you.'

'And does the voice frighten you?' asked Menkh.

'Oh no,' replied Pershivon, 'it comforts us and tells us that all will be well. I like the new voice. We are part of the City, too.'

'Indeed, you are, and all will be well. Your mother and I must go for a short time, but we will see you again soon.'

Tishan took Drenyk and Pershivon's hands. 'Your return was well timed; they are both ready to depart the hatchery. I will take them to the refectory with the others and then join you in the gathering.'

Menkh hugged them both again before releasing them. 'Good. I will travel to the viewing room and take stock of the situation.'

Tishan nodded in reply. 'Don't be too long.'

Menkh gave one last smile and then, concentrating on the viewing room in the Complex, he appeared there moments later.

The walls around him shimmered before coming into hard focus. He saw immediately that thousands of Dorath Mar had forded the Caxaphalc and were crossing over a metallic bridge they had constructed. Menkh also saw that there were other things present whose purpose was not clear; but knowing that they all contained the tortured life essence of his people instilled a slow build-up of rage.

'*Be calm, Menkh. The time of reckoning draws near, balance will be restored, and the spirit of your people released.*'

'*Can we be sure of that, Crixac? What if we falter at the last and these abominations are our downfall?*'

'*Then we will have done all we can in this balance war and the quest that we have been given.*'

Menkh's emotions settled. It was the guiding and malevolent intelligence that was the real foe here, the battle to be joined was just a precursor to that confrontation. Menkh spent some time looking closely at the variants of the Dorath Mar. There were those whose purpose appeared to be the construction of roadways, squat and multilimbed, that worked in close concert with others whose prime task seemed to be the creation of some kind of building material which was used to fashion a roadway. Still others carried tubelike metallic cylinders, but these stood by passively, appearing to stand guard.

'Can you shed any light on these others, Crixac?'

'Your thoughts regarding them are reasonably accurate. The rather stationary creatures carry energy weapons, similar to your staff. Direct your attention upwards, Menkh. Is there anything in the sky above them?'

Turning his attention skywards, Menkh could indeed see several black objects floating on outspread wings above the activity below and occasionally ranging ahead of the main body.

'The Talixit Ven appears to have corrupted some of Tarvuli's raptors to its purpose, using them to scout ahead. They also carry an energy weapon, but I suspect some of Tarvuli's larger flying raptors would make short work of them.'

'What of the City, could they spy us out from above?'

The voice of the Shard interjected, *'The City's shield is strengthened; these creatures will not sense our presence. The force sent against us is strong in numbers and might, but I have unlocked the first armoury and the force it contains. They will be on their way to you shortly. I have already set their interface so that they will follow your instructions implicitly. Their power should be sufficient for us to defeat this first assault long before it reaches the gates. It is important that we do not reveal our full strength to the creature. Such knowledge will be shared with its kind and will give them insight into what opposes them.'*

'And what is this power that you send to me?'

'You will see, Menkh ab Dur,' replied the Shard.

'You would appear to have much in common with Crixac. He, too, likes to have his little surprises.'

'*Really?*' replied the Shard. '*Then, like me, your symbiote knows that seeing them will save a lot of unnecessary explanation. Once you have seen them, then you may ask further questions as to their capabilities.*'

With that the voice was gone.

'*I can see that dealing with the Shard is likely to be an interesting experience,*' remarked Crixac.

'*Hmmm … coming from you, that should give me rise to serious concerns. One thing at a time, however. It worries me that the Dorath Mar will encounter the Benshin. I must ask Tishan what contact we have had with them. I wish I had not lost my staff on our journey to the red crystal, I fear I will have need of it.*'

'*Lost?*' replied Crixac. '*It is not lost, Menkh. You have had no real need for it till now, so I have neglected to mention it to you. The staff will return at your call. When it is not required it will, of itself, phase out, but is ever alert. If you want it, simply hold out your hand and summon it in the same way that you focus on a location and shift there.*'

Following Crixac's instruction, Menkh put out his right arm and concentrated his will on the staff. In moments it appeared in his grasp, somewhat cool to the touch but as solid and real as if it had never left him.

'*It will rapidly warm itself now that it is back in phase. The staff is quite a remarkable device. It is a great sadness that the Kareems and the others all died so needlessly. Their technology was quite remarkable.*'

'*Well, let us hope that the Shard is right. We still have much to do if we are to defeat the Dorath Mar and the creature that manipulates them.*'

Now Tishan's voice echoed in his mind. '*Menkh, we are all assembled. There is much fear amongst the people. I have not told them you are back.*'

'*Very well. Will it cause further consternation if I transfer back and appear in their midst?*'

'*I will prepare them. They have already seen me do this and they have grown somewhat accustomed to it as more City magic. I am still surprised by how much of this they are able to embrace.*'

'There is a reason for that which I will explain later. Make your announcement and then call me.'

Some few minutes later, Menkh appeared next to Tishan, standing on a small dais overlooking a crowd of Graavens who had been seated in the hall of the refectory building. As he looked over them, he was moved to see many hatchlings interspersed amongst the adults and his heart, though warmed, felt that now the stakes were even higher than before in thwarting disaster.

Horven and Mareen stood alongside Tishan and both embraced Menkh fiercely.

'Zaltec, I don't know whether to hug you or hit you! Mareen and I have been so worried.'

'We never gave up hope. When you didn't return, we followed your orders most reluctantly. Our Xotic friends were also concerned but aided us in returning to the Benshin. It will not surprise you to learn that Haran and Kuhltar were both waiting for us once we had crossed the Mother Water and bore us swiftly back to the city. We are beyond words that you have come back to us, though Fendrax said to the Stragosh and to us that you would eventually return from a distant place.'

'I am so sorry, both of you. The journey beyond the doorway led to a place where the time appeared to pass by differently than here. I am glad that the Tamut La carried you back safely. There is a tale to tell of yours to me and mine to you. Some of it you will glean from this meeting, but we will sit and exchange our stories very soon.'

As Menkh spoke to Mareen and Horven, the noise around them gradually increased as the Graavens spoke amongst themselves. A sense of excitement was permeating the room until every Graaven present was standing and a chant of, 'Menkh ab Dur,' thundered in the air from every voice.

Menkh turned and faced the crowd, smiling, and raised both his arms for silence. Slowly the noise subsided and, one by one, each Graaven sat once more.

'My friends, there are no words that would convey to you my feelings at having returned safely and my apologies at not being able to communicate with you. Having left in such a secretive way, let me begin by telling you that I have journeyed to distant places on a quest that was set, in a way, by the City itself. The true reason for this quest was that the source of power for all that we have come to know here was dying. There was no way, given what we face now, that the force which shelters us could also defend us against the return of the Dorath Mar.'

Muttering amongst the assembled Graavens interrupted Menkh as they digested this news. Again, Menkh lifted his arms and silence once more descended.

'I may tell you at once that the quest, with the support and assistance of Horven and Mareen Var,' and here Menkh indicated their presence with a sweep of his arm, 'along with our Benshin allies and our new friends, the Xotic, was successful. The magical source that powered the City was slowly dying. The quest that we set out upon was to find a new source of power to ensure the City's survival and the future for us, its new citizens. Even now as we speak, that new source of power has invested the City. Now we can turn to the issue of dealing with the invader, knowing that our home and our young ones will be protected.'

A palpable sense of relief could be felt running though the gathered people and, once again, the sound of voices exchanging views on this news increased so that Menkh had, again, to raise his arms to allow for questions to be heard.

A voice called out from the crowd, 'Zaltec, great as you are, what we can we few do against what comes before us? We can perhaps muster 300 Sagit and as many again who were of the Baran Mec. But against a host?'

Again, the Graavens spoke amongst themselves until Desh stood and called out to the assemblage, 'The words of Korm may ring true, but the Stragosh and Zaltec have called us together to hear their plan for our defence. Let them speak!'

Slowly the Graavens stilled in response to Desh's voice.

'Thank you, Desh. Your faith in me, indeed all of you, has been the source of strength that has enabled me to continue our struggle every day since we fled. But, my friends, I have no plan for defence.'

Here, Menkh stood silently and a complete hush, a profound silence, descended, with every eye focused on Menkh.

'Ankh, be so kind as to open the doors to this hall and let in what you will find waiting on the other side.'

Ankh had no words to utter. Automatically responding in a crisp Baran Mec salute, he walked rapidly to the end of the hall and threw open the doors. He stood, momentarily quite still, and then moved to one side as a figure, which had been standing motionless outside, advanced along the aisle that led through the now-gaping Graavens towards the dais where Menkh stood.

Into this silence, as the figure approached, Menkh spoke in a strident voice, 'No, I have no plans for defence, I am only interested in attack!'

Now the figure had reached the dais and it halted before Menkh. A voice like liquid metal echoed from its head and in perfect Graaven speech it said, 'At your command, Zaltec.'

'Very well. Turn and face the people. Let them see you clearly.'

Now the Graavens peered intently at the figure before them. That it was crafted from some crystalline substance was unmistakable. Vaguely Graaven in form, it stood seven spahn tall on two sturdy legs with feet that appeared to be composed of five separate appendages, somewhat like toes, that extended out from where the bottom of the leg met its foot. Its hands were the same, with a similar set of fingers that extended out from where the arm met the hand. From top to toe the skin of the creature was translucent and colours could be seen flashing continuously underneath. In the middle of its chest a constant red light pulsed, like a visible heartbeat. Above all this sat a head that was devoid of features except for two eyes that shone redly. It was an unsettling presence and its humanoid shape did nothing to dispel its alien aspect.

Menkh addressed the creature, but his voice spoke to the Graavens, 'What are you, and why have you come here?'

'I am First of the File. I and those of my file follow your commands.'

'You will fight for us and follow my commands precisely?'

'That is our purpose.'

'You will die for us?'

The creature's head moved and tilted slightly. 'This concept has no meaning. Should I be rendered dysfunctional the Second of the File assumes control under your command.'

'How many are you?'

'We are a file, that is to say, 5000 tetrans.'

At the word "5000", muttering amongst the crowd swelled.

'What is a tetran?'

'I am. We are.'

Menkh rethought his words. 'What is your function?'

'Obliteration of your enemies.'

'Who are the enemy?'

'Whoever, whatever, threatens the safety of the City and the Graaven people.'

Menkh allowed some time to lapse before he issued his last command. 'Very well. Return to your file and await my further instruction.'

'As you command.'

The First of the File departed, moving with a fluid grace. Each foot rose to the end of each separate toe so that it moved up and down as it progressed forward in a wavy action, like a trained dancer.

Tishan spoke for the first time, modulating her voice so that all in the room could hear her words. 'Zaltec, what do we know of their capabilities?'

Menkh answered but kept his attention on the Graavens gathered before him. 'We are going to find that out over the next few meh'chaal. Now we must prepare. Along with our tetran force, we will take a core of Hoplex. Volunteers all. The rest will stay here in the city to watch over our young. Over coming days, those who have volunteered will be armed by the City in the same manner as were Horven, Mareen and myself for our journey. In the meantime, we must communicate with our friends the Benshin and warn them. Though I have no doubt they are already aware of the invader.'

'Draachnull of the Benshin is already here, Zaltec,' said Tishan. 'He and a small group are camped outside of the city. They arrived yesterday.'

Menkh nodded. 'That is fortuitous. Are there any further pressing questions?' he asked the group. Heads turned and comments were exchanged, but no-one spoke out.

'Very well. Any questions that may arise will be answered by myself or the Stragosh. Now is the time to prepare to meet our foe and deal them a hammer blow that they will not forget!'

As one, the Graavens stood and called out their approbation, turning to leave the gathering and talking in excited groups.

Menkh turned back to Tishan. 'Let us make our way to the Benshin now and speak with them.'

Directing his gaze to Ankh, Menkh gave further instructions. 'Take the names of volunteers for the expedition. We will leave as soon as possible, but no later than three meh'chaal from now. Horven, you and Mareen will take our volunteers to the arming room. You remember how to get there?'

Horven saluted crisply. 'It will be done. Will we be able to pass through the statues that guard the approach?'

'Wait,' said Menkh, and turning his thoughts inwards he sent words to the Shard, '*Are you there?*'

'*Always,*' came the response. '*I have heard what you have said. Your people will be able to pass and I will guide them to the arming rooms if required. All the materials needed are here. There are other things that need to be done and other powers available to you in time to come. We will speak of this later.*'

Menkh turned his attention back to Horven who had stood patiently, though with a curious expression on her face.

'The short answer is yes, Horven. The crystal will guide you if needed. You may find a more direct interaction with it than with the previous source.'

Horven exchanged a look with Mareen. 'Still full of surprises, Zaltec!' she exclaimed.

Menkh smiled at them both. 'My name is Menkh, remember? Although, in present circumstances perhaps Zaltec is more appropriate.'

'There will be more volunteers than are required, Zaltec,' said Ankh, approaching. 'Might I suggest we favour those without offspring as far as possible?'

'Make it so, Ankh. Now, Tishan and I will visit the Benshin and see what they have to tell us.'

Ankh saluted. 'As you command.'

Leaving Ankh and the others, Menkh approached Tishan. 'If the Benshin are camped in their usual place outside the city we can transport to the city outskirts and then walk out. Is this agreeable?'

Tishan smiled and disappeared abruptly. Menkh laughed to himself.

'*Apparently she agreed with you, Menkh. Best go after her, then,*' echoed Crixac's dry voice.

Abruptly Menkh also vanished from sight and almost immediately appeared on the outskirts of the city, where it opened out to the fields that surrounded it. Walking out, he saw Tishan waiting for him and, a little distance ahead, a group of hide tents indicated where the Benshin had set up camp. Approaching the camp, Menkh saw that Draachnull was accompanied by three other elders who stood waiting for them.

'Greetings, Menkh ab Dur and Tishan Dar,' said Draachnull as they came before him, bowing in greeting in the Benshin way. 'Mrellin of the Lightning clan and Kethra of the Thunder Water clan you have met before. This is Pallak of the Smoke clan.'

Taking each of their hands in his individually, Menkh replied, 'Greetings to each of you, too. It is good to see our Benshin friends in difficult times. You know of the invader?'

They all sat on the earth around the fire that the Benshin habitually lit when they held council.

'We do. The Shadow Hunters have been tracking them across our lands. They bring with them a malaise of death. Wherever they tread we feel the land groan and the life of the plants and animals diminishes. Whatever these things are, Menkh, we are powerless to stop them. The Shadow Hunters set twelve mellax against them when they first entered our lands, bringing their taint with them. The voice of Varthansh Mek moans through the forest. The mellax caused them great damage but even their terrible ferocity was no more than a temporary hindrance. Now we fall back before them, though it causes us much grief.'

'These are the same creatures that destroyed our home and annihilated our people. Hearken closely to me now. These things may be fashioned of blood and bone, but they have been transformed into an abomination, creatures of nightmare. They were created for only one purpose, which you can clearly guess. The power which animates them has trapped in each one the life essence of many our people, slaves to the will of their master. The others of our people it has consumed. It feeds on life, emptying the lands it infests until nothing is left.'

The Benshin exchanged fearful looks but did not interrupt Menkh's account.

'You must leave their destruction to us. The City is powerful, and its energy is renewed. This was the purpose of the quest from which I have but recently returned. In three meh'chaal we will go against these we have named the Dorath Mar. I believe that the city is a safe place. You and all the Benshin are welcome to come here. The lands around the city are wide and lie under its protection.'

The Benshin elders bowed gravely from their waists, their beaded hair touching the ground.

'We thank you, Menkh and Tishan. We will consider your offer and it may be that we will send many of our children and their mothers to this place. We can sense the power that runs through the earth here and feel reassured. You and all the remnants of your people will understand our grief at being forced to leave our lands, our sacred places left to the desecration of a profane presence. But we will endure as best we can. With your permission we will send some of our warrior shamans with you. Let none say that the Benshin gave no aid to their friends in time of war, little though that aid may be.'

'We would welcome the presence of your shamans. The Graaven people admire the strength and cunning of all the Benshin clans. But we are not alone. The City has fashioned its own army to fight this foe and the weapons that will be unleashed will be something that none of us have experienced before. I must tell you, though, that even when we have eradicated these invaders I will not stop until the menace that is the real threat has been obliterated. Only then can we truly be safe.'

Draachnull and the others stood. Each elder nodded to the other. 'Then we shall make blood pact with you in this matter. Hold out your hand, Menkh ab Dur and Tishan Dar.'

Deftly, Draachnull whipped the blade of his belt knife across the palms of Menkh and Tishan's hands, drawing blood. This action was repeated until the six of them had similar cuts. Holding all their hands together so that their blood mingled, Draachnull spoke in a deep and sonorous tone. 'Here do we six make pledge. In the name of Varthansh Mek we will aid each to the other, providing comfort and shelter, food and warmth, healing and light to our friends.'

Then Mrellin spoke in the same formal tones, 'Back to back, side by side, constant, faithful, shall we stand united against this foe until our own death be upon us.'

Kethra took up the refrain, 'Here do we six make pledge. In the name of Varthansh Mek we curse the enemy who defiles our lands. Death, destruction, despair, unceasing enmity, neither pity not mercy shall we show to these invaders.'

Pallak continued, 'Varthansh Mek, aid us, your children, and these our friends. Hold us in your hands, guide us, nurture us, help us.'

'So do we pledge,' spoke Draachnull, then each of the Benshin, and finally Menkh and Tishan echoed the words.

When they released hands, a solemn silence descended on all.

'Words such as these carry great power, friend Menkh. We have today made solemn pact, each to the other. So,' and here Draachnull smiled, 'a drop of brandy would not be amiss, I think, to truly seal our pact.'

Some general laughter and nodding of heads lightened the mood, and after the cup had gone around it was lighter still, even given the circumstances that had led to the pledge being made.

'Now we shall take council as to who shall accompany you and who of our people will journey here,' said Draachnull.

'Good. Then we shall depart and oversee preparations for our expedition. We shall speak again soon.'

'Then there is one last message that I was charged to give you. Shashn of the Xotic sends greetings on behalf of his people. They sought word of your safe return which we can now gladly send back to them.'

'Thank you, Draachnull. Their aid enabled me to fulfil the first part of my quest in re-energising the City. Let us hope for happier times and a renewed acquaintance,' and, nodding to each of the Benshin, he and Tishan headed back to the city. Once out of sight they took hands and transported back to the Complex to assess the progress of the Dorath Mar and to continue planning.

It was clear from their later observations that the Dorath Mar were making steady advances. They had already passed the point where Menkh had first met Draachnull and were deep into the lands of the Shadow Hunter clan. Like the Graavens before them, they followed the remnants of the pathway that led, eventually, to the city. Scanning the path ahead of their lead elements, Menkh came to a place where the land around the pathway compressed. Back down the path a steep ravine tangled by fallen vegetation bordered the left, two bowshots from the path, whilst to the right the land climbed steeply upwards until it met a wall of rock which continued for some distance – a forerunner of the cliff walls that formed the outer defence of the city itself.

'Here is a good place. It forms a natural choke point and prevents our smaller force from being encircled. With our tetrans we should be able to nullify the enemy's greater numbers. At a Graaven marching pace it will take around one dak'chaal to get to this point.'

'You may find the Shard to be of assistance in the matter of travel,' interjected Crixac. *'We could translocate immediately but we cannot singlehandedly take the entire force with us.'*

The voice of the Shard entered their minds. *'Your symbiote partner is correct. I will provide you with a device fashioned partly from the remains of my predecessor. The device compresses time and distance. Whilst it has limitations, at this range there should be no issue. When activated it will open a gateway between the muster point here and the desired location. Step through the corresponding gate here and step out there.'*

'*I know this is merely advanced technology, but it really is like magic to me,*' Tishan mused. '*I cannot even comprehend how this works — but as long as it works, then that is the main thing.*'

'*On the third level, Tishan, you will find a research facility and entire library which will tell you in detail about the work that the Kareems undertook over generations on this,*' replied the Shard, '*though even accessing the database is likely to leave you without enlightenment, given the complexity of the subject. Crixac may have a better understanding.*'

'*I could not access anything on the third level, or indeed any of the levels below ground. My movements were extremely limited. But, Tishan, even though I have a more complete knowledge than you, I, too, lack the understanding that the Kareems had. They themselves formed an elite amongst their people. Eventually, of course, it led to their downfall.*'

'*So, I assume then that we can transport the device to the preferred location ourselves easily enough?*' queried Menkh.

'*Yes, the device can easily be carried. It is perfectly stable until it is activated, which you can achieve with your staff. Give the device a wide berth as the gateway establishes. 100 paces should be sufficient.*'

'*What of its twin? Do we establish that here first?*' queried Tishan.

'*I will take care of the gateway here,*' responded the Shard. '*The grassed fields down from the city's outer gates will provide ample room. Once established, the gateway here will be dormant until the time when you activate yours. Then they will link, and your force can deploy. Those details I leave to you. You will know when the link is forged simply because you will be able to see each other through the gateway.*'

'*How long before the first gateway is completed?*' asked Tishan.

The voice laughed in its fluid way, '*It is already done.*'

'*Then as soon as we have the device, we can start. Getting to the place well ahead of the enemy will give us time to prepare the ground. What of observation from above?*'

'You will be shielded, in the same way that the City is shielded. Nothing will observe you. I think you may find the Benshin useful to you if you wish to eradicate the Dorath Mar's aerial observers. They are not limited to controlling mellax. Ask them.'

Menkh nodded thoughtfully. *'You can depend on it.'*

'As to the device, it is already in your quarters. Begin whenever you are ready. I will aid you as I can.'

Translocating to Menkh's quarters in the Complex, Tishan and Menkh found the device sitting on a table. It was square in shape, around ten talit long on each side. Like the congealed remains of the dead crystal, it had no colour but was rather an opaque black which seemed to absorb the light into itself. Cool to the touch, its surface felt oily yet was perfectly dry. In all other respects it was unremarkable and, for that reason alone, Menkh and Tishan treated it as if it might suddenly explode.

'Crixac and I will translocate. I have the chosen point clear in my mind. Once we have opened the gateway we can step through and assist as required with moving our forces. Any questions?'

'No. I think we have been through everything. I will speak to the Benshin regarding the Shard's remarks.'

'Well,' Menkh smiled briefly, 'then, to it. Let us hope that I can carry it one handed.'

'I have already augmented your muscles. Unless it is exceptionally heavy you should not have an issue,' Crixac assured him.

Whilst the object was surprisingly heavy for its size, Menkh, with Crixac's assistance, was able to lift the device with his augmented strength. Dismissing his staff until needed and with a last smile at Tishan, Menkh translocated. Tishan looked for some little time at the spot where Menkh had been moments before, till she, too, disappeared in search of the Benshin.

CHAPTER NINETEEN

Menkh stood near the pathway at a point where, some 200 paces to his left, the ravine plunged downwards to eventually meet a boulder-strewn bottom. To his right, about 500 paces off, the cliff wall rose upwards approximately 100 spahn. At its top, cycads and other ferns grew in abundance. Similar dense growth crowded the far side of the ravine and the cries of small animals could be heard above a gentle wind. It was altogether peaceful. Above, the violet sky was cloud free. Avlar was reaching its zenith whilst the face of Colunda had disappeared below the cliffs to the north.

A tawny shape that had lain silently near the cliff wall now rose lazily and stretched before approaching where he stood.

'Fendrax!' Menkh exclaimed in complete surprise. 'How good it is to meet old friends, though I cannot begin to fathom how you knew I would be here.'

Fendrax also bowed gracefully and, approaching Menkh until they were nose to nose, sniffed delicately in the way of the Tamut La.

'Greetings to you, friend Menkh, Crixac. I echo your feelings. It is no great mystery. Several nights ago, as I was journeying back to your city, a voice came into my mind and told me to come to this place and wait. I have seen the creatures that you intend to face. A miasma of corruption and death precedes them, slowly killing all in their path. You will need to be careful; they are many and they are strong.'

'I, too, have been observing them from afar. We will be as prepared as we can. But what of your litter? Are they well?'

'They still hunt under the suns. They have taken my grandchildren and all our kin and fled to the north. Though they did so reluctantly and only at my strongest bidding. For now, they are safe – but that will depend on you and whatever force you have to face down this menace. What is your purpose here? Though you are strong, I do not think that you will stand long before that which approaches.'

'We are establishing a doorway between here and the city. Perhaps it is best to sit here whilst that happens. I suspect that the process will invoke some force which we cannot predict as it sets up.'

Menkh turned his thoughts inwards, '*Back there a way, I think. That will give us time to stage our forces as they arrive and be far enough back from the position I will set them in.*'

'*You are the Zaltec, Menkh. It seems a pity that such peace and tranquillity will soon be shattered, but then, the alternative is unacceptable.*'

Menkh placed the device on the ground and, retreating the suggested distance alongside Fendrax, he summoned his staff. Then, gripping it in both hands he focused his thoughts upon the device. A beam of yellow energy shot out from the staff and upon hitting the device seemed to be absorbed into the box-like structure.

'*You are becoming very proficient with that staff. But there is still power there you have yet to tap, I think. The power of the staff is dependent on the strength of will of the wielder and their capacity to focus their thoughts upon what is required.*'

'*Are you not supplementing my focus, Crixac?*'

'Only when critical. If I were to do that, the combination of what I shall call your "ignorance" of the how and why with great power could be catastrophic. No, Menkh, you learn well, but better to learn slowly with a little assistance from me. Soon my knowledge will become your own, as if it had always been there. Yes, balance is everything, don't you think?' Crixac's voice had a wry tone. Menkh snorted in response and was about to reply when the device began to exhibit a reaction to the energy beam.

For the first time, bright colours could be seen to flash out from its previously opaque surface. With each flash of light, the box expanded in size. Vibrations could be felt through the soles of the boots that Menkh wore and the ground shivered so that small stones and other scattered debris moved about. With a sudden whoosh of air, a brilliant white light, painful to the eyes, hid the expanding box from sight. Just as the wave of air hit Menkh with enough force to make him stagger backwards, it sucked back with such force that Menkh, already off balance, fell to his knees. When he had gathered himself and climbed to his feet, he saw that where the device had sat, a doorway now stood, similar in structure to the one where he had travelled to the Balancepoint earlier in his quest.

In the space formed by the doorway, which was some twenty spahn across and ten high, it was black and opaque, identical to the surface of the device prior to its activation.

'200 paces would have been better. Methinks the Shard was playing another one of its little jokes.'

'Yes,' responded Crixac, *'it does appear to have an oddly endearing propensity for surprises.'*

'Not unlike a certain symbiote of my acquaintance,' remarked Menkh drily.

Suddenly the blackness between the door posts disappeared and Menkh could see Tishan peering at him from the other side.

'Step through and join us,' Menkh spoke to Tishan. Tishan raised her hands to her head to indicate she could not hear him.

'*Interesting,*' commented Crixac, '*the doorway has compressed the distance, but sound appears to be another matter.*'

Menkh beckoned to her to step through. Tishan, visibly taking a deep breath, stepped through the doorway. It was interesting to watch as she appeared to walk through in a kind of slow motion. The action of stepping through was not instantaneous but took a few seconds to accomplish and as she completely cleared the doorway she staggered slightly. Taking another deep breath, she looked at Menkh. 'Well, that was interesting. Like wading through thick mud and feeling like part of your body is slightly behind you. The tetrans will no doubt be fine, but our people will find the experience a challenge.'

'Seeing as we know the doorway works then I believe we can all return to the city. We do not need to deploy our forces until the enemy are nearby and we can monitor their progress from there. Meanwhile, Ankh can step across with a team of workers and look at adding some amusing diversions for our friends once we engage with them,' said Menkh.

'Will you join us in the city, Fendrax?'

'No, I will stay here, I think. There is good hunting to be had and I can keep an eye on things and guard this side of your doorway.'

'Very well then.'

Menkh nodded in assent and, following after Tishan, stepped through the doorway himself. It was, as Tishan had described, an interesting experience. In the first place, for the few seconds it took to step through it was utterly silent and still. This was coupled with the rather familiar sense of coldness. Additionally, it took some effort to push through and there was a feeling, exactly as Tishan had described, that his body was being stretched between two points. It was not a pleasant sensation but was over very quickly. As he left the doorway, everything snapped back into place and the effort that he had used to push through the door made it easy to stagger on the other side, if unprepared.

Tishan had a wry smile on her face. 'So, how was it?'

Menkh smiled in return, 'Yes, interesting,' he agreed, and then they both laughed. Ankh stood with a bemused expression a little to one side with the small Graaven force he had with him. Snapping a salute, he addressed Menkh, 'Orders?'

'Yes, Ankh. Please step through with your team and see what you can do over the next few days to shore up our position. I am sure you will be able to come up with a few ideas. Oh, and if you haven't already seen her, Fendrax is going to keep you company. Remember your manners when she approaches you.'

Ankh looked slightly worried but, drawing a deep breath, responded, 'With alacrity, Zaltec,' and, indicating that his Hoplex should accompany him, he walked up to the doorway and passed through it. Menkh and Tishan watch closely as he staggered through on the other side. Bending over to catch his breath he then turned with hands on hips to give Tishan and Menkh a rather disgusted look.

Tishan raised her hands as if to say, 'Well, there you are,' and both she and Menkh laughed again. Turning her attention to the fifty or so Graavens who had hung back, she indicated they should join Ankh. 'Away with you, it is an interesting experience but not harmful. I think you will get used to it over time.'

Nodding warily, the group moved forward. Several walked through at the same time, emerging with more or less the same reaction on the other side.

In the time left to them to make final preparations, they observed the progress of the Dorath Mar towards the ambush point. In simulated combat the tetran force proved to be both deadly and capable of responding instantly to Menkh's commands, combined with independent action when the situation called for it.

Finally, when the enemy were only several chaal away from the location Menkh had chosen, the mixed force of Hoplex and Sagit, three praka vek in total, passed through the gateway and deployed into position on the other side to await the arrival of the enemy.

Each Graaven had been fitted out in suits almost identical to those which Menkh, Horven and Mareen had been equipped with for their earlier journey. One praka vek, comprising 100 Sagit, carried war bows, their sheaves of arrows modified by the Shard. In addition to the forty shafts they each carried in a sheath which hung at their waists, a further 15 000 shafts had previously been transported through the portal.

The tetran force was equipped with a kind of opaque crystalline shield and each carried a long, tubelike device, which was similar to that which Menkh had observed being held by the statues that stood either side of the causeway approach to the Complex, as well as some of the newly modified Dorath Mar.

The tetrans were deployed in a line which stretched across the gap that lay between the edge of the ravine and the cliff wall. Placed one alongside the other, allowing enough room to deploy their shield and weapon, they were arrayed in ranks 200 wide and twenty-five deep. Behind them, and stationed around Menkh, were the Graavens.

Menkh stood upon a slight rise in the ground so that he could clearly see the approach of the enemy. Having already checked his helmet communications with the tetran commander and Graaven field commanders, he now stood silently. Alongside him were Tishan and Ankh. Horven and Mareen hovered behind him, his constant protectors.

Menkh looked about him. It was another cloudless day but there was a chill in the air. The Season of Waning was upon them. Soon it would grow much colder and banks of dense cloud would begin to form. Taking a deep breath, Menkh raised his right arm.

As he did so, the Graavens donned their helmets and checked their communications.

'You may deploy your Sagit, Stragosh.'

'As you command,' came Tishan's response. 150 Sagit moved forward, somewhat into place, to the rear of the last tetran rank.

As time passed, the tension mounted amongst the Graavens, who stood silently. Then Menkh's voice could be heard, such that each Graaven felt he spoke to them alone. 'Men and women of the City, warriors of the Graaven Empire, my friends. Today we stand in defence of our new home which has nurtured and protected us and given us new hope. Its magic surrounds us. We have fought and bled together, watched our comrades and people perish, and seen our nation reduced to utter desolation and ruin. Today, we stand together again! Today, it is we who will deliver justice! Today, it is we who will triumph and, when we have swept this field clean of the filth that comes before us, then we shall carry vengeance forward and destroy the menace that dared raise its hand against us. Stand now with me, strong in your courage. Fight now for the memory of those we have lost and for the loved ones we have left behind.' Menkh paused for a moment. 'What say you?' he asked.

A muted roar came back through his helmet.

'What say you?' he called again, and this time the echoing roar was louder.

'What say you?' he called again, at the same time raising the staff he held in his right hand, emitting a flash of red light into the air as the staff reacted to his emotion. 300 arms lifted into the air with clenched fists and cries of, 'Menkh ab Dur,' echoed in his helmet.

'*Nice speech. That quiet was unsettling them,*' remarked Crixac.

'*Well, we shall see now, my friend, because our guests are arriving, and it is time to welcome them.*'

So it was that the leading Dorath Mar came into view. Rank upon deadly rank, silent except for the sounds of their feet hitting the earth. If they noticed the deep ditch that had been dug across the ground in front of them, there was nothing to indicate any pause in their steady progress. Beyond the ditch, dozens of crystalline rods had also been dug in with their tips angled towards the Dorath Mar's approach. They would cause the enemy to break ranks in order to pass through them.

The ranks of the enemy slowly compressed as they approached the trench. It was exactly 500 paces from where the Sagit stood, and within easy range of their war bows.

'Nock!' came the cry, and 150 arrows were fitted to 150 bow shafts.

'Draw!'

As one, the bows were pulled taut and aimed upwards towards the sky.

'Loose!'

There was an audible hiss in the air as 150 shafts leaped with tremendous power from the strings of the bows.

'Nock!' came the command again. Unhurried, methodical and deadly, shaft upon shaft was sent towards the enemy.

As the first wave of arrows reached the top of their flight, a humming sound was emitted. The crystal tip of each began to glow and light sprang from shaft to shaft. As they struck the enemy there was a huge shock of air and individual Dorath Mar were literally blown to pieces. Individuals marching in behind the leading ranks were, in turn, blown apart as wave after wave of arrows hurled destruction upon them.

Still they came on, climbing over shattered remnants and over body parts which now filled the trench before them.

'Most satisfactory, Zaltec,' remarked Tishan in a professional tone.

'Yes, they have still to pass through our little garden. I cannot help feeling that this is too easy. Be prepared for surprises,' responded Menkh.

The first surprise came from above them in the form of a swarm of black spheres which approached at speed. As they came above the tetran force, beams of energy shot down from the spheres and several tetrans were blown apart. It was then that the tetrans raised their shields above their heads. A shimmering light emanated from each one, coalescing with its neighbour until a blazing barrier of energy which emitted a reddish light appeared above the whole force. Now the energy beams aimed at them were deflected back. At times, a random beam of reflected energy would hit one of the spheres which exploded with a dull thud. Other beams hit the ground with a loud concussion, blowing fragments of stone and earth into the air. The Graaven suits initiated their own defensive aura but they were less effective than the tetran shields and a number of Graavens were knocked down with enough force to render them unconscious.

'These suits of ours are strong but they will not take repeated blasts, I think, and must eventually prove insufficient,' remarked Menkh to Crixac.

'Yes, I think you may be right. Still, your Sagit are giving them something to distract them from their aim.'

The Sagit had turned their attention to the sky and were shooting at the spheres overhead, but they moved quickly and hitting one was no easy feat. Meanwhile, blasts of energy continued to shake the ground and more Graavens were thrown violently into the air or were slammed down onto the earth.

It was then that the Graavens noticed a black mass approaching out of the sky from behind their position.

'If that is a further force of the enemy, we are going to be hard-pressed, Crixac.'

'You have not yet used your staff in this conflict and our main tetran force is yet to engage. We must wait and see what this new force is.'

The fluid tones of the Shard echoed in Menkh's mind, *'They are no force from the City. Your Benshin allies have prepared their own surprise to nullify this new threat.'*

The black cloud proved to be a mass of flying raptors. Benshin flute players appeared, walking along the path behind the Graaven position. Their strange music could be heard even above the noise of the blasts from the enemy spheres. Then the music stopped, and the individual raptors swept down amongst the spheres. Mighty beaks full of serrated teeth crushed the spheres as they were caught. Other raptors were blown apart in blasts of energy as the spheres moved to engage this new force, but the impact of losing the raptors that fell was negated by the sheer numbers of them. The attack of the spheres was completely disrupted as they were dispersed across the sky, the raptors pursuing them relentlessly.

Draachnull jogged up to where Menkh stood. 'Greetings, friend Menkh, it seems our arrival was timely.'

'Indeed,' responded Menkh, 'though I am curious as to how you knew of this threat?'

'That is interesting. Several of us were visited by a strange dream several days ago. In the dream a voice spoke and told us that we would be needed, and where. This gave us the time to gather many bartung from their nesting grounds and get here at the appointed time. It is a wondrous thing.'

'Yes, just another surprise in what seems a long succession,' responded Menkh drily.

The Dorath Mar had continued their advance, even hampered as they were by having to cross over the shattered fragments of those who had been destroyed. Now they were less impeded by the arrows of the Sagit, who had been forced to turn their attention to the black spheres.

By now, they had entered that part of the approach where the crystal rods had been planted. As they advanced in their silent way, they moved around them, had almost cleared the field, and were in close proximity to the first of the waiting tetran ranks.

As the leading ranks of the Dorath Mar reached the very end of the crystal field, the rods flashed into blistering light and hundreds of the enemy simply dissolved into nothingness. One minute they were almost within attacking range and the next they had vanished. Any human force would have retreated from this new threat but implacably, silently, ranks of Dorath Mar stepped forward and advanced. A dozen times more they experienced the same result but, as time progressed, it became clear that the light and power of the crystals had begun to diminish. Eventually, they were totally drained of all power.

Now the front rank of tetrans, moving as one by unheard command, replaced their shields on their backs, lifted the tubelike devices they carried to the horizontal and began to move forward through the crystals before them.

As the tetrans advanced, what at first appeared to be a cloud of dust slowly moved up from behind the Dorath Mar, where they continued to advance over the detritus of those which had been destroyed. The read outs that glowed on the inside of Graaven helmets flashed a warning of its approach.

'What is that, do you think?' Tishan spoke into her helmet.

'Nothing good,' came Menkh's response.

The cloud rolled over the tetran force which calmly advanced towards the first of the foe before them. Both they and the approaching enemy appeared unaffected by it. Not so any remaining bartung which, flying low as the dust reached them, emitted a harsh shriek, became instantly lifeless and fell out of the sky. Their bodies crashing into the ground were as much a menace as the enemy, as Graavens ran to avoid falling bodies and the shields of the tetran force, as yet unengaged, deflected the bodies away from them.

Benshin flutes played again and what was left of the bartung departed, fleeing before the dust cloud.

'Draachnull, get your people through the doorway behind us and back to the City. There is nothing more you can do here, and I do not want any Benshin to die today.'

'As you say, friend Menkh,' Draachnull reached out and gripped Menkh's gloved left hand in both of his. 'May Varthansh Mek watch over you and your people.'

So saying, he called on the several Benshin with him and, waiting until they had passed through the doorway before him, followed them through the portal. It was eerie to see them standing on the other side of the doorway looking anxiously back.

'Fendrax, I fear you, too, must leave this place until this dust has dispersed. Our suits will protect us, I think, but I would not have your death on my conscience.'

'As to that, the choice of living and dying is mine to make. Climb upon me, Menkh ab Dur, your staff will provide a shield over us both and we will battle this foe together. Let none say that She Who Hunts left friends to fight alone and ran off. If I do not stand with you now, then I deserve to die!' and, briefly touching her snout to the transparent visor on Menkh's helmet she lowered herself. Menkh climbed on and observed the fight from the higher vantage point his seat now enabled.

The dust cloud rolled over the Graaven position. A hissing sound could be heard as the Graaven suits sealed themselves and began to filter the air that they breathed and Menkh caused a greenish-coloured shield to envelope both him and Fendrax. The dust obscured their vision. It flowed over and around the doorway and shield but could not penetrate it. Leaves on plants and grasses underfoot withered and died, small creatures and insects fell to the earth and lay lifeless, and Menkh began to feel a rage building inside himself.

Now the tetran first rank had made contact with the still-advancing Dorath Mar. There was a sound like nothing Menkh had ever heard. A buzzing, low-pitched hum that made the ears vibrate even from within the confines of his helmet could be heard. From each of the tubelike devices a red beam of light shot out. Upon contact, the light punched a hole through the outer skin of the Dorath Mar, reducing it to a smoking ruin. The tetran force, now advancing behind their front rank, lifted the fallen bodies of the enemy and with frightening power heaved the shattered remnants and flung them over the heads of the Graavens down into the ravine. Their remains crashed through the once verdant undergrowth, now dead from the effects of the dust cloud, and fell amongst the rocks and boulders far below.

Menkh sat astride Fendrax, coldly and calmly watching all unfold. The tetran force needed no commands from him. Like the Dorath Mar, their advance was accompanied by complete silence other than the sound of their weapons. A few black spheres, those that had survived the raptors, had returned and the Sagit had engaged with them. Menkh had just turned to speak with Horven and Mareen, who were standing near him, when a blast of energy from one of the last of the spheres struck Mareen.

Mareen was smashed violently into the ground and Horven was blown from her feet. She staggered drunkenly upright. Tishan and Ankh were running towards them as Horven leapt towards Mareen's lifeless body.

The anguish in Horven's voice was clear as she desperately called Mareen's name. A rent could clearly be seen in the fabric of Mareen's suit. In ordinary circumstances she would have been injured but the invasive dust was no ordinary circumstance and its deadly miasma had stolen Mareen's life away.

A wave of sadness came over Menkh as he watched Horven kneeling over Mareen's body, desperately calling her name over and over. Vaguely he heard Tishan's voice ordering that Horven be assisted in getting Mareen's body back through the portal.

Menkh turned his attention to the field where some few lifeless Graavens also lay, unmoving. Other Graavens carried them to the safety of the doorway.

Now the rage that Menkh had felt building inside him turned incandescent.

Tishan turned to look up at Menkh, as the weeping Horven was escorted through the doorway accompanying the body of her sibling, to find that he had disappeared. What she now saw abruptly stopped any words she may have uttered.

The air shimmered slightly, and a figure suddenly appeared in Menkh's place. Its skin appeared to be made of a red, crystalline substance which glittered in the light, its body clad in flowing robes that matched the colour of its skin. The figure's features had an alien cast and it gave off a palpable menace. A red glow now enveloped both the rider and the form of Fendrax. Had Tishan not been on a field of battle she would have turned tail and run as far and as fast as possible following its precipitate arrival. Instead, she stood glued to the spot. In the creature's hands a tall staff blazed with many colours which flashed within its core, whilst eyes of a piercing blue traversed the field ahead where the tetrans continued to advance against numbers of Dorath Mar. Beams of energy from both the tetran force and the Dorath Mar flickered through the fog-like air and now some tetrans were falling victim to the Dorath Mar assault.

A baleful gaze turned and fixed Tishan, but the voice that she heard in her head was the voice of Menkh ab Dur. 'Get behind me. Get all the people behind me, Tishan. Now!'

Tishan pulled herself together and issued the command. Rapidly, the Graavens cleared away and fell back. With an earth-shattering roar, Fendrax leapt into the air, bearing Menkh aloft as he swept the staff around and held it out before him. The bolt of energy that leapt out from the staff was indescribable. It blazed like a thousand suns. A thunderclap, like a mountain falling, pierced the air and as it swept forward from Menkh, it grew in strength and power. As it struck the rear of the tetran force it seemed to absorb their energy and use it to magnify its own. The tetrans crashed to the ground, robbed of all power. As Fendrax returned to the earth, having leapt over all of the tetran ranks before her, the wave of force struck the Dorath Mar. The impact was like the energy field of crystalline rods, only far greater in strength. The Dorath Mar were obliterated. Rank after rank, every Dorath Mar dissolved into a cloud of vapour which dropped to the earth and evaporated away. As the energy struck the first rank, so it leapt to the second and the third. Relentless and implacable, its terrible power ran unabated. Within mere moments, not a single Dorath Mar was left. Slowly, the dust dissipated and silence descended. The Graavens stood bewildered and Tishan, turning her attention back to the transformed figure of Menkh, blinked her eyes as he disappeared from sight, leaving Fendrax standing alone and roaring her defiance so that the very air seemed to throb with the sound of her rage.

CHAPTER TWENTY

Menkh reappeared. His crystalline skin reflected the cold light of Orvasne as it peeped its serene face through one of the many windows that were set in the walls of a vast and lofty hall. The cold light of Menkh's gaze was offset by a more roseate glow which heralded Avlar's arrival and the break of dawn.

The illusion that Crixac wove around him so that he still looked like a Graaven had been thrown off in his rage but its effect on his people was a problem for another time.

'Welcome, Crixac, to the Hall of the Emperors in the city of Tarmech, one-time capital of the Graaven Empire. Here it was that I left Pershiva as she led the last of the army to war whilst I fled to the east.'

Menkh moved towards a set of doors that opened on to a stone balcony. As Orvasne dropped down toward the horizon, the soft light of Avlar lit up a desolate scene.

A vast city lay before Menkh's gaze. In his mind's eye, he could see the crowds of people that had once flocked the temples and markets. Travellers from all over the Empire milled in its streets to trade goods or carry merchandise up from the wharves which abutted the banks of the Camchak, the great river, that flowed eternally to the long lake far to the south.

Not a living thing could be seen. Withered plants and shattered stems marked where once great parks had stood. Ornate fountains, which once had flowed with life-giving waters, were forever stilled. Everywhere walls and pavements were cracked, and masonry had, in places, fallen in. The city had the appearance of an abandonment that stretched back centuries, an ancient ruin where only the echo of an echo of life could be imagined. A mournful breeze blew around the buildings, raising dust that gathered in small drifts in doorways and against walls. All was desolate and silent but for the movement of the air.

Menkh stretched out his senses, tenuously feeling for life.

'*This place has been sucked clean of life. Even the very ground is rendered sterile,*' remarked Crixac.

'*Yes. Not entirely dead but so close to it that the stones themselves fall into ruin and decay. I can feel it being drawn away. All the life essence of the land sucked along lines like veins that flow across the land.*'

The figure disappeared again, leaving the empty hallways and the memory of an obliterated people behind.

The air shimmered. The figure appeared again, this time in the midst of a great plain. To the north, thousands of withered stumps marked where a vast forest had once stood. To the south, a lakebed, long devoid of water, stretched into the distance. Between the two, thousands of desiccated bodies dressed in rusty mail lay amid ragged banners.

'*Here it was she led them,*' remarked Menkh, '*protected by the waters of Garmeer to the south and the forest of Parmet to the north. Had it been any other enemy it would have been good ground. Against the Dorath Mar, they didn't stand a chance. Here they lie where they fell, their very bodies leached of all life.*'

Crixac was silent. There were no words that could assuage the horror or alleviate the feeling of despair that was felt. Menkh walked towards the centre of the line where the Graavens had stood. Here the bodies were piled deeper, until finally he came upon that of Pershiva, still wearing the royal diadem on her wasted brow. Menkh stood silently for many minutes as bitter tears washed down his face.

'I knew she was dead, of course. It is the reality of it. What despair she must have felt as our people fought and died alongside her.'

'Perhaps not, my friend, perhaps not entirely. She had placed all her faith in you. Let us believe, rather, that her last thoughts were of you leading the last of her people to safety and wreaking vengeance on that which had laid all so low.'

Menkh reached down to tenderly remove the diadem from her brow but even his delicate touch caused her body to subside into dust.

'Remember now that her memory lives on in Pershivon, in your offspring, and that of your people, safe now in the city where you have led them.'

As Menkh stood silently holding the diadem in his hand, his mind wandered …

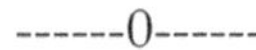

He paced up the centre of the Great Hall and throne room, flanked by Baran Mec. His hands, bound lightly in chains of chaldec, a precious metal, were mute testimony of his guilt. Around him were gathered the nobility of the Empire. Peremon ab Shallic barely contained the cynical smile of triumph as Menkh passed him by. Menkh, however, had eyes only for his sister Pershiva, newly crowned Pohlan Kar and puppet of the Shallic, Persavic, and Mellish clans. A title rightfully Menkh's but lost to him in the vicious politics of the Court.

He halted before the throne and bowed low. He noted a ring of guards that stretched around the hall and to his right, at the bottom of the raised dais where sat Pershiva, stood Tishan Dar, Kalvak of the Baran Mec. Their eyes locked briefly before Tishan diverted her gaze.

'Remove the chains from this, our prisoner,' called Pershiva, though her voice sounded tentative. Peremon took this as his cue and, stepping forward and bowing, he spoke, 'Supremacy. Menkh ab Dur is a traitor, he should be left bound.'

'Menkh ab Dur is of the blood royal and my brother and his fate is yet to be determined,' responded Pershiva.

Now Fazor of the Persavic stepped forward and his bow was the merest inclination of his head. 'Pohlan Kar, this is not seemly. Menkh ab Dur has failed in his duty to the Empire, sparing the enemy instead of annihilating them as commanded by your father, of honoured memory.'

A muttering swept around the hall as those gathered exchanged whispered comments. Recent events had destabilised the Empire. The sudden and unexpected death of the Emperor had led in swift succession to the deposing of Menkh as successor and the setting up of Pershiva. Doubt and rumour surrounded the death of the Emperor Dur ab Shemma.

Now, Hema of the Mellish clan stepped forward, his bow non-existent. 'We must insist, Supremacy, that you take affirmative action with this traitor!' he called out.

Peremon and Fazor nodded their heads in agreement and they glared upwards at the diminutive figure of Pershiva.

Slowly Pershiva rose from the chair and stood silently for a brief time. In a much stronger voice, which seemed to echo around the hall, she spoke directly to the three nobles standing beneath the dais. 'So, it seems I must act on your advice and make judgement on traitors?'

The three exchanged pointed looks. 'Yes,' said Peremon.

Pershiva turned her gaze to Menkh who stood calm and composed before her, and her eyes did not leave his face.

'Very well. Kalvak Tishan, hear the words of your Pohlan Kar. The sentence for traitors to the Empire is death. The sentence to be carried out immediately.'

Menkh did not stir. If the thought of his imminent death troubled him, he gave no sign of it. A total and expectant hush fell on all those assembled.

'At your command, Supremacy,' Tishan Dar responded with Baran Mec salute. 'Tremm, Jessic, Paltor you have your orders. Carry them out.'

The three guards saluted and, drawing the stabbing sword each carried in their belt, they advanced on Menkh, standing just beyond the figures of Peremon, Fazor, and Hema who stood smiling smugly.

At first, so rapid were the blows, the look of smugness stayed on their faces before turning to looks of horrified surprise on each as the swords were thrust into their bellies and sliced viciously upwards. Their muted screams as they gasped for air and their jerking movements rapidly subsided as they fell to the ground.

The Pohlan Kar stood unmoved. Her gaze had never left Menkh's face whilst the dispatch of the three nobles was occurring. 'Clear this carrion from my halls and cleanse the floor,' she ordered, before finally turning her eyes to her Kalvak.

'Tishan Dar, have you obeyed my instructions for the traitors' families?'

'It is done, Supremacy.'

'Very well.'

Her gaze swept around the hall and the muttering and gasps of surprise were stilled as her eyes met those that stood there until, once again, they fixed on Menkh.

'Menkh ab Dur, will you bow to the will of the Pohlan Kar?'

Menkh went down on one knee, 'I am ever the servant of the Pohlan Kar. Gladly do I submit to your sentence upon me.'

'Stand then, Menkh ab Dur. Beloved brother and son of the Empire. Guards, remove those chains, they offend my sight.'

A brief moment passed while the command was followed.

'Here is my judgement upon you, Menkh ab Dur. For allowing the enemy to be released and sparing their people you are sentenced to exile.'

Mutterings and cries of surprise went around the hall.

'Silence!' shouted Tishan Dar. 'Who dares question the will of the Pohlan Kar?'

Not one voice was raised in the silence that fell following these words.

Pershiva spoke again. 'Two sem'chaal shall you be banished to dwell on the island of Firma in the midst of Ter'Malloch, the Great Lake. When that time has passed shall you return to us here, to be proclaimed Zaltec of all Graaven forces. Do you submit to our will and to our judgement?'

'So shall it be,' responded Menkh.

'Very well,' Pershiva lifted her gaze to the assembly in the hall, 'know you all that the traitors Peremon, Hema, and Fazor conspired in the foul murder of our beloved father, Dur ab Shemma. Through their lies and intrigue they contrived the arrest of Menkh ab Dur and sought to set me up as their puppet. Now, they are dead, and their families declared to be terrac, outcast, shunned and reviled. None shall aid them on pain of death. Tishan Dar, clear this hall. Menkh ab Dur, remain and await my further instruction.'

Several semmit passed as the hall cleared. The departing Graavens trying to bow to the Pohlan Kar and those calling out words of fealty were ignored. At last, but for a handful of guards, only she and Menkh remained.

When the doors closed with a hollow boom, Menkh swept forward and caught Pershiva in his arms as she broke down in tears.

'Shh, dearest one,' he spoke soothingly. 'You have done all that we planned and our father is avenged. Hush now.'

After some moments in his embrace, Pershiva pulled back. 'Menkh, thanks be to Bekkor that you were here. I could feel your strength coming to me through your eyes. I could not look as those traitors were put down.'

'All will be well. The horror will pass, and you will be a great Pohlan Kar. Together, we will work as we have planned. I will go to my exile, but we will keep in touch. Two sem'chaal is not so long and all is calm here.'

'Yes, you are right. Nought but some vague rumours from out of the extreme west. All else is well.'

'Rumours?'

'Nothing to be concerned about and nothing concrete. You know what the frontier is like. Come, let us have a last meal together before you depart.'

'Yes,' replied Menkh, tentatively rubbing the ache in his belly. 'Think about promoting Tishan to Stragosh. She is loyal and dependable, and you will need someone with sensible council here in the capital who is not of noble blood.'

'It is already done,' she replied as she took his hand.

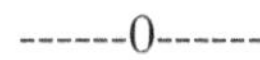

Slowly the memory faded until his senses returned to the lifeless plain and the forlorn remains before him. The rage within him grew once more until he felt that that the whole world could not contain it. 'Help me, Crixac. I will not leave them all here like this. Help me raise a monument to them.'

'Take up the staff, Menkh. Focus all your rage, your grief, your love into it and unleash its power and we will see what we can fashion.'

The staff thrummed with power; its glow intensified until no Graaven eye could have borne to look at the light that now poured forth. A whirling dust storm rose high into air and a vacuum formed at its centre, drawing in the thousands of bodies that lay on the ground and which themselves fell into dust with the movement of the air. Great heat melted the gathering sand and within the very heart of that heat and light a three-sided pyramid arose, its base planted firmly upon the plain, to some twenty spahn in height.

As the newly formed material cooled it created a translucent shell through whose sides, as you walked around it, the individual faces of Hoplex could be seen, rising to the surface and then falling back into its depths. As Menkh stood transfixed, the face of Pershiva, perfectly shaped, her lips lifted in a small smile, rose to the surface. The royal diadem and crown of the Empire upon her head, the face seemed to gaze at him for some moments before it, too, sank back into the depths.

'Now that is what I would call a fitting monument to all that fell here,' remarked Crixac.

Menkh had no thoughts or words, spoken or otherwise, to convey his emotions. He turned his attention back to the veins he could feel in the ground and the direction they led.

The figure again shimmered and disappeared, leaving the monument standing alone amidst the desolation of the plain until the world should fall or life spring up anew.

CHAPTER TWENTY-ONE

Menkh travelled in the place between. Here time and distance meant nothing, the world around him an insubstantial reflection of the real world outside this one. It was neither light nor dark – a strange kind of drab twilight held sway. Suspended in the air, the ground below him rushed by, but that was the only indication of movement. There was no feel of wind as he travelled, all was utterly still and silent. The veins in the earth which he followed pulsed eerily as the life they stole travelled along them towards their ultimate destination. A kind of languor crept over him in the place between, nothing seemed to have any urgency, reality had no application. Here, nothing ever happened nor ever would. Lose focus in this place, he realised, and you could be trapped forever.

'Snap out of it, Menkh. Never lose sight of why we travel here. Think of Mareen, think of Pershiva, and focus on those veins.'

Menkh's thoughts had been drifting into a kind of malaise but Crixac's voice brought him back to wakefulness.

'Thank you, my friend. My thoughts were drifting far away. This would not be a good place to lose your way.'

Now in the distance Menkh could see that a myriad of veins all drew together. Some veins pulsed strongly, others had barely any flow at all, but ahead was the final point where they all met. It was time to slip out and back into reality.

The air shimmered and Menkh stood once again on the earth. As before, the ground around him was devoid of life. Withered and desiccated plants and grasses stood forlornly. Before him, a vast dome reared into the air like some monstrous egg, its skin pulsing with a lurid purple light. With each pulse it seemed to expand a little, pushing out across the earth. It was many spahn tall and its circumference was such that to walk around it would take an individual several chaal, like walking around the walls of a small city.

Menkh turned his thoughts to Crixac. *'What now?'*

'Now, my friend? Now we must enter this thing and seek out what resides within. Now that you are partly crystal, your body will adapt to the environment inside and I will calm your mind as we make the changes. You must once again focus on your staff and will us inside. We cannot cut our way in; to do so would result in the atmosphere inside leaching into this world. That would not be desirable. Are you ready?'

'Am I ready to enter a poisonous egg, travel through a toxic atmosphere, and confront a malevolent entity? What do you think?'

Crixac chuckled drily but he did not respond. Menkh focused on the staff and willed himself inside. His senses were overwhelmed. Had Crixac not been with him to calm his thoughts he would have gone insane. His mind cried out that he could not breathe nor move, and he was desperate for air. His body made rapid adjustments as he floated in a loathsome slime. Finally, he tried to open his mouth to suck in the liquid, only to find that his mouth had disappeared. He felt calmer as his newly modified body absorbed all that he needed from the liquid he floated in. His own skin had become jelly-like and as he willed himself to move through the slime, his body pulsed and propelled him forward. He sensed the environment around him. Hair-like filaments replaced his eyes and built an accurate picture in his brain of his surroundings.

Within the fluid he travelled, more solid structures, somewhat like the roots of a tree, could be discerned. Like the veins he had followed to the egg, so the roots guided him towards his goal.

Ahead now, suspended between the roots in a grotesque parody of the crystal room within the Complex, hung a black mass. Its surface rippled obscenely as the life force that fed it pulsed into its body. Menkh could sense its intelligence. Like a fisherman delicately resting a finger on his line to sense movement, so this creature stretched its consciousness along each of its lines and into the world beyond.

Menkh had expected to encounter an evil and malevolent presence. The reality was, in some ways, worse. An utter and complete indifference to everything except its own needs, a complete disregard for everything combined with a supreme will that could dominate and overpower the minds of other lesser creatures.

'So here we are, Crixac. I seem to have lost my staff so I am at a loss to see what we can do to destroy this thing.'

'In the first place, your staff now forms part of your body. It is simply a case of focusing your will when the times comes. However, we will not try to destroy it, but to contain it. Then we can cast it out into the place between.'

'A noble plan. What are we going to contain it in? I have nothing to hand. Actually, I am entirely lacking hands, but I sense you have thought of this?'

The black shape gave an agitated movement. Something impinged on its outwardly directed thoughts, a perception that something was not right, although it could not place what it was. It focused its attention on the strands of power that it manipulated. It sensed an annoyance along one of its threads, a resistance that it had not expected and that must be dealt with.

The fluid voice of the Shard entered Menkh's mind, *'You both must keep even your thoughts hushed. It senses a wrongness but cannot place* it. You are going to contain it, not destroy it. You already have the vessel that can achieve this. It is the royal diadem you retrieved from the body of your sibling.'

Menkh was perplexed no less than Crixac. 'That is, indeed, ironic and remarkable. I would say it was an amazing coincidence that the very thing that could defeat this malevolence was in our grasp all along,' remarked Menkh.

'Let us say that it was an extraordinary coincidence that when your ancestors fled the City, they stole one crystal and took it with them. Legends grew up around the sacred diadem and how it "fell from the stars", as such things happen when real origins are lost in time, or people wish to forget. In fact, it is a shard of great power, though in a different way to the power which is invested in me. Your ability to utilise the staff allows you to unlock it and that is what we will contain it in.'

'You mean as big as it is the diadem will hold it?'

'Menkh, you could contain this entire world within that shard. You have the means to do so, it merely takes the will and the focus. I will aid you in this.'

The black shape moved again. The feeling of wrongness was growing though it could sense nothing untoward in the filaments that fed life back to it. A seed of an idea began to form, at first rejected, but slowly growing, that the sense of wrongness was here with it. In this place where no life, other than its own, could exist, its senses began to probe the liquid in which it lay suspended, looking for that which did not belong.

'So, what must I do? I cannot see or feel the diadem. Do I focus my will upon it?'

'No, Menkh. First you must excrete it into the liquid around you.'

'Excrete it? Do you mean it is inside me?'

'Indeed. Like your staff, it was incorporated into the form you currently occupy. Think of the diadem, form a clear picture of it in your mind, and "push" with your will. The diadem will be expelled from your form. Once it is outside of you, you can focus your will and the power of the staff on containing the creature. The staff will form a band of energy which will trap it and slowly compress its form. The shard will ignite with the energy created and will draw the creature into itself. There it will be contained.'

'And this thing will sit meekly back and allow this to happen?' asked Crixac.

'No, Crixac. It is going to fight and its will is overwhelming. That is where you and I must work together to reinforce Menkh's mind and to enable him to maintain his focus.'

Suddenly the Shard's voice shouted an alarm, 'The creature has scried your whereabouts. Menkh, you must act now!'

No sooner had the warning been issued than a vast weight settled on Menkh's mind. It was like a mountain falling on top of him. His mind compressed, all rational thought left him, and terrible pain arced throughout his body. Insanity was but one tenuous thread away as Menkh gibbered in a distant corner of his mind.

Somewhere in the dimmest recesses of what remained of his sanity a voice spoke to him. The voice was comfortingly familiar, one that he had not heard for a very long time, but which evoked deep emotion and feelings of love.

'I am here with you, Menkh, dearest brother. Together we shall fight this thing. Come now. All is well. Focus your will. Lift yourself beyond despair, beloved one.'

Menkh fought out of the terrible despair he was trapped in. 'You are here with me, Pershiva?'

'I am in the diadem, Menkh. In the last moments when life was leaving me, the diadem called to me and held my spirit close, waiting for the time it knew was coming. Together, you and I shall harness its power and rid our people of this menace.'

Menkh felt his strength and purpose returning. He pushed back against the mountain that sought to overcome him. He felt the diadem leave the confines of his body, exiting through the gelatinous membrane that formed his skin. He felt a joining with the mind and spirit of Pershiva, and together they focused their will on the staff. Still the power of the creature was overwhelming as it fought back and sought to overcome them. He felt the Shard join with him and Crixac and Pershiva, reinforcing their will, and slowly they pushed back together.

A golden beam of pure energy leapt from Menkh's body. It arced through the liquid and swept with blinding speed around the black form of the suspended creature. At the same moment, the diadem exploded into brilliant light. A scream of utter rage echoed through Menkh's mind, briefly accompanied by a last push of the creature's will, instantly dampened by Pershiva and the Shard.

The energy which surrounded the black shape compressed, bulging here and there as the creature thrashed around endeavouring to free itself. As it compressed, a tendril of force connected with the blazing light of the diadem and was drawn inside it. With infinite slowness, the creature was sucked slowly, inexorably, into the diadem until it had disappeared altogether. The filaments and lines which had previously attached to its form now hung motionless in the fluid which had supported it.

'*Well done, brother,*' echoed Pershiva's voice triumphantly, '*it is done!*'

The diadem, moving now of its own accord, pushed itself back inside Menkh's form and, with a final effort of will, Menkh transported himself back to the world outside where he collapsed on the ground in a state of exhaustion.

Menkh's mind drifted. It was not an unpleasant sensation. Memories from the past floated up from his subconscious and he looked at them objectively like some third-party observer. They had no hold over him and they drifted away from his conscious mind. Again, a persistent voice echoed in his mind.

'*Pershiva?*'

'*Yes, dearest one. I have come to say goodbye. I am free now to travel on and you must return to your reality, there is much still for you to do. Know also that the life force of our people, trapped within the abomination of the Dorath Mar, have also been freed. The obliteration of their vile form freed them and now that this creature has been contained, I will lead them to the place of renewal.'*

'Will I see you again?'

'Perhaps one day. Till then, look into the eyes of Pershivon and there you will also see me. Farewell, dearest one. Take care of our people.'

'Always. Go in peace, beloved sister. My heart travels with you.'

Pershiva's voice faded, 'I am at peace, beloved.'

A profound sadness settled upon Menkh, but he could not resist the pull back to consciousness and he opened his eyes to a sky filled with ominous looking clouds. A cold wind blew over him.

'Weather to match your mood, my friend. Welcome back,' remarked Crixac.

'Was I out for long?'

'Not that long. But so distant in place and time that not even I could rouse you. But come, see what our magic has wrought this day.'

Menkh stood and leaned on the staff which had been next to him on the ground where he had lain. In his right hand he held the diadem. He felt remarkably refreshed and his melancholic and introspective mood lightened, knowing that the spirit of Pershiva and many of his people journeyed towards a new beginning. He surveyed his surroundings but there was no sign of the giant egg that they had entered.

'No. Interesting isn't it?' mused Crixac. 'Turn your gaze onto the crystal.'

Menkh lifted the diadem level with his eyes. Its perfectly translucent depths now had a black heart which swirled and pulsed.

'There it is, egg and all, contained inside where it can do no harm.'

Menkh concentrated on the swirling blackness. *'It is passing strange that this thing has no name. Even the Shard refers to it rather obliquely.'*

'To give it its true name is to invest it with power. It "is" and that is enough. Besides, Talixit Ven is an accurate enough description, and Dorath Mar for that matter.'

'Yes. What of them? Have we more to fear from them?'

'Of the Dorath Mar? No. As soon as this creature was contained, the will which drove them or might have created more was cut off. They have fallen, never to rise again. The spirits of your people trapped inside have been freed. As to the Talixit Ven? There we must wait and see.'

'I can never tell our people the truth about the Dorath Mar, Crixac. They must never know what was trapped inside.'

'Nor shall they. They have conquered the Dorath Mar and they have survived. The Time of Renewal is at hand for all of us.'

'One last question then, if you know the answer. How did the Dorath Mar come into being?'

The voice of the Shard interposed itself into his thoughts. *'The creature that now lies trapped within the diadem created them, Menkh. Such is the force of its will and its power; it can manifest into physical form that which it imagines. When it arrived and consumed the first of your people it evaluated what was required to defeat you. The life essence of those of your people it did not consume itself were contained inside the body of the Dorath Mar. This was a form that captured all the martial skills of your people in a body, virtually indestructible when facing Graaven weapons. There was an added element of horror for your people — are not the Dorath Mar themselves reminiscent of the creatures from some of your folklore? Your people hunted down by the very creatures used to frighten them when they were young. "Beware the Dorath Mar who haunt the dark places!" Isn't that from one of your Graaven stories?*

The fact that you managed to disable some is itself a remarkable feat. There were a myriad of ways it could have laid your civilisation low but, in part, it also feeds off the terror and despair it creates, so a slow conquest was preferable to a quick one. If it had known of Kareem Vastar and all that lies within it, its approach would have been very different. Every race this thing, and the others of its kind, has ever consumed have yielded up their knowledge. You are lucky in one sense that the creature's arrival here was a random act that upset the Balance and it had no knowledge of the City or its origins.'

'I would not call the violent death of hundreds of thousands "lucky",' responded Menkh.

'True. But do not forget that your empire was founded on the violent deaths of hundreds of thousands. You yourself have wrought destruction on those you saw as the enemy.'

Menkh sighed and was momentarily silent. *'You are right, of course. Pershiva and I were brought up as true Graavens. But I am no longer that person. We both rejected what our race had become. Together, we would have changed our society.'*

'I do not rebuke you. I merely point out to you the facts. In the end you have effected the changes you desired, but in ways that could not have been foreseen or contemplated. There is much here that shows the hand of the Intelligence. Come. You must return. Your people worry after you and there is much now to celebrate.'

'What of the diadem and its contents? Shall I return with it?'

'No. You travel in the place between. Leave it there as you journey back. Let it lie undisturbed in that place. It is fitting.'

'Very well then.'

The voice of the Shard withdrew.

'Are you ready, my friend?' asked Menkh.

'As ever. I must admit that even I will be glad of a rest. All these new experiences have been quite illuminating but I am ready for the mundane for a while.'

'This from a creature that spent 2000 years cohabiting a pet animal?'

'Yes. Well there is no need to remind me. Besides, I did a lot of reading. I mean, a lot.'

Menkh laughed, the air shimmered, and the figure disappeared.

EPILOGUE

Across the lands that had once formed the Graaven Empire, life slowly began to trickle back into the earth. It would take generations to renew, but here and there a few stalks of grass would occasionally appear as testament to its slow revival.

In the city the Graaven people continued to thrive. In the new society they had formed, the Graavens were not limited to mating only with those of their own caste. Their society was stronger for it. Slowly the Graavens occupied more of the city as their population grew. The bond they formed with the Shard grew stronger with each new generation.

Menkh spent increasing time within the Complex. His and Tishan's offspring were often in his company, exploring the Complex and accessing the stored knowledge that lay within its archives. They were familiar with Crixac and would often ask him directly regarding any number of things concerning his past, which inevitably led to long evenings of discussion.

Tishan proved herself to be as able a civil administrator as she was Stragosh, and the affairs of the Graavens and their bonds with the Benshin and Xotic grew ever stronger. Fendrax brought some of her offspring to live in the lands outside the city, and Horven would sometimes take long journeys with her to visit the Benshin and Xotic. Horven had mourned the passing of her sister but, as she conceded, 'She died a true Graaven, Menkh, in defence of our home, and it was a quick and honourable ending.'

As to the "strange creature" that appeared during the confrontation, the Graavens who had been present concluded that the "spirit of the City" had manifested itself in their defence. Little more was said about it, such was the relief of their victory over the Dorath Mar.

Then, some three sem'chaal following the containment of the creature and the defeat of the Dorath Mar, Menkh was seated in one of the archives along with Tishan reading about the founding of the City when the voice of the Shard echoed in his mind.

'Menkh, you must come to the viewing room. Now.'

Tishan and Menkh exchanged looks. As ever, the voice of the Shard was fluid and delivered in even tones so Menkh could not glean any great sense of urgency. Sighing, he returned the knowledge sphere to its resting place and, smiling at Tishan with a whispered, 'I will be back shortly,' he willed himself to the requested location in the Complex.

Standing in the centre of the room, the walls around him were black except for several floating, silvery objects.

'What am I looking at?'

The wall shimmered and the floating things leapt into sharper focus. Shaped somewhat like a fish, with curious bulges in their skin resembling the horns of some strange animal extending out of the body, they were undoubtedly some kind of vessel moving through the depths of space.

'What are they?'

Crixac's voice answered, *'That, my friend, is a fleet of ships. My guess is that the Shard has discerned something disturbing.'*

The Shard's voice echoed in his mind. '*The time of our preparation is over; this is the response I have been waiting for. Come, we must take the next step in our quest to reset the Balance.*'

Menkh's form shimmered and disappeared.

To Be Continued …

Acknowledgements

My father was the first person who said to me that, in life, it isn't what you know but who you know that is important.

I have held this as a constant throughout my life and the writing of this novel has been no different.

My wife, Marilyn, has ever been my rock through good times and bad and who, throughout the past thirty-five years, has been my constant support no matter what I have endeavoured to do. Without her steadying presence this book would have remained an unfulfilled ambition.

To Ian Andrew, who has given so unstintingly of his knowledge and experience, both as a published author and as a friend and mentor on this journey, my deepest and enduring thanks.

This Work is dedicated to these amazing people. Thank you for being in my life.

About the author

R obert C Littlewood was born in London in 1957, emigrating with his parents and sister – all now deceased – to Australia in 1964.

Prior to completing a Bachelor of Education at Murdoch University in 1992, he undertook many different jobs. After attaining his degree, he worked as a state schoolteacher for a number of years before leaving teaching to take up other interests, including semi-professional work as an opera singer.

Robert is married with three grown children and resides in Bunbury in the south west of Western Australia.

Deviance is his debut novel.